Soul of

Fractured Fate

SOUL OF FRACTURED FATE

J. Grenz

Copyright

This is a work of fiction. All characters, organizations, and events portrayed in this story/novel are products of the author's imagination or are used fictitiously. Any similarity to real persons, living or dead, is coincidental and not intended by the author.

Soul of Fractured Fate

Book one

Copyright © J. Grenz 2024

Cover and header artwork by J. Grenz

Trigger warnings

Auburnigh

Colire
Light
Amara
Dreanigh
Drakome mountains
Moradi
Shadow
Lupos
Marapor
Dialigh
Faeglo forest
Auroras
Wilkno
Samarria
Selk
Decantous
Serbea
Illa
Gloom grove forest
Tomarapos
Aquaveno
Lumoscavar
N
W
E
S
Eneara →

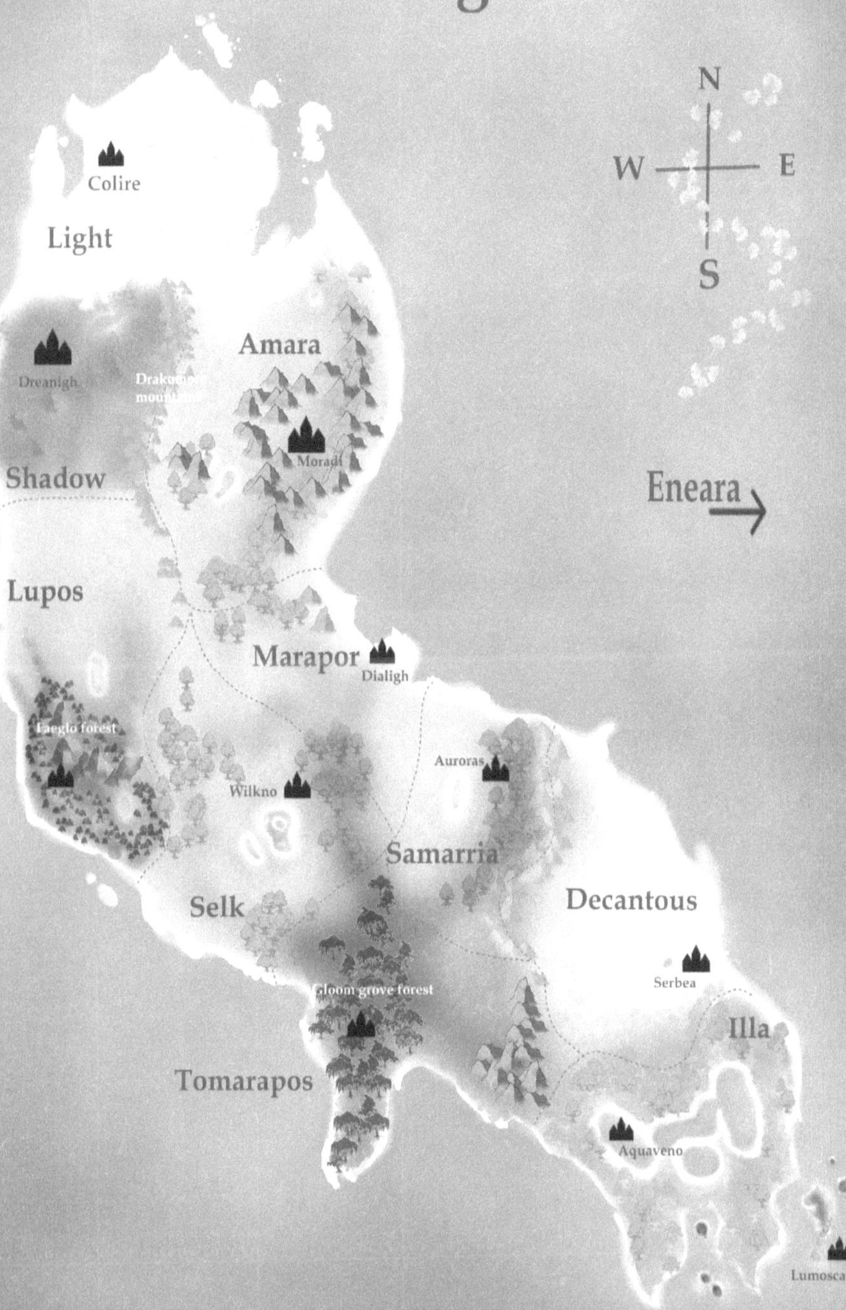

Chapter 1
Jade

I look at the small stack of paperwork the clerk hands me. Excitement and apprehension coil through me. "Is this it? It's done? Final?" The gentle tremor beneath my skin makes it a challenge to get the words out.

"Yes, final as of this morning, nothing else you need to do." The clerk smiles. I clutch the paperwork to my chest and walk back out of the office. It's done; I'm free. After five years, I'm free, and it's never felt so good. It's over. I straighten my jacket as I step outside into the brisk air, the breeze tossing wisps of my black hair around me, and I smile as the sun warms my face.

As soon as I reach my car, I jump in and pull out my phone. Putting the call through the speaker, I shift the car into gear. "Mom!"

"Are you divorced? Is it done?"

"Yes! I'm free!"

She squeals, as excited as I am. "How are you celebrating? You have to celebrate." I take a moment to think it over, unsure what to do next. Step one—pick up the final decree. Step two? I have no idea. On the road ahead is a coffee shop. I smile.

"I'm gonna get myself a nice big coffee or maybe a chai latte."

"Oh, good choice."

"Now, what do I do?"

"Get coffee." She snickers through the speaker.

"Mom—"

"I know what you meant. First, you get coffee. Then, you go home and get ready to go out and celebrate with Cat tonight." Cat, my dear friend, helped me through this entire process. Yes, she and I have big plans for tonight. None of them involve being sober.

"Hey, you can tell people you're a di-vor-cee now," Cat says, putting a lot of emphasis on each syllable. I grip the warm paper cup; the spicy aroma of chai dances around me as we walk to the front door. I'm so glad she decided to meet me here before we go out. The wind plays with loose tangles of Cat's icy blue hair as I grin at her. I pull out the key to my apartment, slide it into the lock, and listen for the click of the tumbler. But it doesn't click. Instead, the door swings open, and my jaw hits the floor. Strike that. It goes through the floor down to the earth's crust.

Stunned.

Speechless.

Carnage.

My apartment is trashed. A hurricane has blown through and left nothing but despair in its wake. Every moving box has been split open. Shreds of cardboard and my life lie shattered everywhere on the floor. And, oh God, the fluff. A fine layer of silky fluff covers everything, turning it into a winter wonderland of death. The bodies of a dozen stuffed animals hang from chairs, countertops, and the light fixture. It's carnage.

I barely take in the sharp inhale of my friend next to me as I walk into the apartment on unsteady feet. I can't stop myself; my feet are moving, but I no longer inhabit my body. As my throat closes, I don't know whether to laugh or cry.

"Everything is destroyed," I deadpan, my emotions numb. Smashed boxes and shredded fabric cover what seems to be a mound of papers. No, not papers; books, or they used to be. Fuck. My grip tightens on the cup as my stomach sinks. "So it seems someone got the notice—" I trail off. Cat knows as well as I do who would do this and steal nothing, Ace.

I sink to my knees as my ears ring, and a wave of dizziness comes over me. The squish of the carpet quickly pulls me out of my panic attack. Cold liquid seeps through the knees of my leggings, spreading in darkened spots that crawl up my legs. "What the hell?" Instinctively, I touch the carpet with my fingers and pull them away wet.

I don't want to know.

I don't want to know.

The aroma hits me; I know. The acidic smell of piss overpowers the room. I'm kneeling in piss. That fucker. "I need to change. I think he marked his territory after he destroyed everything I own," I groan.

"Tell me that's not—" she says, her pale blue eyes crinkling in disgust. I give her a savage look that confirms her suspicions as I pull myself to my feet.

"Okay, well, you can wear some of my clothes tonight. Because we are not gonna let this stop us from celebrating. You can buy new stuff, but you only have one first night of freedom." Cat is smiling again, or at least trying to. Out of the corner of my eye, it looks like the grimace may be winning. I struggle to register what she is saying. The world is coming back into focus as I see the carnage that has taken place here. All I can do is nod in agreement. "I know it sucks, but we can install new locks tomorrow and figure out the rest later. Come on, let's go to my place and get ready so we can drink to celebrate a new beginning." I follow her out in silence. For how much trouble he gave me to retrieve my stuff, I guess there's no sense in mourning the things I never thought I'd get out of our house in the first place. Squaring my shoulders and lifting my chin, I give Cat a resolute nod, locking the door again.

"I mean, we kind of assumed he'd pull something today," Cat says, shifting the car into drive. "He was never going to go down without a fight. Honestly, you got lucky he even agreed to sign the paperwork."

"He signed the paperwork because he had a piece on the side worth jumping ship for."

"I know," Cat sighs. "But it was the out you needed. Fuck him, fuck the stuff he destroyed. You can chill at my place until you find an apartment he doesn't have the address to."

I fidget my fingers, not knowing how to respond to any of this. All of my belongings are ruined, not that there was much to begin with. Clothes, books, and makeup are all replaceable. Okay, focus on the positive; I'm free. My heart skips a beat as my earlier happiness returns to me. "Holy crap, I'm single. I just realized it. I'm free, and I'm single!"

"On that subject, you know that there are gonna be a lot of really hot guys at the bar tonight."

"No, too soon. I have only been single for a couple of hours." I roll my eyes. We may have split a year ago, but today it's official. Why would I want to get tangled up in another relationship so soon?

"True, but you have been miserable for years. I'm just saying it couldn't hurt to test the waters. I'm not saying jump right back into another big relationship. Just lay the groundwork." She is grinning at me the way she does when she knows she's going to get her way, and I will have no say in the matter. This is how she talked when I said I would divorce Ace. She boasted that she was right about him being a scumbag. The only thing I can do is laugh. "Also, I'm stopping at the store on our way because we need snacks while we get ready." Snacks, always snacks. Cat is a tiny little thing that should be the size of a whale with how much she eats. But she's smiling at me, and snacks are starting to sound great.

"Snacks." I nod in agreement.

Chapter 2
Jade

"You sure I don't look like a raccoon? This smoky eye got a little away from me." Looking in the mirror at the dark glittery shadow I expertly applied to my lids. In all honesty, I looked pretty good. The years of being put down about my looks make me second-guess everything.

"You look hot! Now let's pre-game, so we are good and ready to talk to the man meat!" Cat smiles wickedly at me while she pops a Hot Cheeto in her mouth. She's lounging on her purple sofa like an empress, holding a glass of who knows what.

Turning back to the mirror for one last inspection, I smooth down my long black hair over one shoulder and check my outfit: black leggings and a green sequin tank top. It's a bit snug in the chest, but also a size too small because it's Cat's. My tattoos are on show, running halfway down my arms, showcasing the badass I once thought I was. Twining roses run down one arm and lilies down the other. Okay, badass is a bit too far, but I think they are beautiful.

Cat's outfit includes black leggings and a red crop top with a cut-out across her chest. Her tattoos are on full display. A mosaic of swirling stained glass wraps up one arm and down her side, peeking out from under her top and then disappearing below her waist. Her long, icy blue hair is curled in gorgeous waves past her shoulders. She's watching one of my favorite K-dramas—the Fairy and the Demon. It's a grumpy sunshine love story where the villain gets the girl.

I plop down beside her, sinking into the soft velvet, and grab the extra mystery drink. "To freedom!"

"To freedom and never seeing his dumb face again!" She and I giggle as I take a long drink. The light fizz of bubbles plays on my tongue as candy sweetness coats my mouth. Fantastic, pink Moscato—my favorite. "Tonight is gonna be legendary."

"Future me is gonna be so hungover," I sigh as I lean back and watch the fairy meet the demon for the first time. The fairy is livid because the demon just cut off her gorgeous hair.

"Oh man, that guy has a death wish." She laughs, "And future you isn't here yet. Let her deal with the consequences of your actions."

"She's gonna be so pissed." Drinking down the last of my glass, I watch the demon pin the fairy to the wall with her arms over her head. "Damn, that's hot. That half-smirk, he's really got that whole brooding thing down."

"Too bad she hates him! If it were you, you would be all—'yes, please, Mr. Demon.' Except for the hair thing, that's a murderable offense." She giggles. I glare at her or try to. I'm sure the heat in my face gives away the plot since she laughs harder. "Or maybe not. Damn, you've got it bad for the bad guys. Explains a lot about Ace."

I groan. "Well, initially, he was nice, considerate, and caring. It wasn't until we got married that he flipped the script on me. While I've dated a lot of assholes, I've never dated a bad boy like the guys from tv or books," I sigh, pouring myself another glass.

"Ah, you got love bombed. Makes sense since he's so manipulative." Cat pauses, tapping her chin. "Maybe we need to find you a tall, dark, and broody. Give that bad boy kink a real try!" She tips back her glass, draining its contents. I bury my face in my hands and take a deep breath. This girl is going to be the death of me. "Alright." Cat slams her empty glass on the table and bolts off the couch. "Empty that, then let's get this party on the road! Dancing, drinking, and hopefully hot guys!"

She bounds across her living room to put her glass in the sink. Her apartment, adorned in jewel tones to offset the white walls, is pretty cramped, but it's cozy. Really, it's just a home for all her books. Bookcases overflowing with fantasy, romance, Norse mythology, and fairy porn line every available wall. Stacks of her newest obsession, vampire smut, are taking over the floor in all the corners. I love it here.

I'm a little less bound up after the wine and fairly full from the banquet of snacks we'd been eating all afternoon. One last look in the mirror has me feeling pretty good about myself. It's time to celebrate.

I'm. So. Hot. Good lord, this always happens. Drinking makes me so hot. Or maybe it's just sweltering in here. So many people are dancing and moving around. On the plus side, I feel fantastic as I dance to the music on my way to the bar for another round of drinks with Cat hot on my tail.

"What will it be, ladies?" the nice grandma behind the counter asks. She looks like a grandma, not my grandma, but a nice little old lady who probably knits in the park, grandma.

"Hi, two cinders, cedars, uh, ciders, please!" I drawl. Grandma makes a face of disapproval. Crap, she knows I've been drinking. I'm in so much trouble. "And two waters!" I add for good measure. Future me is going to be so happy with that decision. She hands me the water. Cat and I gulp it down greedily. Wow, has water always tasted this good? This place has the best water. Grandma looks pleased as we finish the last of our glasses. I'm glad. I hate it when

Grandma is mad at us. She slides over our ciders and walks away to help someone else. "Oh man, I thought we were in trouble with Grandma." I laugh.

Cat slides onto the recently vacated barstool next to me. "Yeah, I thought she was about to call our moms to come get us!" She bursts out laughing, wiping a tear from her eye as she tries to regain her composure. Her face drops into a grin. "I think Mr. Tall, dark, and broody wants to have a word with you." She points behind me to a gorgeous man whose shirt looks painted onto his muscles. He has long black hair tied back in a low ponytail and honey-golden eyes set against his deep skin tone. Holy wow, is he smirking at me? It can't be at me? His smirk turns into a full-on smile. His teeth seem to sparkle in the dancing lights. "And he's walking over. Be cool."

"I can't be cool," I hiss. "He's hot, and I'm—" I trail off, pointing up and down myself. "Oh hell, I'm way past tipsy," I whisper-shout at my friend through the music. Suddenly, there is heat at my back, yet a chill runs down my spine. I slowly turn and look up, locking gazes with Mr. Honey eyes. He is barely inches from me, leaning over my back to flag down Grandma.

"Well hello, beautiful," he purrs. How can a man like that purr words? "Sorry, I'm not trying to get into your space, but this place is packed." I squeak out some sort of acceptance of this. I am lost in his eyes as his gaze takes me in. Oh no, I'm staring, probably blushing, being an absolute moron. "Hi, I'd like three of whatever the ladies are drinking." He winks at me, *winks*. Then, he glances to his other side as a couple vacates their seats. "Here, sit next to your friend. Seats open." He backs up to put his hands on the two barstools to my right.

"Oh, uh, thank you," I stammer, sitting next to Cat. Honey eyes takes the other seat beside me. "I'm Jade, and this is Cat."

"Charmed, I'm Warrick." He is once again smirking at me. "What brings two ladies such as yourselves out tonight?" He leans an elbow on the counter.

Cat leans forward, setting down her drink to scoot her barstool closer to me. "We are celebrating!" She picks up her cider and takes a swig.

"Celebrating? May I ask what we are celebrating tonight?" His brows raise in anticipation.

"Freedom from matrimonial hell!" Cat thrusts her bottle up in the air, and I can't help but do the same. "Jay here got the official divorce decree today! She's free!"

Warrick makes himself more comfortable, leaning on the bar towards me. His eyes pierce right through me. "I see. Well, this is something to celebrate. May I join you?"

"Hell yeah, you can!" Cat shouts and grabs the fresh bottle of cider Grandma brought over. She leans over and whispers, "Close your mouth and stop staring before you drool on him." My hand jumps to my mouth, and I laugh. God, I need help. I pick up my cider and take a big gulp, hoping it will help clear my head a bit. Help me focus on something besides the man sitting in front of me.

"To freedom and escaping the bonds of matrimony!" Warrick raises his bottle of cider, and the two of us clink our bottles with him. "Now, since the question of whether you two are single has been answered, may I ask you to dance?" My heart just jumped up my throat and ran out the door. I'm a little dizzy and can't tell if it's my nerves or the case of alcohol I've put away. Dancing means touching, and touching means those muscles. I'm in trouble. I'm so out of practice with all of this.

"She'd love to!" Cat cuts in before I can even worry myself into a panic about this. She is shoving me out of my seat, taking my cider, and putting my hand in his. All the blood in my body rushes to my face. I really hope my makeup hides the fact that my face looks like a tomato. With my hand in his, he stands, and I'm just now noticing he's tall. Towering over me, and I'm not that short. He has got to be six feet and then some, six-four? Six-five? Shit, I'm just staring again. I get my feet to move to follow him back to the dance floor. Some mix is playing that I can't place, and the beat is all over the place. I can't look that bad since everyone here is pretty toasted.

Closing my eyes, I sway to the music and revel in this moment. His hand slides around my waist, warm and inviting. I run my hands up his chest and down his arms before I realize I'm totally copping a feel, and my cheeks heat again. But when I look up, he's just got that sexy grin on his face, like he finds me amusing. I squeak out an apology, and he chuckles and pulls me in closer, the look in his eyes looking almost predatory. Now, I'm pressed against him, which is borderline obscene in public. I mean, most couples are dancing this way. But I just met him, and I'm groping his muscles. This wall of a man pressed against my body, and damn, it's hot. It feels like no time, and a lot of time has passed.

Over the music, we talk and dance. All at once, oh no, I'm hot. I'm melting. I need air and water. It's far too hot again. "I need to sit for a bit. It's too hot," I explain to Warrick, who nods as a bit of sweat trickles down into the collar of his shirt. I trail it all the way down with my eyes. And I'm being a creep again. Damn it. I locate Cat, who has moved our drinks to a table in the corner by a window. Wonderful—air circulation. I sit and enjoy the breeze coming in. I grab my drink from the table and notice it's full. "Did you get me a new drink?"

"Yeah, you two were dancing for a while. So I finished it, danced with that guy over there, and got us fresh drinks when I saw this open table," she replies. Were we dancing that long? Wow, time is getting away from me. I pull out my phone; it's already past one in the morning. Cat is motioning for a cute blonde guy to come over to the table, curling her finger seductively, beckoning him. He smiles and walks over, sitting down next to her. "This is Chris. Chris, this is Jay and Warrick. We are celebrating tonight. Sit with us for a bit." He nods eagerly and sits. Leaning in close, he and Cat whisper to each other. I see Cat has found her prey for the night.

An arm wraps around the back of my chair as the faintest heat whispers past my ear. "Are you feeling better, Jade?" His voice is low as he leans into me, sending a chill down my spine. I grab my cider, hoping liquid courage will come to my rescue.

"Honestly, this has been the best day, minus the–all my stuff getting destroyed part. I just get really hot when I drink." I can't tell if my slurring is getting better or worse. Maybe it's time for more water.

"What do you mean all your stuff got destroyed?" Warrick looks appalled.

"Just what she said. That creepwad of an ex of hers got into her apartment and committed genocide on everything she owns." She slams her cider down, very annoyed. "Then he peed on it! And she sat in it!" She practically yells that last part. I groan and rub between my eyebrows, mumbling about kneeling, not sitting in it. "That's not even the worst he's done to her!" I groan inwardly, as I know this tirade is nowhere near done. There is no stopping her now that she has the men in her thrall with wide eyes. Both men look back and forth between the two of us expectantly.

"Okay, so this one time, correct me if I'm wrong. He had started an argument about how clean he expected the house to be. It was not up to his *standards.*" Cat emphasizes with air quotes. "She works a full-time job and usually does a lot of overtime, so who cares if the dishes didn't get done one whole night!" I lean back in my chair and take a sip of my cider. I know which story this is and have no intention of stopping her. It's embarrassing, but it's so ridiculous that it's validating when people are outraged on my behalf. Shit, if this table were alive, it would be outraged on my behalf.

"So this argument devolves from there, pretty much anything this fucktart can think up to be mad about. And whenever she defends herself, he just changes gears to prove his point. Till he stuns her fucking stupid. This guy legit mid-argument, says–" She pauses either for dramatic effect or just to collect herself. "Well, I put your dildo in my mouth and sucked it. Blowjobs aren't that hard." Stunned silence. Cat is smirking with her job done, arms crossed, point made.

"Wait, wait, wait, wait, this guy sucked a dildo to prove a point?" Chris' shocked expression says it all. I nod and laugh. "Who does that? Why? What did that have to do with anything? Were you even arguing about blowjobs?" I shake my head as I continue to giggle. "Who does that?"

"I believe your ex is gay," Warrick chuckles. He looks so confused; it's almost endearing. Cat may have broken this poor man I just met. Hi, I'm Jade. My ex sucked a dildo to prove a point. Fuck my life, you just can't make this shit up.

"That's what I said!" Cat exclaims. "It's insane to just throw that out there out of nowhere. I hope he comes out, so maybe he'll stop being such an asshole."

"Even if he's not gay, it is kind of strange to just come out with something like that during an argument." Warrick is still trying to rationalize this. His pensive gaze lands on me. "Well, I may not understand the whole situation. But I can guarantee I've never ended an argument like that. What did you say?"

"Well, at first, I was just stunned stupid. It was so out of left field, I didn't know what to say. Then I told him to go ahead and do that for half an hour and see how his jaw feels." I laugh. God, this story never got old—one for the highlights reel of my life.

"Well, this calls for another round of drinks! I don't know how anyone could stay sober after a story like that." Chris quickly stands, swaying a little, and makes his way over to the bar. I was not sober, hadn't been all night, but I wasn't about to stop him. Smiling, I look over at Warrick and once again get lost in his eyes. His gaze has gone predatory, making me squirm a little. What was it with this guy? He exudes predator in the best way.

He leans over again, trapping me between himself and the wall.

He's so close I can smell him—cedar and water, like the woods. His half-smirk widens to a full grin as I realize he noticed me smelling him.

Kill. Me. Now.

Drunk me is embarrassing. "See something you like?" he growls so low I'm pretty sure I was the only one who heard him. Heat flushes my cheeks. I am so busted and so bad at this. I make yet another sound that is a confirmation, but mostly a squeak. Judging by his low growl in response, he wasn't exactly turned off by my answer. Visions of tearing his clothes off dance through my head, warring with the very dull voice in the back of my mind saying—you don't do stuff like this. You do not sleep with men you just met in bars, no matter how hot they are. However, the idea of what he looks like without that shirt on, what those muscles would feel like. No, he appears to be a player who knows how to pick up women. A player who is probably exceptional in bed. Who you will never see again. Maybe...now, just hear me out; perhaps that's not a bad thing. Okay, voice of reason, you are fired and entirely unhelpful.

"How about we get out of here and get some food in your stomach to sober you up a bit? Continue this celebration in another location, where we can talk more?" He glances between Cat and me, lifting an eyebrow. Cat perks up at the mention of food. Smiling to myself, I nod.

"I'll just grab Chris, and we can go." Cat moves to stand, but Warrick gently grabs her wrist.

"That won't be necessary," he says with a wide smile. My heart speeds up a tick, and I swear, from this angle, I see a fang. But it must be my imagination. The world starts to tilt a little. I must be way drunker than I thought. "Chris doesn't want to go where we are going." Confusion is an understatement for the look that passes between Cat and me. We don't share men, so where does he think this is going? Cat looks like the world is tilting, swaying in his grasp. I wonder if someone slipped us something. Oh god, have we been slipped something? Warrick chuckles at my panicked expression. "No, you haven't been drugged. Don't worry, I'll take care of you. A little food, and you'll be right as rain."

Did I say that out loud? Oh god, the room is spinning.

This time, the whole world seems to shift on its axis. I grab onto Cat and Warrick to keep my balance. Cat holds onto my arm as tight as I have her hand. I hear the table screech across the floor. Warrick's warm arms wrap around us, but everything is spinning and turning. The room is getting foggy, and I can't see straight. If this keeps up, I'm going to be sick. The world flips one last time, and our screams are all I hear. Then everything is black.

Chapter 3
Jade

I glance up from my computer to a knock on the wall. My husband stands in the archway to my office, stark naked, smiling with flushed skin. He suggestively sways his hips as he whips a tie around like a helicopter. The glazed look in his eyes is the result of far too much rum.

"I'm working," I giggle. "I have to have this report done by midnight or it's my ass."

"Seriously! You're laughing?" he bellows. He turns and storms out of the room.

I stare at my unfinished report and the empty archway with my chest deflating. I can chase him down and explain, but I've got twenty-five minutes until my deadline. Damn it. I know if I go after him, I'm gonna miss my deadline, but if I don't go...

Fuck!

Not again.

I walk down the hallway to the music of shattering glass, with the bass of loud crashes. My palms sweat as the air grows thick, and I slow my steps. The door to our bedroom hangs ajar from the bottom hinge, the metal bent and holding with its last bit of strength. Glass litters the floor from the picture frames that have exploded like fireworks against the walls. A cold sweat runs down my spine as my eyes widen in horror.

"I was trying to be sexy, and you laughed!" he booms as a shot glass explodes against the dresser. The hot-pink glass glitters on the carpet as tears well up in my eyes. That was a gift. My mom gave me that.

"I giggled because it was cute," I hesitate. "If you'd given me a minute, I'd have told you to wait till I finished my report. I don't understand why you are so mad."

"You would have been too tired when you finished! I was trying to get you before then."

My stomach drops. He knew I needed to finish this before midnight, that I was almost done. This isn't fair.

"All I ask for is a little attention, Jade. When we got married, you made a verbal agreement with me. That we would have sex every night. But no! You've always got a report due, or research for a meeting!"

"Well, you might understand what that's like if you had a job, Ace," I send his vitriol right back at him before I can think better of it.

His face turns red as his head cocks to the side, and his jaw clenches.

Shitshitshit!

"Excuse me?" A wry smile spreads across his lips. He balls his fists, slowly clenching and unclenching as his knuckles turn white.

"N–nothing," I stammer as I take a slow step backward out of the doorway, unable to blink as I watch the predator in front of me.

"You wanna cast stones? Jade. I don't hear the dishwasher going, just gonna leave the dishes for me? Even though that's also your job?" He glares at me as shock takes hold. What the fuck do dishes have to do with anything? He steps closer to me, crunching the glass under his feet. I flinch as I wrap my arms around my middle.

"I'll do it tomorr–"

"You know," he cuts me off. "I sucked your dildo just to see what it was like for you? I did that so I could understand what you go through better." He sneers.

What?

What the fuck?

"And you know what, Jade? It wasn't that fucking hard," he scoffs.

I stare at him. The beat of my heart thunders in my ears as I try to make sense of how the argument got here.

Stunned silence greets his declaration.

"I—wait, what? Seriously?"

"You heard me—"

"Well, come talk to me when you've sucked on it for half an hour straight and see how your jaw feels. It's yours now." I grimace. What the hell am I supposed to say to that? This is so embarrassing. I can't even ask my friends for advice.

He pushes past me with a wad of clothing in his hands as he heads for the kitchen. I stand and watch as he gets dressed, pours a glass of rum in a cup, and downs it as he snatches up his keys. "I'm going to Chase's house. Go ahead and finish your work." He makes air quotes like I'm not working. For fuck's sake.

The door slams, and his engine roars as he leaves, drinking and driving. Great. I stand in silence as I stare at the door. My chest shakes with the effort to stop crying as I glance at the clock and wipe away the tears from my face, but the knot in my throat gets lodged as I see it's twelve-fifteen.

Not again.

Crack.

It's too bright. Why is it so bright? Did I forget to close my blackout curtains last night? I pull the covers over my face to shield myself from the light bleeding through my eyelids.

"Oh, you're awake!" a soft female voice says nearby, shocking and jolting me out of my half-sleep state of awareness. I push my covers down, sit up, and blink rapidly, trying to adjust to the light in the room. My vision blurs as the sun wages war on my retinas.

Oh shit.

Not my room.

"Calm down, you're safe. Everything is going to be alright." My eyes land on the woman standing a couple of feet from the bed I'm sitting on. She's got her hands up like she's coaxing a wild animal. "I know this all seems strange, my lady. I'm Lorelai, and I'm a healer. Tell me what you remember." I gawk at this woman, taking in the sight of her cream gown and starched white apron. She has blonde hair tied up in a tight bun and piercing blue eyes. Are her ears pointed? No, I'm hallucinating again. Where the fuck am I? What the hell happened? "My lady?" She moves forward, so I scramble back against the headboard. "Please, my lady, this will all make sense momentarily. Please, tell me what you remember about last night."

Okay, seeing as how this cannot be real. "Last night, I was out celebrating with Cat. Oh my god, Cat!" I frantically look around the immense room.

"She's fine, I assure you, and you'll see her as soon as we are done here." Bringing my attention back to her, she moves to sit on the side of the bed, smiling and nodding her encouragement.

"Okay," I hesitate, but decide to continue. Maybe trying to remember will give me some answers. "So we were celebrating and drinking. A lot. We danced for most of the night." Scrunching my face, I try to recall what happened next. "Then we went to sit at the bar to get more drinks and relax a bit. Oh! And this guy showed up and started talking to us–Warrick! So I started talking and dancing with him for a couple of hours. And Cat did the same with this guy, Chris." I get out in a rush and stop to think again. "We sat down at a table, the four of us, and chatted for a while. Then Chris went to get us more drinks," realization hits me. "That's when the world got fuzzy, and I got really dizzy. I think one of them slipped something into our drinks!"

"What did you talk about right before you got dizzy?"

How about we get out of here and get some food in your stomach to sober you up a bit? Continue this celebration in another location, where we can talk more. "Warrick asked us if we wanted to go to another location to eat. He must have drugged us. Oh god, what did he do to us?" My heart is racing at the thought, and the air becomes thick. The pressure of imminent tears clouds my eyes.

Lorelai laughs. Laughs? What the hell? She composes herself when she notices me glaring at her, but is still smiling. "And what did you say when he offered you this deal?"

"We agreed to go get food. It sounded like a good idea at the time." I glower.

"Warrick, that scoundrel," she's laughing again before quickly composing herself. "I can assure you, you were not drugged, aside from the copious amount of alcohol you consumed. You see, you gave consent when you agreed to go to another location with him." My jaw drops as I look down at my crotch. "Oh! No, not that kind of consent," she hurries to explain. "No, no. No one has touched you like that. What I mean to say is that you gave your consent to be brought here. You and your friend."

Relief goes through me. I was not drugged and raped, but this is still insane. I have no idea what you're talking about, but I'll humor you. "And where exactly is here?"

"Not my place to say, but you'll be told everything you need to know soon. In the meantime, like I said before, my lady, I'm Lorelai. I've cared for you and your friend since you arrived." She stands as she talks and moves around to the end of the bed. "I've taken care of what would have been a nasty hangover and removed that very strange ink poisoning you and your friend seemed to be afflicted with." Wait, what? I'm staring at her in confusion as she points at me. "You had the toxins all over your body. I'm surprised you didn't notice. All down your arms and even in your hair. No matter, I've removed it, and you are good as new again."

All down my arms? The fuck is she?—Oh. My. God. I shoot my arms out in front of me and see skin, blank skin. Throwing the covers off of me, I inspect my legs—all blank. Holy hell. My. Tattoos. Are gone. "What the hell! Those were expensive! I loved my tattoos!" I don't even know if the rage I should be feeling is touching the shock that this could even happen. "How? Why?" But before I can go on with my tirade, I notice the white tangling over my arms and draping over my chest. My heart sinks. "My hair! Ah, what did you do?" I shriek.

She looks almost put out; is that annoyance on her face? "I removed that strange pigment and restored your beautiful hair. This Silvery white color is so unusual and beautiful. I really don't understand why you seem so mad."

"Have you never heard of tattoos or hair dye? I look like an old lady!" When my hair turned white as a teenager, I was horrified. This is next level.

She tisks, *tisks* at me! "Archaic practices. We have much better methods that don't involve damage to a person's body. Ink in the skin, honestly." Laughing, she turns to head towards a door, but looks back. "For your safety, you must remain here in your room. However, this door here leads to an adjoining suite where your friend is. Soon, someone will come to collect both of you to explain why you are here." She smiles. "Through there..." She points towards a door, "is the bathing chambers. Might I suggest you wash up and pull on something appropriate from the wardrobe? You do not want to be-" She hesitates, "presented, in your underwear." I'm still stuck on archaic practices as she leaves the room through a third door, and the lock clicks. What the fuck just happened?

With my heart hammering in my chest, I slowly climb out of the bed and take in my surroundings. The expansive space dwarfs Cat's entire apartment. The walls are cool gray stone, adorned with tapestries depicting dragon battles in an overall theme of red. An imposing four-poster bed, crafted from dark wood, is draped in luxurious bedding in deep shades of crimson. Most of the floor is covered with a huge onyx rug adorned with intricate floral patterns reminiscent of brocade designs, matching the large draperies around the windows. To my right, two cozy burgundy chairs sit beside floor-to-ceiling windows, with a small table between them. The area is begging to be read in. Across from the foot of the bed is the door that Lorelai mentioned leads to the bathroom. A few feet over is the door she said leads to Cat. An enormous ebony fireplace and two more chairs are to my left, completing the room's aesthetic. It's a remarkable space and a gothic Victorian dream.

As I look around the room, I spot a giant cabinet. I'm assuming this is where I find clothes? Because Lorelai was correct, I am, in fact, in my underwear. Fantastic. I sigh. At least it's the underwear that I put on last night. The armoire is stuffed full of dresses. Long dresses of various colors, most looking like they have corsets. A prom dress store threw up in here. "What the hell?" No pants, no leggings. Right, okay, breathe. Pulling out a less fancy-looking dress, it's a simple thing with a more fitted look, rather than a ball gown. It looks like everything in here will fit me, at least, but wow—everything is so fancy. Holding up the more petite dress, it occurs to me this is a slip—more underwear, not clothes. "Bloody hell." I resume rifling through the closet.

Finally! A dress that doesn't go to the damn floor. Tucked between a canary taffeta nightmare and an ice queen wedding dress is a little inky number that will hit just below the knee. It's a light fabric with some layers to fluff it out and a corset top. Okay, Vampire Barbie it is. I grab some matching flats in the cabinet next to this one; I'm pretty pleased with my choice. However, the shoe closet has some enjoyable options. I think there is a shoe for every dress in the previous closet. Interesting. I drop the clothes on the bed, intending to head towards the bathroom, when the ensuite door bursts open with a bang.

"What the hell!" Cat is in her lacy underwear, looking as feral as

I probably do. I scream at my friend's sudden noise and appearance before running to her and wrapping her in my arms.

"You scared the shit out of me!"

"Me! You mean this place! What the fuck! They won't tell me anything! Just–oh, by the way, we took your tattoos and fixed your hair. The fuck! It's my natural color; that shouldn't even be possible since I bleached it to make it blue. Not a damn split end in sight, too. What the hell did they do?" She's holding up her strawberry blonde curls as evidence. Her eyes grow wide as she looks at me and reaches for my hair. "Holy shit! You weren't kidding when you said all your hair went white. Actually, it has a silvery quality to it. Why couldn't my natural color be like this?" she whines.

Huffing, I pick up a strand of my hair and turn it over in my fingers. "I think you're missing the point here." I look at her, a little worried. "We have more than a little bit been kidnapped."

"How does one get a little bit kidnapped?" She's got a grin on her face that says she's got a point. "Yeah, this is crazy. Any idea where the hell we are?" She walks over to the window to look out. I hear an audible gasp leave her before I rush over.

"Wow, you *really* do have terrible taste in men," Cat gasps. The emphasis wasn't necessary. "I knew that guy was bad news when he smiled at you, but I figured, what's the worst that could happen in a crowded bar?" Cat muses.

"This?" I squeak. A nervous laugh escapes us as we look out the window at the all-too-close, or too-big, moon. It would have just felt off, or a trick of the angle, if not for the second smaller moon beside it. The second one is seemingly suspended mid-explosion, broken in half with a couple of smaller pieces hovering above. This could quite possibly be the worst-case scenario.

"I don't think we're in California anymore, Toto." Cat slowly turns to look at me. Another uneasy giggle escapes us. Nope, definitely not.

I walk over to the bathing chamber, with my mind reeling from the implications of what this could mean for us. "Oh, no."

"What?" Cat has her arms crossed in that tell me there isn't more bad news, way of hers.

"A chamber pot," I cringe. Cat doubles over in laughter. She's laughing so hard she may begin crying, clutching her sides. "What?"

"You—you're concerned about indoor plumbing?" She barks out another laugh and wipes away a tear. "There are two moons; our tattoos and hair color have been removed and restored to factory default settings. We were kidnapped, and no one from our world will ever find us. And the first time you say: 'Oh no,' it's to the lack of a toilet." She resumes her laughter while I stand there dumbfounded.

"Well...I mean, it's all shit. No, it's worse. But on top of everything, never mind, it's all bad." I can't help but laugh as well. "I need coffee."

Chapter 4
Jade

"Maybe they're aliens, or—" Cat trails off, and excitement comes to her in a wave. "Or vampires!" Oh, dear, I've lost her. She's lounging in the chair by the window in my room, wearing a deep red velvet dress. The neckline plunges low, but the hem falls just below her knees, like the black dress I picked out. We had both taken a luxurious bath in the clawfoot tubs in each of our rooms and gotten dressed. Cat's room was the exact mirror of mine, but in purple instead of red.

I'm brooding in front of the fireplace, holding a shoe in each hand. "I highly doubt your dream vampire just magically showed up and kidnapped you," I groan, looking back at the fire that never seems to die down or need tending. At least I was wrong about the chamber pot; it was a trash can, and upon further inspection, there was a small room with a toilet. Thank hell for small favors and such. A toilet didn't make up for the whole kidnapped-and-probably-not-even-on-Earth thing, though. Who am I kidding? We are so not on Earth anymore. "Maybe you have a point about aliens. Guard your butt." I give Cat a pointed look.

"I'm just saying, none of this makes sense otherwise. From what I can see out the window, we are locked up in a tower in what appears to be a castle. I mean, that garden down there doesn't even look real." She points out the window. "The trees are all pink, the grass is purple, and the water is a *very* unnatural shade of blue. I mean, I see normal trees beyond the garden, and then—boom! Two moons! I'm telling you, aliens or vampires." She crosses her arms and gives me a pointed stare right back.

I turn as I hear the lock click and the door open. And look who it is, Mr. Kidnapper himself. "Oh, hell no!" I shout as I throw one of my shoes at him. He quickly pulls the door shut and uses it as a shield; my shoe bounces off the wood and tumbles across the floor. As the door opens again, I throw the second shoe through the opening, and a distinct thud sounds as it makes contact.

The door opens the rest of the way, and Warrick steps inside, holding the offending shoe. "Shoes? Really?" He cocks his brow in question. Smiling, he takes another step inside and closes the door behind him. "Hello, ladies."

"Oh, fuck you," Cat snips. "Where the hell are—" She trails off as she stands and takes in the sight of him, cocking her head to the side like a bird. "Holy shit, are—are your ears pointed? Wait, no, they weren't like that last night." She stops and takes a very slow step back. "What are you?"

My attention flicks to his ears, and there is no mistaking what I thought was a trick of the light or far too much alcohol. Now I see it: his ears are pointy, very pointy. He's just standing there smiling—smiling—oh, "I knew I saw fangs last night!" This? This is what you choose to voice first? "Holy shit, you might have been right, Cat." My eyes dart to her, then back at Warrick, who now seems much more dangerous. Because he wasn't dangerous before? "Umm... I'm sorry about the shoe. Please don't bite us," I say slowly, like I'm trying to calm a rabid dog.

"Shoes." He shoots a glare at me.

"Huh?"

"Shoes, plural. You threw two of them at me." He looks amused now. "Calm down. I know you're probably mad."

"Probably? Probably! Yes, I'm mad! Where in the hell are we? What exactly did we *consent* to?" I rage at his words. My blood boils. Crap, that's right, he is a dangerous man. That thought is enough to cool my jets. "Sorry, please don't eat me," I whisper with my head down. Good job, Jade; let's make the big man, monster? Whatever, angry. Between being pissed off and scared out of my mind, I don't know how to respond to any of this.

"Eat you?" He booms a laugh, making Cat and me step back. "Okay, first, I'm not going to eat you." He has doubled over; he's laughing so hard. "Not unless you ask me to," he says with a wink, continuing to laugh. "Cat, please come sit next to Jade by the fire, and I'll do my best to explain what is happening." He takes a step back and motions for her to move.

Cat scurries over to the chair in question, and we sit and look at him. "Welcome to the land of Amara. You are currently in the castle of Moradi, the City of Radiant Moonlight," he announces with a flourish of his hands. "I am Warrick, Captain of the Guard for his royal majesty, King Corbin."

My jaw drops at the same time Cat's eyes grow large. King? Castle? What the hell? "Why are there two moons?" I point towards the window. Seriously? This is what you are focused on. He just told you you're in a kingdom you've never heard of.

He grins and continues, "Because that's how many moons there are here. As you may have guessed, we are no longer in your mortal realm. Last night, when I said we should go somewhere else, I may have omitted the part about that other location being another realm." He looks a little sheepish.

"So you *are* vampires," Cat interjects. "Or aliens?" She shrugs and leans forward.

Warrick bursts into laughter and sits on the side of the bed facing us. "No, I'm not a vampire." He composes himself. "They exist, but none are currently in Moradi. And no, not aliens. We consider ourselves fae." Fae? Great, I closed one crappy chapter in my life and jumped genres.

"I knew it!" Cat jumps out of her seat. "I knew something was different about you and Lorelai; I should have guessed with the pointy ears! How did I not think of it sooner!" She stops, looking over at Warrick, who has a pensive look on his face as he regards her. "Sorry, I'll sit. That was probably really rude."

"It's to be expected. I was sent to your world to find highborn ladies to participate in a little experiment," he says. My eyes bug out of my head as I pull my legs up to my chest in the chair. My heart is surely going to beat right out of my chest. "Bad choice of words; don't worry, it's more of a courting setup of sorts. Lords, ladies, you get the point." No, no, I do not get the point. What I understand is that this fucker was bait, and I fell for it.

"First, we are not *highborn* anything, just two normal girls. Second, *what?*"

"I'm not explaining this well. The queen will do a much better job in a little bit. Anyway, I came to apologize for seducing and tricking you into coming here. But as promised–" He smiles and walks towards the door, opening it and walking out. He returns a moment later with a cart full of food that smells divine. "Breakfast." He smiles devilishly. "I promise it's safe to eat, just as I promised I'd take care of you." My stomach rumbles loudly, reminding me I'm starving. Well, it can't get much worse. I get up and stomp my way over to the food. Warrick is smiling as if I presented him with a puppy.

There are pancakes, waffles, and various fruits; some I recognize, some I don't. Plus, meats that resemble sausage and bacon. It all looks and smells delicious. "Thank you," I mumble.

"You are most welcome. Again, I'm sorry about last night, but I promise this will be worth it." He smiles again. "I mean, any guy has to be better than your ex, right?"

"Huh? Any guy—wait, courting? As in dating? Are you out of your mind!" Furious, I flail my arms, wielding a fork towards him.

"You brought me here to date? Fae? Date fae men? Are we even compatible? You kidnapping, catfishing, son of a bitch!"

He moves towards the door. "Well, it's been great! Enjoy your breakfast. I'll return in an hour to take you to the official announcement. Shoes go on your feet, not out the door," he calls as he quickly closes and locks the door.

"No promises!" I shout. Grabbing a plate, I load it with pancakes, fruit, and bacon before looking at Cat, who is doing the same. We sit and eat silently for a moment, trying and failing to forget about our troubles and savoring the incredible flavors. "Damn, this is good," I swoon. Cat nods in agreement.

"Did that sound like the pitch for a terrible reality dating show to you?" Cat muses. I nod, creasing my brow. "So fae. We are here in a fae land, to date fae?"

"I have no idea. This is ridiculous. Warrick is ridiculous. This room is ridiculous." I angrily shove another piece of pancake in my mouth. "What the hell are we supposed to do?"

"Find out from the queen why we are here. Then, what? Decide whether we will go along with it or try to get home?" She picks up a strange pink fruit in a triangle shape and inspects it before popping it in her mouth. Her eyes light up as she chews. "You gotta try some of that." She walks over to the cart and heaps more of the strange fruit on her plate before sitting down again. "Or we just ride it out and see if they send us home when we don't find anyone to *court*." She makes air quotes.

"Well, Warrick is on my shit list, so I certainly hope he doesn't think he still has a shot with me." I take a bite of the pink fruit to punctuate my point, but damn if that isn't the best taste ever.

Chapter 5
Killian

"Are you sure this is what you want to do?" Mom is pacing. She always paces when she's worried. Her long gown billows behind her, making her look ethereal. But I'm not concerned. This plan is brilliant.

"Yeah, I'd much rather try my luck at finding a real mate than just have an arranged marriage. I want a spark, ya know." I flop down on her bed, sprawling out on my back. "Like, I'll just see her across the room and know." Plus, the last time they tried to set me up was a disaster. I came on too strong, and she ran for the hills.

"That's not how love works, dear."

"But that's how *my* love is gonna be. It will be magical. Like it's written in the stars." Just like in the books. I've read so many books about love and romance. The princess is constantly distressed, and the guy shows up and saves the day. Only I don't want my mate to ever be distressed, which is why we invited them here. I'm a gentleman like that.

"It's not always the happily ever after you read in books, Killian." She's pinching the area between her brows like she always does when I have a great idea. "This is the first time you've been around multiple eligible females your age. Just take it slow, and don't rush in like a dragon on gold." Her blue eyes pierce me with her severe gaze.

"Oh, I won't. I'm gonna talk to all the women and win them over one by one if I don't know which one is mine right away." My mom doesn't look convinced, but I can't tell her about the young ladies Rodan and I used to sneak out to meet. She'd be so pissed. "Don't worry though, I'll know." This is a turning point in our kingdom's history. This will be the moment when everything changes for the better—leading to me taking the throne and my life partner being there beside me. We will bring the kingdom back to its former glory.

"Corbin, please tell me you had that *talk* with your son." She looks at my dad, who's lounging by the window. The sun shines off his golden hair the same way it does mine. He's smiling because he knows I'm right. He slowly nods to my mom, confirming we talked about the fish and the bees. Mom huffs and turns back to me, smoothing down her chestnut hair even though it's never out of place. "Can't we just arrange a nice wife for you? It's not too late to back out." Her pleading eyes make me want to cave, but this is a way better plan.

"Don't worry, Mom, this is gonna be great! Plus, I can't just leave the other males to fend for themselves. In case you've forgotten, there are no women left in our kingdom." No one knows exactly what the curse did, but fifty years and not a single female born in the kingdom pretty much sums it up. So we invited females from all the other kingdoms here; it's brilliant. There will be so much love in the castle, it'll burst out the windows.

"I have not forgotten. I just think you have unrealistic expectations." She sits on the bed beside me, patting my knee. It's so cute that she's worried. "Are you sure you want all the males to take the memory potion? I know you don't want anyone to know which of you is the prince, but this seems extreme."

"Absolutely, I know the females won't know, but any of the lords or dukes could let it slip. If they all take the memory potion, the enchantment will make it so no one is quite sure. They may even think they are the prince. It evens the playing field, and the women will give everyone a chance. I mean, one look at me, and I'm sure they will want me anyway." I shoot Mom a wink. Really, it's the only way; it seems totally unfair to the other guys otherwise. Every woman wants to marry a prince. "In a couple of months, when I'm ready to reveal myself to my mate, we'll reverse it. It's foolproof."

"Famous last words," Mom mumbles. I almost missed it, but I have keen hearing. She sighs. "So just you and Rodan will keep your memories?"

"Yep. He's not going to tell anyone." Rodan is my oldest and best friend. I need him to help me in this, and I need him to know me to do that. If I wiped his memory of me, it would be almost his whole life. Whereas the others I've only met in passing. Man, this is gonna be fun.

Mom rolls her eyes. It's another of her tells that she loves my plan. "Warrick returned last night with the mortals. I still don't understand why you wanted mortals."

"He's back? He got them?" With excitement coursing through me, I jump off the bed. He actually got two mortal females to agree to come here. I can't believe it. Although I have never seen one, I'd venture to guess that Warrick found the most attractive ones. "I can't wait for Warrick to tell me everything! Okay, first the announcement, and then tonight we have the first ball."

"Warrick wasn't very forthcoming with information on the females." Mom looks a little annoyed. I'm honestly surprised Warrick was brave enough to keep the details secret. He's saving it for me, though. I know it. "Lorelai, on the other hand, said his methods were questionable, and the mortals were not pleased. Maybe we should send them back."

"No way." I give my mom my most no-nonsense look. "They stay. Just make it worth their while." I have to find a way to keep them here. "Maybe if they don't fall instantly in love with me—" I smile, knowing that could never happen. "When this is all over, we just send them home with a ton of money. I mean, mortals are super into money, right?"

Mom groans, pinching her brows again. I know I've won. "Okay, fine. Go get ready. The announcement is in an hour. I've got to prepare," she mumbles to herself again, and it's the cutest thing.

I hug my mom, lifting her up off the floor, and kiss her on the cheek before setting her down. She straightens her corset, giggling quietly to herself. She loves it when I do that, even though she pretends she doesn't. I run over to Dad and hug him, too. He grunts and pats me on the back. I can feel his pride in me. I am so ready to present my most dashing self.

As usual, the atmosphere in the throne room is genuinely lavish, and it never fails to captivate. The sun's rays illuminate the room with vibrant rainbows through prismatic glass. They combine with the celestial ceiling and flickering golden chandeliers, creating a magical ambiance of swirling light. The meticulously polished cobalt floor adds to the allure, resembling a serene ocean reflecting the candlelight. It's enchanting to look at. This chamber was designed to mimic being underwater, and it's utterly magical. Standing to the right of the dais with all the other males, we are ready for the ladies to arrive.

"Stand still. You look like you need to piss," Rodan hisses, always looking out for me. His dark brows furrow as his deep forest eyes seem to flare brighter. I stop bouncing on my toes; I didn't even realize I was doing it.

I catch a glimpse of white in the doorway and freeze. Here they come, the first two girls. The one on the right has bright red hair, and next to her is a girl with pale golden hair. Both of them are in white gowns with fur hoods.

As the females begin to file into the throne room in pairs, their elegant gowns and graceful demeanor add to the room's magic. Each echoing step they take fills me with anticipation. Beside me, the men are softly murmuring to each other. Excitement is thick in the air as we wait.

"The ladies Scarlette and Beatrix of Colire," a guard announces. I ignore who got that job today, only seeing the women taking up the spots across from us. They are gorgeous. Both of them have legs for days. One is a beautiful redhead with full lips, doe eyes, and a sprinkle of freckles over her nose. The other, a stunning blonde, that looks fierce, even with a smile on her face.

"The ladies Maysant and Loreena of Dialigh." My breath catches as I spot the next two; their exposed skin glimmers in rich, deep tones, and I wonder if they taste as sweet as they look. I'm dazzled by the pale gold and blue dresses they wear, flowing like water around their feet, and that long dark hair. Are all the women this gorgeous?

Lost in my daze, I miss the next four women who file in. Two in dazzling and colorful dresses of crimson, gold, and orange with lots of sparkling accents, and two who are as colorful without the sparkle in tones of green, aqua, and violet. The sparkly ladies look like twins; that could be fun. Two for me, none for you.

"Princess Owari of Aquaveno and Princess Yudoku of Lumoscavar." Oh! The sirens! I can't believe the sirens came. The lavender-haired one is definitely the lake siren; her lavender dress sways as she glides across the ground. They really are graceful; no wonder so many males are drowned by them every year. She's beautiful, like a marble statue. The one with teal skin is super cute; she must be the sea siren. Her small button nose, plump lips, and wide eyes give her an almost childlike appearance. I could just eat her up. She's so precious, but I have a feeling she'd eat me first. An icy chill runs down my spine, and sweat builds on my brow. I'm sure it's okay; they agreed to be here after all.

The next few to file in are the fox spirits from Wilkno and the fawns from Gloom Grove Forest. I'm definitely gonna have to talk to all of them. I can't believe how breathtaking all these girls are.

"Princess Juniper and Princess Nucifera of the Faeglo Forest."

"Oh. My. Gods. Pixies? They are adorable," I whisper to Rodan, who responds with a grunt. He's not even looking, staring straight ahead with a bored look on his face. Come on! I've never even seen half of these fae outside of books! I'm guessing the one with blue hair is a water sprite. They are so small, they can't be more than four feet tall. And they have little wings that flutter so fast.

"The ladies Jade and Catria of the mortal realm." I am gobsmacked by my first view of the mortals. A collective gasp rings out among everyone, and low murmurs of conversation echo around the room. The one mortal has long silver hair that glistens like molten metal in the sunlight. She is wearing black in contrast with her ivory skin. Her dark blue eyes are smoldering with rage. The light is dancing off the curls of the strawberry-blonde girl walking beside her friend. Her light blue eyes fill with wonder as she takes in the throne room in a stunning crimson dress. I cannot believe I'm actually seeing mortal females.

Warrick escorts the mortals to the side where the other females are waiting. Speaking quietly to the silver-haired one, he slips his hand to her lower back, trying to direct her. "Don't touch me!" She pulls away quickly and walks over to the wall. Oh, she looks fun, little firecracker, that one. She leans against the wall and crosses her arms over her chest. He leans in again to say something in her ear, and—is she mocking him? Her lips are moving with a grimace, darkening her features, subtly bobbing her head from side to side. I let out a short laugh. Is she truly making fun of the Captain of the Guard? Oh, this is fantastic. Warrick smiles, shakes his head, and walks away from her, returning to our side. I'll have to find out what he said to her later to elicit that response. The blonde looks around the room, taking in everything and everyone with wide eyes.

I hear the side door to the dais open, and Mom and Dad walk out. Oh boy, it's time. Mom will make her announcement, and then we can actually talk to these women. It's almost time to find my mate. Man, I thought I'd know on sight, but I guess not. They are all so pretty that I don't even know where to start. Dad sits on his throne while Mom steps forward, clearing her throat and calling the room's attention to her.

"Fifty years ago, a curse fell upon this land. The kingdom of Amara has not seen a female born since that fateful day. This can go on no longer. As we continue to work towards ending this curse, our males grow older with no prospects for marriage and, thus, no heirs.

"In the past, lords and ladies would have met within these hallowed halls and courted. Or they would have been betrothed through political alliances. We've invited each court of the realm to provide two ladies of their court to help further alliances and continue the peace we have meticulously maintained. Rather than arrange marriages, we'd like to give a chance to love matches. I anticipate this will take time, as not everyone experiences love at first sight." She pauses, and I know she's thinking about me. "During the season, we will hold balls and events. Otherwise, the castle amenities are at your disposal. You are all adults. I expect you to act as such." I can hear snickering from the guys beside me; she gives a pointed look at our side of the room.

"Gentlemen, you are forbidden from revealing your station or title, as we'd like to keep things fair and not have every girl clamoring for a prince. Ladies, you may speculate all you like." She winks at the females. "But the men have been temporarily enchanted not to know who among them is a prince, as there may be more than one. This should make things—interesting. All men are in the south wing. Ladies, you are in the west wing. Please remain out of the east wing, as those are the royal quarters," she finishes, once again looking at our side of the room.

My father stands and steps beside Mom, putting his hand in hers. "Let the courting season begin!" he booms, stepping aside to lead his wife back to her throne.

Chapter 6
Jade

This room is spectacular, but I feign disinterest. Everything is shades of blue with gilded accents. Opulence as a word doesn't do it justice. The floor glitters as the echoes of footsteps bounce around the room. With Warrick walking beside me, I locked my eyes forward and took in as much as possible. Men to the right of the room, ladies to the left. Apprehension, front and center.

As the queen stepped onto the dais, I couldn't help but gawk. I've never seen royalty outside of TV, and she is radiant. Her cream gown flows around her regal form, with touches of red that add to her stately appearance. Her mahogany hair is swept up off her shoulders, with light wisps framing her face. Dark eyebrows frame her piercing blue eyes. She is tall and majestic, given even more presence by the onyx, spiked crown upon her head.

As she makes her speech, I'm captivated by so much, from the queen to the devastatingly handsome king who sits behind her, hanging on her every word. He has perfectly styled short blonde hair and a purposeful shading of stubble on his face. King meets rugged model. Seriously, they are both so stunning that they are almost painful to look at.

I drag my eyes from the dais, and the queen talks of finding a love match. "Right, sure, that sounds perfectly reasonable. For fucking kidnappers," I whisper to Cat as I try not to stare at the fucking mermaids and fairies that walked into the room beside me. I land my eyes on the men across the room.

"They are staring." Cat leans into me, nodding towards the men.

"More like leering. Lord, help me."

"Some of them are gorgeous. Like, should be illegal gorgeous."

I put on the most disdainful face I can muster as I appraise them. Nearest to the queen is a man with long, golden, wavy hair, in a puffy, long-sleeved white shirt and leather pants. "That one reminds me of a pirate," I snicker under my breath.

"Don't laugh; most of them are dressed like that," she says, trying to hold in a giggle.

"Pirate chic," I snort as Cat almost loses her composure.

Next to him is a guy who looks shockingly like the demon from my favorite k-drama. "Seriously, did he just walk out of a fantasy romance?" I motion to him, admiring his nearly black hair that looks like it's almost down to his ass. His dark eyes look bored. He's the only one who doesn't appear to be checking out the buffet of women across from him. Here is the tall, dark, and surly man I expect to find in a fae realm, with what looks like muscles to match. His outfit is almost identical to the blonde beside him, but all black. I quickly avert my eyes as my libido starts getting ideas.

"Breathe. While he may look like a walking wet dream, bad boys are never the good choice, no matter how attractive they may seem at the time." Cat smothers a smile.

"I have a severe problem. Oh, put a leather jacket on a smolderingly hot guy and have him brood, and I melt like fucking butter. What the fuck is wrong with me! I've been kidnapped. This is not the time to check out the merchandise," I whine in exasperation.

Moving down the line as nonchalantly as possible, I see drop-dead gorgeous men with silver hair like mine. Actually, I see about four men with hair like mine. Interesting. A man with short honey-blonde hair like the king, with his shirt unbuttoned low, giving me a peek at his very muscular physique. "He looks like sex on a stick. Okay, next, before I drool." I pull Cat's attention to the guys I'm looking at. Next to him is a man who looks very similar but has dark red hair, looking amused as he notices me checking him out.

Crap.

Slowly, I turn my head as if I don't care. A majority of the men are breathtaking to look at. "Like, how are they all so hot?" Only a few bring me back to reality: a squat, broad man who appears to have no neck. A man who looks old enough to be my father—ew. Some men appear to be less muscular and more reed-thin. Most of the men are attractive in their own right, but only a few stand out.

"I finally get my first taste of freedom in five years, and now the fae have kidnapped me to date these men," I lament. "On one hand, damn, some of these guys are gorgeous. On the other—what? The. Fuck. Maybe the queen will hear me out?"

"I love reading about this kind of thing in books, but in reality, I'm ready to pee myself."

"Fuck Warrick, if I ever make it out of here, I'm done with men." I scowl at Warrick.

"Let the courting season begin!" the king booms, jolting me right out of my stupor. Shit! Now is my chance.

I give Cat a look, and we both rush for the dais. "Your Majesty! Your Majesty!" We run to the bottom of the platform. "Please, Your Majesty!" As they turn, the queen cocks an eyebrow, and we both freeze, dropping into what I'm sure are the worst curtseys.

"Ah, the mortals. May I help you?" The queen stares down her nose at us as she sits beside her husband. He rests his elbow on the armrest, leans over, and whispers in her ear before setting his chin in his hand. The queen smiles; it's vicious and has me taking a small step back.

"We would like to go home, Your Majesty," I manage to get out in a rush. Cat nods vigorously.

"Warrick did state that he didn't exactly explain what you agreed to," she pauses. "However, due to the curse in our lands, we are willing to try anything to break it, including mixing mortal bloodlines with our own. If in a few months, you have not made a match with any of our fae, I'll let you return to the mortal world. Your world is capitalistic, yes?" I'm confused by the queen's question, but nod anyway; it's pretty accurate. "Then, if things don't work out here, we will send you home with a king's ransom. Stay here and try to find love. If you fail, return and live like queens in your old world." She smiles. "If that will be all, you are dismissed. Go mingle." And she turns to her husband.

Well, fuck, now what?

We slink away from the dais and over to the side of the room furthest from the crowd in the center. "So, stay and find love, or go home rich in a few months?" Cat muses. "Yeah, um, that solves the problem of, we are probably gonna be fired by the time we make it back." She laughs. "I may be able to live with this."

"Live with this? Are you serious?" My mind is reeling. How—why—what do we do? My heart is still thundering in my chest. The idea of meeting and giving a chance to fae men. Hot fae men. Nope! Get your head in the game. No more naïve decisions that get you into bad situations. Going home rich would be nice, though.

As I'm contemplating all my life decisions that led me to this moment, a flurry of color comes careening towards me. My vision is taken up by a barrage of blue floating before me. "Oh, my gods! You must be the Mortals!" The blue pixie has her hands on my cheeks, pinching my mouth together as I stare wide-eyed at her. Her hair is a dark blue that ripples like water in the light, tied back in a high ponytail. She turns my head left and right, getting a good look at me. Out of the corner of my eye, I can make out a blur of green, holding Cat by her shoulders as she flies in circles around her. "What's the mortal realm like?"

"Do you have parents?" the green one asks. We are both frozen, not sure what to do. What the hell is going on?

"Did you hatch from eggs?" Blue follows up.

Huh? Seriously?

"How many toes do you have?" Green looks down.

The blue one grabs my arm by the wrist with both hands, vigorously shaking. "Do you have magic?" She turns my hand over. "Where does it come out?"

"Are you shifters?" Green continues in their flurry of questions. "Oh, maybe they are sirens; look at the hair!" she points at me. Holy shit, what is going on? I'm looking back and forth at these pint-sized pixies, who change which of us they inspect with each question. It's a blur of colorful interrogation. I'm dumbstruck.

"Ladies, ladies, let the poor mortals be. I'm sure they will answer all your questions and more soon." The blonde guy with long, wavy hair makes a shooing motion with his hands while he smiles at them. The pixie's faces drop into a frown as they flutter back down to the ground and walk away dejected. They're not as small as I'd expect a pixie to be, standing about four feet tall.

"Thank you. I wasn't really sure what to do." I say, relieved at having been saved from the questioning.

"My pleasure, ladies. I am Killian," he says with a bow. "How are you finding our kingdom?" he winks. I'm unsure how to respond to the wink; it's left me flustered. "I hope the accommodations are to your liking. Warrick mentioned you told him you like books, so we made sure your rooms were across from an entrance to the library." He gives a big smile, which is kind of cute but also a little unnerving since he also has fangs. I wonder what those are for. It's probably a predator-type thing like lions. Why am I intrigued by this?

"The library is across from our rooms?" Cat is beside herself; I can feel the excitement radiating off of her. She is bouncing on her toes as she beams at this guy.

"Of course, we wanted you both to be comfortable." He gives her a lazy smile before putting all his attention on me. "You don't seem happy, Emerald." His brow furrows with sadness.

"My name is Jade, and I'm not sure how I feel, having been kidnapped and all."

"Yes, but emerald is my birthstone, and they are both green." He grins and winks again. "Warrick told me what happened." He laughs, and I scowl. The hell? "I know it's not what you were expecting. I promise it's so much better. It's like the start of a great romance. Whisked away to a faraway land to fall in love with your mate." With his hand held to his heart, he's got a dreamy look in his eyes. What planet does this guy live on? "It's gonna be great. You'll see. There's a ball tonight, and everyone will fall madly in love under the stars. It's how these things go. You are gonna love it." He looks as excited about this wild idea as Cat does about the books. Delusional, both of them.

The man with the long dark hair walks up behind Killian, patting him on the shoulder. "Ah, Rodan! Meet the mortals—Emerald and Catria." Killian gestures to us.

"It's Jade, actually." I shake my head at Killian. This guy.

"Charmed, I'm sure." He bows with one arm behind his back. It's such a smooth motion; his hair stays perfectly in place down his back. As he rises, I notice the lazy smile he has painted on his lips, like this is amusing to him. We make eye contact, his smile falters, and I am trapped by his deep green eyes that seem to grow darker by the second. My breath catches; I'm choking on air. The further I fall, the more the butterflies rise in my chest.

"Hi Rodan, it's nice to meet you." Cat cautiously steps forward, breaking the spell between us.

Rodan sneers as he steps back. "Right. I must go." He turns on his heel and walks away, heading straight for the door.

"Yeah, he's not much for social pleasantries. But I am. I'll escort you to the ball tonight, seeing as you don't know your way around yet." He smiles and walks away before I can respond to any of it.

"What was that?" Cat looks at me.

"Which part?"

"The part where you and k-drama-dream-boy eye-fucked?" Cat puts her hand on her hip.

"Do what? I—I didn't—I have no idea what you are talking about! Did you see the look on his face? He was repulsed by me," I stammer. Cat crosses her arms, unconvinced. "Anyway, what was up with that Killian guy? Seems he's got a few screws loose."

"Seems a lot of people around here do." She gives me a pointed look before turning her attention back to the room at large. "We got accosted by pixies."

"They seemed—nice." I laugh.

"Should we go back to our room and wait for some of the chaos to calm down? Maybe let the novelty wear off?"

I sigh. "Do you really think it will?"

"No." Cat looks around helplessly, spotting Warrick and waving him over. He smiles as he walks towards us. Cat closes the distance. "Can we get out of here? This is overwhelming." I nod in agreement.

I take another cursory look around the room and notice a few other guys looking at us and talking. "I don't think I want to deal with any more introductions. Those men look like they want to eat us."

Warrick laughs as he leans over and whispers, "Some of them do." He smirks while I glare at him. "Fine, fine, I'll walk you back to your room. But from here on out, you two are free to go where you please within the castle. Unless you want me around to escort you everywhere?" He waggles his eyebrow suggestively.

"Not a chance, but better the enemy you know." I half grin as we follow him towards the large double doors we came in through.

A hand snakes through mine from behind and closes, stopping me in my tracks and spinning me around. My breath catches in my throat as I'm caught off guard. Now, in front of me is the man with short blonde hair and his shirt open to his navel. Up close, I can see every muscle peeking out of the opening in his shirt, and lord, there are many of them. He's as tall as Killian and Rodan were. With him standing so close, I strain my neck to look up at him. Most of these men must be well over six feet tall. He's peering down at me through long lashes with a blush-inducing smile that spells trouble. Everything about this man screams danger, from his chiseled jawline to his rock-hard abs. "Hello," he purrs. "I was hoping to welcome you before you left. Excuse my impertinence." He brings my hand to his lips and lightly kisses my knuckles. "I am Bravos, and you are?" His words are slick as oil.

"Um—hi—I'm Jade." The look this man is penetrating me with is bringing out my shyest self. I make a poor attempt at getting my hand back. But the butterflies are back and dropping as low as the opening in his shirt.

He chuckles as I realize he's noticed me admiring him. I mean, come on. Who looks like that? And I am at eye level with his pecs. Also, about six inches away from him, it's time to take a step back. "Like what you see?" His smile grows broader and more dangerous. "I look forward to seeing you tonight." He brings my hand back up to kiss it again, but I pull it out of his hand and clutch it to my chest. "Save me a dance," he says with a slight bow and a softer smile.

"Umm, okay," I mumble before turning and running after Cat and Warrick, who are waiting by the door with raised eyebrows. "Don't say anything," I bark at Warrick, who raises his hand in defeat.

Chapter 7
Jade

It's been a couple of hours of peace and quiet in my room. Cat has been lost to the library, which I'll probably check out tomorrow since it appears we will be here for a while. At least the room is nice. As much as I want to kick Warrick's ass, he nailed my dream room.

I sit by the window to contemplate my next move. I guess I'm stuck here. The options could be worse, though. Stay here and find love. Ha, okay. Or go home rich for my trouble. I kind of like the idea of never having to worry about money again. Cat is going with option number two: go home rich. I'll be lucky if I ever get her out of the library. It's a whole new world of books at her disposal. I'm pretty sure I'll be right there with her, but for now, she's convinced me this is an excellent opportunity to get my feet wet in the dating pool again. Okay, I don't really agree with her, but maybe it's not a bad idea. Who am I kidding? It's a terrible idea. I have the worst taste in men. I always put myself out there and get hurt--badly. But there is no harm in having fun for a little while. At least I don't have to worry about running into my ex, which could be a dream scenario. I doubt any of these guys will be interested in me anyway. Some of those guys, my god, are gorgeous. I don't think I've felt my body react like this in years. This is dangerous.

One thing I don't have is a way to protect myself. I look around the room for anything that could be used as a weapon. It feels futile, but I hate feeling helpless. All I want is the comfort of knowing I could protect myself if something went wrong. Plus, I'm in a fae realm. Isn't that super dangerous for humans? In all the books, they make you dance till your feet bleed and drink fae wine, and–fuck, I need a weapon. All I see are closets full of clothes, shoes, and accessories. There isn't anything on the bed that is sharp, nor in the bathroom; soap and makeup won't help. A chair leg would make a good club, but all the chairs are pretty sturdy. However, the chair in the bathroom for the vanity might be easy to break. I wonder if nails are holding it together? Don't most stories about the fae have some mention of iron? I may be on to something here.

Looking out the window, I see the moons in the distance peeking out behind the mountains, a firm reminder that escape is futile. From what I can tell, the castle rests in a valley. Right beneath my window lies a garden that appears as if it's from a fairy tale. The gentle breeze makes the bubblegum pink trees sway gracefully amidst lavender grass, and patches of cobalt and fuchsia flowers bloom along the pathways. Surrounding a cerulean blue pond is dark amethyst ivy, while a lovely blush-colored weeping willow stands tall at its center. The entire garden is adorned in captivating shades of pink, blue, and purple, making it the most stunning and magical sight I've ever seen.

The dance is still a few hours away, but I get up to pick out a dress for tonight's festivities. I'll take my sweet-ass time getting ready, since I've got a closet full of clothes and a vanity full of makeup. I guess why not try to have a little fun? Maybe I'll see about busting up that chair after I do my makeup; it seems senseless to do it before. Then I'd have to drag another chair in there.

The collection of ball gowns in that closet is genuinely remarkable. I chose a breathtaking icy blue dress featuring a corset bodice embellished with iridescent crystals, which glisten like rainbows. The sleeveless design boasts a sweetheart neckline, and the enchanting crystals cascade down the voluminous skirt. With my hair elegantly braided and wrapped from one side of my head to the opposite shoulder and subtle makeup highlighted by a bold, berry-toned lip, I exude the aura of a fierce ice queen.

Cat was still in the library the last I saw. I have no idea if she's coming tonight, but she insisted I go. I think about the fact that she's a hypocrite as I drag the small vanity chair out of the bathroom to the center of the room. It's time to get out some aggression and get some nails. Hopefully.

I grab the back of the chair and lift it high above my head before slamming it down on the ground. I hear a crack and a thud, but nothing breaks. I bring it up again before getting similar results. "What the fuck?" I slam the chair repeatedly in my frustration, resulting in zero damage.

"What." Thud. "The hell." Thud. "Kind of." Thud. "Chair is this!" I slam the chair again. This was way easier in theory and much harder in a ball gown.

"What did that chair ever do to you?" a voice says behind me. I drop the chair with a thunk, spinning around to face the door, shocked to see Killian and Rodan standing in my doorway. Killian is grinning and trying to hide his amusement with his hand.

"Such violence," Rodan says, casually leaning against the door frame with a smirk playing across his mouth. I get little butterflies at the sight of them.

I stand up straight, putting my hands behind my back. "I...uh...I was just—" I search around the room for any excuse for the lunacy they walked in on. "There was a bug?" Don't question it. I smile more confidently. "There was a bug."

Rodan practically snorts. "A bug?...Interesting. Since there is an enchantment on the castle that keeps pests out." He sneers at me. "Although they let mortals in, so anything is possible." Yep, that one hates me. What bug went up your ass? It's probably where they keep the bugs they enchant away.

"Rodan, go find Catria so you can escort her." Killian dismisses Rodan, giving him a look before turning back to me. "Wow, you look lovely. I was banking on you wearing black again and tried to match." He looks down sheepishly at his incredible suit. It's almost like a modern style with flourishes that mimic medieval style. He is gorgeous.

I smile. "Well, I like your outfit and how it looks on you." My cheeks heat. "I mean, how it's the opposite of my look." I blush brighter. God, I hope this makeup conceals it. I've never met anyone who blushes as red as I do.

His smile is beaming. "So you like how I look?" He gives me a devilish once-over, "and how I'll look with you." Lord, help me. I'm not religious, but a girl needs a hand here. He walks towards me like a predator sizing up its prey. Stopping mere inches from me, he grazes his fingers down my arm, giving me goosebumps. I swallow hard. "Hi, Emerald." His voice has gone gravelly.

"Hi, Killian," I squeak out. What is going on with me? I'm bumbling for words, scared, and a little turned on.

He grabs my hand and beams again. "Are you ready to go to the ball? We are gonna have so much fun. You'll get to meet everyone you missed earlier today. I hope you're feeling okay. I was worried when you disappeared." He's semi-dragging me out of the room as he rambles, and I officially have whiplash from the abrupt mood change.

I glance around the hallway, expecting to see Rodan brooding, but there isn't a soul out here. I stumble as I try to keep up with his pace. "Umm, could you slow down? This dress isn't exactly easy to run in. And you are tall as hell."

"Oh, sorry." He laughs, slowing down to my pace. "So Warrick said you used to be married but aren't anymore?" He gives me a quizzical look.

"Uh, yeah. I'm no longer with him." I really don't want to talk about this with him right now. "What about you? Any ex-girlfriends I should be worried about?" Because you're interested? Why would you ask that, Jade? I'm apparently listening to hormones now?

He casts me a long, appraising look and smiles. "Nope. I'm a lone wolf. I've never left the kingdom, and there aren't many girls around here." He's still smiling but looks kind of sad, like a kicked puppy.

"Oh, so you've never—dated?" Please tell me I'm not dealing with a ballroom full of virgins. I can't handle that kind of pressure. I'm sure my face conveys my worries because he arches a brow and laughs.

"This isn't the first time ladies from other courts have been brought here, just never on this scale." He winks. I guess that answers that question. "Most of the other guys have traveled to other kingdoms, but this is the first mass experiment. Close quarters and all that should help the sparks fly," he says with a flourish of his hand. I can't resist a laugh. This guy is a hopeless romantic.

As we turn to exit the corridor my room is on, we go out onto an open-air hall. From this vantage point, the night sky appears positively stunning, with the moons casting a radiant glow that renders the lights almost unnecessary. Majestic arches crisscross the ceiling, ending in grand marble columns, creating an enthralling sight. The gray-blue granite floors glimmer under the moonlight, adding to the enchanting ambiance. It's a beautiful hallway, evoking a sense of dark allure and spellbinding my senses. I stop to stare at the moons in wonder, truly appreciating the sight for the first time. I can't believe I'm in another realm.

"It's beautiful, isn't it?" He sighs, and I startle, forgetting for a moment I'm not alone. Killian is looking out at the moons with wonder in his eyes.

"Yes, it's breathtaking. I was just taking it in. This is all still so crazy to me." I look at him, the moon's light tinging his features in a light blue haze. "Thank you for walking me. This place is so big, I'm sure I would have gotten lost."

There's that fifty-megawatt smile of his. "No problem. I'm glad you let me escort you. I know I can come on kind of strong sometimes, but I don't think I've ever been so excited. I really want to find my mate, and breaking the curse would be nice, too. I've been alone for so long, and this is kind of my last hope before an arranged marriage." I can't help but smile as we turn and continue walking. Yesterday, I picked up divorce papers. Today, I'm attending a bachelor-style ball. What life is this?

I steal a few looks at Killian as we walk. He has not stopped smiling, and I can't help but notice the revealed dimples. It's cute. I wonder if all the girls here are being escorted by someone. Or if Killian is trying to stake his claim. I guess I'll find out. Some part of me wants to believe the best in people and assume he's simply being nice.

"So why, may I ask, were you beating up that chair?" Killian casually asks as we round yet another corner. My cheeks heat; damn it, I figured he'd let that go.

"I was looking for nails," I admit a bit sheepishly.

"Nails."

"Iron," I correct myself

"Why iron?" His look has turned serious.

"You know, iron...hurts fae...I was looking for something I could use as a weapon."

"Ouch, that's not nice." His sad puppy-dog look breaks my heart. "But there were no nails in that chair anyway." He smiles and continues walking like nothing ever happened. I clench my jaw in frustration and have to scramble to keep up.

"Well, the legs would have worked like clubs, if they would have broken off," I mutter.

He stops and looks at me, cocks his head to the side, and bursts out laughing. "Oh, you are fun." He turns, guiding me through the hallway again, all the while snickering to himself. I am apparently an idiot. "If you would like to learn how to defend yourself, just ask. I'd gladly teach you. No chairs needed." He glances at me and gently brushes the back of my hand. The butterflies have returned to wreak havoc on my insides. That is actually a kind offer. If I'd been able to defend myself in the past, things would have turned out very differently.

"Are you okay? You seem to have gone deep in thought," Killian says, pulling me out of my head.

"Yes, sorry, I'm good. I was thinking about your offer. I appreciate it."

"It's only an offer." He stops and looks down at me. "There's no pressure. I'd like any excuse to get to know you better." His shy smile melts all the bad memories away.

"I'll think about it." I smile. "This is all a lot. I wasn't planning on dating for a very long time." If ever. I look down at the floor, unwilling to meet his eyes.

"Can I be your friend and start from there? I know I'm a lot when I'm excited. Just keep an open mind. I promise we really meant you no harm by bringing you here. If there is ever anything you need, just ask," he says, lightly lifting my chin with a finger to meet his eyes. "Let's go have some fun." He gives me a hopeful smile as he brushes the back of my hand with his again. I follow him as we continue walking.

After many more hallways and turns, we reach a spectacular outdoor atrium. Colorful lights dance in the air, creating a kaleidoscope of rainbows around the space. Tables and greenery surround a large marble dance floor. At one end is an orchestra playing upbeat music more akin to pop than classical. At the opposite end are tables laden with trays of food: meat platters, breads, pastries, candies, and a fountain flowing with red wine. This may not be the worst thing.

Everyone in the room looks ethereal. There is magic in the atmosphere I can't ignore. Ladies are dancing and seem to almost float. They are so graceful. I see the two pixies, still in their respective colors to match their hair, in long, form-fitting gowns with backs so low it's almost scandalous. Their wings draped down their backs like cloaks. Two girls next to them are talking and laughing, wearing what can only be described as winter bridal gowns. Their dresses are adorned with lace and fur. They look like goddesses next to the tiny pixies.

Transfixed by the scene around me, I startle when Killian speaks. "Romantic, isn't it?" The look on his face is pure bliss. "How about some wine, and you can mingle with the fae you haven't met yet?" He motions over to the table filled with glasses. "I must divide my attention, but save me a dance?" He casts me a wicked smile before bounding away towards a group of men.

"I—um. Okay," I stammer as he leaves me. Mingle...yeah, I'm great at that. Not. I sigh as I go towards the table. This won't be awkward at all.

"Wine, my darling?" a smooth voice cuts into my thoughts. I look up to see Bravos moving towards me with a glass in each hand.

"Yeah, thank you." I take the wine, intending to upend it, before pausing right before it hits my lips. "This isn't like—dangerous for mortals, right?"

He shakes his head, a smirk playing at one corner of his lips. "No, those practices died out eons ago. I assure you, I'd never put you in danger." His gaze bores right through me. I cast my eyes down to avoid the intensity. Are all fae this intense?

I take a long drink of the wine; it's heavenly, sweet, aromatic, and smooth. Liquid courage, here I come.

"How is it? Up to your standards, I hope." He's still staring at me intently. I nod in confirmation. "Good, come dance with me. I'd love to get to know more about you." He reaches for my empty glass and sets it on the table while taking my hand with his other. "You look ravishing tonight. I noticed you the moment you walked through the doors."

"Thank you. I really love this dress."

"It complements your beauty well," he says. I don't know what to say, so I follow his lead onto the dance floor. It's not until we are there that I notice the tempo of the music has turned slow, and men escort women out to the floor all around the room.

He pulls me into him, pressing me against the hard planes of his body. "I don't know the dances of your realm."

"I lead; you just follow along." He wraps one arm around my waist and takes my hand with the other. Looking around, hardly anyone is dancing this close. However, the positioning is the same. "Tell me about yourself, princess." He angles himself to whisper in my ear, sending a shiver down my spine.

"I'm just a normal girl, not a princess." He's pressed so tightly to me, I'm sure he can hear me. "I work a good job and make enough money to support myself. Or at least I did." I'm sure that not showing up to work today will put a wrench in that.

"Humm, work. Doing what?" How is this man making it sound dirty? It's just a question.

"I am, well, I guess, was an executive assistant to the CEO of a big company."

"What is a CEO?"

"Oh, umm, like a business owner, he was in charge of everything. And I helped him."

"This man owned you?" he growls.

"No! No, I worked for him and got money in exchange." Okay, not an easy concept to this fae, got it. "Anyway, I didn't do much else; just hung out with Cat when I wasn't working."

"Cat? The other mortal. You enjoyed working?" he says, like it's disgusting. I can't help but smile. Has Bravos ever worked a day in his life? What do these guys do?

"Nope, hated it. But the money made it possible to support myself and divorce my husband, so it's not too bad."

He pulls back, looking at me with astonishment. "You are mated?" A crease forms between his eyebrows.

"No! Not anymore! In my world, if you get married and it doesn't work out, you get divorced. I'm divorced." The culture shock here is gonna take some getting used to. He grumbles and pulls me back in tight. This is a little unsettling. Hopefully, not all the guys here are this forward.

"Good, I'd hate to think I didn't have a chance." He smirks at me.

"So..." I say, trying to break the tension. "What about you?"

He stands a bit straighter, making eye contact with me. "I am glorious. Trained like a warrior, I have stunning good looks, and while I can't remember, I'm pretty sure I'm a prince. I've lived a great life, traveling, partying, meeting fine ladies like yourself." He winks at me. Seems a bit full of himself, exactly how I'd expect a prince to be. He leans back down. "What do you do for fun?" His voice low and gravelly again.

My mind goes to dark places, things I'd like to do for fun, like run my hands down—stop. Don't fantasize about the hot guy you don't know. Warrick should have been lesson enough. I really need to stop drinking around hot guys. Collecting my thoughts, "I like to read and watch shows."

"Read?" He sighs at the word like it offends his sensibilities. "Go on a picnic with me tomorrow."

Direct. "Um, why?"

"Because I want to spend more time with you, and if I don't ask you now, someone else might." His face has become solemn.

"But I'm spending time with you now." I shrug.

"I'm not allowed to monopolize your evening; none of us are.

Queen's rules," he says with a roll of his eyes. "So tomorrow, picnic in the enchanted garden. I'll send for you." He steps back as the song ends, lifting my hand into a soft kiss again, which sends butterflies through my stomach. Bravos walks away without another word. I guess that's that.

I grab another glass of wine and take in the spread of food on the table. Wine will be future me's problem. The food looks delicious. Holding a plate, I pile it with as many things as possible: skewers of meat, steamed veggies, and a heap of desserts. With plate and wine in hand, I walk to an empty table and sit, ready to feast.

My attention is taken by the two lovely women who walk over and sit on either side of me, both holding plates piled as high as mine. "Oh, thank the gods, another lady who eats!" The one who speaks has a rich caramel tone to her skin and beautiful chestnut-colored hair flowing out of a headscarf of deep burgundy; her gown is forest green and drapes around her form like a Grecian goddess.

The other girl is wearing the same outfit with the colors reversed, and the scarf is draped over her shoulders, her curly, light brown hair cropped below her chin. They look like they strolled off the pages of One Thousand and One Nights. I recognize them from earlier, but can't recall their names. "I know," she says between mouthfuls. "They just look longingly at the food but never touch it. Bless their hearts." Is that a Southern twang? It can't be. I guess I didn't think about regional differences in fae. So much to learn.

"Oh, pardon our manners. I'm Lyra, and this is Arlin," the first one clarifies, taking a big bite of a tart. "We really don't know anyone here yet, and you were all alone. Been waitin' an hour for someone to make the first move on the food." She looks towards the wine fountain and waves her hand in the air. A glass lifts off the table and fills itself in the fountain before floating over the heads of the other guests and into her hand. Holy shit, that was cool. Is it rude to ask how the hell she did that? I don't think I'll ever get used to these people and their magic.

"I think a lot of them ladies are afraid to mess up their dresses." Arlin grins.

"Or their figures. I heard that the ladies of Colier rarely eat. Cold stomachs, cold hearts, cold beds," Lyra says with a devilish wink, popping a bite-sized cake in her mouth. A bit harsh for people you haven't met yet, but who am I to judge?

Tipping her head back in laughter, Arlin interrupts, "You can't say stuff like that in polite company, Lyra." At this, I laugh with them. As I taste every wondrous thing on my plate, I feel more relaxed. I think the wine is finally settling my nerves.

Cat comes careening into the table, nearly dropping her plate as she sits beside Lyra.

"Whoa, girl, what's the rush?" Lyra laughs.

"Edgar tried to talk to me," Cat grunts and motions over her shoulder. "Told him I was late for dinner with Jade. Only just escaped a dance. That guy is gross." She shudders.

"The ogre with no neck?" I grimace while Cat nods, taking a bite of her food.

"Oh, he's no ogre. They are very polite. Quite lovely actually, once you get past their um faces." Arlin giggles.

"Truly, Arlin has dated a few. Such sweethearts. But Edger..." she groans, "he is a different breed. He asked me for a roll in the hay right off the bat earlier. Well, I never." She flutters her long, dark eyelashes with her hand over her heart. "I may not be a blushing violet, but that is just crude." I have to shove a laugh down. This is too much. Cat looks stunned, wide eyes searching mine. "You made the right choice." Lyra pats Cat's knee.

"I wasn't expecting you to leave the library tonight. What changed?" I say as I slide my glass of wine over to Cat, who obviously needs it. Lyra has four more glasses of wine float over to the table and settle in front of us. It's such a handy trick.

Cat downs a glass in one gulp. "Rodan," she huffs before shoving a tiny cake in her mouth and chewing angrily. "That asshole took my book, picked me up, and threw me over his shoulder. Then he took me to my room, pulled a dress from my closet, threw me and the dress on the bed, and told me I had five minutes to put it on or he'd dress me himself." She throws her hands up in exasperation. "So I put on the fucking dress because who knows if he'd make good on that threat. I have no desire to find out." She downs another glass of wine and looks around, standing as she spots the fountain. "So here I am, participating in this shitshow. You want another glass?" I laugh and nod as she storms off.

"Boy, she's like whiskey in a teacup." I give Arlin a blank look because what? "You know, all ladylike on the outside but feisty on the inside?" she clarifies. I roll with laughter while nodding.

"I heard that Rodan fella doesn't want to participate. He's only here because Killian asked him to be," Arlin muses. "He's sizzling, though, if you like insufferable jerks." I can't help but laugh with them.

Cat returns with the wine and digs into her food again. "So, are we the first mortals you've met? I imagine, based on the stories in our world, we can't be the first ones here."

Arlin and Lyra look at each other before looking down at their plates. Arlin speaks, "You're not the first mortals to come here, darlin'. It happens occasionally for this reason or that," she pauses and takes a sip of wine. "Sometimes mortals follow a fae unwittingly through a portal." She shrugs and leans in like she's telling a secret. "Sometimes they are kidnapped," she says lower. I exchanged a look with Cat. "Sometimes it's a changeling situation." Taking a long drink of wine and looking nervous. "But you are the first we've met."

"Changelings? Like the stories of swapping human children for fae children?" Cat's eyes are bright as she looks at Arlin.

"Oh, I'm afraid that was our kingdom," says a voice behind me. We all look up to see the beautiful dark-skinned fae, dressed in shades of purple, standing beside our table. She looks a bit sheepish. "We don't do it anymore," she quickly adds, sitting next to Arlin and sweeping her long, dark, curly hair over her shoulder.

"Why did you take children?" I ask.

"We were at war, and the heirs were usually a big target. So to protect them, we would swap them out with a mortal and then swap them back when it was safe."

"Children were targets?" I don't even know what to say.

"Oh yes, especially babies. They are easy targets and weaken a family line if one is lost. But don't worry, we gave back the mortals that didn't die." My eyes widen at the thought.

"And what would happen if it was never safe to bring them home?"

"Oh, the mortals would just stay here, and the heir stayed there. Happened a few times." She laughs, "I'm sure there are tons of people running around your world having no clue that they have fae blood. It happened a lot." Wait, did it happen a few times or a lot? How much is a lot?

"How long ago did you stop stealing children?" Cat looks a little pale as she stammers out the question. I take another sip of my wine.

"Oh, maybe seventy or so years ago." She shrugs.

"Why didn't you swap them back when they were older?"

"Usually, we forgot, and there was a new heir by then." She shrugs as if it's no big deal and smiles. "Dark topics—this is an interesting table to be discussing politics during a party. By the way, I'm Maysant." She kicks her feet up on the chair beside her and grabs her wineglass off the table.

"Hi, I didn't realize it was a political topic. You said it was your kingdom that did it?" I don't even know where to begin with this information.

"Well—" Lyra interjects, "it was most of our kingdoms." She smiles. Turning to Maysant, "You're from Marapor, right? We traveled through there on our way over here. It was a beautiful country."

"You didn't bring a portal master?" Maysant looks confused.

"Oh, we did!" Arlin interrupts. "But we really wanted to see Dialigh since we've never been. It's so beautiful."

"Ah, makes more sense, a short vacation before the pageantry." She rolls her eyes as she finishes her glass of wine. "Now, if you'll excuse me. I am required to dance with no less than three men at each of these balls, and I've got a grand total of zero so far." She flashes a wicked smile that tells me this is not her idea of a good time. She walks up to a man brooding at another table and runs her finger through his long hair, tucking a piece back into his top knot. She's brave because that man looks like a barbarian warrior out of a fantasy novel, all hard muscle and stern features. He gets up and walks behind her, watching her every step as she sways her hips. Boy didn't know what hit him. She's good.

Chapter 8
Rodan

This. Is. Stupid.

The whole damn thing. There's a gods damned curse on the kingdom, and they are playing matchmaker. I want to support Killian, but this is seriously the stupidest plan he's come up with yet. This will not work. This will not break the curse. Collecting the mortals will fix nothing.

After being dismissed by his royal ass, I found the other mortal sitting in the library reading a book. I attempted to ask her to get dressed and let me escort her. She fucking refused. So I dragged her ass here. She seemed about as pleased as I felt about it.

As soon as we walked in the door, she was accosted by Edgar. I almost laughed as I walked to a dark corner. I hate that guy, but I'm guessing few people like him. He has been trying to get one of the women into his bed all day. Thinks he's god's fucking gift to women. The mortal ran off and escaped to a table of other women. To the table with Jade—that girl is trouble.

I was amused earlier when I saw her trying to break an unbreakable chair. Had to hand it to her; she was really trying. I don't think I'll tell her the furniture was enchanted after a drunken night with Killian and me a few years ago. We broke a lot of furniture, and the queen was pissed. Thinking about it almost brings a smile to my face, but that's not sending the right message to these dumb fucks. Gods, I hate balls.

Standing in the corner, I can see everything that is going on. The pixies Juniper and Nucifera are not flittering about for once and are calmly talking to Sorrel and Ambrose. Bravos is off talking with his brother, Hawkin. Those two are insufferable twits. Ellis and Calazar are sitting at a table deep in conversation, probably talking about how much gold it takes to host a ball like this.

Killian and Ryker are talking to the ladies from Colire and Gloom Grove Forest. The fawns from Gloom Grove Forest are an interesting sort, a little skittish, but the horns, long ears, and freckles make them intriguing. Even in their fae form, they strongly resemble deer in their features. The elves from Colire—well, they dressed as if it were their damned wedding day. The redhead is pretty, with dark red hair curled perfectly into ringlets, freckles over her cheeks, and an innocence in her eyes that's all show. As for the blonde, she has a certain allure to her, with her full lips and green eyes, but the overly styled hair ruins it for me. I don't trust any of the women who have been brought here.

Mortals and Sirens, Killian has lost his damn mind, and I refuse to give any more thought to the mortals. Especially Trouble. My gaze drifts to the table where the silver-haired mortal sits. She's laughing as if it's a typical day. She is unaware of the danger she's in. Not that I care. I refuse to spare that woman a thought. But did she have to wear a dress that pushes her chest up like that? It's bad enough she's the curviest girl here; does she really have to flaunt it like that? Fuck, I need a drink.

"Rodan. There you are." Fucking Killian. "Isn't this the best?" His smile is almost blinding as he walks up with Ryker.

"I hate that you required me to be here," I grumble.

"Ah, but you wouldn't have come if I hadn't." He gives me that stupid puppy-dog face; it almost makes me smile. "Anyone catch your eye yet?" His smile returns like this is the cat's pajamas.

"No," I grumble.

"What do you know about the mortals?" Ryker looks their way. I can see the intrigue in his eyes. I roll mine.

"They seem a little standoff-ish, but I think we'll wear them down. I really like the feisty one with silver hair. But I don't think she's interested." Sadness sweeps over Killian's features. Of course, he likes her. Just my fucking luck.

"The other one, drinking wine like a soldier and eating like a barbarian?" Ryker asks, staring intently at Catria.

"She's a brat." I shrug.

"Seemed nice to me, but good luck getting her attention away from the library. Rodan had to practically drag her here." Killian gives me a smug smile.

"Practically, try literally. She hissed and scratched the whole time, too," I deadpan.

"Ask her to dance." Killian nudges his shoulder.

"Really gonna throw him to the wolves like that, Killian? She probably bites." I smirk.

A low growl comes from deep in Ryker's chest; I'm unsure if it's a warning or arousal. Ryker upends his glass of wine, gulping down the contents, and turns on his heel, stomping across the dance floor, headed straight towards Catria. Gods help his soul with that one. She's in a pissy mood, thanks to me.

Killian and I stand and watch the show. I await the carnage that is sure to ensue.

Ryker approaches her, and she gulps. He leans down close to her ear and whispers something. She slowly leans back with wide eyes and pink cheeks. What the hell did he say to her? I almost want to laugh at her expression. He holds his hand out to her, and to my surprise, she accepts it and stands, following him to the dance floor.

"Huh, kind of expected him to get slapped," I grumble in disappointment. I like Ryker. He's a gentle giant but has terrible luck when it comes to talking to ladies. He's the strong, silent type. I'm surprised he said anything to her and didn't walk up, grab her hand, and drag her out.

I turn my gaze to Killian, who's practically got hearts in his eyes. "Why aren't you dancing, puppet master?"

"I wanna dance with Emerald, but she's still eating. I also wanna ask one of the sirens, but I'm scared. Why aren't you dancing?"

"No," I grumble while watching Ryker and Catria. He's holding her close and kind of swaying. I guess neither of them knows how to dance, morons. She's chattering away, and he already looks like a love-sick pup. Great. It's almost comical the way he towers over her. His six-three frame with her being what? One hundred pounds soaking wet? He has at least a foot on her and probably a hundred pounds. She twists his long hair in her fingers that I doubt he bothered to brush, let alone tie back.

"Come on, just pick a girl. One dance, everyone else is required no less than three," he pleads. I come out of my thoughts and glare at Killian.

"For fuck's sake, will it make you shut up about it?" I growl.

"Yes. Oh, my gods, this is so great." He's bouncing on his toes again. "This is merely the beginning. We will melt that cold heart yet." He slaps me on the shoulder, and I wipe the idea of punching him from my mind. Killian is simply excited, I remind myself as I search for my prey.

A flash of silver catches my eye. Trouble is scurrying away from the wine fountain back towards the table Catria was at. Edgar is strutting after her, a man on a mission. Trouble looks back and makes a sharp turn towards one of the pillars. She's trying to hide. This brings a dark grin to my face. I don't realize I'm moving until I'm across the room, rounding the other side of the pillar she ran to.

She comes careening around the pillar and smacks right into my chest. Clearly startled, she braces herself on my chest before looking up, panting. I stare down at her and smirk.

"Oh… I'm so sorry." Her chest is heaving, and I have a feeling she's been scurrying around longer than I realized. I like this breathless rasp in her voice. I feel my dick twitch; apparently, it enjoys the view of her chest heaving as she struggles to breathe.

"Going somewhere?" I bring my hand to her waist to steady her.

"I was trying to get away from Edgar." She flails her hand behind her. "He creeps me out." She brings her hand to her chest, drawing my attention back there. A little bead of sweat trails down and disappears between her cleavage. I tighten my grip on her waist. She still has one hand firmly planted on my chest; realizing this, she steps back and drops her hand. "How's your night going?"

"I hate these things."

She turns and peeks around the pillar before spinning around, looking panicked. "Dance with me."

"What?" I deadpan. I'm caught off guard. And I have a bad feeling that if I agree, my dick will take over all rational thought.

She grabs my hand and tries to spin me towards the dance floor. She pulls with all her might, but I'm firmly rooted in place; all she manages to do is extend my arm. "Please, he's coming. Just stop being a brooding jerk for two seconds and help a damned damsel in distress," she practically growls at me. This elicits a laugh from me. She stops, juts out a hip, and puts her hand on it. "What's so funny?"

"You, a fucking damsel in distress. Right. I saw you beat the hell out of that chair. That poor defenseless chair." I know I'm taunting her. She's staring daggers at me as I laugh and retake her hand, leading her out to the dance floor. I am going to regret this.

I pull her into the dance position and begin to move. She stumbles a bit but eventually figures out the rhythm. "Do they not dance in the mortal realm?" I smirk at her.

"Yes, they do. But I don't know your fancy dances." She sneers at me.

"Obviously," I taunt. "It's like trying to dance with a rhino."

"You're really charming, you know that," she says flatly.

I smile, showing her my fangs. "I'm no such thing and never said I was." Pulling her in closer, pressing her body into mine as I lean close to her ear. "This is no fairy tale, Trouble." This close, her vanilla and sugar scent washes over my senses. With her body pressed against mine, rational thought is leaving the building.

She stiffens her posture. "Oh no? Well, you've certainly got the beast trope down."

I give a low laugh. "You have no idea," I whisper in her ear. I can feel the shudder roll through her body, her scent changing slightly, going a little spicy—interesting. Trouble likes to play?

We spin around the dance floor for another song in silence. Her face gives nothing away; I have no idea what she's thinking. What I do know is that her scent is intoxicating; I want to bury my face in her neck. I want to see how strong it would get if I kept taunting her. Keeping my hands from wandering is proving more difficult than I thought. Especially with her pressed against me. But I've never touched a woman that inappropriately without permission, and I won't start now.

"Do all fae dances require you to dance so close?" She pushes back a little, not going anywhere in my hold. I've caught a little mouse. I'm gonna play with it.

"No, why?" Amusement fills my chest.

"Because Bravos ground himself up against me, too," she grumbles like she's not enjoying this. But this strikes a nerve. Bravos? She danced with Bravos? Of all the simpering fae here, of course, the bastard was after her. I almost feel sick at the thought of that man putting his hands on her. She doesn't belong here; the sooner she leaves, the better.

With a sneer, I gaze at her as I withdraw. "You let that filth touch you?"

She looks slightly taken aback before she turns her features to indifference. "Not that it's any of your business, but yes." That smug expression on her face says it all; she liked it, too.

"I guess you're as empty-headed as I thought. Mortals don't know a real fae when they see one, nor could they handle one if they tried." Before she can say another word, I spin her away from me, pointing her towards the wine, and walk off in the other direction. Let her think the worst of me. She is better off that way.

There, I danced.

Fucking Bravos. Not that I should care. Who gives a damn who Trouble dances with? She was a means to an end. Now Killian will leave me alone. I sit down at a table where I can see most of the room.

"You look like you could use a drink, Rodan." Warrick takes the seat beside me, sliding over a glass of wine. He casually sips his as he looks around the room. He's overdressed, like everyone in the room, wearing the dress uniform of the guard. "Saw you dance with Jade. How'd that go?" His grin says he already knows.

"She's insufferable. Heard she hates you."

He laughs and slaps the table. "You have no idea. I took her the night she was celebrating her divorce being final." He takes a sip of his wine. "She was very drunk by the time I found her. I liked her spunk, though."

"How'd you convince them to come to this charade?" I take a sip of wine, watching the lavender-haired siren talk to Ellis. She's draped herself across his table to get his full attention, the slit in her form-fitted gown gaping open, showing off the entire length of her leg. He is beet red. I'm guessing he won't be standing up for a good while, or that siren will get a nice view of the tent he probably has in his pants.

"I may have been a bit cryptic on the details." Warrick laughs. He sips his wine and follows my stare. "Looks like Ellis is in trouble. She hasn't taken her eyes off him all night. I guess it is true what they say about sirens. They like their men intellectual over brawny."

I stifle a laugh. "Damn, poor guy. He probably already smells his doom. Fuck, every one of these halfwits is fucking doomed."

Looking back at me, Warrick leans back in his chair. "That include you?"

"Fuck no. I've got bigger things to worry about than women." Like trying to save a kingdom.

"If you say so." Warrick grins at me.

"What about you? You participating in this bullshit?"

"Am I supposed to?" He lifts a brow. "I was just sent to collect them. Bait." He laughs, "Portal master's job is never done and all that shit." He takes another swig of wine. "Jade is pretty hot. I had a good time with her in the mortal realm, but I'm pretty sure she wants to castrate me." We both laugh. I mean, if what I heard is correct, I wouldn't blame the girl. "Maybe try my luck with foxes. The redheaded one is pretty cute."

"You, with a fox shifter? You'd break her in half." I laugh as I try to picture it. "If you could catch her, that is. They are pretty quick."

Warrick glares at me. "Better than Beatrix. That girl is convinced she's gonna sniff out a prince. Says she's got a sense for it." He gives me a look that says we both know that's bullshit. "Beware of that one."

"The blonde one from Colire?"

"That's the one. She's been sniffing around like a dog in heat." He nods towards her on the dance floor, fawning over Hawkin. Hawkin has his hand barely above her ass, and from this angle, I can't tell if he's whispering into her neck or sucking on it. It's a disturbing image. I guess I know who she is shacking up with tonight. Hawkin is Bravos' little brother; both of them are pompous, arrogant asses raised by pretentious, smug parents who sew deceit into the kingdom at every opportunity. Let the royal chaser think he's a prince; serves them both right.

"Looks like Killian is trying his luck with Jade again." Warrick points his glass towards the two of them, talking off to the side of the fountain. She's drinking her wine and smiling at Killian. After a bit, he sets down her glass and takes her out to dance. They are both all smiles, and the sneer returns to my face. Of all the females here, why is he so smitten with the damn mortal?

"She's trouble," I grumble.

Warrick raises an eyebrow before settling into a smirk. "Jealous?"

"No, disgusted," I deadpan.

"Oh, my mistake. I'll get more wine while you brood." Warrick walks away with both glasses in his hand. Asshole, why would I be jealous? I can't stand the girl. Jade is an opportunist who is here to make things worse. She is going to break Killian's heart and leave, and make the rest of us pick up the pieces. She will run for the hills and never look back at the first sign of trouble. It's how they all are.

In a dark corner, I let my gaze travel about the large atrium. Edgar has the twins cornered, although they are both touching his arms, and I'm disturbed to think they might be hitting it off. Quickly averting my eyes from that train wreck, I spot Ellis with the siren now in his lap. Holy shit, go Ellis. Unless she eats you, then RIP, man.

Scanning around, I see the redhead from Colire, Scarlette, talking to the russet-complexioned fox with short, bronze, curly hair. They are walking towards one of the gardens and giggling. Before I lose sight of them, the fox kisses the redhead and bolts out the door. The other girl gives chase, and they both disappear into the dark garden. That brings a smile to my face. It was cute and the first genuine interaction I've seen tonight. I'm no romantic, but a small part of me wants to see them work out—a tiny part of me. Fuck, I'm going soft.

Warrick returns with the wine, setting down both glasses before turning around and stalking away. I look in the direction he's headed and see the other fox, Fennec. She's talking with the fawns and a group of guys. Good luck with that, man.

Many glasses of wine later, Killian is still dancing with Jade to a slow melody, but it looks like he's practically holding her up. She's either drunk or that tired. It is getting pretty late. Ryker is still dancing with Catria; she's still chattering away while he stares at her adoringly. Fuck, I've lost them both.

I sit enjoying my wine, waiting for the night to be over. Then I'll have at least a week before the next ball. So long as the queen doesn't get any bright ideas about more group activities.

As the night grows late, Killian walks up to me carrying Trouble in his arms. "I need you to escort Jade back to her room for me."

"Why don't you do it?"

"Because Warrick needs my help to escort the sirens back to their rooms; they are drunk." He goes pale, and I bark out a laugh. I guess I didn't draw the short straw tonight.

"Why doesn't Ellis do it? He was cozied up to one earlier."

"Because he's passed out in his room. The siren came back down a few minutes ago," Killian explains. Oh, shit. I hope the poor fucker is still breathing.

"Fine, hand her over." I stand impatiently, taking Trouble from his arms and adjusting my hold on her. This enormous dress makes it hard to find her beneath the skirts.

"Ah, fuck no," she slurs as she cracks her eyes open.

"How much wine did you give her?" I lift an eyebrow at Killian.

"Only like three or four glasses." He shrugs.

"And how many did she have before that?"

"Only like three or five," she trails off before smiling innocently. So, she is entirely tits-up drunk then. Wonderful. I guess I can't blame her. I'd likely be blitzed if I woke up in another realm, too.

Killian is already turning to go help Warrick wrangle the sirens. The teal one has her arms wrapped around his neck and is petting his hair. The lavender-haired one is hissing at him as he tries to hold her around the waist. Killian slowly approaches and bows to the lavender-haired one. Says something to her as Warrick lets her go. She cozies up to Killian, and he escorts her out. Warrick has scooped up the other one, who has gone limp in his arms. They walk out of the room.

I look down at Jade, who struggles in my hold. But with my arm under her knees and the other around her back, she's not getting anywhere. "You're drunk."

"You're observant." She glowers at me as I walk towards the hall. "You can put me down."

"Nope."

"I can walk."

"Nope."

"Why are you like this!" she squeals, and I crack a grin. She's got some fight in her, I'll give her that.

"Because I don't need to be responsible for your face-planting in the hallway." And because it pisses you off, and I like it when you're angry. She groans and tosses her head back.

I tell her. "If you're a good girl, I'll get someone to remove that nasty little hangover you're gonna have tomorrow." Her jaw drops open, then quickly shuts, like she's thought better of her answer. She goes quiet and glares at me. Her eyes struggle to stay open. Her head bobs as she resists sleep. She gives up and rests her head on my chest, passing out.

As I open the door to her room and step inside, she stirs. "Please don't let him hurt me," she mumbles, eyes still shut. She talks in her sleep? "Don't let him in here. I can't fight him off." Setting her down on the bed, I unzip her dress, covering her with a sheet as I attempt to remove her clothing. I can't imagine a corset being comfortable to sleep in. It's difficult, but I manage to get her under the covers without getting an eyeful of her body. Don't need to be giving my dick any ideas.

I walk the dress over to a chair and drape it there, pondering what her words could mean. She sounded so small, so scared. I turn to walk out when I hear her moan again. "Please, not again."

She thrashes and rolls over. My brow creases. "No, no, no, no, no, not again." She lets out a sob before I leave her room.

It would do no good to wake her. She's drunk and having nightmares. But still, I feel conflicted as I stand outside her door. What does she mean, not again? Who was hurting her? I run my hand down my face and shake the thoughts from my head. Not my problem. She is not my responsibility. I got her to her room. That's all I had to do. Then why do I feel like I'm doing something wrong by leaving her there like that? Fuck.

Chapter 9
Jade

The warmth of sunlight pours in through the window. What time is it? Reaching over to my bedside table, my hand bumps into a glass. That's weird. I crack an eye open to see gray stone walls and a fireplace on the far wall. Oh, so I'm still here. Great, it doesn't matter what time it is; I'm not getting up. I roll over and groan. I was honestly hoping it was all an elaborate dream. The pounding headache tells me I am very much awake, though. I guess any more sleep is out of the question. I throw off the covers and make my way into the bathroom. Walking past the vanity tells me I look as bad as I feel. Wonderful. Well, I guess I'll take a bath and then go back to bed because I'm already done with today. I turn on the water to fill the tub and grab the vanilla-scented oils from the shelf; at least living in a castle has its perks. I sink down into the warm water, and the tension melts away.

I leave the bathing chamber a while later, feeling much more alive than when I had entered. My heart skips a beat, and I stop dead in my tracks as I spot two bright green eyes staring at me. Is that a panther? An enormous cat? Good god, it's the size of a pony.

I am going to die. My tombstone will read: Eaten by a cat.

"Umm...hi, kitty," I squeak out. Yep, I'm definitely going to die. I've established myself as prey. "Nice Kitty? Any mice or rats are all yours." Yep, I'm officially a moron.

This beast looks almost annoyed. Can a cat look annoyed? One ear is cocked backward, and its eyes are narrowing to slits. The end of the tail taps and swishes. It takes a step forward, and my entire body flinches. It sniffs in my direction, then looks at the door leading to the hallway. Its muscles ripple beneath the shiny black fur as it bolts across the room and jumps through the window. My heart is beating so hard I think my ribs might crack. I collapse onto the floor, my legs no longer functioning. My ears begin to ring, a high-pitched noise blasting through my head, adding to my lightheadedness.

"How many times have people told you not to get near the danger kitty?" Okay, to be fair, I didn't touch it, but somehow I had one in my room. I could have died. I mean, what a way to go. The zoo had large cats, but that one was next level. Had to have been bigger than a tiger. I get up and cautiously approach the window, looking at the three-story drop. How the hell did it get in here? Looking away from the ground, there's a tree about twenty feet away. There's no way. That's too far. Maybe someone let it in here? But why? I close the window and make sure the latch is locked.

A knock on the door startles me, sending my head spinning again. "Miss Jade, it's Lorelai. May I come in?"

"Come in!" I call across the room.

She steps into the room and looks me up and down. "My, you are white as a ghost today. Come sit, and I'll take care of that nasty hangover. Then we can get you dressed for your date." She moves over to a chair by the fireplace.

I sit in the chair and tuck the towel I forgot I was wearing around myself more securely. "Wait, my what?"

"Your hangover." She walks over and presses two fingers to my forehead, and the pressure in my head and nausea dissipate. It's heavenly, and I sigh, okay, this is pretty nice. She walks over to my closet and pushes clothes aside.

"Do you think I could get some pants? Just for, like, relaxing in? I mean, dresses are cool and all, but I live in leggings."

"Of course, I'll make some for both you and Cat. She made the same request this morning." She smiles at me and pulls out a yellow dress. "How about this one? It's nice and light and flowy, perfect for a picnic."

I grimace. "I don't really like yellow. I like the style of the dress, though. I'm more of a jewel tones, black, and pink kinda girl."

She looks a little disappointed and glances back at the gown.

"Don't get me wrong, I like everything else about the dress," I hurry to add, and her smile returns. "Also, what picnic?"

She hangs the dress on the bedpost, flips her blonde hair over her shoulder, and then rubs her hands together, looking intently at the fabric. "Your picnic with Bravos—the man won't shut up about it. According to the maids." She places her hands on the dress, and pink leaches out all around them, slowly changing the color. I stand up and watch in shock. What was a bright yellow dress is now pastel pink. It flows with layers of tulle and small ruffles at the bottom. The fabric is covered in outlines of roses in sparkling light blue; with its tight bodice and puff sleeves, it does look like a perfect dress for a picnic.

"Okay, that was awesome. Did you make all the clothes? I thought you were a healer?"

"I am." She laughs. "But I have many talents and different things I can do with my magic. Like manipulating fabrics." She smiles, holding out the dress to me. "Seeing as you and Cat are not from this realm and didn't bring anything with you, I was assigned to help and clothe you. I'm just glad you're not as helpless as some of the ladies. I've heard some of them don't even get dressed or bathe by themselves." "You may not have magic, but at least you aren't helpless. You'll see, the longer you are here, just how helpless some of these lords and ladies truly are." She smirks at me, and I smile back. Okay, I like Lorelai.

"And what is the deal with the picnic?" I press again.

She groans, "Fine, fine. I'm to show you out to the garden in a little bit. Bravos will be waiting there for your date." She takes in the blank expression on my face and sighs, "Apparently, you agreed to it last night at the ball. I don't suggest standing him up."

"Oh."

"Yeah, oh. So get dressed. At least you're already bathed."

I move towards the clothes closet to get underwear and start getting dressed. Lorelai goes through my wardrobe, changing the colors of my dresses, removing everything yellow and orange. I note only a few pastel tones left when she walks away from the closet, satisfied. "So, right before you came in, there was a giant cat, like a panther, in my room," I say.

She raises an eyebrow as she sits in the chair by the window. "A panther," she deadpans. "In your room."

"Yes, is that normal?"

"No, are you sure it wasn't just one of the queen's cats?" she asks skeptically.

"Are they giant?" I say while stepping into the dress.

"No...Maybe you imagined it?"

"I don't think so. I almost had a heart attack," I say, clutching my chest.

"What did it do?"

"Looked at me, then jumped out the window." I motion the direction it went with one arm as I put the other in a sleeve.

She seems to consider this and then shakes her head. "It must have been one of the queen's cats; they are quite unique. Plus, I don't see how a wild animal could have gotten all the way up here. and—" she trails off.

"And what?"

"The panther shifters all died out long ago," she sighs, standing up to help me button up the back of the dress.

"Wait, panther shifters? As in shifters? like werewolves?" I spin around to look at her.

"I guess, kind of like that. But none of that full-moon nonsense. Shifters don't go rabid. They are fae in another form. Some lines died off, though; those bloodlines were lost—like the panthers. That's why I said- It must have been one of the queen's cats," she sighs. "Probably stress causing your imagination to run wild. I assure you, no giant cats are walking around the castle. I'm sure you'll feel normal and less stressed about all this in a few days."

I sigh and walk into the bathroom to do my hair and makeup since I guess I have a date today, and I've already started the day off with hallucinations. My stomach growls as I put the finishing touches on my lipstick and brush out my hair. "Will there be food at this picnic?" I call out the door.

"Wouldn't be much of a picnic if there wasn't, but probably a fair question with any of these lords," she muses. "Yes, I saw a maid packing it up before I came to see you."

Thank god. At least I had that to look forward to. Bravos makes me nervous. I mean, all of them do, but he is too slick, too attractive, and I don't trust that. God, I can't believe I'm going on a date. I have zero desire to get tied down again. The year of therapy I needed during the divorce would have been enough to put anyone off.

Of course, the universe had other ideas; I muse to myself. But wait, there's more: behind curtain number two, you've won an all-expenses-paid kidnapping to fairyland. Where you will date desirable men you're not ready for, because your karma apparently sucks. Hearing the Price is Right announcement play through my head, I grin.

We exit the castle into a thick cluster of evergreens. The day is already warm, and the light dances through the trees. The air is sweet and fragrant, a mix of pine and flowers. Lorelai stops at the door and points me down a path that leads to the garden. The path is smooth cobblestone, worn down from centuries of use. Patches of flowers are scattered by the tree trunks, and small animals rustle through the thicket beyond the trail. It's a short walk before I spot the purple grass swaying in the breeze, and a garden that looks made of cotton candy greets me. It's so much more beautiful when you are standing in it. From my window, it's pretty, but being immersed in it is magical. Butterflies hop around from flower to flower, while petals are carried by the wind. The pond off in the distance shimmers in the late morning light, and lily pads float in little patches along the shore.

As I make my way to the clearing, I see Bravos stretched out on a large white blanket on top of a purple grass hill. I follow the path and turn to walk up the small hill. When I reach the blanket, I stop short. The man is shirtless. His eyes are closed as he basks in the sun, a slight sheen of sweat sparkling across his abs. I take in his short blonde hair reflecting the sunlight like glitter, and his tan skin glistening. From this angle, it's easy to admire his sharp features. The man looks as if he were chiseled from stone. Lord help me, he's hot.

"Hello, pet," he purrs, cracking an eye open.

"Hello, Bravos, how are you today?"

"Please sit." He sits up and motions to a spot on the blanket. I drop down next to him, looking down at the basket that he has brought. "Are you hungry, beautiful?"

"Yes, actually, I'm famished. Did you have a good time at the ball last night?" I'm not really sure what to talk to him about. I don't really know anything about him.

He pulls things from the basket: an assortment of cut-up fruit in a bowl, little sandwiches cut into squares, a small box with chocolates, and a bottle of wine of some sort. This honestly reminds me of a date from The Bachelor—a romantic setting with bite-sized foods. I resist the urge to look for a hidden camera somewhere. Wouldn't that just be the kicker? This whole thing is some elaborate reality TV show, and I'm the unsuspecting victim. It takes all the restraint I have not to laugh at the notion, but I can't control the smile tugging at my lips.

"I had a great time at the ball, even though I wish I'd spent more time with you. I found the other women rather dull." He looks up and winks at me before pulling out two glasses. My face heats. "What about you? I saw you dance with a few of the guys. I hope none of them will be competition for me. Although I'm not sure anyone could outmatch me," he says.

I can't help but think about Killian and Rodan. Killian was charming, and when he calmed down, he was nice to be around. Rodan may have been a bit of a jerk, but thinking about him makes my stomach flutter. I have a feeling that Bravos doesn't want to talk about other men, though. What have I gotten myself into?

"Yeah, I had a good time. I'm still getting used to the whole idea of being here. This is all kind of way out of my comfort zone," I pause. "This garden is beautiful. I've never seen purple grass before, at least not this shade of purple." I skirt around his question and reach my hand out to run it over the soft grass. It's silky and delicate.

"I'd love to show you around some more. I could show you all sorts of things you've never seen before." He has a smile as bright as the sun painted on his face as he passes me a glass of bubbling liquid. I tentatively take a sip; sweetness floods my senses as bubbles assault my tongue. Pretty sure this is some sort of sparkly wine, the kind that frat boys give naive girls at parties. I set down the drink. It's a bit early to get trashed on wine; at least, I think it is. I have no idea what time it is. Noon maybe?

"I knew there was something special about you when you walked into the throne room. I'm sure you felt it, too. Last night, I should have spent the entire evening with you. It was a mistake to let you out of my sight for even a moment." He smiles while I look at him wide-eyed. I take a bite of the small cucumber sandwich. "But you know how it is. I had to talk to everyone to be sure." He waves his hand, dismissing the idea. "I'm delighted I asked you here today, though. This way, we can get to know each other better." I nod slowly in agreement, not sure what to make of this.

"Okay, so what do you like to do for fun?" I try to move the subject somewhere safer.

He puffs out his chest and smiles. "I am an expert hunter. I can kill anything," he beams, and I shudder inwardly.

"Cool..."

"Chocolate?" He holds one up to me, suggesting he feed it to me. I pluck it from his fingers before popping it into my mouth. It melts, and I nearly dissolve into a moan. Why is the food here so good? His eyebrow raises as he studies my face, licking his lips and drawing my attention there. His gaze is heated when I move my eyes to his. My heart flutters as my face tingles from my blush. I take another tiny sip of the wine. "With my hunting skills, you'd never go hungry. Plus, their skins are useful, and the ones with horns are great for decorating."

"Right–"

"It is a pity that we are in a time of peace. If we were at war, I'd be the best general. With my fierce determination leading my men to victory, slaughtering our foe," he continues, looking up into the clouds. The sun gleams off his tanned chest. As I eat, he drones on about battle tactics, and I nod to encourage him occasionally. "I'd be the hero prince, a true warrior. Maybe sometime you could watch me in the sparring ring." He smiles at me. I give him a half-hearted smile in return. "Anyway, tell me more about you." He runs the back of his hand down my arm, giving me goosebumps.

"Well, let's see, I wasn't expecting to be dating so soon." Take a hint, please, and slow down. "I don't hunt, but I'm pretty good at cooking. I read a lot, and I used to draw." Searching my mind for anything I could tell him, my mind is blank. "I watch a lot of TV and hang out with Cat."

"Cat?"

"My friend...the other mortal here..."

"Oh! Her, yes, the other one. Go on."

"I don't know what else to say. It's been a very long time since I've been on a date." Feeling embarrassed, I stare at the pond rippling a few feet away.

"You don't have to be so nervous." His brow creases with a look of concern on his features.

"Sorry—"

"I find everything about you interesting. You are nothing like anyone I've ever met. I like watching the wonder in your eyes at every new experience." He reaches out and slowly tucks my hair behind my ear, causing my heart to beat faster. "I like that I can hear your pulse quicken when I touch you," he says in a low voice. His hand moves from my hair, fingers trailing down my spine, sending a shiver through me. "Because being around you makes my heart skip, too." He leans over and places a chaste kiss on my shoulder. I freeze, not sure what to do. This is all moving way too fast.

"Maybe we should go for a walk? You can show me the rest of the garden," I squeak and grab my glass of wine. Apparently, I'm going to need this. I can't keep stuffing food in my mouth, hoping to make this less awkward.

"Sure, we could walk around. I have a bunch of great things planned for today." He smiles at me.

"Like what?"

"Wouldn't you like to know?" he says, wiggling his brows. He stands and holds out his hand to help me. I stand, straighten my skirts, and look towards the pond again. "You like the pond?" he says, taking my hand. I sip my wine and nod. The ground is soft beneath my feet and a little steep, but easy enough to walk on. I'm definitely glad that Lorelai insisted on flats.

"This is the pink garden. There are four on the grounds, all with a different theme. I thought this one would be the most romantic. Plus, the saltwater pond is in the night garden, and I think Yudoku is currently there." He sneers.

"The sea siren?"

"Yeah, she's been hanging out there since she arrived. Water folk always tend to gather there to recharge or whatever. She's a bit bitey for my taste," he shudders, and I turn away to hide my smirk.

"Is it true that sirens lead men to their deaths?"

"From what I've heard, it's like a rite of passage for them," he says dismissively, helping me to the path around the pond. I can't help but take in the weeping willow swaying in the breeze on a small island in the middle. The cerulean blue water looks so clear and inviting, I can see multi-colored fish swirling in its depths. "You are brilliant to know so much about fae folk."

"I only know the rumors and fairy tales of my world. I never expected any of it to be true," I say honestly.

"And me? What do you know about me?" He gives me a wicked grin when I glance over at him.

Ducking my head and gazing back towards the little island, I see some small pink birds flitting in and out of the branches. "I don't know much yet. You seem strong and are good at hunting."

"I've spent nearly my whole life training for battle. It's the way of the fae to be the strongest. Like I told you before, I'm pretty sure I was raised as a prince. I know I had the best education and training available. I've traveled all over and been to almost all the kingdoms. Met all the fine females the lords had to offer, but you are the first to catch my eye."

"Um—thank you." The nervous flutters have returned. The butterflies in the garden flutter about in a mockery of my insides. I take another drink of my wine, the bubbles tickling my nose. "Where is everyone else? Seems like a lot more people would be taking advantage of such a beautiful area."

"Other than Hunter, who's at the hot spring with Beatrix, I'm not sure." He shrugs. "Are you looking for someone?" His gaze bores into the side of my head as I refuse to meet his eyes. Killian's face pops into my mind. I wonder what he is doing right now. Is he on a date with one of the other women? Is Rodan? I guess they should be, since this is why everyone is here.

I shrug indifferently. "No, just curious. There are a lot of people here, but I guess the castle grounds are vast."

"Owari is over on the far shore." He points to a figure across the pond. Her lavender hair is dark from being wet, and her tail splashes lazily in the water. She is relaxing on the shore, a vision, sunning herself with rainbows gleaming off her silver scales. "I saw her piranhas earlier, so I figured she was somewhere around here."

Stunned, I turn towards the water again. "Piranhas?"

He laughs a low chuckle. "Yeah, I wouldn't recommend getting too close to that water. She never travels without her pets."

"Pets? Piranhas? I–okay then, not putting my feet in the water, got it." I have so much to learn about all of these fae.

We walk for a little while in silence while I take in my surroundings. This landscape is gorgeous. I stop to smell a light blue flower. Its blueberry scent wafts around me. Bravos leans over and picks it up, sliding it into my hair above my ear.

"I like you in flowers. Are you sure you're not a flower sprite?"

I let out a genuine giggle. "Yes, I'm sure. Just a normal mortal." I shake my head as we enter a thicket of pink trees. Up close, what I thought were white trunks are actually soft blue bark.

"There's nothing normal about you. You are exquisite." He turns, stepping towards me. I instinctively take a step back, finding myself up against a tree. Pulse quickening, I'm unsure what to do as his glistening body takes up my vision. Is it common for fae men to be shirtless on a date? "I have something for you." I gaze up into his dark blue eyes and see sincerity shining back at me. He pulls something from his pocket that I glimpse briefly as I'm trapped in his eyes. "I had my brother make this for you from his earth magic. He's quite talented with jewelry." I look down to see a silver necklace. It looks like rose vines intertwined together. The red gemstones take the place of roses. It's small and delicate, with tiny leaves and thorns throughout. I'm speechless. It's gorgeous, but why would he do this for me?

"Why–? Don't get me wrong, it's lovely, but why would you get me jewelry? We've only just met."

"Because I needed something to impress someone as gorgeous as you. I hope you like it." He steps closer, only inches between us, as he reaches to put it around my neck, leaning his head over one shoulder so he can see. It fits like a choker, much smaller than I thought it would be. I hear a soft click, and then it loosens ever so slightly. It's so delicate I barely feel it. At least it's comfortable.

"Thank you, Bravos," I breathe out. I'm overheating from his nearness; I'm sure it's showing on my face. I can feel his breath on my ear. With him this close to me, and his hands brushing my neck, my whole body flushes.

"It is my pleasure," he whispers, causing the butterflies to fly lower in my belly. He presses into me, his chest hard against me, arms on either side of me on the tree. And then his mouth is on mine, soft at first and then hungry in intensity. The shock wears off quickly as my body takes over for my mind. His hand wraps around the back of my neck while he deepens the kiss, tasting the sweetness of the wine on my lips. His other hand encircles my waist, pressing me into him. He licks and nips at my bottom lip, eliciting a low groan from me. My god, can this man kiss. I drop the wine glass, forgotten in my haze, and bring a hand up to his chest, feeling the rugged plains of his muscles. I bring my other hand up around his neck, pulling at him. He breaks the kiss for a moment to grab me by my ass and pick me up.

Leaning me against the tree with my legs wrapped around his

waist, he kisses up the length of my neck. Nipping the soft skin in gentle bites, leaving me struggling to catch my breath. His lips crash into mine again. Kissing me long and slow, like he's savoring it. His hips roll against my core, and I'm suddenly aware of his hardness. The shockwave of the contact brings my body to life. A low growl rumbles through him as his kiss turns demanding. Grinding his length into me again, making me wonder what fucking a fae would be like. The idea of it turns me on as much as the half-naked fae in front of me.

I'm lightheaded and euphoric as I lose myself in the feeling of this man. His hands roam my body, one trailing up my side to cup my breast, the other stroking up and down my thigh. The thrill of his touch rockets through me as I rock against his length, no longer in control of myself. I need a release. For so long, I'd forgotten this sensation, this need. But something is off, like I'm about to take a dive off a cliff that might have jagged rocks awaiting me.

His hand pulls at the skirt tangled between us as if he can read my mind. This breaks the mind fog. What am I doing? "Wait." I break away from his kiss. This isn't what I want. "Wait," I repeat, breathing heavily. He stops and looks at me hungrily. "It's too fast," I pant. "Too soon," I say as I struggle to put my legs down. He steps back and runs a hand through his hair.

"I'm sorry, I don't know what came over me." He drags his hands down his face before shaking his head. He takes another step back before readjusting his pants, his erection impressive through the material. I avert my gaze as I straighten my dress. "Shall we resume our picnic?" A flash of anger shades his features before calm indifference takes over.

"Yeah, sure." I smile at him as I duck my head, not wanting to make eye contact.

Chapter 10
Jade

"You kissed him!" Cat exclaims, much to my horror, the sound echoing off the library walls.

I grimace. "I know!" Holding my face in my hands, trying to make sense of it. "I don't know what I was thinking. I don't even know if I like him." Recounting the events of my morning with Cat has been taxing. I feel as though I've been thrust into this situation, and I'm drowning. After my hormonal escapades, we returned to the picnic blanket and talked for a while. Or shall I say he talked? Bravos went on and on about his skincare routine and how much work it was to be as handsome as him. Needless to say, I was not amused and felt like a moron for kissing him. I made an excuse that I had plans with Cat for the afternoon. He begrudgingly let me go after a lot of coaxing. I can't help but think that going out with Bravos was a mistake. On my way back inside, I ran into Killian and quickly asked him where I might find Cat. Then, I went straight to the library entrance across from my room.

The library is grand, a three-story room of spiral staircases and balconies opening up to the vast expanse of the great space. There are nooks tucked away in multiple areas with chairs and tables, a whole room with desks, and row upon row of books winding into what seems to be an eternity of shelves. Multiple fireplaces keep the place warm, allowing for even more cozy reading areas. The whole place is topped off with an elaborately painted domed ceiling. I understand immediately why Cat never wants to leave this space; it's heaven.

"Well, it's not like you need to pick anyone immediately." She picks up her glass of water. "This is the first time you've been single in a long time. Test the waters." She swishes the water around her glass to emphasize her point. "Don't try to have anything serious for once. It will be fine."

"I know; I just can't believe I did that. I don't know anything about him. He's vague when I ask him about himself, and I don't know what else to ask."

"Yeah, I get that. What about Killian? He seems to like you," she says while rummaging around in a plate of chocolates, looking for a particular flavor, I'm guessing.

"Where did the chocolates come from?" I smirk.

"Don't change the subject." She looks pointedly at me. "Ryker brought them."

"Ryker?" I ask, shooting her pointed look right back at her. That man looked like a Viking in a suit. His long blonde hair was wild, and his beard barely tamed. He is what I'd imagine Thor would look like. He is also the type of guy that is Cat's kryptonite.

She groans. "Yeah, he's been bringing me snacks here all day. It's kind of sweet," she grumbles. Miss I-don't-do-serious-relationships may be getting a run for her money.

"Sounds like someone likes you–" I smile at her.

"Don't," she barks. "I'm going home rich and not interested in finding a *mate*," she makes air quotes as she says, mate.

"You could always have a little fun while we are here. He looked like he wanted to have a lot of fun with you last night." If you want to play dirty, I can play dirty too.

Cat's face turns red as she opens and closes her mouth like a fish out of water. "I haven't thought about it. I–" she trails off before clearing her throat. "So, any thoughts on Killian? He seems nice."

Deciding to let the topic go, I concede, "Killian is very nice, kind of a hopeless romantic. It's adorable. But last night, he handed me off to Rodan." Anger bubbles up inside of me. "That man is a pain in the ass. Seriously, what is his problem? He wouldn't even let me walk back to my room. He carried me; it was embarrassing."

"Um–I heard you passed out before he got you there. Maybe that was a good thing." Her tone is placating as she takes a slow bite of her chocolate.

"He also chastised me for dancing with Bravos. He never says anything nice. He's a jerk."

"A jerk you danced with–" she says, raising an eyebrow.

"That was different," I bark, and both of her eyebrows lift as she levels me in her stare. "I was trying to get away from Edgar."

Cat devolves into laughter, buckling over in her chair. "Okay, okay, fair."

Thankfully, after my dance with Rodan, I spent most of the night dancing and talking with Killian. Edgar found other women to annoy. Ryker ended up walking Cat back to her room, but she has remained tight-lipped about how the ball went with him. I know I was pretty drunk by the end of the night. I was having such a good time talking with Killian that I lost track of how much I drank. He told me about his hopes for the future and how he wants to travel. Some of his hobbies are reading and knitting, which I didn't see coming. He also told me about how he and Rodan grew up together. He said his parents adopted Rodan when he was a baby. It was sweet listening to him. He's so passionate about everything.

"So, are you going to pick a guy to actually test the waters with soon? Because if you do, I want details." Her suggestive tone makes my face heat.

"Are you?" I retort.

"Complications to getting rich," she sighs and slouches back in her chair.

"How so? And how is it different for me?" Seriously, this isn't the Jade dating show; you are in the same damn boat, Cat.

"I'm curious, but I'd much rather go home rich." She waves her hand dismissively.

"That's not an answer. I'm curious too, but having a little fun doesn't mean we can't go home rich."

"I knew it. I knew you were thinking of sleeping with one of them. Which one?" Cat sits up straight, expectantly awaiting my reply. She fucking played me. She knows she played me, and I fell right into it. Fuck.

"What?" I stammer. "I have not—" She cocks an eyebrow, a knowing smirk playing across her features. "Fine, yes, I've thought about it. Do you know how long it's been since I've even wanted to?" I groan.

"Too long. So, which guy? I mean, you were like halfway there with Bravos, but do you have someone else in mind to pop your fae cherry?"

"Ew."

"Yeah, that sounded a lot hotter in my head. Pretend I didn't say that." She grimaces. "So—"

"I don't know—I haven't put much thought into it."

"You'll figure it out, or your hormones will when you have the right amount of liquid courage pumping through your brain."

"Is that what you are gonna do, Cat? Just let alcohol decide?"

"I wish I could say no, but sometimes it sets the libido into overdrive." We both devolve into laughter. What else are we going to do, trapped in a castle with a bunch of hot guys? Cat has always been the instigator. I've always been the worrywart; we work well together. "Any idea what you'll do for the rest of the day?"

"No, I came here because I needed to clear my head after spending the morning with Bravos. Sadly, that man knows just how hot he is and uses it like a weapon."

"How's the weapon in his pants?"

"Cat!" I shriek, face going scarlet.

Cat laughs with delight. "Oh man, your face! I'm joking!"

I grumble. "It's not funny. They all seem to know exactly how to turn me on. I don't get it. I'm never like this."

"You need to get laid; that's why."

"I don't even like sex; you know this: it hurts, it's boring, and I get nothing out of it. Why is my body acting like this?" Plus, it's too soon. What if I ruin everything by jumping into bed too quickly, like before?

"Maybe it thinks a fae guy might satisfy it. Your clit is curious." She grins mischievously. "You are always so in your head about it. Listen, we are going home in a couple of months. You'll never have to see these guys again. It's not like we are looking for love. You just need to experience good sex. Seriously, your description of it is so wrong. It should never be like that." She waggles her eyebrows. Lord, help me with her. It's not like I don't know that I jump from bad relationship to bad relationship. It's honestly never my intention. I wish I could be like her and not care and be free to explore. Plus, I don't see Cat jumping into bed with anyone right now.

"You are delusional and far too interested in my sex life when you have a perfectly capable fae guy barking up your skirt."

"Touche." Cat gives me a grin. "I'll report back my findings." Both of us devolve into fits of giggles again.

Wandering around the library, I find texts on everything: history, geography, mathematics, fiction, romance, mortal and fae books alike. This is genuinely the most extensive, beautiful library I've ever seen. Rich mahogany shines on every bookcase, every shelf full. I could wander the rows for hours and still not see all of it. Every chair is cushioned in rich jewel tones, inviting me to sit and stay a while. Small reading lights are perched in every sitting area.

I turn down another corridor, looking at a row of books on magic, and run into a wall. Hard. Stepping back and rubbing my head in confusion, I look up. No, not a wall, fuck, it's someone's back. I stumble back a few steps and slowly lift my gaze, feeling my face flush hot. He slowly turns to look at me. If looks could kill, I'd be dead on the spot. Shit. If I thought Rodan looked dangerous before, this was a whole new level I didn't know anyone was capable of. I stammer out an apology before he turns and storms away. Leaving me and my heart, trying to break free of my rib cage in his wake. How long has he been here? Did he hear my conversation with Cat? Oh god, I hope not.

"Hello, Emerald." I jump and spin around to find Killian leaning against the bookcase. "Interested in magic?" He pulls a book and flips through the pages.

"You scared me, Killian," I breathe out, trying to slow my heartbeat.

"Sorry, saw you over here and wanted to say hi." Looking at me, he cocks a slight grin.

"I was just wandering around, taking it all in. There are so many books, I don't even know where to start. Does everyone here have magic?"

"Yes." He brightens. "Check it out." He raises his hand and lays his palm flat, producing a small sphere of flames, bright and flickering, warming my face. This is so cool. I stare at it as I bring my fingers up to his. "Don't touch it; it will hurt like hell unless you have fire magic." He laughs, pulling his hand away from me.

"Oh, sorry. I've never seen anything like that before. How does it work? Bravos said something about earth magic earlier, so I guess not everyone has the same powers?" My eyes are still glued to the little fireball. I have to know more. I want to learn as much as I can about the fae before I go home.

Killian closes his hand, and the little ball disappears. "I'd love to tell you more over... tea?" He smiles and bounces a bit, the move endearing. He is so sweet. Kinda reminds me of a puppy most of the time, barely able to contain the excitement in his body.

"I'd love to." Smiling, I take the offered hand to walk with him. His hand is warm and smooth in mine. "Where are we going?"

"Over here to one of the reading areas. It has a table, and I can get us some tea." He points to a set of chairs cozied up next to a fireplace with a little table in between. "Wait here. I'll be right back." He bounds away, and I watch him as he goes. With all that muscle, he's built like a football player. It's hard to believe someone built like that is bouncy. I smile to myself at the thought as I sit down and pick up the book that Killian left on the table. Magic for Younglings, of course, he picked up a book meant for children to help him explain. I guess everyone has to start somewhere, I laugh to myself. Opening up to a random page, I see an illustration of a mermaid with her arm out and an enormous wave of water going over a ship. Well, this should be interesting.

I look up from the book at the sound of purring. I look around me but don't see anyone. Strange. What is making that noise? The library has been so quiet that this sounds almost deafening. It sounds like a cat. I get up and search the base of the fireplace, and turn to look under the table. I spot a flicker of movement out of the corner of my eye. It's a long black tail, flicking back and forth. I get on my knees and bend to look under the chair I had been sitting in; light green eyes meet mine. As the small creature moves towards me, the light catches on shiny ridges poking out through glossy black fur. Its enormous ears are almost comically large for its tiny head. The purr intensifies as it emerges into the light. This small thing looks like a kitten but has reptilian aspects. The little spikes on its head continue down its back and tail, each spike surrounded by patches of little black scales. Where the shoulder blades are, little wings sit tight against its body. The front paws look more like a kitten's, whereas the back feet have more of the strange black scales. My mind is trying to wrap itself around what I'm seeing. It's like a cat and a dragon had a baby; the cutest thing ever came out of it.

"Hello, little thing," I coo at the creature. I reach out slowly, letting it sniff my fingers. Admiring the scales that travel between the fur, I see a small billow of smoke puff out its tiny nose. The little thing reaches up and puts its paws on my leg. I tentatively run my palm down its soft back, the scales slick beneath my touch. The purring intensifies again as it jumps fully into my lap, arching its back into my hand. "You like that, do you?" I shift so that I am fully sitting on the floor, and it kneads the skirt of my dress, getting comfortable. "Hum, you're a lot like a normal cat, aren't you?" I muse, scratching under its chin. It makes little chirping noises as it makes itself cozy on my lap. Curling up into a ball and closing its eyes, I wonder what this little guy's name is.

"Are you okay?" I glance up to see Killian setting a tray down on the table, a troubled expression on his face.

I beam a smile at him, looking at the animal on my lap. "I'm great! What is this?"

"That is a book dragon, also known as a dragon cat. It's a small breed of dragon. It's one of the queen's cats. He didn't hurt you, did he?" He looks uncertain.

"No, are they dangerous?" I'm unsure how anything this cute could be.

"They can be? Usually, Pop just likes to hide under things and singe your shoes." He gives it a pointed look.

"Oh, so you're a mischievous little thing, huh?" I coo at the little dragon cat while stroking his head. "His name is Pop?" I look up at Killian as he sits in the chair next to me.

"Yep, that's Pop. A bunch of them are running around the castle, but Pop likes the library. Thankfully, he hasn't set too many books on fire." Pop looks up, and smoke trails out of his nose again.

"Yeah, you know you did it. Proud of it, too." Killian laughs, and Pop puts his head back down, apparently done with this conversation. "I'll move him if you are uncomfortable. Would you like to sit in a chair?"

"I'm comfortable, don't worry. I honestly think he might be the cutest thing I've ever seen."

"What about me?" Killian looks offended.

"What about you?"

"I thought I was the cutest thing you've ever seen," he pouts.

"You are a person and not a cat. Dragon cat? You know what I mean." Killian slumps back in the chair and crosses his arms, making me laugh. "Fine, okay. You are the cutest." I smile. "Happy now?"

"I guess. I mean, I know I'm the cutest. I'll prove it too. You just haven't seen me at my cutest yet." He winks, and I'm left wondering what the heck he means by that. He leans over and hands me a cup of tea. "I hope you don't mind. I didn't know what you liked, so I picked my favorite; it's kind of sweet and spicy."

Cinnamon and cardamom fill my senses. "Mmm, smells wonderful." I smile. "So, how does magic work? Is it limitless? Do only certain fae have it?"

"Okay, so magic, I'm like the best to explain this. So, all magic is elemental. Everyone is born with it. The stronger the power, the stronger the fae. So, like, the royal families are the strongest." I nod and sip the tea, the spices tingling on my tongue. "I like to picture power like a well inside of you. If you use too much, it goes empty, and you must wait for the well to fill back up."

"So, your power is limited?" I sit like a good little student and listen to him. He is so in his element. I could listen to him talk about his world all day.

"Yeah, but sleep and time replenish it." He smiles. "Stronger fae can pull from their element and use that if it's around, but it's tough to do that if your well is empty. Like, really fucking hard, only the strongest fae can do it." I nod. It makes sense, I guess. "If your well is full, you can pull from your element as much as you want. I have Fire, so I can use the fire around me at minimal cost to my well."

"What about what Warrick did when he brought us here?" I ask, brows furrowed.

"Ah, that. He's a portal master, a powerful one. It's an air-related magic. He can make portals to anywhere. He's also a healer, as all portal masters are. It's a protection from wartime. Healers can't be targets, so if a portal master is a healer, he's safe to evacuate the soldiers. He had to use a lot of power to bring you here," he says sheepishly. "Sorry about all that. Anyway, most fae can learn at least a little healing. It depends on how powerful they are."

"So, you can learn other things?"

"There are spells that can be learned, like healing, moving things, shielding, stuff like that. But some stuff is forbidden, like curses. That's dark stuff. Aside from the curse on this kingdom, I don't know much about it. Any other questions?"

"What can you do with fire besides the little ball?" I take another sip of tea, watching how excited Killian is to tell me all this. I can't believe I'm having a conversation about magic.

"I can do small things like light candles, heat water, heat bodies if it's cold." He lifts his eyebrow in a suggestive waggle, which makes me laugh. "But I'm pretty powerful, so I can also make giant fireballs and breathe fire. There's a lot of cool stuff. My power is actually more extensive than most. Pretty much anything you can think of involving fire, I can make it happen," he beams.

"I see. So, mighty powerful fae, what other powers do people have?"

He gives a little chuckle. "Okay, I'm not that conceited. Other fae have earth magic. People can grow stuff and make stuff from plants, dirt, or rocks. Depending on power level. Every element has different sub-sects that do different things. Some earth magic can work with metals or make pretty much anything, like clothes or furniture. Water magic fae will be able to do everything from making water out of nothing to causing a tsunami." My eyes widen, imagining something like the picture in that book. "Air magic is pretty cool. A powerful enough fae could levitate with enough air around them."

"So every power is related somehow to the four elements."

"Yep. Some bloodlines died out long ago, so certain abilities were lost, but they were all related to keeping the world's harmony."

"Do you know which ones were lost?"

"Some, but not all of them. Shadow-wielding was lost. I guess it was pretty cool. I think storm fae were also lost. They could control the weather, but died out centuries ago. Now we have fae that can do some weather-related stuff, but I guess it's nothing like what the storm fae could do. Oh, and soul renderers—they could borrow anyone's power with a touch. Scary fucking fae if you ask me."

"Wow."

"I know. It must kind of suck not to have powers at all. A fae without power wouldn't even survive here." He laughs.

"If they wouldn't survive, then how do mortals live here?" This is kind of a concerning point.

"Don't worry, Emerald. I'll protect you. No one will challenge you to a duel." He smiles and drinks his tea as if the idea is absurd. I guess it kind of is, though. His smile is infectious, the light dusting of stubble on his chin making the hard lines of his jaw even more pronounced. I'm captivated by how the golden glow of the fireplace shines in his long hair. "This book is for kids but will cover all the basics." He points to the book on the table. "You can take it to your room to look at later if you still have questions. Or come find me. I'm at your disposal for anything you want." He leans toward me, not losing eye contact, and pets the cat in my lap. I let out a breath and try to hide my shaking hands by taking another sip of tea. His eyes follow as I lower the cup, but stop at my neck and darken. "Where did you get that necklace?" he asks, his tone even.

I reach for my neck, feeling the necklace Bravos had put there earlier. "Bravos gave it to me." I run my fingers over the chain, uncertain if I've somehow offended Killian.

"May I see it?" His face is so severe, unlike the Killian I've seen since I've been here.

I nod and reach around my neck to unhook it. As I feel the leaves and thorns, I can't find anywhere that feels different. I can't find the clasp. Killian's eyes bore into me as I feel around, my heart beating a little faster as I realize I have no idea how to get this off. "Can you help me?" I pick up my hair with one hand and point at the back of my neck with the other. "I can't find the clasp." He stands and moves around behind me. I make one last attempt, feeling for anything that could make it come undone, but it's a futile attempt. I slip my finger under it and give a little pull, thinking maybe it hinges somewhere. The necklace tightens, and a sharp prick of pain greets my finger. I yelp as I pull my finger from my neck, blood running down the pad, stabbed by one of the thorns.

"What did you do? It wasn't this tight before." Killian runs his finger along the nape of my neck, the pressure of the necklace noticeably tighter.

"I don't know; I tugged on it, it cut me, and now I feel like it's getting tighter." My heart is pounding in my ears as I scratch at the necklace, but I can't get a finger under the barbs. The space between the metal and my skin is gone. "How do I get it off?" I breathe hard against the constriction.

"Calm down," Killian says softly, rubbing circles on my back while he sits behind me. "Don't mess with it, or it will get tighter," he sighs. "It will get looser if you relax. Then I'll get it off of you. Don't worry." His hand trails up my back, massaging as he coaxes me to keep breathing. "How about after this, we go get dinner? We can have a nice quiet meal, just the two of us under the moons?" he whispers in my ear.

"Okay, food would be nice." I breathe out and feel a little prick of pain in my leg. I look down to see Pop extending his arm across my leg with his little claws out. He looks up at me expectantly. "I'd love to stay with you, Pop, but I need to eat at some point," I giggle, and the pressure around my neck eases.

"Hold your hair way up," Killian's gruff voice cuts in, and I do what he says. "Hold really still," he instructs. An uncomfortable heat sears the back of my neck, and I scrunch my eyes at the pain of it. Sucking in a breath through my clenched teeth. With the tears in my eyes threatening to break free, the necklace drops into my lap, and the pain subsides to a dull ache. "I'm sorry. My intention was not to hurt you." I feel the heat of his body before his lips press softly to the back of my neck, replacing the pain with warmth. Killian wraps his arms around me in a hug, burying his head in my hair. "Don't accept jewelry from anyone but Lorelai from now on, okay?"

"Wha–what was wrong with it?" I stammer out.

"Just a minor flaw. Try not to worry about it. These things can happen." He hugs me tighter, and I lean into his embrace. "Dinner?"

"Yeah, that sounds nice, Killian."

Chapter 11
Killian

"He put a fucking collar on her!" Outrage does not begin to express how I'm feeling right now. "He is already trying to make claims without her consent. She didn't even know what it was." I throw my hands up. This whole thing makes me want to pull my hair out, and I love my hair. A growl rumbles deep in my chest. "Who does he think he is? You can't treat females like property." Those collars are dangerous. The more you try to tug it off, the tighter it gets until the person passes out from lack of air. Magic is the only way to remove it; easier done if you have earth magic, but I don't. So I had to melt it off of her. Then, I had to heal the burn I put on the back of her neck. I roar in frustration. "Those collars are archaic, used hundreds of years ago to control mortals. Bravos was out of line, pulling something like that." I slam my hand down on the table, causing my wine to slosh and drip down onto the wood.

"We should kill him," Ryker says somberly, sitting at the table across from me, in the small meeting room.

"We can't kill him." I want to, but it would be a big mess to clean up with his parents being lords and all. I sigh as I slump down into my chair and grab my wine from the table.

"We can kill him just a little." He shrugs as he strokes his beard.

"How does one kill someone just a little?" Rodan smirks at him over his wineglass, while Warrick laughs in amusement.

"We can't kill him," I groan.

"He's right. If Bravos is the prince, it could be disastrous," Warrick says, resigned.

Rodan snorts, trying to hide his grin behind his glass of wine, and I shoot him a look.

"We kill his brother then, since he made the damn thing." Ryker laughs. "Makes no difference to me." I groan, shaking my head and running my hand down my face. "Then we kill his pet." He grins.

"No. No killing, and don't go telling Catria about the collar either. I don't want Jade to know what he did to her. She's already shaky enough about being here. If she knew, she'd never trust a single fae again." I give Ryker a pointed look, and he shrugs. He's been spending all of his time trying to get Catria's attention, going so far as to bring her food in the library to have an excuse to be around her.

"You mean she won't trust you." Warrick smirks. "Speaking of, how was your dinner with Jade?" Warrick smiles knowingly at me. I'd asked him to set up the terrace overlooking the night garden for a romantic dinner to get Jade's mind off the necklace. I also thought it would be the perfect opportunity for us to have an actual date. I relax into the memory. The moons lighting up the sky and the bioluminescent trees and flowers at night are incredible. Who wouldn't fall in love looking at it? Her eyes lit up as she looked out over the garden. The glow of the leaves on the trees lit up the night. The neon colors of all the flowers carpeting the ground glisten magically, together with the way the saltwater pond glows a brilliant blue on a still night, is enough to make even the most stone-hearted person fall in love. The best thing of all was her. She was enchanting. Warrick said I may be laying it on a bit thick, but I'm just getting started. I've got a plan to win her, and it's not playing dirty like Bravos.

"It was magical," I sigh with contentment. Fluttering my eyes closed as I relive every detail with her.

"He's got it bad," Warrick chuckles. "Knew he'd like her."

"She's mortal." Rodan gets up, walks over to the window, and looks out. His forearm is against the glass, head resting on it as he glares into the horizon. The moonlight illuminates his porcelain face, making the contrast of his dark hair even more apparent. He's been uneasy ever since he met her, retreating more and more into himself. He needs to meet the right girl, and he'll be right as rain again.

"Something about her pushing your buttons?" Warrick retorts, and I lift an eyebrow. "It's not like you're trying to court a female. What does it matter to you?"

"She doesn't belong here. She is mortal. Do you really think she will stay just because you like her?" Rodan doesn't turn as he speaks in a low tone.

"Well, I think when she falls madly in love with me, she will stay." I know Rodan means well, always looking out for me. We were raised together since we were babies. He just doesn't want to see me get hurt.

"There are other, more suitable women here. Why don't you take one of them on a date?"

"Because I just have a feeling, you know? It's like that time we went hunting for deer, and I was like, there is definitely gonna be one over in the clearing, and it was right there. I knew it was gonna be there." I smile, thinking back on that day.

"We all saw it run over there," Warrick deadpans, rolling his eyes, while Ryker bursts out laughing.

"See, I knew it would be there." I don't know why they are fighting me on this. They were there. They saw the deer clear as day in that clearing. "So, back to my date. I ensured we had a super romantic dinner to go with our romantic setting. Steak, wine, chocolate-covered strawberries, the works. She loved all of it. After tonight, she's definitely falling for me. I mean, who could resist?" I smile. She told me all about growing up in the mortal world, being a kid, and not having any idea of magic, but pretending like she did. We spent the entire night telling stories about ourselves and comparing them. It was exactly like in the mortal romance books. Every detail of tonight went perfectly. These details are for me, though, not these assholes.

"I don't know if one night will win her over, man. She seems pretty skittish, and I don't think people fall in love that fast," Warrick interjects, much to my annoyance.

"How do you know? Have you ever been in love?"

"No, have you?" Warrick shoots back, laughing.

"No. Of course not. I'm saving that for my true love." I take a drink of my wine. What a silly question.

"Oh, I see. I forgot you're the expert here. Guys, make sure you save your love for your true love only." Warrick booms a laugh before polishing off his wine and pouring himself more. I lift mine to him, scowling, and he fills my glass.

"You just don't get it." I slouch back in my chair. None of them gets it. I want the love from the books, one true love, and all that. "Just help me keep an eye on the mortals so stuff like that collar doesn't happen again. They are in danger here if only because of their ignorance of our ways."

"That's why they shouldn't be here," Rodan growls from his perch over at the window. "More trouble than they are worth."

"Damn, Rodan, what crawled up your butt?" I laugh.

"One of the queen's cats, apparently," Ryker responds, and we all bust up laughing. Rodan looks none too amused by our antics. He shakes his head and continues his brooding.

Chapter 12
Jade

Light filters through my lids as morning breaks across my room once more. I groan and fumble for my phone, wondering what time it is, only to knock over a glass of water. Opening my eyes, I once again realize I'm not in my world and close my eyes again. Still not a dream. With a groan, I go to turn over, but my legs won't move. There's a weight holding them down. What the hell? I open my eyes and let out a startled yelp. A giant black mass of fur is on my legs, and its bright green eyes open into slits. It slowly lifts its head while keeping eye contact with me, then all I see are teeth. I'm gonna die. I can't move, and those teeth will be the last thing I see.

To my astonishment, it's a yawn. Its big arms are stretched over my legs, where its head was resting. It shifts its weight and slowly gets up, the light from the window making its coat sparkle like stars. It's the giant panther from yesterday. Everyone told me it was my imagination. But here it is, crouching down as it stretches. Stretches—like a cat, a typical cat, not a going to eat my face cat. My heart thunders as I watch, petrified in place. It walks off the bed and jumps out the window again. Wait, I closed that window. I know I did. What the hell is happening, and why is this cat, panther, thing stalking me? Oh god, is this how it hunts? Is it just going to torment me until it's hungry?

Here lies Jade, an enormous cat said she tasted like chicken. Well, I'm awake now.

A knock sounds at the door, and I jump. The door swings open, and Arlin strolls in, her curly hair hanging around her face. "You're still in bed, Sugar? That just won't do." Her singsong voice makes me smile as she walks over to the wardrobe and rummages around. "Heavens to Betsy, you just have to see what the boys are up to."

"What do you mean?" I'm not sure I want to know.

"The event that the queen put on today is a hoot. All the men had to cook, and you just won't believe what some of them were doin' while gettin' ready. I just had to come get you. Here, put this on." She throws a silky, form-fitting dress at me in a pretty forest green. The little cap sleeves and calf length give it a somewhat daytime-appropriate look. I run to the bathroom to fix myself up and put it on. Putting my hair up in a ponytail and painting red lipstick on, I look pretty decent for only spending five minutes getting ready.

"So, what is going on?" I don't even know what to think. The men are cooking? Why does Arlin make it sound important that I see this? I'm not awake enough for this. I miss coffee.

"Today's event, Sugar. The men have to prove their cooking prowess." She throws me the pair of flats I've been living in, which were by the fireplace. "Apparently, the queen arranged it. I think she did it to torture them. Cuz they look like a bunch of fish outta water, flappin' around like they don't know what to do." She's bent over laughing.

"Does Cat know? I feel like she wouldn't want to miss this." I giggle, thinking about it.

"Lyra went to find that girl. She's fixing to search the library, cuz she wasn't in her room." Arlin looks me up and down and smiles, apparently finding me suitably presentable. Grabbing my hand, she pulls me out the door. "You look pretty as a peach. Now come on, we don't want to be late. I'm sure they're all as busy as a cat on a hot tin roof." I laugh while running alongside her down the hall and stairs, following her lead to wherever we are going.

We stop at the doors to a parlor, the room fairly crowded with the women who have arrived to watch the show. Everything in this room is pink and floral. It reminds me of how my grandma's house was decorated, but fancier. A large, round table with the numbers one through 20 sits in the middle of the room, presumably where the food will be. There is another table set off to the side with plates and silverware. The smaller tables and chairs occupy the perimeter of the parlor. A box with papers stacked neatly next to it is down at one end of the room. Perhaps we will be rating the dishes? I have to admit, this does sound fun. I like food. What could possibly go wrong?

"Oh my god, are those sticks?" I poke at a bowl that looks suspiciously like short sticks in water with crumbled leaves on top, and try to stifle a giggle.

"Maybe it's like a fae delicacy?" Cat looks at me, a little worried.

"Most certainly not. Those are just sticks, Dear," Lyra interjects, crinkling her nose as the four of us try not to laugh. Lyra picks up one of the offending sticks and sniffs it. Looking over at Arlin, "Sticks and water. I dare say, I had hoped he'd tried to season this abomination at least." Lyra wrinkles her nose. A laugh escapes Arlin, which sends us all into giggles.

"Who do you think did it?" I say as I glance behind us at the men lined up proudly against the far wall, conversing with one another. They aren't allowed to talk to any of the women until all the votes are cast. The winner gets to take any female as his date to the beach tomorrow, and none of the other males can interfere. As everyone is going to the beach, that may cause some drama with the guys. The one with the fewest votes, which I'm guessing will be

Mr. Sticks, can't ask anyone to be his date. The whole thing is silly, but overall, it's pretty fun.

Cat giggles and leans in close. "Edgar." All of us snicker at her response.

"Or maybe," Arlin whispers, "Mika or Rosard, I doubt those two have ever stepped foot in a kitchen." Both men remind me of weasels. Mika, with his handlebar mustache, and Rosard leering like a creep. Both are so prim I doubt they've done a hard day's work ever in their lives. They are pretty likely candidates for the sticks.

"Do you think it's the prince?" I whisper back.

Lyra considers this and leans in. "No, I was given lessons in the royal kitchens as a youngin'. Unless he's too big for his britches, most royals know a lil' somethin'." I guess the princess would have a better idea than I would. It's the first time I've thought about one or more of these guys being princes.

The idea of dating a prince is almost absurd. Though some of these men could fit the bill. I don't know how I would feel about dating a prince. I'm still getting used to dating in general. Killian has been so sweet and has helped put me at ease here. I don't even want to think about Bravos. Then there is Rodan, who is so hot it should be a crime, but he keeps giving me the cold shoulder.

Our giggles continue as we move around the table. Some dishes are simple, and some are complex. There are strawberries with whipped cream, a rather soupy crème brûlée, cupcakes, cookies, a platter of steaks, cream puffs, fruit salads, a bowl of chocolate crumbles, a peach cobbler, and a tray of cut-up veggies. There is even a tray with a fish. I'm unsure whether it was cooked or simply plopped down. Each man had a few hours this morning to plan and create something. The creation we all agreed was the best was some sort of chocolate mousse; it had layers of caramel and was topped with meringue, reminding me of a decadent pie. After tasting and ranking all the edible foods, we cast our vote sheets. Some of the other girls are still making their way around the table and hadn't even sat down to eat yet, so it would be awhile before the results were in.

"I heard you went on a picnic with Bravos yesterday, Mortal." Beatrix saunters over to our table, her long blonde hair flipped over one shoulder. She looks like every Instagram model with a live, laugh, love sign in her house. Her haughty tone tells me everything about how this interaction is going to go.

I smile up at her and nod. "Yep."

"Do you know who I am?" She glares down at me.

"No."

"I'm the girl Bravos is here for. I was out with his brother Hunter. You know that they are royalty. Bravos is the eldest, as in the heir," she drawls, and I lift an eyebrow. "As in, he will be king someday, and I'd like you to stop whatever it is you think you are doing. He is way out of your league." I hear Cat snort beside me as I give Beatrix my undivided attention. "I'm just saying, Bravos will be mine. He just doesn't know it yet. So kindly—back off. This isn't a game for me," she huffs and storms away. I don't even know what to say. I don't think I'm even into Bravos, but that shit is funny. Who the fuck does she think she is? I turn and give Cat a questioning look as she snickers.

"The fuck was that all about?" I ask.

"Apparently, you stepped on someone's toes." Cat grins.

"She was madder than a wet hen," Lyra says, watching her go.

Arlin gives me a worried look. "You do not want to make an enemy out of that one. She could start an argument in an empty house," she muses. I shrug; she's like every bully I've dealt with my whole life. I don't let girls like that get to me.

"So, who are you interested in?" I look at Lyra and Arlin, who look down at their plates.

Arlin turns her head quickly towards the men and back. "I've been talking to Flynn. He is a writer," she sighs. "Wouldn't know it by looking at that dreamy physique, though. I'm fixin' to ask him out soon if he doesn't do it, though. He's the one I keep getting all gussied up for." I take a quick look at the guys, seeing Flynn. His long, dark hair is tied back in a low braid today, and he has a dark and mysterious look about him. Definitely attractive, cute even. "I love days like today when he wears shirts without sleeves. Those arms are somethin' else." She fans her face.

"And you, Lyra?"

Lyra looks nervously at the guys. "Well, originally, I was looking at Puck," she hesitates. "He's more my type. But I reckon with Sorrel barkin' up my tree day and night, I'm all cattywampus." She puts her head in her hands. Sorrel and Puck stand at opposite ends of the men. Sorrel is stern-looking, with his white hair brushing his shoulders. While Puck, with his rich brownie-colored eyes and hair, could be the Aladdin to Lyra's Jasmine.

"I know the feeling."

"You do?" Lyra says, looking up hopefully.

"Well, yeah, I'm not sure if I like Bravos, like at all. We have nothing in common. But the attraction is there. Then there is Killian. He is super sweet, we have a ton in common, but…"

"But what? Does he not get you hot and bothered?" Lyra looks at me sympathetically.

"No! No, not that. I would just feel bad if he got attached, and I left. I don't think I'm right for him, for anyone, for that matter."

"Sugar, there's not a pot too crooked that a lid won't fit," Lyra says, patting my hand.

"Huh?"

"What Lyra is tryin' to say is, don't worry so much about it. Things will either come together or they won't. Just go with the flow," Arlin interjects.

"That's what I've been trying to tell Jay. Just have fun. While Bravos isn't my favorite, kind of reminds me of every other bonehead you've dated. The point is to get out there again." Cat smiles.

"I'll be honest, Sugar, Bravos thinks the sun comes up just to hear him crow," Arlin says.

"That man should marry himself." Lyra laughs.

"Or a mirror." They all burst into laughter at Arlin's joke. I can't help but crack a grin. Sadly, they may be right. I glance over and see him checking his reflection in a window; he's preening like a damned peacock. Something about his behavior sends up familiar red flags I can't quite identify. I look back at the girls and nod towards Bravos, flexing in the reflection. Which results in another bout of laughter. I think I'm gonna have to cool my jets on that guy.

"I don't think I could compete with himself for his affections."

"It's okay. I don't think anyone could." Cat smirks. "Have you seen Rodan recently?" She wiggles her eyebrows.

"Not since I smacked into him in the library."

"You smacked him?" Lyra looks stricken.

I giggle at the idea. "No, I ran into him. I wasn't looking where I was going. I didn't see him."

"So, what happened?" Cat leans in.

"Nothing, I apologized, and he stormed off. There's nothing to tell. He doesn't like me; that much is clear." I watch him talk with Killian. He smiles as they talk, and I'm struck by how much I wish he'd smile like that at me. Of course, I'm attracted to the one who doesn't want me. Why am I so captivated by assholes?

"Uh-huh." Cat leans back in her chair, crossing her arms over her chest. "Feels like some sexual tension to me."

"What? No, it's nothing like that. That guy hates me." I wave my hands in front of me. Why on earth would she think that? Whenever he talks to me, he tells me to go home, that I don't belong here. Or he glares at me and makes himself scarce. I won't deny that I think he's gorgeous, but that doesn't mean anything.

"So you're telling me that if Mr. Tall, dark, and broody tried to take you, you'd say no?" Cat lifts an eyebrow as Lyra and Arlin lean in. I flush red instantly, the temperature in the room rising. When did it get so hot in here? Cat laughs. "My money is on that one. She can't resist a bad boy." My face gets even hotter as I bury it in my hands.

"Shut up, Cat," I mutter.

"Ladies and gentlemen! Your attention, please." The room goes silent as the queen walks in. "I have the results of today's events. Most of the men provided lovely treats. Some of the showings were abysmal." Her regal brows scrunch together. "The most abysmal dish goes to Edgar, really Edgar, sticks? Even Calazar placed a basket of apples on the table. Those were at least edible." She shakes her head and continues praising and critiquing different dishes. "... Ryker's bowl of chocolate was a passing attempt." Cat smiles. "...Bravos, your plate of steaks was interesting, but perhaps season them." Low giggling wafts through the room. "Hawkin, fish needs to be cooked." She looks pointedly at him. "And cleaned. Warrick, your cupcakes were delicious. Ellis, the crème brûlée should not be soupy." I can agree with this. "Killian, your cobbler was divine, but not enough to beat our winner."

All murmuring stops as we realize who has not been critiqued yet. "The winner of our cooking competition is Rodan. Congratulations, your chocolate mousse got the most votes, and I must agree, it was decadent yet light and full of flavor." Applause rises from all the women in the room, the men half-heartedly clapping.

The queen waves him forward. He moves slowly to stand beside her, a smirk playing at the corner of his mouth as he bows low. "Thank you, Your Majesty."

"For your prize, you have your pick of dates for tomorrow's outing. Ladies, this will be one of the few times you don't get a say in the matter," she pauses, giving the room a pointed look. "Keep an open mind; your heart will not lead you astray. Now, Rodan, who will accompany you?"

He smirks, "Jade." One simple word, and my stomach drops.

"Wonderful! This concludes today's activity. Tomorrow, everyone, be prepared for the beach. And please be respectful of one another," she says and walks out of the room.

I look over at Killian, who is staring at Rodan in confusion, you and me both. Rodan has a smug curl to his lips as he looks at me. What the hell just happened?

"Jay?" Cat shakes my shoulder. "Hey, you okay? You're looking a little pale." I slowly nod. "Don't worry, it will be fine." She winks, "I told you he doesn't hate you."

"What the hell?" I stammer out under my breath. I look over towards Rodan, who is still smirking at me. Why? I don't get it. I'm too stunned to voice any of this. Rodan stalks towards me. I barely see my friends stand to make themselves scarce, mumbling their goodbyes.

Rodan stops in front of me, holding out a hand. "May I escort you back to your room?"

"I was going to go to the library," I say as I take his hand and stand.

"Then I'll walk you." He guides me out of the large parlor. Almost everyone else has cleared out. I see Juniper, the green pixie, walking with Alvar, his hulking form dwarfing hers as she floats beside him. The fox shifter, Corsac, and Scarlette disappear up a staircase. We walk along in silence for a little while.

Moans echo down the hall, coming from an alcove to our right. I squint through the darkness. I can just make out a large form moving. Rodan snorts a laugh and pulls me along.

"Who was that?" I hiss, annoyed I didn't see.

"That was Oberon fucking Maysant. Didn't realize you wanted to watch. I can take you back for the show. I doubt they'll mind."

My face flames red, and my heartbeat speeds up as embarrassment floods me. "Oh. No. I didn't realize–I–" He pulls me around a corner and guides me into an alcove.

"You don't realize how things work around here," he growls.

"I didn't realize people had sex in hallways, but I guess I shouldn't be surprised. I suppose I'll never get used to things here." I go to walk around him, but he blocks me.

"Leave if you can't handle it."

"What is your problem, Rodan? You're hot, then you're cold. I'm getting fucking whiplash dealing with your bullshit. Tell me why. "

"Mortals are weak and pathetic. You are selfish and only out for yourself. You won't last a week here before you're on your knees begging for someone to send you home," he spits out.

"How dare you. I never asked to even be here."

"But here you still are all the same."

"Fuck you, asshole." I'll stay to prove you wrong and wipe that smug look off your face. "Maybe I will find love here." I hate that he's getting a rise out of me.

"This isn't a fairytale, Trouble," Rodan growls at me. "This is real life. What do you even know about the real world, princess?"

"You know what, fine," I growl right back. I've had enough. You want to make assumptions about me without knowing me? Then I'll tell you the truth. "I *was* obsessed with fairytales and happily ever afters. A couple falling madly in love, and everything going perfectly. The real world is far from that. It's ugly and mean. Relationships are hard and messy and often abusive and tragic. At least in my experience, nothing good comes from falling in love. You can watch all the rom-com and princess movies you want and dream of a better, beautiful world, but it doesn't change facts." I realize too late that I've got a tear running down my cheek, but can't find it in myself to care. "So, yes, Rodan. I know this isn't a fucking fairytale. I know that I'm not going to get a fucking happily ever after. It's never been in the cards for me. I know, okay?" I lift my chin in defiance of him, angrily wiping the tear away, and swallowing the lump that formed in my throat.

Rodan walks forward, pinning me against the wall. "You know nothing," he says in a low tone, his face unreadable. I move my hands to block and hold him back, seething at his words.

He grabs both of my wrists in one hand, pinning them above my head. It happens so quickly that it almost doesn't register. "What the hell?" I bark at him as I kick and buck my hips. "Get off me," I growl.

"Make me," he growls back with a dangerous smirk playing at one corner of his mouth. His knee slides between mine, causing my body to respond to his touch. I struggle, but I'm thoroughly pinned to the wall by his body. Breathing heavily, all I can smell is him. It's like the ozone smell before a storm and amber, a dark scent with promises of danger. Having him pressed against me is definitely giving me ideas I don't need to have right now. I can't stand this guy, but I still wonder what his mouth on me would feel like. Fucking Cat, of course, she was right. Pinned to a wall by an insufferable jerk, all I can think about is how I want him to keep going.

His dark grin deepens as he leans his face dangerously close to mine. "Something tells me you don't want me to stop," he purrs. And he is so right—no, we are not going there. I growl and struggle in his grip. The hard warmth of his body is pressed against mine, my body responding to his proximity. What the hell is in the wine here? Struggling only makes it worse; grinding against him and the hard stone behind me only adds to my arousal. His gaze feels like it's boring into me. "I think you like being pinned, Trouble," he whispers in my ear. I fight not to show him what his words and proximity are doing to my body.

"No," I snap.

He gives a soft chuckle before leaning in and slowly smelling me from my shoulder to my ear, sending tingles down my spine. My breath catches, and my spine straightens. "Your body begs to differ." Another soft chuckle leaves him as he releases me and walks away. Shock has frozen me in place, my face hot. He can smell it when I'm aroused? Fuck me. That is so not good. And why the fuck did that turn me on? If anything, it should have been a trigger, a huge red flag. Not a fucking turn-on! Asshole.

Chapter 13
Jade

After my run-in with Rodan, I returned to my room to bathe and cool my jets. I don't know what his problem is. Why the hell did he pick me to accompany him tomorrow if he wants me to go home so badly? For that matter, what the hell was that in the hallway? I can't get his burning eyes out of my head.

Sinking beneath the water, I want to erase the image from my mind. The ghost of his touch still lingers on my skin, holding me to the wall as he slowly inhaled up my neck. I break the surface, taking in a breath. Nope, I'm not thinking about that. Anger returning once more, I furiously scrub at my scalp, mourning the loss of color once more as I look at the silvery strands. It's been so long since I've seen my natural hair that I didn't realize it had gone completely white. Fucking magic.

As I dry off and get dressed again, my mind returns to the conversation with Killian. Everyone here has magic except us. I wonder what else these fae are capable of. The wars that have been fought. The curses, for that matter—everyone keeps saying the kingdom is cursed, by what?

I sit beside the fire to dry my hair and pick up the picture book. Flipping to the first page.

Earth magic wielders can manipulate plants, grow crops, and build our cities. Fucking children's books. Some fae have an affinity for metals and can make weapons and other fine things. The picture is of a fae building a castle, while another grows crops on a farm. Thanks, Killian, but I think I'd like a more detailed book. I snap it shut, intent on going to the library.

Voices carry down the hallway as I open the door. "I'm gonna go try my luck with Miss Jade today. I want to treat her like the queen she is and show her what I can do."

"I don't think you're her type, Ed," Warrick says.

"We just need to build that intimacy. I'm kind of an expert in it." Edgar says.

Warrick laughs, "Good luck, man, you're gonna need it."

I don't need to hear anymore as I bolt across the hall and into the library, running down the staircase and into the depths of the stacks. I run as fast as I can, making turn after turn, hoping he never saw me enter the library but knowing I'd have no such luck. Slowing to a stop only once I reach a dead end, it's a room full of dusty, worn books, all bound in leather and cracked with age. Hearing someone nearby, I turn frantically, looking for somewhere to hide. Darting around the side of a bookcase, I slam into Rodan's chest. Again.

"Do you always run in libraries with your eyes closed?" he drawls.

"My eyes weren't closed. I didn't see you there when I came around the corner." He lifts an eyebrow and glares at me. "Ugh, I heard Edgar coming and ran, okay? I really have no interest in a one-on-one with him." He crosses his arms. "I don't even know why I'm explaining myself to you. If you weren't just creeping around pretending to be a wall, this never would have happened."

"Creeping?" A ghost of a smile is playing on his lips.

"I'm looking for a place to hide, okay? You could help me, you know."

"I could, but watching you squirm is more fun." There it is, that annoying smirk.

"Gah! You are infuriating. What are you even doing here?"

"Not playing hide and seek." He lifts an eyebrow. Okay, hilarious asshole. I march over to a chair and sit in a huff. "That's my spot." His annoyance roughens his voice.

I look around, exaggerating the movement. "I don't see asshole written anywhere."

"Careful, Trouble." His tone is warning, but I don't care.

"Seems like a nice spot for reading. Any good books in here?" I give him a sardonic smile. He stands there with his arms crossed. "Aren't there any books in this library with..." I pause to figure out how best to convey this. "Any spice?"

"Spice?" he deadpans, suddenly looking very confused. "We do not spice our books here. Not really sure why you'd want to."

Uncontrollable giggles take over my body, got him. "Sex." I continue to laugh as my face heats. "Books with sex scenes." A flash of pink hits his stoic face. He drops his arms and storms away.

Worth it.

I get up and browse the books in this area of the library. Most of them are records of the kingdom and are better suited to someone with a background in the subject. So, I go to find the section on magic again. I walk along the stacks, taking in the various books and titles, taking my time. Finding my way back to the main rooms is proving to be a challenge. I didn't realize how many turns I'd made. The sound of giggling draws me to a stop. I peer down the corridor to my left, and more giggling gives way to moans as I peek around the corner.

Ellis kneels in front of a girl splayed over a desk, her skirts pulled almost up to her waist. My breath catches as I see them, pale blonde hair cascading over a stack of books. She arches her back and moans even louder. I spin around, pressing my back against the shelves. I did not need to see that. Her moans grow louder as I tiptoe away.

"Ohhh, my prince! Yes!" Oh god, that's Beatrix's voice. I have to stifle a laugh. I hear them moving, the thump of a book.

"Let's go. I told you I don't have time for your games, and I've entertained them enough," Ellis says.

"Fine, fine. Where is this place you just have to show me?" she grumbles.

I look around frantically for somewhere to hide and crouch behind a low bookshelf. I pull out a book so I don't look like I've been eavesdropping on a girl getting eaten out on a desk. Moments later, I hear a low rumble and footsteps, followed by another rumble. I sit and wait. A high-pitched chirp comes from above me, a sound vaguely familiar. I look up to see Pop looking down at me curiously from the top of the bookcase. I smile at the little dragon cat as it walks along the shelf and hops down on the other side.

After a few minutes, I slowly stand; they didn't pass by me. I peek around the corner and see the little room and desk empty. No people, no stack of books, and nowhere to go. I look all over the space as I enter, but it's another dead end. There was no other way out. They should have passed by me. Maybe one of them has that portal magic. Fucking fae.

"Why does it smell like sex in here?"

I jump, heart hammering as I spin. "Bravos, you scared the crap out of me." Holding my chest as I try to breathe, he arches a brow and stares at me. "Beatrix and Ellis were in here a moment ago." I shrug, trying to look nonchalant. "Maybe you smell them?"

He stalks over to me, staring down at me. I avert my eyes to the floor. He reaches out, tipping my chin up with his finger. "So, it's not you then?" His dark eyes bore into me as I back into the desk. I grimace as I realize I touched the spot where Beatrix was sitting.

"No, of course not." This is the face of embarrassment at walking in on someone else.

"Seeing as you are alone, I'll believe you. I was afraid I'd find you here with Rodan." His expression set in a snarl.

"Why would I be here with him?"

"Because of your date tomorrow," he spits, hands balling into white-knuckled fists.

"Oh, yeah. That." Alarm bells go off in my head. He is angry. I may not know the dangers of fae, but I know the risks of possessive men. I have to get out of here. This area is far too secluded. His posture tenses as his jaw clenches.

"I was hoping to be your date to the beach. There are many hidden alcoves and places to disappear to," he says, his tone suggestive.

"Well, that sounds very nice, Bravos," I say as I slowly circle around him towards the exiting hall. "I look forward to seeing the beach tomorrow. It's a pity I won't be your date, though." Stepping away, I convey the most sympathetic face I can muster. "I really gotta get going, though. I've been here for hours, and I'm supposed to have dinner with Cat."

"What's the rush? You could always stay and have dinner with me." His tone suggests anything but food. He snakes his arm around my waist, pulling me towards him. I put my hands up, pushing on his shoulders. The need to put distance between us is acute. Sweat beads down my back as I try to keep my breathing steady. "I haven't stopped thinking about you since our date. You've been very hard to find. I was thinking we could pick up where we left off in the garden. You, me, a bottle of wine under the moonlit sky. Make it clear that you are with me to the others."

"Seriously, I need to go." I push as he pulls me flush with him. "Really, we can have dinner another night." His face has gone serious, and I don't know if he believes me. I try to stay calm. I know he can hear when my heartbeat increases.

"Ahh, what the fuck!" he shrieks and lets go. I back up and look down to see his ankle is smoking, and flames lick the bottom of his pants. I say a silent thank you to Pop, who must have been under that desk, as I run out of the room.

"It was great to see you, but I gotta go," I shout behind me as I run. Okay, maybe Rodan was right. I spend an awful lot of time running in the library. But not with my damn eyes shut. I run until I reach the stairwell that leads up to the door by our rooms. I open the door a crack to listen before I bolt over to Cat's room and dash inside. A quick glance around tells me she's not here, but this is the perfect place to hide for now.

I walk over to the sitting area by the window and browse the books she has stacked there, finding a book on magic that looks much more thorough than mine. I open the window, pull a chair next to it so I can enjoy the breeze, and flip to page one.

"You're my wife," he snarls. "I own you. You've never done your wifely duties. And now—" Ace seethes, getting in my face. "Now I know you're cheating!"

"What? No. What are you talking about?" My heart is racing. I can't catch my breath. "I would never. Where did you get this idea—"

"I just know. I know the signs," he cuts me off. "You're just like my ex. Who is he? Huh? That guy you work with? Your boss? Your so-called friend?" His icy stare bores into me. He's gay, I want to shout, but he's talking so fast I can't get a word in. I don't understand. Where is this coming from? "Since when do you let your phone die? You never let your phone die! Ever since I've known you, you've never let it die. Jade." His face red with anger, snarling my name like a curse.

"It—"

"No, you say you're working overtime. Always at work, never at home. Can't do anything around the house. I had to do my own laundry today so I wouldn't stink at work tomorrow." Emphasizing his point, he kicks the laundry basket next to the bed. "You're never in the mood, always too tired."

"I am working overtime! The project is due next week—"

"Whatever. Jade." He sneers at my name. My mind is reeling, trying to catch up. To defend myself. But I can't remember half of what he's said. "Who is he? That guy from your work trip?"

"There was no guy. It was just me and Molly—" I plead.

"You never want to cuddle with me after. It's always gotta be a quickie because you're too tired! I always have to ask you, pester you. I tried giving you time during the day to get in the mood. Texting you."

"You sexted me at work! When I'm working! That's not hot; it's frustrating. I have work to do."

"See, it's never enough! You say you want to spend time with me. But where are you while I play video games in the evening? Cleaning? If you wanted to spend time with me, you would!"

"You always yell at me if the house isn't clean! When else am I supposed to do it?" I can't seem to hold on to what I'm trying to defend myself for. He's moving too fast.

"I'd rather live in a pigsty than not have sex," he spits. "It all makes sense now, though. Just know, I'll find out who it was and kill him." There is no guy. This makes no sense. "I don't know if I can ever forgive you for this. You're my wife! Your body belongs to me!" I try to collect my thoughts, but I can't. Where do I even start? Oh god. I'm shaking with anger or fear; I can't tell. "What, you've got nothing to say?" He grabs my arms, pushing me flat against the bed.

No. Not again.

I can't move.

Crack

I wake with a sob lodged in my throat, sitting up and scrubbing at my arms to get the feel of his hands off me. I'd hoped the nightmares wouldn't follow me here. My past haunts me, making me relive every horrible moment. I hiccup loud sobs, not caring if anyone can hear me. Why does my brain torment me with these memories? Why can't I simply live in peace? I didn't fucking cheat. But now I realize I should have, so I'd be punished for something I did. Then, I might have a different kind of torment in my sleep. Instead, I was forced to suffer and relive years of abuse. What did I do to deserve this? Hot tears run down my face as I reach over to turn on the light.

Still here, still not in my own room—the room I didn't even get a chance to unpack. I groan as I move to get out of bed. The bed shifts beside me. I turn my head slowly, my pulse rising at what I might see. Bright green eyes and shiny black fur. Oh, fuck me.

"If you're gonna eat me, just fucking do it already and put me out of my misery!" I yell at the panther. It stares unblinking at me. "What do you want?" It stands and moves towards me, and I freeze. The giant cat slumps down next to me, laying its massive arms across my legs and resting its head on them. I don't know what to do. Fresh tears pool in my eyes as I put my hand on its head and pet it. Fuck it, I may as well. I doubt petting it will be the deciding factor on whether or not I'm a midnight snack. "I'm just gonna assume you're one of the queen's cats," I sniffle. It continues to look at me.

"Why is everything so hard?" I moan. It blinks and folds its ears down. "What? It was a nightmare. God, why am I explaining myself to a cat? Why are you here? How do you keep getting in?" I ask, sniffling. Silence, yeah, what did you expect? I continue stroking its soft fur, feeling my heartbeat slow. "Well, for what it's worth, thank you for distracting me with your presence. Although I could have done without the heart attack." Sighing, I slowly lay back down, careful not to disturb the cat.

I continue petting its head, listening to it breathe. I guess this isn't so bad. It doesn't seem too dangerous yet. Maybe it really is just a pet. It shifts, laying its head on my stomach with one paw across me. I suppose this works. It's warm. Before long, it falls asleep. I need to find out its name so I can stop calling it- It. I'll be honest; the company is definitely helping. I close my eyes and let its presence and steady breathing comfort me.

Chapter 14
Rodan

While going to the beach may not be my idea of fun, the look on Trouble's face yesterday when I said I'd take her was. I stalk down the hallway, intent on picking up my prize. She may have had the last word in the library yesterday, but today, it will be mine. Walking down this hallway, steps echoing off the walls, I'm reminded of watching her squirm in the alcove. My dick took over my brain function as her smell intoxicated me, and I nearly lost my control. Why did that turn her on? I can feel a smile tugging at my mouth. She has so much anger toward me. It's almost too easy. Give it time; she'll go home, and everything will return to normal. Normal, a fucking cursed land, but normal. A small part of me is unhappy with the prospect of driving her away, but it's necessary. The main point is keeping her away from Bravos. I don't trust that guy, not after the incident with the collar. Naming her as my date today was a kindness when I think about it.

Killian wasn't too happy with the stunt I pulled at the competition, but this is also for his own good. He needs to spend time with the other females, so he realizes the mortals are just a fantasy. Little girls who will run at the first sign of danger. Killian has deluded himself with fairytales. I'd rather he did not get slapped so hard by reality; however, the more I look into the curse, the bleaker the possibility of that becomes. I can't find anything about how all of this started. Nothing in the records shows any plans for war with the Shadow Kingdom. It's all the same: the Shadow Kingdom was cursed and, in turn, cursed the Kingdom of Amara in retaliation. Then, the Shadow Kingdom fell, leaving Amara with no answers on how to break the curse. So, who cursed the Shadow Kingdom to begin with? And why?

I arrive at Trouble's door, shaking the thoughts from my head. I can worry about this later. I raise my hand to knock when I hear voices coming from the room next door and pause.

"Jade is too open. Too forgiving. But she's broken. I heard her crying again last night." Cat's voice carries through the door, and I lower my hand, trying to hear the low murmuring. "–He was cheating on her the whole time. Then, accusing her of it. Years she put up with that crap." Moving closer, I try to listen as her voice lowers again. "I think something in her cracked that day. Or maybe it fractured every time something bad happened. She doesn't talk about it, ya know, but I think he used to hurt her. She never had bruises or anything like that. But something was going on."

Her voice goes quiet, and I creep closer again. "I think he forced or verbally berated her until she gave in. And she has mentioned a few times that every guy does the same thing. I–I don't know for sure, but I'm pretty sure everyone she's ever been with has abused her." A low growl rumbles involuntarily through my chest. "I'm afraid for her. That she's gonna keep trying to find the love she's looking for in all the wrong people. She just attracts narcissists. That's why I've been encouraging her to just have fun here. Because when we go, she doesn't have to worry about facing them again. She won't be jumping into another bad relationship. Maybe she will find someone who can show her sex doesn't have to suck. I don't know," she sounds defeated. "Should I just tell her to stop? To keep to herself till we go? She's a romantic at heart, but she's just been beaten down by the world. She used to be so much...more. A force to be reckoned with. She was so obsessed with romance movies. She wanted that kinda love." Like Killian, I sigh. "I just wanted her to have some fun before we leave."

"Don't go." Ryker's low voice rumbles through the door.

"I don't do relationships. I've told you that. I like you a lot, but I've seen too many like Jade's end in disappointment," Cat's voice sounds pleading.

I stand up straight and move back towards Trouble's door. I shouldn't have listened to their private conversation. Fuck, that explains why she looks so scared all the time. The reason I can always smell fear on her. Why her heart races when she talks to any of the guys. She might put on a brave face, but her body gives her away. She's right. I am an asshole. I'm an asshole for not putting it together sooner. Fuck.

I reach up and pound on her door a little harder than I intend, move to the opposite wall, and lean back. Taking a deep breath, I shake the thoughts from my head once again. I cross my arms over my chest as I wait.

The door opens, and she is a vision in black and pink. A flowy black top wraps around her, giving the most gorgeous view of her cleavage and the bikini hidden beneath. The bottom of her swimsuit is a shadow under sheer pink pants that shimmer in the morning light. I shift to hide the erection that is growing in my pants. Okay, maybe the beach date was not my best idea.

"Hello, Trouble," I say, giving her a half grin and appraising look.

"Hi, Rodan."

I take a step forward, offering her my arm. She huffs and closes the door behind her as she moves to walk down the hall. "Someone's excited." I give a low chuckle. That earns a glare shot back at me. I love how easy it is to rile her up.

"For the record, I am not interested in courting you, Rodan," she quips as we descend a staircase.

"Trouble, I'd rather kiss a basilisk." I smirk at the disdain I see in her eyes. "Plus, I know you have a thing for Bravos."

She turns towards me, brow furrowed. "I'd rather fuck a cactus," she says simply and continues walking. "Sideways."

A laugh slips from me. I was not expecting that. "What, did he offend your sensibilities?"

"No, he is too much like every other self-centered asshole I've dated." She pauses. "What? Do you think I've got him wrong?"

I continue laughing as I try to respond, "Trouble, you just surprised me, is all. A cactus is quite extreme." I stop walking as I double over in laughter. She looks back at me and cracks a smile, the beauty of it causing a stir in my chest. I straighten, trying to regain my composure. Clearing my throat and motioning to the left, "We are going out that way, to the stables."

"We aren't walking there?"

"That would be a very long walk."

"Oh."

We step outside into the fresh air. The day is sunny and warm. It will be a few hours before the others take the carriages to join us. One of the perks of winning yesterday's competition. The other being she couldn't refuse my offer. This is the only way I can see to keep her away from Bravos, although I thought it would be a lot harder. We walk the path to the large stables where my horse is saddled and waiting for us. She's a large black steed, her mane and tail a striking white, both braided and laced with tiny blue flowers. "This is Nightingale."

Trouble slowly walks up to Nightingale and strokes her neck. "She's beautiful," she breathes. She is so tiny next to my horse. Continuing to pet the animal as she greets her, she brings her hands to the horse's muzzle and strokes its long nose. "I haven't been on a horse since I was a kid." She smiles and looks around. "Only one?"

"You ride with me."

"Of course I do," she grumbles.

Motioning for her to come over to the horse's side, I help her seat herself in the saddle. I admit I'm impressed that she got up there mostly on her own. Climbing up behind her and pressing her body flush with mine, I reach for the reins. I can feel her breathing, every movement of her body, her sugary vanilla scent making my dick twitch. I may not have thought this through. Too late now. I wrap an arm around her waist and kick the horse into a gallop toward the gates. She lets out a yelp of surprise as one hand finds mine and holds on tight, the other going white-knuckled on the pommel.

When we reach the city, I slow the horse. "Welcome to the city of Moradi," I say as I turn the horse down towards the main road.

"There's a city—"

"Of course, there's a city. Did you think the castle held the entire population of Amara?"

"I—no, I didn't really think about it," she says in awe, looking at the stone buildings towering around us. Most of this stretch of road has two and three-story buildings, with shops lining the bottom floors and homes on the upper. Every structure is unique in the color of stone it was hewn from. I had a feeling she might like it.

"I've never seen anything like this before," she breathes. "It's gorgeous. How do they make them sparkle like that?"

"This is the Gemstone Quarter. Every building is made with earth magic. They sparkle because of what they are made of." I slow the horse and point out a milky light green building tucked between rose quartz and blue agate buildings. "That one is made of jade."

"Oh, my god. Really? That's so cool." She bounces, rubbing against my cock. I regret taking one horse. I pull her to sit more in my lap as I readjust in the saddle. She squeaks out of surprise but doesn't protest, too mesmerized by the city surrounding her. "What kind of shops are there? Where are all the people? Is this a nice place to live?"

"It's a very nice place to live. It's early yet, and the shops are not open. The people are probably in their homes. As for the shops, everything people could need. Although with the population dwindling and people moving to other kingdoms, I'm not sure how long this city will be this way."

"Because of the curse?"

"Yes."

"Will you tell me about it?"

I sigh. "You really want to know? It's an unpleasant topic."

"Yes, no one seems willing to talk about it."

"It's not that they are unwilling. Most have given up hope. Many of the men at the castle will move to other kingdoms with the ladies they choose, hoping to foster heirs that they can move back to start the cycle again. Amara is reaching a critical point."

"So what is the curse?" She presses as we exit the Gemstone Quarter and enter the central city of white marble buildings. People are starting to appear, cleaning the shining homes and roads with water magic. Her hand tightens on mine in excitement.

"It started with the Shadow Kingdom a little over sixty years ago. A curse was cast by someone very powerful. A death curse—it ravaged the land and its people. It was slow at first. Fae started dying in droves on the outskirts of the territory. Then, more and more; in ten years, a quarter of the population was gone. After thirty years, all that was left were the people in the castle. Their wards only held out for so long, though. So sometime in the first ten years, the Shadow King cast a forbidden curse to punish the kingdom he thought had cursed his land. He cursed Amara. From that day on, no females would be born in Amara. Fae don't have children often, so it took a while for everyone to realize what had happened. By then, the Shadow King and everyone in Shadow were long dead. So, nobody has a clue about how to lift the curse on Amara.

"How do you know that the Shadow King cast the curse?"

"He wrote it in a letter to King Corbin right before he died. All it said was, 'Now your kingdom will fall, too.' By the time it arrived, everyone in Shadow was dead."

"What happened to the land left behind after everyone died?"

"It's a death curse; spend more than a few days there, and you'll be cursed to die. It's a barren land no one dares enter anymore," I reply. At least no one enters to anyone's knowledge. It would be taking way too big a risk.

"And no one knows how to break the curse on Amara or Shadow?"

"That's what I've been trying to find out. It's why I was looking at the records yesterday. Before, I was so rudely interrupted and accused of being a wall," I deadpan as I poke her in the ribs.

She laughs, leaning her head against my chest. "You do make a good wall, though." I crack a grin as Nightingale picks up the pace, and we near the city's edge. "Does the king have any idea of what happened back then? Did his father tell him anything useful?"

"The king's father had long since retired by that time. King Corbin is as confused by all this as the rest of us."

"Then who was king fifty years ago?"

"King Corbin."

"But—he would have been a child," she makes it sound preposterous.

"I assure you, he was not." I stifle a laugh.

"Then how old is he?" her tone incredulous. "He looks like he's forty tops."

"He recently celebrated his two hundredth year."

"What?" she shrieks. "Wait, wait, wait. Then how old are you?" She tries to turn to face me, but struggles in my hold. I do not need her falling off the horse.

I lean towards her ear. "Are you worried?"

"Yes! How old do fae get? Oh my god, tell me I'm not dating a bunch of super old guys. I have no interest in a May-December relationship," she groans. I have no idea what that is, but her reaction is priceless.

"Thirty."

"What?"

"You asked, I'm thirty," I say.

"Like thirty thousand, a hundred and thirty—?"

"Thirty. As in thirty. Am I to assume you are a hundred and thirty?"

She laughs. "No. Just twenty-nine. But—how long do fae live if the king is two hundred?"

"In our realm, people age a lot slower. All creatures age slower from adulthood. Most fae live to be about five hundred. Most are mated between thirty and forty. A few of the men at the castle are older, as there has been a significant decline in available women in Amara."

"Oh."

We ride in silence as we depart the city. She is taking in the view of the mountains as we travel through the pass. Leaning her head on my chest, she remains in my lap with my arm around her waist. She seems comfortable, which I wasn't expecting. I thought she'd fight me the whole way. The lush green trees reach towards the sky while the morning fog burns off. I watch the shadows drift over her hair as the tendrils brush my arm, the urge to run my hands through it and pull almost overwhelming. From the path, I see a little clearing in the trees. I envision stopping the horse and taking Trouble there. Silencing that quick tongue of hers with my mouth as I bring her to ruin.

"So, what powers do you have?" She breaks the silence and pulls me out of my trance.

I pull my hand from her waist and run my fingers down her arm, letting my power lick her skin lightly, bringing all the little hairs to stand on end. Her spine stiffens, and she lets out a slight gasp. I incline toward her ear and whisper, "electricity." A whiff of that intoxicating scent she gives off when she's aroused hits me. Interesting.

"Oh," her response is breathless, and I find I quite like that. "I thought all magic was elemental."

"It is. I wield air, but my specialty is electricity. Been studying up on magic, Trouble?"

"Just curious about it. I've also been reading about the history of Auburnigh. Where is Eneara?" I'm surprised she's looking at our land's history, not only Amara but the whole of Auburnigh.

"Eneara is the continent that lies east of here."

"Is that where the vampires are?"

"Who told you about the vampires?"

"Warrick."

"And why would he do a thing like that?"

She groans, "Because when we first got here, we thought he was one–"

I laugh harder than I've laughed in years. Warrick, a vampire! "Trouble, you are something else." Still chuckling. "Yes, all the vampires and such are in Eneara."

"Glad my kidnapping by a man with fangs is amusing to you," she deadpans, crossing her arms.

I pull her in tighter to me, eliciting another tantalizing squeak out of her as I fight to keep myself under control. "Why history? Kind of a dry subject."

"I studied history in my world. It's what I got my degree in. It's amazing how similar yet different the history is here."

"How is it similar?" I ask, intrigued by this enigma in my arms.

"Mostly the wars. It's the same in both worlds, usually a play for power, land, control, stuff like that."

"Smart girl."

Chapter 15
Jade

As we crest the pinnacle of the last incline, I'm greeted with the sight of the sea. The briny breeze envelops me as I take in the picture. The ocean sprawls in front of us, clear and calm, shades of blue rolling on the tide up the rosy sand beach. The view is unreal, the sandy coast resembling the softest strands of cotton candy rather than sand. Turquoise pools nestle amidst sparkling sea glass stones in a mosaic of pastel colors. The water is so pristine in areas that I catch glimpses of coral. Coves peak out from the rugged mountains, with waterfalls cascading down into crystalline lagoons. I have never seen a more beautiful sight.

We ride along the shore, and I listen to the slow, quiet rhythm of the water rolling up. The early morning sun sparkles off the water, illuminating the spray of the waterfalls. Our pace is slow as I take in the scene, moving towards one of the alcoves. We pass a calm and deep lagoon, its center almost ink-like at its depth. Around a stone cliff that juts out is another lagoon with a waterfall cascading down the front of a ridge covered in ivy and flowers.

"This is breathtaking," I breathe. Rodan's grip tightens around me once more as he stops the horse.

"I thought you might enjoy it here," he says as he gets off the horse and gives me a hand to get down. His hands graze down my sides as he lowers me to the ground.

We walk along the beach in silence for a while, listening to the sound of the waves in the distance. It doesn't roar; it's a soft murmur. It's peaceful and quiet. I walk along the path of glittering sea glass and admire the colors. They are smooth like stones, all of various sizes. Rodan occasionally picks one up and skips it across the water. Sometimes I swear I catch him casting furtive glances my way, but I must be imagining things. Down the mountainside, there are trees and flowers similar to those in the pink garden but growing wild, mixed in with the greenery.

Rodan looks serene here, the hard edges smoothed away until it seems the calm has penetrated his soul.

He glances towards the path we came in on, cocking his head to the side and shaking it. "The others are coming," he grumbles.

"How do you know?" I look back at the path but don't see anything.

"I can hear them."

I sigh, knowing that the peace we've enjoyed for the last hour or so will be lost. I'm not wrong; a line of carriages arrives at once, and all the fae inside pour out, running for the water and yelling in excitement as they strip. Most women wear something very close to a bikini, like the suit Lorelai provided me with this morning. The material is a little different, but the same concept. The men, however, wear minuscule shorts that leave little to the imagination. While some wear, oh dear god, the fae equivalent of a speedo. Edgar is in a fucking speedo. I need to bleach my eyes out of my head. I cringe and avert my eyes while trying not to gag.

"Are you okay?" Rodan asks, following my gaze. "Oh, for fuck's sake," he grumbles as Edgar dances at the lagoon's edge, thrusting his hips. His belly almost covers the small piece of fabric that hangs from his waist. On second glance, the thing he is wearing is closer to a loincloth, and a very small one at that. Seeing him almost naked sheds light on his squat appearance; he has to be related to a troll. "Come with me."

"You don't have to ask me twice."

I follow Rodan back to where we had left the horse. Nightingale lies in the shade of a large blush tree by the water. The loud roar of the waterfall deafens the other people's sounds on the beach. The area is serene and secluded, away from everything. I marvel once more at the clear aquamarine of the lagoon.

"Now would be the time to strip, Trouble." Rodan takes off his dark shirt, revealing the tight planes of his muscles beneath. The light dances playfully across his broad shoulders as he reaches for the button on his pants. Holy hell, I snap my eyes down as my mind wanders to dangerous places. He is built like a god; his alabaster skin glistens in the sun, reminding me of a marble statue.

"What?" I squeak out.

"Unless you want to swim in your clothes, I'd suggest stripping." A sly grin plays across his face. Flushed, I take off the top that covered my black bikini. It isn't anything elaborate. The straps wrap around my neck and back, covering everything except my cleavage. I drop the light-pink pants in the sand next to me, revealing the matching bottoms, and look up to find Rodan's dark stare pinned to me. I have never felt so naked as I do under that gaze.

To hide my flushed skin, I turn and put my feet in the water. It's warm and inviting. I feel him behind me. Before I can react, I'm lifted off the ground and thrown in. I screech as I hit, water engulfing me.

That son of a bitch.

"Asshole," I breathe as I surface, looking around at the shore for my assailant.

"Getting all wet for me, Trouble," his voice carries from behind me. I spin to see him swimming backward towards the waterfall. He ducks under and disappears.

I grumble as I swim towards the waterfall, looking for him. The water is so clear I should be able to see him, but I don't. I swim under the falls and come up behind the flow of water, holding on to the rocks as I wipe water from my eyes.

"Hello, Trouble." The low purr of his voice pulls my attention up. He's standing in a cavern behind the waterfall. He leans down and offers me his hand. I'm tempted to pull him down into the water again. "I want to show you something."

I reach up and let him help me into the hole, climbing the slick rocks as carefully as I can. When I finally stand in the cave, I'm struck speechless. I stand, my face going slack at the sheer expanse of the cave. A myriad of stars, like shimmering diamonds, embellishes the inky canvas of every surface. The whole cave sparkles with celestial illumination on midnight blue stone polished smooth as glass. I am standing in the night sky.

"What is this place?" I whisper, afraid to break the serenity.

"My favorite place in all of Auburnigh. I found it as a child. Someone long ago must have hewn the cave and every surface in it smooth." A soft smile spreads across his face. "I've never shown it to anyone. I used to disappear here for hours."

"It's magical. Everything here is so beautiful," I breathe as I walk further into the cave, staring up at the ceiling and watching the lights sparkle. I run my hand over the smooth wall. Why would he show me this wonderful place he's kept secret for so long? "You're being nice." I turn and look at him skeptically. His eyes darken as he stares at me; no secret that he's been watching me.

"Do you prefer it when I'm mean?" he purrs, making a shiver run down my body. That voice does things to me I don't understand.

"It's unsettling," I stammer out as I watch his breathing increase with mine. The water drips from his hair down his chest and trails to his waistband. My heart is fluttering in my chest as my gaze wanders back up. I take in the curve of his jaw as he licks his lips, bringing my attention there. Want swells in me as his gaze flicks to mine.

A low growl emanates from his chest as he stalks forward in two long strides. "Fuck it," he growls before his mouth collides with mine. Stealing my breath away, my eyes flutter closed. He wraps his hands around my face before sliding one to the back of my neck and deepening the kiss. I don't know how we got here, but I don't want him to stop. I burn for whatever this is between us.

I run my hands down his sides and pull him flat against me, eliciting another growl from him that sends a thrill down to my core. Kissing him is electric, worlds colliding and collapsing. I give in to this dark desire that plagues me. This fevered kiss feels like a cataclysmic inevitability that we've both been fighting for eternity.

He presses me against the wall, smooth against my bare back. I kiss him with a hunger I didn't know I had. I let sensation cloud my judgment as I claw at his back. He breaks the kiss, trailing his mouth down my neck, unhooking the straps of my top. I let them drop as he runs his mouth down my chest, making me want more.

"May I?" he gruffly asks as he tugs on the strap around my back, holding my top on. I nod. My top falls away in moments, and his mouth is on my nipple, gently nipping and sucking. I groan at the slight prick of pain as he bites. He brings his mouth back up my neck before kissing me again, this time gentler.

I'm lost in his destruction of me, my walls falling down around me. My breath hitches as I run my hands through his hair, pulling him into me. I want more. I want him. Rolling my hips, I grind against him. I'm aching for him. He groans in response, pressing firmly into me, growing harder as he rolls against me in return. He growls, catching my lip in his teeth. The pressure builds within me as I run my fingers down his abs and explore every muscle as they flex under my touch. Shudders ravage his body with every light caress. When I reach his waistband, he breaks the kiss and grabs my hand.

"Careful, Trouble." His gruff voice and warning tone send a thrill through me. He pins my arm above my head and leans his forehead against mine. "Can I touch you?"

I stare at him wide-eyed and give a slow nod, my shallow breaths making me dizzy.

"Use your words," he purrs as his gaze darkens and a grin plays at the corner of his mouth, rolling his hips into me again.

"Yes," I whisper. My heart is pounding, and my body is beginning to tremble.

"Good girl," he whispers in my ear, sending another wave of shivers down my spine.

Slowly, he trails his other hand down my arm, sending little shocks of electricity skating across my skin, his power licking me. My breathing grows more shallow as I watch him look at me. His eyes dilate, the little bit of green hidden. He hooks his finger in the side of my swim bottoms and cocks his eyebrow at me. I nod, and he pulls them down my hips. Letting go of my arm, he slips them down my legs agonizingly slowly until I can step out of them, completely naked. I shiver at my vulnerability as he slowly stands, taking in every inch of my body, a rumble sounding through his chest. The look in his eyes is carnal as he appraises me.

He gently raises my arm above my head again, lacing his fingers through mine. He leans in slowly and kisses me, intensifying the burn within me. Every kiss, every caress, like a magnetic connection pulling us together. He explores my mouth with his, rocking against me, rolling his hips. His hard length rubbing my clit through rough shorts. He glides his hand down my side, igniting every nerve ending. Shockwaves of anticipation dance through my senses. His hand circles my stomach above my center.

"Are you wet for me, Trouble?" he murmurs against my mouth, before he runs his fingers down my folds and growls, deepening the kiss once more. He pushes my legs apart with his knee as he slides his finger up and down, barely touching my clit before moving again. I gasp as my eyes fall shut, and he gives a low chuckle as I buck into his hand, intent on getting more. He slowly slips his finger inside, and it's agonizingly slow as he pulls back.

"Eyes on me," he whispers, low and seductive. My eyes open, and he watches me, sinking his finger in deep before pulling out again and circling my clit before doing it again and again. I let out a soft moan, needing more. Pleasure rocks through me in pulses as pressure builds. My breath comes out in short bursts as I try to remember to breathe. He keeps his eyes trained on me as he adds a second finger. I feel the stretch as I buck against his hand.

"So tight," he growls. "I'd ruin you if I took you," he says so low I barely hear it. But I can't concentrate over the feeling of his fingers as they curl within me, hitting a spot I didn't realize existed. I moan louder as his thumb pushes on my clit simultaneously as his fingers hit that spot within me. He works his hand harder and faster as he circles my clit. The pressure is building, and my breaths become shorter. He slows down again and kisses me gently, caressing my lips. I reach for his pants again, wanting more. He pulls back and shakes his head slowly, letting me know with the dark look in his eyes to do as he says.

He withdraws his fingers from me, leaving me feeling empty, wanting. He slowly licks them, and my legs tremble with want. "I knew you'd taste as good as you smell." He grins. My pulse hammers as I watch him through hooded eyes.

He collects both my wrists in his hand above my head, pinning me to the wall. Something about being pinned like this makes me even hotter. He runs his fingers back down my center, and suddenly, there is more pressure at my core as he slips three fingers slowly inside. I wince at the stretch.

"It's too much," I breathe. The sensation overwhelms me, and I'm lost to it as my heart beats faster.

"Trust me. You can take it," he whispers in my ear before he bites my neck. In the shock of the quick, sharp pain at my neck, I feel him fill me up. The bite sends a shock of pleasure through my core. I feel bliss as he pumps in and out of me.

My back arches into him as he holds me in place with his body. The pressure is building again; it's more intense than before. He touches my sensitive clit, and a slight shock like static electricity sends me over the edge. Fireworks explode through my body. He continues pumping as I ride the wave and come apart in his hand. Before I come down, he curls his fingers, and I feel that little electric shock run through the inside of me again, sending me over. I scream his name as the climax retakes me.

My moans are smothered as he kisses me roughly, continuing to shock me before every wave ends. I'm panting, writhing, and seeing stars as he sends another little shock through me as I ride his hand, unable to stop. I think I might die when he bites me again and sends a bigger jolt of power into me. I cry out in ecstasy. This is the apocalypse of my body, and I will gladly die here.

"Good girl," his low growl sends shivers through me.

He kisses me slowly as he gently removes his fingers from me and helps me slide down the wall into a heap, my body buzzing, yet wholly undone. My legs are shaking so badly I don't think I could walk if I tried. Holy shit, I didn't know that it could feel like that. Aside from a few toys I've played with, it wasn't anything like that. I've never come so hard or for so long. Definitely never multiple times. That was just his hands. I shudder to think what actual sex would be like with him. I think I'm starting to understand why people enjoy sex now.

He pulls away and looks at me. "Now you can report your findings to Cat," he says with a self-satisfied smirk.

It takes me a minute before it dawns on me, and mortification takes over. He heard us in the library talking about sex. My face flushes hot as I cover it with my hands. I don't even know what to think about this. Yesterday, I was convinced he hated me. I do not know where I stand with him, but I want more.

"W—What did you do to me?" I stammer, rubbing my neck where he bit me, sure his fangs had pierced the skin, but finding the area smooth and unbroken.

"From the sound of it, the men of your realm have done you a great disservice. I took it upon myself to rectify that." He gives me a devilish smirk, picks up my swimsuit, and helps me put it back on. He leans forward and kisses my forehead, then helps me stand back up on shaky legs.

A sharp scream breaks through the sound of the waterfall, freezing us both in place. Then, a roar so loud it shakes the cavern echoes into the cave. Rodan snaps his head and looks out towards the opening, runs, and dives out through the waterfall. Unsure what to do, I scramble after him, climbing back into the water. I swim under the falls to the shore, and when I surface, I hear a cacophony of sound. I run onto the sand and around the side of the cove. The main area of the beach comes into view.

The sight causes me to stumble sideways, fall into one of the lagoons, and freeze.

An enormous white dragon sits on the shore. Its scales shine like pearls in the sun. Spikes run up its long nose and end in long horns pointing back towards its large folded wings. Spines run down its back and end in a tail that thrashes dangerously. The dragon's roar shakes the ground, causing the surrounding water to ripple. A mighty blast of blue fire erupts from its mouth towards the sky. Above the flames, the pixies flit back and forth, deftly avoiding being hit. Nucifera douses the flames with a torrential downpour that cascades from her hands, while Juniper creates large wooden stakes that she whips at the giant beast. The dragon cries out and rears back before slamming its front legs down on the ground, narrowly missing a golden wolf at its feet.

The wolf backs up with a vicious snarl before flames explode from its mouth, turning the talons of the dragon black. The dragon's black eyes turn towards the wolf as it swipes its claws, barely missing the tail as the wolf bolts out of reach. My heartbeat is the percussion of war drums.

Bellows sound through the air.

Roaring eclipses all thought.

The crackle of power, a cacophony of battle drums.

Fae run towards the carriages as the cries continue. Edgar waves the crying twins into a carriage with Lyra and Arlin close behind. Poppy and Hyacinth run for the forest and change into deer as they leap for the treeline and out of sight. Cat runs for a carriage but trips and falls. Ellis picks her up and keeps running. They both get into the carriage, and it takes off down the path. I move further into the water, sinking down to hide. Running would require getting too close to the dragon. I'm too scared to move as I watch the chaos ensue. The world seems to go quiet under the ringing in my ears and the hammering of my heart. My head goes foggy as I try to take in air.

Oberon and Ryker run towards the dragon's tail as they throw their hands up in the air. Giant pillars of stone form around the tail like a cage, stopping the wild thrashing. Beside them, Fennec and Corsac both turn into fox-type creatures. Fennec's red fur shows like fire as her numerous tails whip into a frenzy of motion. Corsac is the ghost of Fennec—translucent, glowing blue. As Fennec's tails alight with fire, Corsac's tail blasts it towards the dragon in a giant wave of wind and fire.

Scarlette climbs up onto a boulder, squatting down with her palms outstretched. She swirls her hands in front of her before she slowly stands. The ground under the dragon's right legs swirls into a molten red liquid before climbing up the ivory dragon and solidifying into black stone.

Beatrix stands on the shore next to Scarlette and pulls enormous icicles out of thin air, which she hands to Bravos. He launches them like javelins—fast and hard through the air. The dragon turns towards them and roars, taking a deep breath. My heart stops as I think they are about to be roasted. Bravos has his hands outstretched, and the blue flames of the dragon go around an invisible dome surrounding them.

Helpless, I crouch down further into the water. This display of magic is surreal. Every strike agitates the great beast; it thrashes and bites. Shields form and fall from different fae as they work together to subdue the white dragon.

Calazar and Ambrose run towards a lagoon that is closer to the ocean. The sirens, Owari and Yudoku, walk out of the water, shedding their tails, joining hands with the two men. The four of them raise their hands toward the ocean. In the distance, the water swells. As it nears the shore, the wave grows taller, reaching over the dragon's head. The surge curls around the dragon, pulling it towards the ocean. The dragon drops to its side with its legs encased in lava rock. The ground trembles as it falls. Like a terrible omen, the power radiates through the beach.

A large crack of thunder rips across the sky as lightning strikes the downed dragon, its roar deafening. The dragon turns its head toward me, and I look for a place to hide or run to. Rodan stands on the cliff above me, electricity crackling around his body. The dragon takes another deep breath, fixing Rodan in its black stare. He looks down, makes eye contact with me, and his eyes widen. He dives into the water next to me and pulls me under into the deep blue water.

I shake as the water temperature seems to drop, the surface above me rippling with the blue fire. Spots fill my vision as what little air is in my lungs burns. I need air, but the fire continues to blast over the water. Panic sets in its icy claws as I reach for the surface, but I don't move. Rodan is wrapped around my body, holding me under, away from the fire. I claw and struggle until my lungs give out, water rushes in, and the world goes black.

"Fuck. Fuck. Fuck." A faint voice comes through the darkness.

"Killian!" The frantic voice calls. "Killian, get over here. Help me!" As the fog slowly lifts from my mind, I realize it's Rodan's voice calling. I crack my eyes open and see his panicked face above mine.

An enormous golden wolf's face appears next to Rodans, and I remember. The dragon, the magic, the fight, and the fire before drowning. The wolf whines and transforms into Killian. My eyes widen in shock as every muscle in my body tenses. Killian was the fire-breathing wolf. I can't control my breathing as the world spins around me. So much noise. So much danger.

"Calm down, Trouble, you'll be ok. We will figure this out." Rodan tries to soothe me, but his panicked expression only adds to my anxiety.

"What? How?" Killian stammers, looking panicked.

"I don't know," Rodan shoots back.

"But—how?" Killian looks at me, eyes wide. My mind reels over everything I've witnessed.

"I don't know." Rodan scrubs his face with his hand.

The dragon roars, shaking the ground beneath me. I wince at the sound.

"You have to get her out of here. Take my horse and find Warrick. Get her out of here." Rodan points towards the horse and looks down at me again, features softening. "Close your eyes, Trouble. Killian will get you out of here, and we'll get this figured out."

Killian reaches down to scoop me up as I close my eyes tightly. I feel so small in his arms. I can hear his heart racing as he runs for the horse. I jostle as he mounts and takes off at a gallop; the wind running over me.

"Warrick. Portal. Now!" he shouts as we slow to a stop. Then the world twists, nausea hits, and memories of the night I met Warrick flood my mind.

With my head still spinning, the horse returns to a gallop as Killian holds me to his chest. He slows and carefully climbs down. I feel every movement, but can't bring myself to open my eyes.

"It's gonna be okay," he murmurs in my ear, before he breaks into a run. I hear doors open and his footsteps echoing off the walls as the floor changes from the crunch of gravel to the pounding steps on stone. "Tell the queen I need her!" he shouts at someone. "In the mortal's chambers. Now," his tone commanding and final. He slows his pace. "It's gonna be okay," he keeps murmuring all the way to my room.

Chapter 16
Killian

What. The. Fuck? What do I do? How did this happen?

I open the door to Jade's room and gently place her on the bed, mind reeling as I pace. I need my mom, fuck; I need a drink. I pull at my hair and groan. Everything was so crazy at the beach. That dragon came out of nowhere. We were kicking its ass. Honestly, running around as my wolf was so fucking freeing. Well, minus almost getting stepped on, but my fire was spectacular.

And then, this.

Jade gazes up at me, and her face is so broken. She closes her eyes and curls into a ball, pulling her hands around her knees. I wince in anticipation. Her eyes snap open as she feels the fur. A loud squeak of terror fills the room. She flips around, looking at herself, getting louder and louder.

"Calm down, Emerald. It's gonna be okay. We are gonna figure this out," I try to coax her down, but she pulls on the fur and gives me a panicky look. Which I have to admit is super cute: that little white face of hers and those big eyes peering up at me.

Then she notices the tail, and a sound like a wail leaves her petite mouth as she picks it up and cries. I step closer to her, but she scurries across the bed.

"It's okay. I was just gonna bring you to a mirror to show you it's not as bad as it seems," I sigh as I reach for her again. She inches forward, lets me lift her off the bed, and place her on the floor in front of the mirror. She slowly walks forward with her head down. When she looks up, I see her wide eyes in the mirror as she takes in her white fur, adorably cute little button nose, and paws. She reaches up to her face, rubbing at her chubby little cheeks and round ears. She looks down, picks up the tail, and wails again, slumping onto the rug in a little ball. "I'm sorry. If it's any consolation, you look adorable." I try to cheer her up, but she only cries harder.

This isn't going like the fairytales at all. The fairy godmother is supposed to show up and turn her into a princess. Or the brave knight is supposed to rescue her, not change her into an animal.

"Killian. What is it? What has happened? Are you okay? Your fa—King portaled out with Warrick, something about a dragon?" Mom rushes into the room, looking concerned.

"I'm fine, M—My Queen. But something happened." I resume my pacing and gesture to Jade.

"Oh, hello there, little one," she coos at Jade. "Who is this? I haven't seen an otter shifter since I visited the courts of Illa years ago. Why are they in the mortal's chambers?" She looks at me quizzically before realization falls over her. She gasps, covering her mouth with her hand. "Oh no," she breathes, taking a step forward. "Is that—" she doesn't finish. "How?"

I groan and run my hands over my head again. "Yeah. I don't know," I grumble helplessly. "And I don't think she knows how to change back." I look over at the little white ball on the rug as she wails again. "Can you help?" I look at my mom with great, big puppy eyes.

"I seem to remember a young prince in a very similar predicament. You have to calm her down; it's the only way until she learns to control the shift." She smiles softly at me before looking at Jade again. "I'm sure I don't help with that, as her heartbeat increased as soon as I walked in. Get her to lie down and tell her a story. Did the other mortal, um—change as well? Most peculiar, this feels like the strings of fate's dirty work." Mom's face twists with distaste. What neither of us says is changeling. The answer is hanging right there in the air. Someone in Jade's family was a changeling.

Footsteps pound down the hallway moments before the door crashes open again, and Catria pours in. "Oh, my god! Killian. Where's Jade? Is she okay? Did she make it off the beach? What was that? Jade! Jade!" Catria screams in the room as she searches frantically.

"Calm down, Catria, everything is fine," Mom says in that calming voice she uses when I've had a bad dream. Catria jumps and appears even more panicked as she stares at my mom.

"Your Majesty. Oh, my god. I'm so sorry." Her eyes wide, she attempts to bow, but Mom waves it away.

"Jade is fine. She is unharmed," Mom pauses. "However, she's having a bit of a hard time right now," she gestures towards Jade, who is sniffling and looking up at her friend with wide eyes.

Catria looks down at the cuddly ball of fluff on the floor and cocks her head like a bird. "Jay?" she questions. Jade nods as more tears stream down her fur. Catria slowly walks over to her and kneels down. "Don't take this the wrong way, okay? But you are adorable." Catria cracks a smile, and Jade squints her eyes at her.

"See, I told you. Isn't she just the cutest?" I smile at Catria, who is looking down at her friend in wonder. Jade slides her glare over to me. Which would probably be terrifying if it weren't the cutest thing ever. I turn around so she doesn't see me smiling.

"Catria, I'd like to have a word with you, if you don't mind. Killian will stay here with your friend and help her change back." Mom gives me a pointed look. "But I have some questions, and I'd like to run some tests to see if you also have a fae lineage. Just so we are not caught off guard again." She stands by the door.

Catria's head snaps up. "Fae lineage?"

"Yes, dear, it seems time in our realm may have woken up the fae blood within Jade. I'd like to make sure we don't have any more surprises. If you would?" She gestures to the door again.

Catria gives Jade a little pat on the head before standing. "Would that be bad?" She takes a hesitant step forward.

"Gods, no child, I would simply prefer you didn't end up crying in a corner because you suddenly have fur." Mom gives a sympathetic look to Jade, who tries to give a half-hearted smile, flashing a tiny fang. I am having a cuteness overload right now. My mom is the best. I watch her escort Catria down the hall, being all mom-like so she doesn't freak her out.

Now I have to figure out how to help Jade. Mom did make a good point in getting her to relax. That's how I figured out how to change back when I was stuck as a pup. Okay, I've got this. I can figure this out.

I quickly walk over and scoop Jade off the floor, who gives a startled yelp. Oops, maybe I should have warned her first. Too late now. As I pull her against my chest, she is trembling. Shit, not good. I need to go slower.

"It's okay, I've got you." I pet her as I walk to the bed and slowly lie down with her on my chest. She's so small. "So, we just need to get you to relax," I say as she looks up at me and blinks. I'll tell her a story, like Mom said. "Would you like to hear how the moon got cracked?" She nods her cute little head and rests it on her paws as she looks at me.

"Long ago, a great war raged in Eneara. Sorcery and dark magic clouded the lands. Darkness reigned, and curses threatened our domain. But I'm getting ahead of myself. There was a sorcerer, Gabriel, who lived in a small village. He was young and aspired to travel and make a name for himself. One day, a lovely young witch crossed his path. She had just been rescued from the mortal realm witch trials and was still adjusting to life in our realm.

"Gabriel didn't like Morgan initially, but couldn't avoid her. She was everywhere; to be fair, it was a small town. One night, she got caught in a rainstorm, and the bridge to the inn was flooded. Gabriel found her by the washed-out bridge and took her to his home. She was trapped on his land for a time while they waited for the rains to stop. Something happened during those days, and they fell madly in love. He vowed to give her the world if she wanted it. When the rain stopped and the bridge was repaired, they married.

"This is where the happily ever after should be, but this isn't a happy story. Damn, I should have told you a happy story. Anyway, over time, Gabriel became restless with the world around him and wanted change. So the happy couple left their small village searching for more people who wanted to see the change they did.

"Over a few years, they had traveled the countryside and rallied many to their cause. Thus started the Great War. Eneara was torn apart. Every kingdom was overthrown until Gabriel and his wife sat on a throne over it all. Auburnigh was under siege and struggling to hold back his forces. He had victory in his sight.

"Alas, Morgan was unhappy. As the war raged on and people were subjugated, she found herself alone. Her husband's power grew to unimaginable levels, corrupting the man that she had grown to love so long ago. This was the crack in the armor that the resistance needed. A vampire sought her out to try to get her to flip sides, but when they met, a bond tugged at their hearts. The Gods had plans, and they were fated to fall in love.

"Morgan left with her lover in the dead of night, breaking Gabriel's heart. He raged at the Gods for taking her from him, for he had done everything for her. So he cast a curse on the Gods in revenge for their slight. The whole world felt the quake that shook the realm as his power shot into the heavens, splitting the moon in two, just like his heart. In their anger, the Gods erupted. Oceans overtook islands, tides changed course, seasons stopped, and the world froze into stasis. The world may rotate, and the days may change, but the seasons stay as they were that fateful day. It is said that only a cursed love can break the curse placed on the Gods. Someone else must suffer the way Gabriel suffered. It's a really screwed-up story. Sorry, I'll tell you a pleasant story next."

I tell her the tale of the dashing beast who falls for a lovely girl, embellishing how I envision the story. I make the beast a wolf like me and tell the beautiful love story between him and the fair maiden. As I tell the story, Jade rests her head on my chest and closes her eyes. I close my eyes as she breathes steadily, and she succumbs to sleep. I listen for her heartbeat to slow with her breathing. Eventually, I feel her shift as her body changes, but she doesn't stir. I wrap my arms around her, not wanting this moment to end. I let sleep take me.

Chapter 17
Rodan

It has been over a week since Trouble left her quarters. Over a week since we found out she somehow has fae blood running in her veins. When I dove into the water to save her from the dragon fire, I thought I'd be battling to get the water from her lungs if we were under for too long. I wasn't expecting her to shift in my arms.

I need her to go home to the mortal world, where it is safe for her. How do I push her to do that when she has fae blood? Fuck, this was supposed to be easy. I couldn't even keep my damn hands off her. Every time she ran her hands over me, I almost lost control. I smother a smile, remembering her pinned against the wall as I tried to keep my damn dick in my pants. Bringing her to the brink, over and over again, before finally letting her fall apart in my hands. Using the most minor bits of my power to push her over the edge. Her curvy, soft body, putty in my hands, waiting for the touch it craved. I've thought about it all week. I lost control in that cave and barely kept enough restraint not to take her right then and there. She was so wet and tight. I can't believe she was so jaded about sex. What the fuck did the men of her world do?

Kissing her will be my utter destruction. World ending destruction. What was I thinking? I wasn't. I let my dick take over, and gods, was it glorious. Every touch electrified me; every moan my undoing. I am ridiculously fucked.

Fuck, I need to stop thinking about this. My dick is already getting excited again. I don't need to be shifting the table fight everyone is working.

Looking through the record book in my hands, I turn the page, but my mind wanders back to that day. My heart stopped when I heard that blood-curdling scream. The white ice dragon that hadn't been seen in a century. So much about the whole ordeal doesn't make any sense. Ice dragons stay in the icy mountains near Colire, so why was it on the beach? Why was it awake? Why did it attack?

Slamming the book shut, I throw it in the pile with the rest. I rub my eyes, deep in thought.

"Dragons don't attack unprovoked after a hundred years. By all accounts, the white dragon was hibernating and would be for another hundred."

Ellis looks up from his tome on the desk with a questioning look on his face.

"Nothing in any of the histories has any record of an ice dragon leaving its den to attack," I go on.

"Well, it happened, so maybe the histories are wrong. That dragon was clearly on the warpath. I barely escaped being burned alive." Ellis looks haunted. His air magic was useless to him out there that day. He can barely put out a candle. However, he is intelligent and has at least figured out how to levitate books to and from shelves, so his power isn't wholly wasted. Ellis had helped Catria escape the beach that day and a few others. "Perhaps it flew here from Eneara, an act of war? Do you think they would break the accords?"

"Fuck, I hope not." I grimace. Aubrunigh and Eneara had a terrible war a hundred years ago, with many deaths on both sides. The sorcerers were making a play for power, and the elven fae were protecting their lands. Many races of fae took sides. The dragons and dragon shifters sided with the sorcerers, making the fight seem impossible. Dark magic was used to devastating effect, and thousands were lost in a single battle. According to the histories, a vampire and a witch seized control of the throne in Eneara during the chaos and struck an accord with the courts of Auburnigh. In that accord, no one would cross the sea. Sorcery was outlawed on both sides, and the sorcerers involved were imprisoned in Eneara. I shudder to think what would happen if the accord were broken. Negotiations on trade and open borders have only recently begun.

"There was something wrong with that dragon's eyes. Did you notice that?" Scarlette puts down her book. "I've seen pictures of the ice dragons that lived near Colire. Their eyes are pale blue. That dragon's eyes were black." Her delicate voice is laced with fear and exhaustion. A few of us have been here every day trying to find answers.

"Strange indeed," Corsac replies. "This is not normal behavior. Its mind was dark and twisted. Nothing but swirls of black." She shudders. I always forget that the ghost fox shifter sees creature's thoughts as colors. She reaches over and laces her fingers through Scarlette's.

"Are you saying it was bewitched?" I had not thought of this before. It could give me a direction to look into that I haven't yet.

"Perhaps," Corsac replies as she stands. "Scarlette is tired. I believe it is time for us to retire for the evening." She leads Scarlette out of the library, wrapping her arm around her shoulders. Many of the men were angry when they realized those two were courting, but with all the panic over the dragon, no one appears to care anymore. The queen is beside herself with joy for them. They went to her asking if they should leave, but the queen insisted they stay for all the festivities. If nothing else, we might see one successful match here.

"I believe I'll retire for the night as well." Ellis stands and stretches his back. "I don't know if we are going to find anything if we haven't already. I'll check in with Sorrel in the morning and see if he's found anything of note."

"I'll be down here a while longer if you think of anything. I need to check in with Warrick to see if the king has any ideas."

Ellis floats a stack of books from the table and walks down the hall, probably going to be reading long into the night. Sighing, I pick up another volume, flipping pages, and looking for any mention of bewitched dragons or creatures.

Killian and his father have been talking with the other courts to see if they know anything. They've also been reassuring the females' families that everyone is safe here. The attack could have caused a massive political incident if one of the females had died. Most of the weaker fae fled the beach; three females were injured. From what I've heard, Mika and Rosard were killed in the initial attack. I didn't know them well, but it left many people shaken. The king and queen have been seeing to their families. Their loss to the council will be felt.

Ryker has spent most of his time with Catria, not leaving her side since the attack. Queen Aleena had Ellis and Lorelai confirm that both mortals were of fae blood. Tracing the magic back to the same changeling, a displaced ice prince from the Great War of the continents. Apparently, they lost track of him after the war. So, with this new knowledge, it is still being determined whether Queen Aleena will permit them to return to the mortal world. Much to my displeasure, I've been trying to convince her they are safer there. *Once their magic emerges, it would be a shame to let it wither away in the mortal world again*, she had chastised me. Killian had, of course, agreed with his mom. He is hell-bent on keeping the mortals around.

Closing the book and giving up on concentrating, I stand to go for a walk. I need to get the damn mortal out of my head. I gave in to the temptation once, but that's it, no more.

As I walk out of the library's lower level, I hear footsteps coming down the hall at a strange cadence. I back into the doorway as they come near. Trouble walks with a slight stumble in her step around a corner. I haven't seen her since that day and am surprised to see her out of her room in the middle of the night. She's wearing a long shirt and pretty much nothing else, like she came straight from bed. Where is she going at this hour?

I follow her around the corner, staying back so she doesn't see me, as she reaches the doors that lead out to the night garden.

She stumbles through the doors, leaving them open behind her. Against the bioluminescent lights, she looks like a ghost as she sways along the path towards the pond. It's then that I notice she has two bottles of wine in her hands that she drinks from. I follow as she gazes around at the glowing trees above her in wonder; the glow illuminating the tear streaks down her face. She slumps to the ground, letting a bottle roll away from her as she looks up, placing the other firmly on the ground next to her.

"What are you doing out here, Trouble?" I say as I walk up to where she sits on the glowing grass.

She startles before leveling me in her gaze. "I needed air," she drawls. "What are you doing here?" She stares back up at the trees, disinterested.

"I saw you walking around in the middle of the night, drunk by the looks of it."

She rolls her eyes and lays down, curling up on her side as she plays with the grass.

I look down at her. "Why don't you go to bed?"

"Because things are just as bad in dreams as they are in the real world. I'd rather be somewhere nice," she whispers.

"It's unsafe to be out in the middle of the night."

"Why? Is the big bad wolf gonna eat me?" Amusement laces her tone as the corner of her mouth tilts up.

I sigh and sit down next to her, staring out at the glowing water as it ripples in the breeze.

"My mom always used to joke that I was a mermaid. She could

never get me out of the pool as a kid." She breaks the silence. "I always thought it would be so cool to change into something else, be a dangerous creature that could drag men down to their deaths," she muses as I think of the implications of what she's saying in horror. She's dragging me down into the depths, and I'm barely hanging on. "But of course, I turn into a fucking otter, another cute, small, pathetic thing," she spits out.

"Otters aren't bad things, and they can be dangerous." Trying to find some light in the situation.

She huffs, "Fat load of good it will do me against men twice my size." Pausing, she takes a breath. "I'm so embarrassed. I just froze on that beach–I can't face anyone after that," she sighs.

Running my hand through my hair in frustration, I watch her. "Everyone was afraid. Most people ran."

"Killian didn't." She rolls onto her back and throws her arm over her eyes, her shirt riding up, showing her lace underwear. "Oh god, Killian is a wolf," she groans. "I can't date a wolf—people turn into animals." She's starting to slur her words.

"Fae," I correct. "Fae turn into animals. But not all fae." I reach over and pull her shirt down before my dick gets any ideas.

"I don't know what to do," she moans.

"Start by sobering up and coming out of your room during the day. Then you can wait until the end of all this and go home."

"Home is worse," she whispers.

"You need to go home. You don't belong here. You are not safe here." I growl at her louder than I mean to.

She looks up at me as fresh tears fill her eyes. "Please don't yell at me. He always yelled at me," she all but whispers.

"Who yells at you?" Anger builds within me at the thought of who could strike such fear into her heart, and remorse at the fact that I caused these tears.

"My ex-husband, nothing I ever do is enough." She sniffs. "It will never be enough for anyone."

"What a miserable excuse for a man," I growl. She curls back in on herself, hair falling over her face as she rolls over. I realize I've scared her again. Fuck, I don't know what to do. I lean over and gently stroke her arm. "I'm sorry. It wasn't my intention to make you cry." Damn it all, this is tearing me up inside. How can I possibly keep my distance if I can't stay away from her?

"I'll go home. When this is all over, I'll leave. You won't ever have to see me again." Tears slide down her cheeks as she looks at me through her hair. I slowly brush the hair from her eyes, tucking it behind her ear. A twinge of pain tugs at me. I wanted this, so why does it hurt to hear her say those words?

"Will you have to see him when you go back?" I ask quietly as I run my hand down her arm.

"I don't know...he just kind of pops up. He still thinks I belong to him. I think he'll find me again. Just like last time." Fresh, hot tears turn into sobs. "I don't think I'll ever be completely free of him."

My body tenses at the fear I feel coming from her. Genuine fear, the same fear I smelled on her during the dragon attack. How could she have been married to someone who made her that afraid?

I stay there next to her as I try to calm down, drinking from the wine bottle she propped on the ground. I let the alcohol cloud my thoughts and dull the ache in my chest as I look out at the garden. Hours go by in silence. The night grows around us, darkness descending as dawn nears.

I scoop her up to walk her back to her room. Her calm rhythmic breathing melts away my tension as her head rests on my chest.

"I'm sure what happened in the cave was a fluke. I know you hate me, but that's okay," she mumbles, and I don't know if she's conscious of what she's saying.

That's the problem, Trouble, I don't hate you.

Chapter 18
Jade

I wake alone in my room. For the first time in a long time, I didn't wake in the middle of the night to nightmares. It's also the first time I haven't seen the panther. It's usually there at night when I wake up, but gone by morning. Since it hasn't eaten me yet, I figure it's safe. For the last week, I've been a mess of emotions. The dragon attack was a shitshow. I was not only shocked by the dragon but by the display of power from those around me. It's one thing to know that everyone has power. It's another thing to see it in action. The whole ordeal left me with a migraine. Lorelai offcred to fix it for me, but I turned her away. I lay there in pain for three full days, but the pain distracted me from the horrors I saw.

Killian stopped by every day with a cart of food, trays of delicious cuisine that fell to ash on my tongue. For the last few days, he brought me books and chocolates to get me out of my funk. But every time I looked at him, I saw that golden wolf spitting fire. He cared for me that night and stayed with me until the next morning. When it was clear he wanted to talk about it, I asked him to leave me alone for a while. Aside from bringing me things, he hasn't breached the subject again.

Cat has been in and out, but she knows how I am when things get bad. She understands I need space for a while. She had her own demons to deal with after everything. Thankfully, Ryker has helped her through the worst of it.

It's been so overwhelming, honestly, too much for me to handle, and I needed things to just be calm for a few days.

I walk into the bathroom and run the water, enjoying the steam filling the room. Everything may be crazy out there, but things are peaceful here. Something I didn't even have in my old life. Peace. I huff out a small laugh at the fact that I feel peace in this room as I sink into the hot water.

Last night, I couldn't take it anymore. I got drunk and found myself in the night garden. Rodan's sudden appearance was jarring; his insistence that I go home, his reminders of how much danger lurks here, made me feel small. Even still, he comforted me and stayed by my side. He might be a jerk most of the time, and I know he only has a physical attraction to me, but I don't think he's a monster. Even there with him, I felt more peace than I had in years. I felt my old self coming back. I contemplated what life here would be like if I stayed, and for the first time, that idea didn't scare me.

A knock breaks the silence of the bath. "I'm coming in whether you like it or not." Cat's voice echoes through the room. Heavy footfalls sound before the bathroom door is shoved open, and a very smug-looking Cat stands there. "Good, you're clean. We need to talk," she huffs as she sits on the chair beside the tub.

"Well, hello to you too," I say as I sink below the water to rinse my hair, then come back up. "Yeah, yeah, I know, it's been a week. Blah, blah."

Cat cracks a grin. "Seriously, though, I've had time to think about all this being fae stuff. Honestly, this is the coolest thing ever. It's exactly like my favorite books."

"In the books, the heroine knows how to fight. They aren't just some normal girl dropped into a fantasy world who can't throw a punch without hurting themselves. We are not children of mafia lords or assassins. You are a librarian, and I work in an office."

"But now we are badass shifters." Her eyes shine brightly with elation.

"Who don't even know how to shift."

"But we can learn. Come on, it's an adventure. We can at least see what it's like, and if it's not for us, we go home as planned. Don't just give up, please."

I get out of the tub and dry off. "I'm not giving up. I'm trying to be realistic."

Cat walks over to the bed and flops down on the end of it, spinning so her head hangs off, hair dangling to the floor. "But I want to try. Maybe we can help. You've always been good at research. You used to love trying to figure stuff out from history books before Ace made you get a better-paying job. Maybe a different perspective will help them break the curse or figure out what happened with the dragon."

I give her a sardonic look. "You're joking. I highly doubt we'd bring anything new to the table."

"But it will give you something else to think about. Come on, we'll go help the others, and then later, Killian and Ryker said they'd help with the shifting. Come on, it will be fun. Please." She gives me puppy-dog eyes, and I laugh.

"Fine, I need to get out of this room, anyway. I'm tired of just sitting here wallowing in self-pity."

"Great, and while you get dressed, you can finally tell me what happened with Rodan when you disappeared from the beach."

"Nothing happened."

"Oh, come on. Nothing? Really? I saw the heated looks he was giving you before you two disappeared. Please tell me you at least kissed him," she groans.

"He doesn't like me. He's a jerk ninety percent of the time."

"And the other ten?" She raises an eyebrow. My face heats as I think about his hands on me, in me—the cave. I turn to hide it, but not fast enough. "Oh my god, you did fuck him." She bounces upright on the bed. "I *know* that guilty face. Tell me."

Now, you can report your findings to Catria. His words dance through my mind.

"I didn't fuck him. He—pinned me to a wall and—used his hands." My face is on fire, "and his power on me. We got carried away. The cave was all romantic, and he was being nice. I don't know how it happened." I get out in a rush.

"Because you wanted it to?"

"Yes." Fucking hell, I'd wanted it. "But nothing has changed. We got it out of our systems, and he's back to hating me."

"I don't think that's true. But I know for sure Killian likes you," she shrugs.

"He's a wolf, isn't that kinda weird?"

"Rykers, a falcon, and I—" she shuts her mouth abruptly.

"Cat! You screwed Ryker?" Spinning around, gaping at her as her face turns red. "When?"

"A couple of days ago," she swoons and falls back on the bed. "When the test results came in, I was all freaked out, and he was there comforting me. I don't know, I just kissed him and didn't stop. Holy hell, it was hot." She leans forward, cupping her mouth in a conspiratorial whisper. "I don't think I've ever come so hard in my life."

I burst out laughing as my skin flushes.

"Yeah. Seriously, what the fuck?" I muse as we both devolve into laughter.

Apparently, a small group has been spending their days in the library trying to figure out this dragon situation and if it's related to the curse. Cat drags me over to the large table filled with stacks of books. Piles of history books and records surround Ellis. Scarlette is going through a history of Colire with Corsac, pointing out maps and features of her kingdom. Corsac is mostly staring adoringly at Scarlette. It's cute to watch the two of them together.

Rodan is bent over a book at one end of the table, tapping his finger as he skims records, not paying Cat and me any mind. I fidget as I cast a glance at him, wanting to talk to him, but this is not the place. I can't get a clear read on him, and it's driving me crazy. Sorrel sits next to him, his head leaning back against the chair, eyes closed in thought or sleep, I don't know.

Cat sits in a chair next to Ryker, leaning over to look at the book he's looking at before cracking open a history of the war between the two continents.

Not knowing how to help, I wander the aisles, trying to see what might have something helpful. There has to be something that they aren't thinking of. Plus, no one knows if the dragon is related to the curse or a random occurrence. From what I've gathered, everyone seems pretty convinced it's a separate problem but a sign of possible danger to come. It's an unsettling situation. One I never thought I'd be researching.

As I browse the books, I notice a subsection marked Fae/Mortal history in the history tomes. There are books on the World Wars, general European, South American, United States, African, and Asian history. To my surprise, next to those are Dracula, Interview with the Vampire, fairy tale books, and many others. Why aren't these in the Mortal Fiction section?

"Find anything interesting?" Killian says from behind me, his voice making me jump. He's rubbing the back of his neck, looking a bit sheepish. I feel bad that I've pushed everyone away. He has been nothing but nice to me since I got here.

I point at the books I've been looking at. "What is this section on fae and mortal histories? Why is Dracula here?"

"Oh, that? That's where our kind have bled into your world." He gives a small smile and scuffs the toe of his shoe on the ground.

"So, Dracula was real?" Taking the book off the shelf, I notice that Bram Stoker has been crossed out and Barnalbe Shooker has been written in. "Why does it say Barnalbe?"

He coughs a laugh. "Because that's his name." He shrugs. I cock an eyebrow in question, looking at the book again. "So, it's not exactly accurate. Barnalbe ran to your world to publish his book and villainize vampires. His wife ran away with one, and he decided to out vampires in the mortal world to get revenge. It didn't really work out the way he planned."

"So, Dracula was revenge fan-fiction?" I burst out laughing at the thought.

"Pretty much."

"What about the rest of these? Fairy tales, Vlad the Impaler, Madame Bathory—there's a lot here. Some look like actual history books, while others are mortal fiction." I say, looking down the row of books on the shelf.

"Oh yeah, most of that is either based on true stories or fae from our world causing problems in your world. Where do you think all of that comes from?" He leans over and nudges my shoulder with his, which makes me smile.

"It's fiction. I figured people just made it up."

"Some of it is that way, but much of it comes from our realm. So, we keep these mortal books as part of our history, which also helps when researching the mortal realm to see what they believe. It's easy to walk around as a vampire unnoticed if you know what signs mortals are looking for."

"So, Vlad?" I ask, pointing at the book.

"Vampire."

"Bathory?"

"Vampire." He smirks.

"Twilight?" I don't see the book on the shelf, but it's worth a shot.

"What's that?"

"Vampires that sparkle in the sun." I mimic sparkling by

wiggling my fingers, then shrug.

"I mean, if you call smoldering sparkling." He grins. I laugh. Good to know.

"Interview with the Vampire?"

"Controversial." His face drops into a scowl. I may need to ask more about that later.

"The Little Mermaid."

"Was a disaster." He scrubs his hand down his face for emphasis. I'm enjoying this little game, though.

"Beauty and the Beast?"

"Depends on which version, but she was really into bestiality." He doubles over with laughter.

I gasp. "You're messing with me."

"I really wish I was." He inhales deep, letting it out slowly, trying to catch his breath. "Like I said, if the book is in this section, it holds at least some truth." He leans on the bookcase and looks at me. "I really enjoy telling you about my world." He reaches over, tucking a stray hair behind my ear. "Can we have dinner again tonight?" There is such sincerity in the question, my heart melts a little.

"That would be nice. I'd like that." I give him a shy smile, avoiding his eyes as the butterflies fill my chest. To keep the fluttering at bay, I flip through the books on the shelf. At least I feel more myself again and less like an overwhelmed mess.

Sometimes, a girl has to wallow in a little self-pity before facing the world with her big-girl pants on. Wrapping my head around this new reality is going to take me some time. I highly doubt last week will be the last time I hide away from the world and let the anxiety control me, but now I'm better prepared for the unexpected. I'm in another realm. Dragons exist. I am part fae and can shapeshift. Four things I've faced and have come out the other side of. Now, I need to figure out how to get back into this courting thing and maybe help my friends.

I skim the spines of the books. I don't know where to start. Dragon Lore, Curses of the Mortal Realm—how will any of this help? I bend down to read the spines and notice a gap behind the books. Pulling out a couple, a small book pokes out, tucked behind the others, likely pushed back by a careless person returning a book to the shelf.

I pull out the small book, only the size of my hands. The Story of the Fates is written on the leather cover. It's tattered, and pages hang out, yellowed with age. Carefully, I open the cover and browse.

Fate is a funny, fickle thing. The first line reads.

"What's that?" Killian leans over my shoulder, pressing into my back. He wraps an arm around my waist as I show him the cover, causing the butterflies to dance in my chest again. "The Fates—they are an interesting story."

"They exist?" I ask, leaning back into his warmth, his presence a comfort that washes over me.

He gently takes the book from my hands, removing his arm from my waist, and I feel its absence. His breath tickles my ear as he leans his head down and opens the book in front of me to a drawing of three witches.

"A long time ago, there were three witches. They were very powerful. Some say the most powerful in all of Auburnigh," he says in a low tone, sending shivers down my spine. "The crone, leader of the coven, full of the wisdom of centuries." He points to the depiction of the haggard old lady. "The mother, full of the power of her coven." He moves his finger to a young woman who radiates beauty. "And the maiden, full of the potential future." His finger lands on a girl who looks about sixteen.

"Like most stories, the power they held was not enough, and they sought more. No one knows how they did it, but legend has it they sought out a god. The god saw the maiden's potential, the crone's wisdom, and the mother's power. The god was neither good nor evil, but it's said that what he did was trick them. A sacrifice was needed to give them the power they desired. They agreed to the terms, with the only caveat being they didn't want to deal in dark magic." He turns the page to another drawing depicting a blast of magic hitting the witches.

"The god agreed. However, the witches became bound to the land, immortal, but imprisoned in the forest where they'd found the god." He turns the page, and I take in a sharp breath as I see the depiction of the witches. "The god turned them into trees. The power he bestowed upon them was in equal measure to the sacrifice they made." He turns the page to a depiction of the three trees with golden strings laced between them and glowing orbs floating in the branches.

"They became the Fates. The mother spun the threads of fate with her power. The crone measured the lives with her wisdom. And the maiden cut the threads, ending the potential."

"The maiden is death," I breathe.

"Yes. She is the embodiment of death. Many tales of the Fates have existed, but this is the origin of all of them. Strange that this book was hidden away." He closes the book and hands it back to me before he wraps his arms around me, resting his chin on my shoulder.

"So, can they tell the future?"

"Past, present, and future, if the legend is to be believed."

"Why not ask them about the curse?"

"Because they are crazy," Ellis cuts in from behind us.

Killian drops his arms as we both turn to look at him. I look at Killian, who shrugs.

Sorrel walks over to Ellis, handing him a book before he turns and looks at me. Sorrel's gaze travels to the book in my hand. He sneers at it. "That book is a bunch of garbage. The Fates weren't created. They were the result of a spell gone wrong. Crazy old bats. Everything they say is nonsense. Not worth your time," he says scornfully.

I shift uncomfortably under the scrutiny. Killian slides his arm across my shoulders. "Let her look at whatever books she wants. Plus, maybe she's got a point." He leans into me and winks when I look at him.

"Waste of time," Ellis scoffs and walks off without another word.

"Careful, the mortal's stupidity doesn't rub off on you, Killian." Sorrel's dark tone, laced with sarcasm, bites at me. I scowl at him and lift my chin in defiance as he saunters away. Asshole.

"Damn Trouble, making a name for yourself already, huh?" Rodan walks around the corner. Why does he always seem to be lurking? My heartbeat goes up a tick. I hate that I react this way to his proximity.

I glower at him. "Why don't you mind your own business," I say, leaning further into Killian.

"Didn't say it was my business, just an observation," he says as he walks over to a bookshelf and returns a book. "You really think you've got ideas we haven't tried," he drawls, not turning around, pulling another book out.

"Have you tried talking to the Fates?"

He turns with his eyebrow cocked. "No, every record says they only provide unintelligible riddles. I'm not interested in their games. But by all means, I'd love to watch you fail." His gaze darkens. I level him with a glare, but the look on his face makes my stomach flip. Why does he have to look so sensual when he's being an insufferable prick?

"Oh, I so want to meet the legendary Fates." Killian's excitement is tangible. "I have so many questions I've always wanted to ask them. It would be like the books, seeing a seer and finding out what our future holds." His eyes light up as he smiles and moves in front of me. "We should do it." He grabs my hands, grinning from ear to ear.

I look over at Rodan, who is rolling his eyes. "Yes, we should." I smile at Killian and watch Rodan's face turn to a sneer. Satisfaction rolls through me. "But if Rodan's too scared, he probably shouldn't come." I smirk.

"Like hell, I'm not letting Killian go on his own," he growls.

"Fantastic!" Killian bounces on his toes. "I'll find Warrick and see if he can get us there. Maybe tomorrow since I've got dinner with you tonight," he muses as he gives me a giant bear hug. "I'll see you tonight." He smiles and walks away.

I look over at Rodan, who is seething. "Checkmate, asshole."

"Maybe Sorrel was right. Your stupidity is already rubbing off on Killian since you got your claws in him so deep," he sneers.

"Maybe you should stop eavesdropping on everyone's conversations," I snip back, enjoying the feeling of getting one over on him. "Just go back to your dark cave and stay there if you're unwilling to help." I give him a contemptuous smile.

He stalks towards me, leaning in close, his breath brushing across my lips. "I'm sure you'd love to visit that cave again," he purrs. Pulling back as abruptly, he turns and walks around the corner. My heart skips a beat at his suggestive tone. Images of his hands all over me play through my mind. My clothes become stifling in the warm room, as precisely how much I enjoyed that cave sparks through me. Damn him.

I walk back to the table the others are sitting at, book in hand. Rodan has some nerve. Whenever I think maybe he's a nice guy deep down, he turns around and acts like an ass. Then he does a one-eighty on me and flips the script again, making me question everything. It's been over a week, and no matter how much he pisses me off, I get hot just thinking about what his power can do to me. What is wrong with me? It's not only his power. I can't stop thinking about him. It's infuriating; I need to stop. You know what? Who cares if the Fates are a dead end? At least it's an idea. I seethe as I sit down.

Cat is immersed in a book, her brow wrinkled in concentration as Ryker sits beside her, stealing glances when he doesn't think she is looking. That man has got it bad, and I don't think Cat knows what to do with him. Her strict no-relationship rules are being torn apart here. While my stance of wanting to have fun and not start anything serious for once is also being challenged. Things are so messy, and I don't know what to do. While the idea of staying here is terrifying, the idea of going home is even worse. Home is where Ace can find me. Where Ace can torment me day and night, I don't believe for one second that I'd ever be free of him completely if I went home. Maybe I should give someone like Killian a chance to see where it might go.

I open the little book on the Fates, noting that the story it tells is very close to what Killian had told me, and I smile that he knew it so well. Maybe he read this book a lot before it got misplaced. Ellis is still deep in a book, his bangs falling over his eyes as he reads. His light brown hair and shaggy haircut make him look younger than twenty-seven. I mostly see him here in the library unless there is a mandatory event. This must be in line with whatever job he did before all of this. Sorrel is next to him, sipping a glass of wine and flipping through pages laid out before him. He wears a scowl, probably permanently etched there since I've never seen him smile. I peer back at the book, taking in the old script and illustrations.

"I don't know why we are even still bothering with breaking the curse. Women flocked here to mate with us," Sorrel drawls as he leans his head back in his chair. "Plus, we can always steal mortals since they are more fertile for breeding, anyway." He closes his eyes.

Cat and I don't move our heads from over our books, but make eye contact over the table. I lift an eyebrow in question but keep my mouth shut. Ryker's posture stiffens in his seat.

Sorrel sighs, flipping his long white hair over his shoulder. "It's just so much easier to take a mortal as a breeder than try to break a curse that prevents females from being born. What's the big deal?

We still have heirs either way."

"The big deal is mortals are not your broodmares," Ryker says in a low tone.

Sorrel shrugs. "Maybe they should be. It would solve the problem. Plus, they would probably like it." He looks at me and smiles. "Wouldn't you, Jade?"

"Fuck off, Sorrel." I flip him the finger for good measure, hoping its meaning is the same here. Cat cracks a grin as she sees his smile fall from his face, and irritation replaces it.

I hear a faint crackling sound and look around for the source. The fireplace is nearby, but I haven't heard it make a sound. I look under the table, making sure the little dragon cat isn't lurking, but all that is there are people's feet. I must be losing it. The sound gets louder, and Cat looks up from her book, searching for the source as well. A loud pop rings out, and everyone looks up as the little book in front of me goes up in smoke. Smoke billows around me as I jump back and knock over the chair I was sitting in, nearly toppling over with it. I cough as I wave at the smoke, trying to see what the hell happened. Ashes rain down on the table as everyone stands and looks at the pile of ash on the table where my book once sat.

"What did you do?" Ellis shouts, his eyes wide, and a horrified look on his face.

"N–Nothing. I just opened it," I stammer out.

"Sure, and it burst into ashes all on its own?" Sorrel says with a sarcastic lilt to his tone.

"How the hell would I have done that?" I bark back.

Sorrel curls his lip. "Stupid mortal." He sneers. I glare at him. "See, all they are good for is breeding; can't even hold a book without destroying it." He laughs as he walks out of the room.

What the hell? How could anyone think I did that? I poke at the pile of ash only to see that nothing remains of the little book. Ellis gives me an angry look before picking up his books and storming out after his friend. Well, shit, this was not how I envisioned helping would go. I've spent my entire life reading books and never had any spontaneously combust on me.

"I'm gonna take this as a sign that I'm done for today," I grumble. "I'll just go get ready for my date with Killian."

"Okay, I'll see you later?" Cat looks mournfully at the book and then at me. I nod and wave to Ryker. "Hey, wear the little black dress," Cat shouts as I leave the room, and I smile, shaking my head.

Chapter 19
Jade

I sit in the long black satin dress that Cat had pulled to the front of my closet, looking at the slit that runs so high that my entire thigh is exposed. Well, not much left to the imagination here. I glance at the stack of books Killian had left on the table for me, but I'm not very interested in reading after what happened earlier. I'm actually kind of excited to see Killian again.

What would life be like with him here? What would life in general be like here? I haven't shifted since the dragon attack, but I'm curious about it. I'm also curious about Killian's wolf. It was scary seeing him like that, but after he took care of me that night, I felt like there could be something there. He was so kind and gentle with me. I get warm and fuzzy thinking about it.

I'd woken up curled up in his arms, still in my swimsuit. He was shirtless, and I may have taken a good look at his muscled chest as he breathed. He looked so peaceful, his hair all messed from sleep. But then everything came back to me, and I started to shake again, waking him up, destroying the little bubble we'd had for that moment.

Shaking my head of the memory, I stand. Time to put on some confidence and go find Killian for our date. Part of me never wants to get married again, but another part of me is drawn to the possibilities Killian presents. While he is more like a friend right now, it may be the right place to start. Unlike with Rodan, we started off on the wrong foot, and now I can't get him out of my head. That deep, brooding stare. The dark rumble of his laugh. That damn smirk that makes me want to punch him or pounce him. Dear god, I need help. I'm fucking hopeless. Am I seriously falling for two guys? Maybe this is future me's problem.

I walk down the hall, steps echoing as my heels hit the floor, following the hand-drawn map Killian left under my door. It's a charming sentiment; the map is crude, but I think I understand where he's taking me.

Turning right, a hand snakes out of a dark alcove, and I'm pulled right into someone's body as I let out a yelp. I struggle and push on the person, but their grip is tight as they wrap their arms around me in the shadows. My breath catches, and my heart thunders as I resist.

"Hello, Princess," Bravos purrs. My heart races as I realize who it is and stop my thrashing. This is not good. How the hell do I shake this guy?

"Still not a princess," I state, annoyed. I lean back, trying to get distance.

"You look good enough to eat tonight." He leans down and licks my earlobe, causing my heart to beat faster. "I hope this dress is for my benefit," he whispers. Dread washes through me as his hand runs down my thigh to the slit. Sliding his hand under the fabric, he growls as he gropes my bare ass.

"I'm sorry, I need to go. I'm late for dinner." I try to keep my tone even, but it comes out barely a whisper as terror consumes me. Even when I attempt to push away, his hold on me is so tight, it's almost bruising.

"But I missed you, Princess," he whispers as his mouth moves down my neck. Every muscle in my body tenses as the panic sets in. "I get why you couldn't deal with everyone, but you should have let my handsome face cheer you up," he says between kisses down to my collarbone.

"I was just thinking about our future together," he says in a low tone.

Kiss.

"Living in this castle. You round with child."

Kiss.

"While five of our strapping young boys run around." He punctuates his point by licking my neck and pulling me closer, squeezing my ass.

"I don't think we are right for each other," I whimper in fear, unable to escape his grip as I feel him growing hard against me. My body trembles as my pulse quickens. No, none of this can happen. Nausea threatens as he speaks.

"Nonsense. Our heirs will be powerful fae. And you will be so beautiful bringing them into this world." He moves to the other side of my neck, continuing his fantasy. "I just knew when Queen Aleena, Mom, announced this experiment, I'd find the perfect breeding partner." He runs his hand down my arm, sending a wave of queasiness through me. Breeding? Is he saying this whole thing is about breeding? No, I can't. It's not even an option, especially with somconc like him.

He puts his forehead on mine. His stare is intense and possessive. My heart shrivels as my rib cage tries to collapse on itself. A cold sweat breaks across my brow as I take this in. This is a disaster. I need to get away from Bravos. I need to talk to Killian. Because if that's what this whole thing is about, I'm in big trouble. The queen mentioned heirs, but I figured, like most couples, it's up to them. Bravos and Sorrel are making it sound like this is a breeding program. Is that what this was all along? Sorrel was talking about kidnapping mortals to breed with. How did I miss this? All of their talk of love matches, mates, and courtship, I thought these guys were trying to find love.

Bravos leans in to kiss me, but I turn my head and attempt to duck as I resume struggling to get out of his hold. "Please, I need to go," I stammer out, so distracted by what he said I almost forgot the more pressing matter: I need to get out of here.

"I need you. Right now," his tone gruff. He pulls me back in with his arm around my waist and moves his hand from under my dress. His fingers drag along the side of my leg before they move towards the front.

"No, I don't want to be with you," I squeak as I shift my hips away from him.

He lets out a low growl, sending adrenaline through my system. I shift violently again and lose my balance on my heels, causing me to stomp on his foot. His grip loosens enough for me to catch myself on a wall and stumble back a few steps. I run before it has even entirely occurred to me—I've escaped. Scrambling down the winding hallway, I try to remember the directions on the map: down a stairway and fourth door on the left.

My lungs are burning, and my feet hurt from the heels, but I count, opening the fourth door, running inside, and slamming it shut as fast as possible. I collapse onto the floor, trying to catch my breath.

"Hey—shit, are you okay?" Killian rushes over beside me, putting his hand on my back. I flinch at the contact and look at him with tears filling my eyes. He immediately removes his hand, kneeling down beside me. "What happened?" His soft tone washes through me.

I reach out and pull him into a hug. His arms wrap around me, petting my hair. His scent fills my lungs as I try to catch my breath. He smells fresh and earthy, like a forest. I hold him, not saying anything until I've calmed down and can breathe again.

"Can we not talk about it? And just have dinner, please." I try to smile at him as I break the contact between us.

His brows furrow, but he nods, letting out a low whine as he stands. He offers his hand to help me to my feet, takes a long look at me, reaches up and wipes the tears from under my eyes. "You look lovely tonight." A small smile plays on his lips.

"Thank you," I rasp as I take in the room around me. The most striking feature is the purple stained-glass windows that cast everything in hues of violet. The dark blue walls and purple sofa give the impression of dark royalty, but the warm glow of the fireplace and sconces makes the room cozy. It is one of the many parlors in the castle, and its colors make it look dramatic. I spin around, looking at the gorgeous room.

A table for two is set up near the fireplace, adorned with glasses of wine and two plates of food. I walk closer. The plates have some sort of roasted bird and vegetables. As the smell hits me, my stomach growls.

"It smells divine." I smile at Killian, who has moved over to one seat and pulled it out for me. "Thank you." I sit and pull myself in as he moves to sit in front of me. His long, wavy hair is down, and he has a fancy-looking tunic on. He looks quite handsome in the firelight. "I'm sorry I was late," I say, dropping my eyes to the table.

"I'm here if you want to tell me what happened, but I understand if you don't want to talk about it." He smiles, reaching across the table and squeezing my hand.

I'd like to tell him everything, but I can't. Choosing instead not to think about it, I want to file it away like everything else and never think about it again. I won't let this ruin our evening. "I liked the story you told me this afternoon," I finally say.

"You did? I never really tell anyone stories, and that one was one of my favorites as a kid. I felt like they were involved in so many of the fairy tales I loved. Everyone always told me that because those stories weren't real, I couldn't have a love story like them. I think that it's possible." His smile grows as he talks. "Please eat. Before your stomach tries to eat you." He laughs as my stomach growls again. Damn, when was the last time I ate a full meal?

We eat our food, continuing to talk about his favorite stories, most of them romance stories involving a beast of some sort. I tell him about my favorite stories from books and movies and the love stories I used to swoon over. We move over to the small sofa to have tea. He sits so close I can feel the heat of his body through my thin dress. With his warmth washing over me, a flood of calm settles in. It's so easy with him, comfortable.

Killian pulls a book from the sofa cushions. "Can I read you my favorite story?"

"I'd like that," I beam, as he pulls me closer. I settle in with my back to his chest, head leaning on his shoulder.

He brings the book in front of us as he begins to read *Beauty and the Beast*, the mortal version. "Once upon a time..." he reads every voice a different way, and I find myself laughing at some of the accents he attempts. The further he gets into the story, the more I melt into him, enjoying this simple, mundane act of being read to. Like he knew how to calm my nerves and put a smile on my face. Erase the day from my bones. He reads so fluidly, I think he's almost memorized the entire story.

As he finishes the last line and closes the book, he wraps his arms around me, and we watch the fire in the fireplace dance for a while.

"Did you grow up in the castle?" I finally break the silence.

"Yep, although I can't say much else because—you know, the forgetting potion thing," he sighs.

"What are your plans after all this? Like your goals?" I sit up to drink my tea again and straighten my dress.

He leans back, thinking, "I want to make the kingdom better. No, like the best. The kind of kingdom everyone wants to go to. Everyone happy and taken care of. I have so many ideas to help people. But the curse is kind of getting in the way, ya know. It's like this black cloud looming over Amara and counting down our days. It's weakening everything very slowly. We won't be able to defend our borders eventually."

"That's so sad." I can see the conflict play across his features. I didn't realize what the implications of a curse like this would do long term.

"Can I ask you a serious question?" I say as I put down my cup, nerves building up as I work up the courage.

"Anything." He gives me a serious look.

"A couple of the guys have referred to all this as something like a–" I take a deep breath. "Breeding program," I exhale the words out.

Killian nearly spits out his tea. He quickly wipes his chin while putting his cup down. He looks at me wide-eyed. "What? No. I mean, yes, we'd like people to have heirs, but it's not required." He leans forward and puts his head in his hands. "Gods, that sounds bad. It's not a fucking breeding program. We didn't have females available. The guys had no mate prospects unless they left the kingdom. Families would be a nice end result, but–" He takes a deep breath, shaking his head. "Gods, I'm so sorry that you got that impression. Things have been hard enough to adjust to without being told you are just here to make babies. I just want to find my mate." He finally says before looking up into my eyes.

I let out a breath, and relief floods me.

"Killian, I just got free from an awful marriage. I don't even know if I ever want to be married again," I say softly, watching his face fall. "But a part of me doesn't want to give up yet."

He leans over and cups my cheek in his palm. "Then don't," he says as I lean into his hand, butterflies filling my chest at his nearness. He reluctantly pulls his hand away, looking a little dejected.

"So, aside from reading romance books, what do you do?" I say, trying to lighten the mood.

"I run as my wolf a lot. It's enjoyable. Or I practice my fireballs and see how far I can throw them." He laughs, and I smile. "Can I show you my wolf? I promise I won't hurt you." His expression turns shy.

I nod, not knowing what else to do. I'm curious but also terrified. It's kind of thrilling.

He gives me a small smile before standing and taking a couple of steps. He winks at me, causing me to laugh even as my heart thunders in my chest. So quick, I almost don't see the change. The golden blonde of his hair spreads as his whole body lurches forward, and I'm face to face with the most enormous wolf I've ever seen.

He sits and cocks his head to the side before a low whine comes from him. His eyes get really big, and he lies down on the floor.

I am in awe. My jaw is hanging open, embarrassed; I snap it shut. Very slowly, I rise from the sofa and take a step forward. The wolf follows me with its bright blue eyes. He lays his head down between his paws and wags his tail as I approach. Up close, he is larger in this form than in his fae form. The golden sheen of his fur reflects the light of the fireplace. I crouch down, petting the soft fur of his head, and giggle to myself. Yep, this is my life, real-life Beauty and the Beast.

Slowly, Killian moves into a sitting position while I pet his head. This is wild. He looks at me, and his face goes into doggie smile mode, tongue hanging out the side of his mouth and all. I laugh. "Okay, you are a pretty cute wolf." I smile at him.

He stands and pounces on me, paws on my shoulders as he flattens me to the floor. He licks up the side of my face while I laugh and push at his fur. "Hey, not fair!" I giggle as he licks the other side of my face, thoroughly covering my face in slobber.

Quick as a blink, the fur is gone, and my hands are planted on Killian's chest with him kneeling over the top of me. I let out a startled breath between giggles. He leans forward, brushing my shoulders with his hair as he places his elbows on the ground on either side of me, keeping his weight off my body. An electric charge runs through me at his nearness, my breaths coming hard as images of his hands running over my body fill my mind.

His eyes lock on mine as he leans forward and brushes across my lips with his, so delicate, like a question. He slowly leans in and softly kisses me, gentle and featherlight. The flutters in my chest explode. So different from the fevered kisses I'm used to. I kiss him gently, slowly, exploring the soft curves of his mouth. I can feel his heart pounding in his chest, a match to my own. Gently, I reach up and pull him down on me as I deepen the kiss. His movements are slow and tantalizing as he lets go. His breathing gets heavier as I nip and suck on his bottom lip. A growl rumbles through him as he slowly pulls back and softly kisses me again.

He gradually pulls away and sits back on his knees again, straddling me. He rolls to the side of me and smiles. I wasn't expecting kissing him to be so soft and sweet. His demeanor is affectionate and romantic, yet easily excitable, kind of like a dog. His wolf shows his personality.

I look up at him as I move back into a sitting position. "You licked me." I raise an eyebrow.

"I licked you, so you're mine." He winks, and I giggle.

"It's getting late, and we've got a date with the fates tomorrow. I should probably walk you back to your room." He stands and offers me his hand to help me get up again.

He leads me back to my room, holding my hand, and I feel safe. Killian makes me feel safe and wanted. I didn't know these were feelings that I needed. He likes to talk about anything and everything, and looks at me like I hold the whole world. Is this what it's supposed to feel like in the beginning?

He opens my door, and I step inside before turning around. "Killian?"

He stops and turns. I rush forward, grab his face, and pull him into a kiss. I release him and rush back into my room. His cheeks turn pink before I hold the door.

"Good night, Killian."

"Good night, Emerald." He smiles as I shut the door.

I wake with a start, heart thundering, sweat making my shirt stick to my skin. I should be used to this by now. The nightmares happen almost every night. Replaying my past in cinematic detail or warping new situations into the old. I wipe the tears from my face as I stare off into the darkness. This would never have happened if I didn't have such terrible taste in men. I wipe at my arms, trying to get the ghost of Bravos' touch off my skin. Yet another incident to add to my brain's arsenal of torture.

Turning on the light, I grab the glass of water and glance over to my right to the large black void curled up, looking at me.

"Sorry, you chose the worst possible person to sleep next to." I give a half smile to the panther and drink; the cool liquid calms my body. Setting the glass down, I turn towards the cat, laying my head down next to his so I can pet him. I scratch behind his ears, and he leans into it. At least I figured out he's a boy, but I don't know what to call him. "I used to have pleasant dreams a long time ago. Back when I still had dreams in general," I muse. "But then life happened. I thought that love could conquer all, that if I loved someone enough, I would be enough."

He lifts his head, blinking at me before nudging my hands to keep petting. I smile as I continue to pat his big head, scratching under his chin as he rolls his head in my hands.

"I don't know why I'm talking to the danger kitty, but at least cats don't judge your secrets." I must be losing my mind, but I've never been able to tell anyone the full extent of things. Afraid to rock the boat. I don't want people's pity. It's my fault I've ended up in this situation. "I think if I hadn't run tonight, something bad was gonna happen. Really, I just got lucky, and he lost his grip when I stumbled. I can't tell you how relieved I was when I found Killian. He made me feel safe. But I couldn't tell him what had happened. He was so happy to see me." I stop petting the cat and look at him, stretching my arms over my head. "I honestly don't know what to do. I feel so lost here. I like Killian because he is so sweet, and I've never had anyone treat me with such care and respect. But I'm torn."

I look over at the cat. He's closed his eyes, so I continue, "There is something about Rodan that I can't ignore. He drives me crazy. I can't help but run my mouth when he's around, like it's a challenge or something. But sometimes, he's kind and cares for me, even if it's just sitting beside me under the stars while I cry. I hate that I like someone who doesn't like me—a character flaw, I guess. Kissing him was electric in so many ways." I close my eyes. "I have never been hung up on two guys at the same time. It's like if they were mashed into one person, it would be the perfect guy. In reality, I should be going for the nice guy who treats me right, so why is this so hard?" I let out a low laugh. "No. In reality, I should be focused on going home, but nothing good is waiting for me there." I take a deep breath.

"You see, my ex won't ever let me go. Not really. It's hard to explain, but I don't want to return to that. I don't want to be constantly looking over my shoulder." I glance at the Void, his eyes cracked open as he listens to me. "I'd rather risk being eaten by a dragon than face that guy again." I huff a laugh. "That's saying something, isn't it?"

"Maybe I've got it all wrong, and I was never meant to find love. Maybe I was just supposed to be the crazy cat lady with a house full of 'em." At least I've got the crazy part down, talking to a damn cat in the middle of the night.

I reach over and turn the light back off. "Thanks for listening, Void. And for always being here when the nightmares come." He shifts next to me. I reach over and pull myself closer to him, enjoying the soft warmth of his coat. I rub my face in the fur of his back as I listen to his slow, rhythmic breathing and fall back to sleep.

Chapter 20
Killian

I could barely sleep last night. Thinking about today's epic adventure and my date with Jade. I can hardly believe I got to kiss her. Her lips were soft and warm, but I didn't want to be greedy. I took things slow to show her she had nothing to fear from me. I'll admit I got a little carried away in my wolf form and licked her, but I was so excited that she didn't freak out. I needed to kiss her. She makes me so warm and fuzzy inside and calms me. Although I need to find out what upset her before she ran in. Why was she running? Why did she have tears marring her beautiful face? Other than that, the night was terrific.

Now, today, we get to go see the Fates.

The actual fucking Fates.

Just like in the books.

An epic quest with a fair maiden to find the answers to our future. I have so many questions for them; I feel like we are gonna need all day. Not just questions about the curse, either. I wanna know about Jade and me, and if Rodan is ever gonna pull that stick out of his ass. Important questions, you know. I've spent my whole life reading about stuff like this, and now I actually get to go do it.

The hard part is doing it without Mom finding out, like Dad knows, because Warrick needed his permission to take us. But

Mom would be all like: *this is not a fairytale, it's too dangerous.* I know how she is.

Moms, am I right?

I stand outside, waiting for Jade and Rodan to come down. Sunlight is cresting the tops of the mountains, casting them in a warm glow, but I couldn't wait. I sent the maids to get them up early. I'm sure Rodan will be mad, but he's always angry. The bag full of food is ready to go. It's an adventure, and who knows how long it will take? Warrick is powerful, but getting through the wards must be done on foot. So he can only get us so close.

Jade finally emerges from the castle, rubbing her eyes at the light. Rodan is following behind, looking like he's gonna murder someone. Gods, I love him.

"It's five a.m. Killian," he growls.

I run over and put my arm around his shoulders. "You must have an early start on an epic adventure. Onward! Warrick awaits." I pull him towards Warrick, who is yawning. "How can you all be so tired? This is the most exciting thing we have ever done."

Jade looks at me through tired eyes, and I feel a slight pang of guilt since I had her up late. "Why is there never coffee? Or hot chocolate? Something," she grumbles.

"Tools of weak mortals. We don't need it." Warrick shrugs.

"Well, I need it. I feel like death."

Everyone will feel better once we get going. This is going to be the best trip ever. I wrap Jade in my arms and give her a nice wake-up squeeze. She squeaks, and I realize I may have squeezed her too tight. Oops.

"Let's get this over with," Rodan groans.

Warrick walks over and opens a portal for us, the glimmering light welcoming and the first step to this adventure. I grab Jade's hand and run through; she makes some sound of protest, but it dies out as soon as we cross. The world flips and spins as we are spit out in a small clearing surrounded by trees. Jade stumbles behind me, looking a little pale.

"You get used to it," I try to reassure her.

"Uh-huh." She buckles over, appearing like she's about to be sick.

Rodan and Warrick stride out of the portal behind her.

"You don't look so good, Jade. Still not used to that, huh?" Warrick smirks.

"Fuck you, Warrick. Fuck your portals, too." She straightens up but sways a little on her feet.

Warrick chuckles before casting a dome over the area that shimmers faintly in the morning light. "The ward is up. When you return to this clearing, I'll know and come back for you." He turns back towards Jade. "Have fun." He smirks and walks back through the portal, which closes behind him.

"Where are we?" Jade croaks out, staring into the trees.

"In the Dracomore Mountains, the Grove of Fate is further in. We have to walk from here." I take her hand in mine, moving west.

"How do you know where to go?"

"We don't," Rodan deadpans as he follows.

Jade gives me a wary look, but I'm not worried. I straighten my spine and follow the worn-down path ahead through the trees. I read the Fates book as a child and remember at least some of the directions listed in it. Maybe not exactly where the grove was, but I know I can find it.

"When I agreed to this, we had the book Killian. Now the book is dust." Rodan has no faith in my memory.

"Don't worry, it's all part of the adventure. We'll find it." I smile and trudge ahead. That was only a minor setback. Who needs a book when they have my keen sense of direction?

Okay, maybe I was wrong. That path may have led us to a lake.

Maybe I was a bit lost, but it will all work out. As soon as I figure out where the path continues from the lake. On the positive side, this place is super romantic for a lakeside picnic.

"I think we should take a break and eat lunch." I stop and look at Jade, who's looking around with a smile on her beautiful face. "Can't pass up such a perfect spot for a picnic." Man, this is working out so perfectly. Romantic setting, with the perfect girl and my best friend. All of us off on an epic quest to save the kingdom. I am so going to get my fairytale ending when this is all over. I don't have a fairy godmother, though—I guess Rodan can fill that role.

Rodan leans against a tree, his usual scowl painted on his face. But I know he's taking in the scenery and hiding how much he loves all this. I pull out the blanket and place the sandwiches down. Pulling out water skins for each of us since this also looks like a good place to refill them.

Jade eats her sandwich, looking out over the beautiful lake. I can't help but watch her. Her silver hair sparkles as her ponytail sways in the light breeze. She looks serene and happy, like she did last night. Today, she dressed for a day of walking in the woods—tight pants over boots and a sleeveless shirt. Something about it is more alluring than all the lovely gowns I've seen her in. She seems so content. So comfortable with herself. Is this closer to how she dressed in the mortal realm? It's damn sexy if it is.

Rodan skips rocks as he walks along the shore, rippling the still water. He's been so quiet since this all began. Not at all like I expected him to be. I wish I knew how to make him happy. Maybe I'll get him a cake when we get back. Cake makes everyone happy.

I hear a rustle far in the distance before an acrid smell fills the air. Rodan's head snaps up, telling me he heard the same thing.

Something's coming.

"Jade, don't panic, but I need you to hide. Quickly." I help her to her feet, searching for a safe place.

"What's going on?" Jade asks, eyes going wide.

"It's going to be okay, but you need to hide and stay there." I spot a fallen tree not too far from us, shrouded in shrubs, and pull her towards it. "Whatever it is, we can handle it, but I don't want you to get hurt if it's dangerous. Please, just hide until we say it's safe." I don't want to scare her, but the smell is getting more pungent. Gods, what is that?

She runs behind the tree and disappears into the shrubbery, peeking between the branches.

"Stay down," I whisper.

The sound gets closer as Rodan stands next to me, his brow furrowed, both of us on alert. We both sniff the air, trying to discern what it is. It's closing in, but all I can smell is rot and decay, like a days-old battlefield. This isn't good. Snapping twigs and crunching leaves rustle; it will be moments before they reach the clearing. Too much sound to be only one. Whatever is coming, there are a lot of them.

A thunderous roar breaks the silence, sending birds flying into the sky.

They are so close.

I conjure fire in my hand, ready to light up whatever comes at us. Rodan is crackling with power next to me.

The trees split, and the putrid smell makes my stomach roil. Coming into the clearing is an abomination of a man, a monster. It drips and oozes from all over, only vaguely resembling a person. Dead black eyes stare at us as its unhinged jaw hangs at an unnatural angle. Its limbs are uneven and clawed. I have never seen anything so gross in my life. I almost vomit on the spot.

"Nope!" I gulp. "That's definitely a nope!" I funnel my power through my body and throw a fireball at it. The fire explodes as it hits, engulfing the creature in flames, but it doesn't slow its pursuit. Even from across the clearing, the smell of burning flesh is added to the reek of rot. It takes everything I have not to be sick. Everything about these creatures feels unnatural. Dangerous.

"There are more!" Rodan shouts as he sends bolts of electricity to two more that emerge from the trees. They shake and stumble, but they don't falter. "Fuck." He forces all three of them back with a gust of air. Giving us some time to regroup as they struggle against the wind.

I pull deeper into my power and send an explosion toward them as two more come running from the woods. When the blast hits, they are blown to the ground. I let out a sigh of relief when it looks like all of them are down, but it's too soon as they rise again. Some are now missing limbs. One crawls towards us, while others stagger. All I've done is slow them down. What the hell are these things?

Rodan pulls his lightning into a ring, spinning it faster and faster while I pull more power. I reach over and add my fire to the large halo that crackles with the addition. The light is so bright it's hard to look at. Rodan leans back before launching it towards the still-standing creatures. The disk of electricity and fire saws through three of them as Rodan directs its path. Decapitating them while setting them alight. Honestly, it's one of the coolest things we've ever figured out we could do together. This is the first time we've actually gotten to use it in a real battle. It's glorious.

Two more step out of the woods as the death disk sputters out. Gods damn it. How many of these things are there? Looking at their claws and their size, we cannot let them get closer, or we will be vastly outnumbered.

"Killian, do the thing."

"Dude, the thing is gross," I whine, gagging for emphasis.

"Killian..." Rodan's eyes grow larger as another steps out of the forest, towering over the others, bending the trees in its wake.

Fuck. Me.

Okay, this is gonna lead to a lot of questions I don't want to answer, but it may be our only choice. The giant melty flesh man is not going to eat us today. No, sir. I pull back all the fire that is consuming the creatures, pulling in as much power as I can because this is going to suck. The fire builds, swirling in my chest like a storm waiting to be released. I create the strings of light, uncoiling them from my body. I cast out the lines to the five beings still coming for us. Each one connects, and I feel their putrid wrongness fill me. Everything about them is wrong—dark. With all the power I have within me, I blast it down the lines. Power travels through their bodies, causing them to stop. I quickly drop my connection. Rodan and I turn and leap to take cover.

I snap my fingers.

The explosion is quick. All five of them explode from the inside out into flames, scattering burning flesh for yards around. I look back to see that all of them are down. Well gone, in flaming pieces, their blood raining down around the clearing. Raining down on us. The clearing stills, no more sounds of movement. I gag on the stench again as I look at Rodan. He's breathing hard but has a smirk on his face.

"You're right, that was gross," he chuckles as he shakes the viscera from his arms.

We both lay down on the grass, breathing hard and laughing.

"Is it safe?" Jade's small voice carries over to us.

"Yeah, but watch where you step," I say as Rodan and I burst into another fit of laughter. I can't believe I did that.

Jade's careful footsteps stop a few feet from us. I look up to see her gag and take a step back. "Oh god, you guys stink. What the hell were those things?" She rubs her arms, clearly still shaking.

"Some sort of constructs," Rodan says. "Nothing natural. I don't think we ran into those by chance." He sits up and looks at the carnage. I've never seen anything like that before. The big question is why we would run into something like that in the Dracomore Mountains. More signs of something happening, something not good.

I slowly reach my feet and pull what's left of the flames back into me. I strain with the effort. I'm almost tapped out and need every bit of power I can take back. Sweat drips down my brow as I pull the last of the flames back into myself, panting with the effort.

"Did those things spontaneously combust? I don't get it. They just stopped moving and exploded." Jade looks around at all the guts strewn about the grass.

"Not exactly." Rodan smirks, looking at me.

"Wait, you did that?" Jade's eyes go wide.

I scratch the back of my head, feeling more gloop in my hair, and shudder, pulling my hand away. "I can make creatures explode by raising their body temperature. A lot." I give a shy smile and a half-shrug. Fuck, she's gonna be so freaked out.

"Holy shit, that's insane. You could wipe out whole battlefields with a power like that." Her eyes are wide with something like wonder. I love watching the gears turn in her head.

"I mean, that would be cool, but I can only do four or five at a time, and then I'm pretty wiped of my power." I look down, feeling a bit sad about my limitations and nervous about my power being known.

Jade's mouth drops open, but quickly turns to a smile. "Oh, only four or five? That's pretty sad. I thought you were more powerful than that."

"I—what?" I look back towards her, my heart on the ground.

Rodan slaps me on the back, chuckling, "She's teasing you, man. Come on, I need to get this shit off me." He turns towards the lake, and I look back at Jade, who is silently giggling.

Damn, I fell right into that one. I wink at her before running after Rodan and tackling him into the water.

We clean ourselves in the lake. Jade turns away while we strip out of our clothes and wash out all the blood, drying them quickly with Rodan's air magic and a little heat from me.

"What makes you think those things were after us?" I say over my shoulder as we trudge on through the forest. On the far side of the lake, I discovered the old stone path once more, which was headed west. I press on, knowing this has to be the right way. I've got a wicked sense of direction.

"Because I read about them in the records from the war. Sorcerers once made foul constructs. Their description sounded a lot like how those looked. They do not have their own will. The sorcerers had power over them," Rodan says.

"So, you think there is a sorcerer after us?" I lift an eyebrow as I push a branch out of the way.

"I don't know, but if they were the same creatures, someone had to be controlling them."

"I thought sorcery was forbidden?" Jade looks back at Rodan.

"It is. There hasn't been one in the land for a hundred years. But that was very dark magic. That's why their eyes were black," Rodan muses.

"Like the dragon." Jade furrows her brow.

"Possibly..."

"Why would anyone be attacking like this? And why now?" I ask, looking at the path ahead.

"Why now, indeed?" Rodan grumbles.

"Do you think they are trying to stop you from breaking the curse? Maybe we're on the right path. But then, why attack everyone at the beach?"

"Because everyone was there," Rodan breathes. "All the nobles were there. If they all die, the kingdom will all but fall. Fuck why didn't I think of this sooner!" Rodan clenches his fists as I stop to look at him. "Think about it: if the heir dies, someone else has to be named. If another kingdom were to attack during the unrest, our chances of survival are limited."

"But why not just target the heir?" Jade asks.

"Because of all the stupid pageantry, no one knows who the

heir is." Rodan gives me a pointed look.

Okay, maybe I didn't think about how that might pose a problem. But how was I supposed to know someone would target me? Why would they? I'd be a totally awesome king. Fuck. This is bad. If we are being attacked, and this isn't random, we could have a war looming.

"We should ask the Fates. See if they know what's going on. Maybe we are being paranoid. I mean, there are lots of weird things in the forest." I give a half smile, not believing myself.

"Uh-huh," Rodan grumbles.

We trek on in silence, solely the birds chirping in the trees and the rustle of leaves to serenade us. It's already late afternoon. How far is this damn grove?

A clearing opens between the trees, and an oval woodwork of branches stands in the middle. They curl around each other, creating a doorway with two stone steps leading up to a watery window that ripples on an unnatural wind.

"The Grove of Fate," I breathe.

"Another portal?" Jade whines.

I laugh and pull her towards the door, excitement lighting up every cell of my body. I can't believe I found it. I was really starting to wonder if I was remembering a map from a different book. Did the book turning to dust have something to do with all these attacks? It was an ancient book. Shit happens, ya know.

"Do you really think this is a good idea?" Rodan looks skeptically at the door.

I smile, take the steps, walk through the portal, and pull Jade with me.

Absolutely.

Chapter 21
Rodan

Fuck.

That damn idiot just walked through a portal to who the fuck knows where. I run my hand down my face as I contemplate what to do.

Oh, I'm sorry, Your Majesty, I lost your fucking son and one of the mortals.

Fuck.

Who walks through a portal in the middle of the damned woods without checking anything for traps? Or, for that matter, knowing where it goes. This. This is why Killian needs a fucking babysitter. And the fucker dragged Trouble in with him. I can't believe he would put her in danger like that. I can't just leave them.

Fuck.

I steel my spine as I walk up the steps and through the portal.

Chapter 22
Jade

We step out onto lush green grass on top of a mountain. The view from up here takes my breath away. Grand mountains dense with trees surround us, with large lakes and rivers glimmering in the valleys below.

"Holy shit," I breathe.

"You can say that twice," Killian says, looking over the cliff's edge.

I turn around to see a path leading into the trees. It looks a lot like the path we took through the forest, but the cobblestones look new and polished. I sure hope Killian isn't leading us into any other danger.

Those constructs will haunt my dreams for eternity. Just thinking about them brings the smell back into my mind. I was frozen in shock when they entered the clearing. I'd entered a horror movie, and I was the girl cowering behind a damn tree like it would protect me. How could I ever think I could do the things I read about? Honestly, what was I supposed to do? Throw a pinecone? Turn into an otter and cute it to death? I snort at the thought.

Killian moves beside me and laces his fingers in mine, looking towards the path with a big smile and bouncing on his toes.

"Are you out of your mind, Killian?" Rodan growls. We turn to see him standing by the portal. "You don't walk through random portals in the forest."

"We're fine," Killian says, exasperated. "Look, the path. We're so close." He pulls me towards the trees.

I hear another grumble from Rodan as he follows again.

The light shines through the trees, making the shadows dance on the path ahead. Birdsong rings through the air as they flutter from limb to limb. The rich scent of pine fills my nose as I breathe in the calm of the forest. The day seems younger here as we walk through. "Is this another realm?" I ask no one in particular.

"I'm not sure. It's possible. I've never seen a portal like the one we went through." Killian smiles.

"And yet you went through it all the same." Rodan's gruff tone shows his annoyance with his friend.

"But can't you feel it? The magic of this place?" Killian looks at Rodan, who huffs in response.

Up ahead, the path ends in a clearing. The trees shroud what lies beyond them. This adventure is exhilarating, although I could have done without the monsters. I can't help but smile. I've never done anything like this. Hiking, sure, but going somewhere with a purpose like this, and hoping that we may get some answers. If they can actually see the future, maybe I can find out if I have a future here. If I'm genuinely supposed to be dating these guys or if I'm simply learning to be myself again before I go home. Or why I turned into a fucking otter.

We walk into the clearing to see three enormous trees standing in the middle. My jaw drops as I look up and take in the sight before me. Each tree is shaped like a woman. A...naked woman. These are the trees that inspire people to worship the female body. The one on the left looks worn and wrinkled with bark, but no less stunning than the others. The middle one is smooth and voluptuous, an hourglass figure carved in wood. The third is slightly smaller, and so smooth her bark shines. Their leaves only come out at the top of the trees, cascading around them like hair. To be completely honest, they look like two-hundred-foot porn star statues.

"They're trees," I breathe.

"They're hot." Killian gapes.

"They're real." Rodan looks up in awe.

I jump as the one on the left slowly speaks, "Choices, choices, many choices. Many different paths still lie ahead." Her eyes glow blue as she looks down at me.

"Much woe lies in your past. What once was is now lost. For the path that brought you here is not done," the middle one's voice continues, their voices ethereal and as strange as the glow of their eyes.

"Breaking the curse is the only way forward, but sorrow lies in this path, soul of fractured fate. For you will shatter before the curse is done. And what has shattered can never be undone," the youngest one intones. All of them speak as if chanting.

Their gazes shift to Killian as they seem to start over again: "The little boy with the heart of gold, locked away for none to behold," chants the oldest.

"Much anguish lies on this road," the middle one says.

"Compromise must be made, for what you know will not be so," the youngest continues.

They all move their eerie glowing stares to Rodan. "Darkness swirls, and hate has festered," the oldest begins.

"What was lost is gone forever. A path of light could be your salvation and your ruin," the middle one proceeds.

"Fighting fate is a path to woe," the last one says with a warning tone.

Their eyes dim, and they stop. The three of us stand there gaping. I am still trying to understand what any of that meant. I can't dwell on that now when we have other things we need to find out. I nudge Killian, hoping he will be able to ask.

He clears his throat and steps forward. "My most lovely of fates, we've traveled far to ask you some questions."

They ponder this as they all look at each other and then smile. The middle one raises her hands and shrinks. She fucking shrank. I stand wide-eyed as I look at her wooden form come to stand in front of Killian, a few inches taller than him. She flips her leaves over her shoulder, revealing her very pert breasts. Sauntering up to him, she runs a hand up his chest and leans into him. Killian straightens but doesn't push her away.

"Hello," she purrs as she cups his cheek while wrapping her other arm down to his ass, pulling him into her.

I feel like I shouldn't be watching this, but have an overwhelming desire to slap her hands off of him, claim what is mine. Wait, what? We are definitely not exclusive, and I'm still not sure what to do about also being hung up on Rodan. Calm the fuck down.

"Why, hello there." Killian smirks.

Unbelievable, a tree? Really? I scoff. Rodan stands there in silence, the pinch in his brows showing he's deep in thought. His jaw dropped when the trees came into view. He is as shocked as I am about all this.

The naked tree lady continues running her hands over Killian. "Man now, questions later," she purrs as she pulls him away. Killian follows her, looking back only to shrug like he has no idea what's happening.

As they disappear into the trees, I turn to Rodan. "Is he... is he gonna put his dick in a tree? Or are we all gonna die here? I'm not sure how I should be feeling right now."

"He is definitely gonna put his dick in a tree," he says, shaking his head. I can't help but giggle. While I'm feeling a little jealous, it's also hilarious. He looks back up at the two remaining trees. "Is Amara under attack? Or are the things happening coincidences?" he says curt and to the point.

The older one considers him for a moment before her eyes glow again. "Dark magic abounds, trepidation builds. For a long-held plan is about to unfold. Beware whom you seek. Beware, old war coming to your keep."

"Who?" Rodan demands.

"Fate is a funny and fickle thing. Ask not the who for your answers but the why."

"Okay then, why?" I ask.

"When the time is right, you will know. Until then, look to the shadows."

Rodan pinches his furrowed brow, shaking his head in frustration. "Riddles. Had to be fucking riddles."

The older tree lifts her arms and shrinks down like the other. I will never get used to that.

"Come, fae filled with darkness, I have a story for you." The older one motions for Rodan to follow her towards a small cottage that was hidden behind her towering form.

I stand in the clearing now, alone with the youngest of the Fates. While they do not present as dangerous, I don't know what to do. She regards me momentarily before slowly sitting in front of me. Not that it did anything to make her smaller.

"Ask your questions," she says, looking bored.

"So, do you really cut the mortal strings?"

"Snip, snip," she chirps, grinning.

"Are you death?" I breathe.

"Yes and no, but mostly yes." She cocks her head to the side.

"Did you used to be witches like the story says?"

"Yesss, long ago. Now we are trapped here, but most powerful. The story is true, just like your book that went boom." She moves her arms in an arch, mimicking the scattering ashes.

"Why don't you give straight answers to most things?"

"The future changes; we do not. One wrong path and wham, new future. All we can do is lay out the best path without changing the future. I saw your path lead here." She walks her fingers across the ground.

"Is that why people say you're crazy?" God, I hope that's not rude to ask. I cringe at myself.

"Thousands of years, just us three, see how crazy you would be. So many futures and possibilities would make anyone a little crazy," she says in a singsong voice.

I sit in front of her and pull at the grass, unsure how to ask my following questions. "I don't know if I'm actually supposed to be falling for Killian or Rodan. I don't know who I'm supposed to be with if either of them. I feel a pull towards both of them and don't know what to do. Can you tell me?"

She gives me a long look. "You also wish to know if you should stay in the fae realm," she says pointedly.

"Yes."

Her eyes glow. "You are entwined in the futures of two. Fate's plan will become clear to you. Open your mind. Let them prove themselves. You know what the right choice is. What will befall you if you choose wrong. But you shall not make that decision. Things are never as they seem. Your darkest days are yet to come."

"I don't understand."

"You will." She smiles.

Chapter 23
Rodan

Once upon a time, there was a girl. She had dreams, big dreams of great love. She grew up watching romance movies and obsessed with the idea of love. The heroes, the reformed bad boys, the: no one puts baby in the corner. High school boys made her feel unseen until a boy noticed her one day. Things were great for a time until he wanted more than she was ready to give.

Crack.

She moved on, but more woe lay in her path with guy after guy taking from her. She got a job after high school at a bookstore, diving deeper into the stories than ever before. Still so profoundly disappointed in reality. With every new heartbreak came another crack in her soul. One day, a guy from high school walked back into her life, her bookshop. Fate finally seemed to be shining down upon her. Everything was just like the movies: romantic dinners, late-night phone calls, walks on the beach, and gifts just because.

Everything was perfect. Until she didn't hear from him. Two long days went by without so much as a text. Then, when she was starting to worry something had happened to him, a single text awaited her—I want to take a break.

Crack.

After months, she didn't understand what had happened.

Heartbroken, she dove into work and watched the days slip by into weeks. Then he slid back into her life as if nothing had ever happened. She was so relieved she missed the giant red flag and pressed on. Everything was just as it had been before. They were deeply in love, and nothing could break them. Soon after, he asked for her hand in marriage, and she agreed. They married quickly, as he couldn't wait. Things were fine for a time. But as most stories go, things were not as they seemed.

Over time, he slowly built walls to contain her, to trap her, make a prisoner of her. It was so slow, so calculated, she didn't notice until it was too late. Until one day, the cracks in her soul fractured and broke.

She told her friends that everything was fine, that what seemed controlling was just how he was. She kept the secrets from friends and felt she couldn't tell them the truth after lying for so long. She was afraid to tell them everything. However, not all of them were blinded by his deception. Some saw the truth through the lies and were determined to help her, even if she couldn't see the cage through the bars. Then, one day, he swept the rug out from underneath her. He no longer loved her. Maybe he never did.

Crack.

The day came when she saw the light through the darkness and escaped, but she would never be whole again.

What the fuck was that? I grip my head as I come back to myself. Flashes of a life that was not mine had played through my head. Everything was slightly fuzzy and fading from my memory almost as soon as I saw it. I had felt every single emotion, every pain that girl went through. I gape at the woman in front of me.

"Did you like my story, dear?"

"No," I grumble, voice gruff with the effort. "Why did you show me that?" The vision fades from my mind as I try to focus my thoughts. The tension it left me with slowly dissolves. As my surroundings return through the haze, I take in the room filled with dim firelight, the helpless feeling melting away with the warmth. The cracking of the fireplace snaps me back into my body as I gaze upon the crone.

"You'll understand soon enough," she quips, lifting her tea to her wooden mouth.

"Who was that? Why would you show me a mortal's life?" I ask, trying to grasp what I can remember. The memory pours like sand through a colander, flowing faster at every attempt to grasp it.

"So you can understand."

"Who was it? Trouble?" Could her life have really been that tragic in the mortal world? No, that girl was nothing like Trouble. I don't see her letting anyone break her like that.

"You may not yet know this girl, but you will." She smiles softly at me, taking my hand and squeezing it. "Stop fighting your fate before it's too late."

"Can you at least tell me about my past?"

"Your answers lie in shadow. Beware seeking them, for every answer will only bring more questions."

I follow the crazy old bat out of the cottage, regretting ever going in there. My head spins as the story slips from my mind, but the feeling of broken hopelessness still clings to me. I thought she would have some answers about my past, not cryptic stories.

I see Trouble sitting before the young tree. She looks lost in thought. Probably got cryptic answers, like I did. Killian emerges from the forest with the other fate, his face a little red. I really don't want to know what they got up to. I'm surprised Jade isn't more put out by his walking off with another woman, but maybe they aren't as attached as I thought. A quiver of happiness at the thought goes through me, but I quickly stifle it.

"How do we break the curse?" I demand. Time to get to the point of all of this.

All three of the Fates look at each other and smile. It's

unnerving. Shit, what now? Their eyes glow a strange purple color as they all talk as one.

>"There is a prophecy foretold
>Light will overcome the dark
>When the last shadow fades
>The valley of the moon will fall
>A precious stone of fated heart
>A shattered soul of many worlds
>When the blood of great love is spilled
>Dreams and moonlight become one
>The fractured orb will mend."

We stand there waiting for more, but no more comes. That's it? Another answer hidden in a riddle. It's time to go.

"For the record, you were pretty vague when you told me about your powers, Killian." Trouble glares his way over the fire. "Well, in your description of magic in general, I saw everyone at the beach. And then today. Did you really think that a kid's book covered that shit?" The light dances across her features, bringing out a glow within her.

I laugh as realization hits me. "You gave her a children's book to learn about magic!" I nearly fall over, clutching my side with laughter. "Seriously?"

Killian glowers at me across the fire while roasting a rabbit we had caught for dinner. "Hey, it was my first magic book. I thought it was a good place to start." He pouts.

Trouble and I continue rolling with laughter.

"Can all fire wielders make people spontaneously combust?" Trouble wipes a tear from her eye as she fights another onslaught of laughter.

Killian and I exchange looks. This would give away the plot. It was a last resort—using that power. But no way was I going to fight those things with a sword. Their reach was too long, and my healing abilities are okay but could be better. I didn't spend much time learning them like Warrick did, nor did Killian.

Trouble seems to notice the quiet between us; her body goes tense. "Was I not supposed to ask that?"

"You weren't supposed to see that," I drawl.

"It's okay, Emerald." Killian takes a deep breath, resolve on his features. "It's a power only present in royal lines," he sighs as her eyes grow comprehensive with understanding. "Each element has a special ability within royal families. They are closely guarded secrets meant only for emergencies." He stares into the fire. "All of them affect a creature or person's body. I have fire, so I can heat every cell in the body to boiling, then to combustion." He looks at her, his face sad.

"So that means you're the prince," she says in a low voice.

"Yeah," he sighs.

"And you knew?" She looks at me, and I nod, leaning forward, resting my arms on my knees. There are so many things I wish to tell her, but it's easier this way. Although it's getting harder to convince myself of this by the day.

"You can't tell anyone about me or the power you witnessed." He gazes pleadingly at her.

"No, of course not. I wouldn't." She considers for a moment and smiles. "Does this mean you can tell me more about your childhood since I know?"

Killian beams at her before going into an extremely long-winded description of his past. I stop listening when he starts with his earliest memories. Hopefully, Trouble can keep her mouth shut about him. With the way things are looming over the kingdom, I'm worried.

We'd had to set up camp when we'd stepped back through the

portal. It was well into the night, and there was no way we were taking our chances with the hours-long walk ahead of us. Warrick wouldn't start to worry for another day or so anyway.

The talk with the Fates had gone as expected. I mean, I honestly didn't think we'd even find them. Having found them, I'd expected riddles we'd have to decipher later. I wrote down everything I could remember when we reached a good place to camp, the prophecy probably being the most important.

Trouble has mentioned that everything directed at her made her nervous. It definitely didn't sound good. Killian, on the other hand, seemed pretty pleased. Although they could have told us nothing, he would have been delighted just finding the Fates. Some of the things they said put me on edge. I was afraid that they would say too much. Instead, they left me with a lot to think about. Such as, why did she tell me to stop fighting my fate? And what was that story about the girl actually about? Why didn't she let me remember it? Damn woman gave me no answers, just more questions.

I stir the little mug I placed next to the fire, ensuring the contents don't burn as I watch Trouble and Killian talk. There is a natural ease to them, like they've been friends for a long time. I see the yearning in Killian's eyes, though. Trouble, on the other hand, is a conundrum. I can never quite tell what she's thinking or what she might do next. Keeping her at arm's length has been challenging, but I won't slip up again like in the cave.

The crickets and other wildlife shift and sing through the trees as I enjoy the crackle of the fire. It's been so long since I've been in the woods at night. It's an unexpected reprieve from the rest of court.

I pick up the little mug and pass it over to Trouble, who wrinkles her brow at it. "What is it?" She looks at the dark liquid.

"Hot chocolate," I drawl.

She sniffs at it and takes a tentative sip; amusement lights up her features.

"What? Did I do it wrong? How hard is it to make chocolate hot?" Fucking mortal bullshit.

"Um, well, this is chocolate. And it's hot." She smiles. "Usually, it has milk mixed in." Her eyes sparkle as she devolves into another giggle fit.

"So it's hot chocolate milk," I deadpan. This was a terrible idea.

"Thank you, Rodan. This might be even better." She winks before sipping it again. Stupid. Girls and their sweets—at least last time I cooked, I could follow a recipe. But no, she tells me only half the details. I fume as I look at the fire. See how much she likes it if I dump it on her. Visions of her naked body covered in melted chocolate float through my head. Now, I want to lick it off of her. Yep, great way to keep her at arm's length, dumbass.

"Can you teach me how to shift?" Trouble looks at Killian with uncertainty.

"That I can do." Killian gets excited and turns towards her. "Close your eyes, okay? Now, I want you to picture a door." I scoff, and he shoots me a look. "Okay, now open the door. In the room is a box. I want you to go to the box." This would have worked with just the door, but whatever, I'll keep my mouth shut. "Don't open it yet. Inside that box is the cutest little otter in the world. You have to want that otter. You want to hold that otter. But the poor thing is trapped in the box." Trouble cracks a grin. "Now carefully open the box and let the otter out, but like, really want it."

Nothing happens.

Trouble huffs in frustration as she closes her eyes. Her face twists in concentration as she tries over and over again. I roll my eyes as I sit there wondering how long this is gonna go on.

"Trouble, it's locked behind a door. You have an ax or something. Be a badass and save the damn thing." I grin, and she closes her eyes again, furrowing her brow in concentration before she's nothing but fluff.

"You made it way too complicated, man," I drawl at Killian, who has scooped up Trouble and is dancing around with her. She squeaks in triumph.

"Now, walk back through the door and close it to turn back." I wave my hand at her.

Her little face makes an "O" before Killian almost drops her human form, falling on his ass. We all keel over in laughter. Trouble sits on his chest, changing between forms. All the while laughing in delight. She is so beautiful. I want to see that smile on her face every day.

As the night wears on, all of us are thinking about what the Fates told us. For a long time, we all sit quietly. Trouble eventually cuddles up to Killian for warmth as the chill creeps in. A pang of jealousy hits me as I watch them together. I grunt as I think about possessing her, but push the thoughts away.

I watch as the two of them fall asleep. She trembles as the chill sets in. I relent and lie down beside her, hopeful that she will warm up between us. She curls into me as I wrap my arm around her. I feel it as her breathing steadies and her shaking stops. I inhale the smell of her and wonder if she will have nightmares again tonight. Cat says she's had them for years but doesn't discuss them.

As I fall asleep, I get quick glimpses of the story I heard earlier. They slip through my fingers like water as I try to grasp onto them. I don't remember enough to know who it was about. All I knew was it was important.

Chapter 24
Jade

Upon returning from the Fates, the boys disappeared to talk with the king and queen. Ryker and Warrick were left with instructions to find anything related to magical stones. We'd missed an event that all the ladies were cooing about. Something about a fashion show. I'm not too sad about missing that.

Cat and I spent the next day trying to figure out what the cryptic messages I got meant. All we've come up with so far is that breaking the curse is essential for my own sake. It's strange; I never saw myself in a place like this, even caring about helping break a curse. How can I deny what the Fates said, though?

Lyra and Arlin joined us for lunch, and we all talked about theories on what the prophecy meant, not getting anywhere. Topics of the men filled the silence when ideas ran dry. Arlin is absolutely smitten, while Lyra has been balancing two men, trying to figure out which is a better match. I can definitely relate, but I'm not going to admit that. This whole thing will sort itself. It's not like both of them are into me anyway. Although Rodan did look a little jealous of Killian the other night in the forest, so I snuggled in extra close to Killian to see what he'd do about it. And that experiment resulted in a big, fat nothing.

It's been a strange couple of days that have left me feeling like I belong. Even Cat has found a rhythm here, although she's still adamant about not having a relationship with Ryker. I won't push. I see how they are together, but she needs to figure it out in her own time. That Viking of a man will win her over in the end.

Cat worked with Ryker on shifting while we were gone, but she won't say anything more than it's going poorly. Ryker said she could turn fine, but laughed when she scowled at him. She won't even tell me what she shifts into, saying only that she's a wild shifter, and it's different from how I shift.

As for the more immediate problem, I haven't made much headway regarding who is attacking or why. From what I've gleaned, Killian is the target. However, whoever is attacking doesn't know that. The reference to the old war has me looking through every record from that time to find a similar pattern. I need to find out whether history is repeating itself.

When the accord was struck, the vampire lord took control, and the sorcerers were magically imprisoned. Most of the followers of dark magic were similarly imprisoned or fled into hiding.

The ideals the sorcerers were trying to enforce were similar to a dictatorship. However, they presented it as a means of freedom from oppression. Many records stated they wanted to enslave less powerful fae to do the work that more powerful fae shouldn't have to. They also planned to do this to anyone who opposed them.

Auburnigh was the biggest obstacle to their plans. All the kingdoms here tax their people with power. One full day's power a week gets funneled into a magic orb that dispenses the magic to various civil projects. There are four orbs, one for each element. Earth power gets directed into farms and infrastructure. While things like water run the aqueducts and plumbing. It doesn't matter how powerful the fae are. The tax is the same. Even the king and queen, the most powerful fae, pay the tax.

Using the power of everyone, they feed and house every fae in the kingdom. Fae work to earn money for luxuries. Jobs like cooking and cleaning are paid. The military is built of people who want to maintain their way of life. It sounds like an excellent system that takes care of everyone.

The sorcerers didn't like that less powerful fae put less magic into the land than more powerful fae. They complained that more powerful fae shouldn't put more power in just because they had it to spare. Hence, they deemed slaves a better option. It made me sick reading about it. How can people be so selfish? If these people are responsible for the recent attacks, I can't imagine things will get better soon.

I shake off the chill gripping my spine as I walk down the hallway.

In an attempt to feign normalcy, the king has decided to continue with the ball as planned and hopes they can figure out who is responsible soon. I can't help but feel like a sitting duck. Killian believes the person responsible is in the castle, as events suggest they are aware of everyone's movements. If he is correct, it would explain why the dragon attacked on the beach. It may also explain why we were attacked in the forest.

I walk into the enchanting ballroom; the lights glistening off the iridescent marble walls and pillars. The grand space has a domed ceiling made of glass, looking out into the night sky. A slow melody fills the space as people trickle in and make their way over to the buffet and wine tables. Surrounding the dance floor are large round tables and sofas for lounging. The large doors that lead to the bioluminescent garden are open wide, letting in the night breeze.

I make my way over to the food and pile my plate with delicacies before grabbing a glass of wine. I find Arlin and Lyra already sitting down with Cat, having what looks like a lively conversation.

"No. You don't say." Lyra looks scandalized.

"She was madder than a wet hen." Arlin leans forward with her hand on her chest.

"Who was mad?" I set down my plate and lean in.

"Beatrix," Arlin whispers, "found Ellis dallying Owari out by the pond. But Owari said it was fair game because she saw Beatrix doin' the dirty in the hot springs with Hunter and Bravos."

"Ew," Cat and I say in unison.

Arlin looks at us in shock. "There are never too many wolves in the hen pen." She winks at us. "My shock is the hypocrisy of her being mad. No claim has been made on Ellis, as she can't figure out which one is the prince. She just keeps barking up all their trees."

"The ew was to Bravos and Hunter, not multiple men," I clarify after a bite of food.

"Oh, so you have dallied two at a time?" Lyra leans in.

"Um, no."

"It's wonderful, makes them so attentive. Best presented as a challenge," Lyra says as Arlin nods her agreement.

Lyra and Arlin continue their gossip as I watch the others file into the room, Beatrix hanging on Hunter like he might escape if she lets him out of her sight. Bravos walks in behind them with his eyes firmly planted on her ass, gross. Why did I ever let that creep touch me? The sirens are over at a table, Ellis talking with Owari, and Ambrose talking with Yudoku. Their taste seems to be for cute, nerdy men. Maysant and Oberon sit at a table to the left of them. She is trying to feed him some sort of small cake, and he looks horrified. Juniper sits with Alvar. He has his arm over her backrest and runs a finger along her wing. Juniper is side-eyeing him and blushing. Looks like a few solid couples or solid fuck buddies.

Calazar, Sorrel, and Alastor are off in a corner talking with Poppy and Hyacinth, the deer shifters. Edgar has his arms around Aurelia and Amber, the twins from Auroras. I shudder when I see them all smile. Really? Edgar? To each their own, I guess.

Scarlette and Corsac sit down at our table as we all sit and chat while we eat.

"Did anyone try that black stuff in the stone bowl?" Scarlette scrunches her nose.

"The stuff that looked and smelled like tar? No thanks," I grimace.

Corsac sneers, "I figured everything is worth trying, but when I put a spoon in, it melted. It just disappeared into the sludge. I don't think it is edible."

"That's odd. Maybe it was put there by mistake. Or it's a delicacy only certain fae can eat?" Cat shrugs.

I pick up a warm roll off my plate only to have it snatched by a hand from behind me. I wheel around to see Rodan taking a bite of it with a smug expression on his face. "You—" I start, cut off as he shoves the roll in my mouth, silencing my protest.

"Bravos is looking for you," he growls low. "Don't look, eyes on me, Trouble. You have two choices: dance with me or deal with him." He grins. "I'd rather you didn't fuck a cactus tonight."

Cat chokes on her wine, giving me a concerned look.

I groan as I stand up, taking his hand, still trying to chew the bread in my mouth. As I go, I wave away Cat's protests. I'll have to explain later.

I give a cursory glance behind Rodan as he leads me to a spot on the dance floor. Bravos has steam coming out of his ears as he glares at Rodan. I can't imagine this will play out well, but I thank Rodan for the save, nonetheless.

"Why did you save me?"

"Like I said. Don't need you calling a healer to get all those thorns out of you." He smirks.

I kick him in the shin. "Prick."

"I mean, if you like that sort of thing, I could give you a prick. It'd be much more pleasurable than a cactus." His smile widens with mischief.

"I don't actually want to fuck cacti, asshole."

"Then what do you want to fuck, Trouble?" He leans down and purrs in my ear. Turning my insides molten.

"Wouldn't you like to know?"

"Nah, I just worry about your taste in partners. Bravos, cacti, whatever else suits your fancy." He chuckles.

"None of those things have been my partners." Outraged by the insinuation, I try to pull away.

He pulls me in tighter. "So you didn't fuck Bravos in the garden?"

"No, I made out with him before I got to know him. It was a mistake," I huff as I give up on escape, remembering who awaits me. I shudder at the memory and every interaction with Bravos since.

"My mistake," he murmurs as he pulls us into a spin. "Beware the rumors he speaks about you."

I growl in frustration. Of course, that arrogant ass is saying something happened.

Rodan keeps me close as we move through the dance. Holding me so tight, I feel the hard planes of his body through my dress. "Killian just walked in. He's coming to save you from me. Be good, Trouble." With one last spin, he twirls me into Killian's awaiting arms.

"Hi, Killian." I smile.

"Hey, Emerald." He smiles broadly as he pulls me into him. Over his shoulder, I see Ryker sit next to Cat, picking treats off her plate while she playfully bats away his hand.

Killian spins me around the dance floor with ease as I relax into the evening. Now that he's here, I shouldn't have to worry too much about Bravos. I scan the room and see Sorrel and Calazar walk out into the garden with Hyacinth and the sirens following behind. We dance over to Warrick, where Killian leaves me to get some food. I can see what's going on here; Killian is keeping me guarded by his friends. Can't say I'm upset about it, as I keep catching scathing looks from Bravos.

"Got your eye on any of the ladies tonight?" I lean towards

Warrick.

"While they are all pretty, none of them are really my type."

"And what is your type?" I lift an eyebrow.

"That is information only for my friends," he says, smirking.

"We're friends." I feign hurt.

"I thought you hated me? You know, for the whole kidnapping thing." He chuckles.

"Well, finding out I'm part fae and can shift, changed a bit. If I hadn't come, I would've never known that."

"I see." He looks at me skeptically.

"Please, I wanna know. You're one of the few here who talk to me like a normal person. Plus, who am I gonna tell? I thought you liked Fennec?"

"She's nice, hot too, but my taste is usually a bit different from that," he whispers, the confusion evident on my face. He leans closer conspiratorially. "My taste runs a little to the left of her."

I scan the people standing next to Fennec, but the only person is...oh my god, "Alistor? You're gay?"

He puts a finger to his mouth. "It's not like it's unheard of, but no, I like both, just more men than women. I just haven't felt like now is the time to declare it. Romance is the last thing on my mind. But the queen insisted I participate."

"Why didn't you just tell her?"

"Because it's not necessary. I'll come out when I actually care to date. For right now, my duty is to this kingdom. So I participate in the balls, but I have no plans to find a wife." He smiles.

"You told me cuz we're friends," I gloat. Warrick laughs at my declaration. "Thank you for telling me, cuz I was totally about to call Fennec over here to help you out." I wink at him, and we both crack up.

"I don't need your help to get a female into bed. Could have had you that first night if I wanted to." He lifts a brow in challenge. I put my hand over my face to hide my blush as he laughs again. Fine, you got me there.

A loud boom rings out as the buffet table collapses in the center. We both whip our heads over to see everything on the table tumbling into the black sludge that is now spilling over the stone bowl, dissolving the table.

What the fuck?

A high-pitched wailing rings through the air, which grows louder by the minute. More screams ring out, causing me to cover my ears as I look around to see where they're coming from.

My heart stops. My breath catches as I look in horror at the doors leading to the garden. More screams ring out as people move away from the door. Everyone covers their ears to muffle the shrieking coming from this monster.

A pile of flesh-colored goop is moving into the ballroom, pulled along by teeth on the ground. Screaming mouths with sharp teeth are scattered all over it. Eyes of all different shapes and sizes look in all directions. This thing is horror incarnate.

I have never seen anything so scary in my life. Fuck the dragon. What the absolute fuck is that?

I run for Cat, who is moving slowly back, wide-eyed. Ryker moves in front of her.

"Get small and hide. Get out if you can," he growls.

I shift into my otter form and look up at Cat expectantly. Her brow creases as she looks at the monster, then at me. After what seems like an eternity, she finally shifts. I gape in shock at her tiny form next to me. I'm not sure what she is: part hedgehog, part lizard?

She has the head of a lizard, but fur tufts out of little round ears on top of her head, and spikes come out of her scaled back. Her whole underside is fluffy with little paws. What the fuck, Cat?

The shrieking of the monster grows louder as it makes its way into the ballroom. We run along the edge of the room to the furthest corner, hiding under a sofa.

The black sludge has started moving, rearing up and splashing forward like waves. Holy shit, this is bad. Ellis runs up and tries to place a shield around it, but it breaks through, and the black sludge surrounds his shoe. He quickly dances out of it and runs, as his shoe disappears into nothing. That can't be good. Ellis climbs on top of a table and throws off his sock as it starts disintegrating.

Poppy shifts into a deer and makes a break for the wide garden doors. She slams into an invisible barrier, slipping wildly on the floor with her hooves. I watch in horror as the monster reaches out a glob of teeth and eyes towards her as she struggles to get outside. It bites her leg and slowly pulls her towards an enormous mouth on the side of its form. More globs reach out, pushing her inside as she screams.

No. No, this can't be happening. Oh god, Poppy. I scream in fright as Cat tucks herself further into my fur.

Killian blasts it with bolts of fire, leaving black scorch marks. Warrick stabs at globs with his sword as they reach out. Bits of the monster fall to the floor as it whips around, screeching.

The cacophony of screams stops as the deer disappears. A new mouth opens up and begins screaming as a new set of eyes surfaces that are the russet brown of Poppy's. Everyone gapes in horror at Poppy's screaming features now on the monster.

What the fuck!

Cat and I sink further to the ground and back up a bit more.

Pounding sounds from the doors leading to the castle. The doors shake with the force of the magic blasting from behind them.

The fairies flitter around the windows high above the monsters. "The windows won't open!"

"There's a barrier surrounding the room!" Someone else shouts.

"There's no way out!" A woman's voice screams.

Shit, shit, shit. This is bad. That means the guards are locked in the hallway. Cat and I exchange horrified looks.

The black sludge surges forward, landing on an overturned

chair. The chair dissolves and disappears beneath.

The monster begins its cacophonous shrieking again as all of its scattered eyes survey the room. Flynn joined Warrick hacking at the arm-type globs that keep reaching out for people. And Juniper hovers at the ceiling, raining down wooden spikes on the creature.

Bravos pulls out his sword and stabs the black sludge—the metal dissolving as the black oozes up the blade. He jumps back, letting go of the sword, swearing. Hunter casts a wooden spear and stabs at it, but the result is the same. The black sludge moves up the spear as it sizzles into nothing. They both run behind a table to regroup as the sludge continues to advance.

Arlin stands near the black puddle, trying to build a rock wall around it. Her face is scrunched in concentration as the earth shifts and hardens. She's got it surrounded by rock almost three feet high. She shakes with the effort to build up the stone into a well-like structure. Black surges up past the wall and over her head, taking her down.

I scream as I see her collapse beneath the black. The sludge goes flat, having dissolved her instantly.

I choke on a sob. Tears run down my face.

"Arlin! No!" I hear Lyra's scream echo through the room.

"Arlin!" Flynn stops, staring stunned at the place Arlin had been standing the moment before. "Ahhh!" he lets out a cry of pain as the monster bites his leg and pulls him off his feet. He stabs wildly as he screams. Warrick furiously hacks at the glob that has Flynn. A wide mouth opens, and teeth clamp down. I close my eyes as his screaming rises and stops. The room goes almost silent, and then Flynn's screams start anew. I don't have to look to know the monster has a new face within its flesh.

Silently, Cat and I cry under the sofa for our friend and her lover.

Ryker comes running at the sludge, and we both step forward as if to stop him.

No. Please, not him.

Cat covers her eyes with her paws, crying while I look on, hoping he has a plan.

Beatrix stands to the side, pushing her magic into the black sludge. Parts of it freeze and slow down. Ryker runs up with a club made of rock and beats it with fury in his eyes. The sludge moves back, trying to pull itself into the stone well that Arlin had tried to encircle it with.

"I can't hold it much longer. My power is running low," Beatrix cries, the strain making her shake. Ryker continues beating at the sludge with the rock bat as the last of the sludge slips over the wall and back into the well with its nearly completed dome. "Close it! I'm losing it, and if it splashes over, we are both dead!" she screams. Ryker smacks at the sludge that's attempting to escape over the other side of the wall. Slowly, the walls curl in, and the dome begins to close. Ryker gives the sludge one more good smack before the rock encases the black sludge.

Beatrix slumps down next to the rock enclosure. "Do you think that will hold it?"

"Sure as fuck hope so. The only thing it didn't dissolve was rock," Ryker says, looking towards the monster that the others are still fighting.

I exhale, seeing Ryker stand unharmed against the black sludge, but pull Cat into me when I see him head over to where the other monster still bites at everyone. He changes his bat into a giant war hammer and swings at the monster, really emphasizing his Viking warrior look.

Blood drips from Killian's hands onto the floor. He pushes a stream of fire at the monster as he blocks its attacks with a sword. The clang of metal on teeth mixes with the shrill shrieks of the creature.

Rodan sends a bolt of electricity through it, momentarily causing it to lash out in all directions before pulling itself back together.

Lyra weeps as she transforms into the most enormous cobra I have ever seen. Her hood is easily three feet across. She rears her head back before spitting a long spray of acid at the monster that sizzles and pops when it hits, leaving a gaping hole in its side.

The monster lashes out and catches Rodan's arm, biting into him. He roars in pain before slicing off the fleshy appendage with his sword and prying off the teeth deep in his arm.

Scarlette gets up on a table, and concentration pulls across her features.

The floor under the monster churns and glows as it turns molten. Red lava marbled with bright golden ribbons flows up around the monster as its screams grow higher in pitch. The liquid rock moves up the body and hardens to black as it goes.

A loud crack sounds as the hardened lava fractures, falling apart into large chunks. The multiple mouths crunch through the rock. Fuck, fuck, fuck, no. Faster than the lava can travel up the body, it's being eaten away.

Juniper swoops down from the ceiling in a blur of green. She spins around the monster at a dizzying rate. I watch as the mouths all fill with a sort of sticky black substance. The screams are muffled as whatever she's doing is choking it. Its mouths beginning to stick shut. The lava glows hot again as each clogged mouth is covered until the monster is encased in lava rock.

Scarlette collapses into Corsac's arms, pale from the effort.

Fennec rushes over to the monster, and the rock turns red hot again. She pours heat into it as the mound shrinks and flattens until a flat puddle of rock remains.

Alvar heats the stone that contains the black sludge, turning it white. The whole thing turns to dust as we wait to see if the sludge survived. The structure collapses, revealing black dust within.

The doors burst open as the guards pour into the room.

Lyra sits on the floor, wailing.

Healers are called.

Cat and I stay curled under the sofa, with tears streaking our faces.

Chapter 25
Killian

"We can not allow this to continue," Dad booms across the sitting room. "These are obvious signs of dark magic. There is a sorcerer in our midst. The experiment must stop. Everyone should be sent back to their respective kingdoms." He sits in his chair next to Mom at the table, rubbing his furrowed brow. He's trying to play big bad dad with me, but I'm far too old to cower to it.

"I agree with your father, Killian. Things are getting out of hand. We could be on the brink of another war. The other kingdoms are ramping up their military activity in preparation." Mom looks pointedly at me. Of course, she is siding with Dad right now. Later, she's gonna hug me, and I'll know whose side she's really on.

"No. We can't show them that they have shaken us. It would show weakness to whoever is doing this." I pound my fist on the table in exasperation. We cannot fail this epically when things are going so well.

It's been over a week since the ball, and we are no closer to finding out who is responsible for the atrocities that attacked. We lost three good fae, and many others, including myself, were injured. Lyra hasn't come out of her room since the incident. Jade and Cat have been fighting, Cat wanting to go home and Jade wishing to stay. Ryker has been with them day and night, attempting to keep the peace and convince Cat to stay. I'd overheard their fight and Jade yelling; *I don't want to go back. I like who I am here. I'm so tired of hiding, not knowing how to fight back. I hate feeling weak. Maybe I can learn how to fight. At least a little. At least to defend myself. I'm not expecting to kill monsters. I just don't want to be helpless anymore.* Cat had asked her who would teach her, and she'd replied that I would, making my heart go all fuzzy. Of course, I'll teach her how to defend herself. Although I can't blame Cat for wanting to leave, a selfish part of me wants them to stay.

Mom takes a sip of her wine, trying to find a compromise between me and my father. We have been going over this day in and day out. Going over every detail with a fine-toothed comb and coming up with nothing. They've even met with the other kings and queens to see if they know anything and feel out who may be involved. "What if we at least stop the group activities that place everyone in the same room? If they are trying to target you, placing you all in the same area appears to be when they attack the most. It gives them higher odds of killing you." I see the concern across her brow as she places her hand on mine and squeezes. I know she just wants to keep me safe. I want to keep me safe, too. Dying would really suck.

"At this point, I guess you're right," I sigh. "Ending everything is just not an option. Our kingdom will die just like Shadow if we don't do this. We need the strengthened relationships with the other kingdoms that marriages would bring." If I bring this up, Dad must agree with me. This is our last hope. If we can't forge these alliances with the other kingdoms, we won't have enough people to defend our borders. If war is coming from Eneara, we are fucked.

Dad makes a noncommittal grunt. "That reminds me, Hyacinth returned to Tomarapos. The court is holding a memorial for Poppy today." He lowers his head, sadness plays across his features, and Mom wipes a tear from her cheek. "That said, Lyra did reach out to her father on our behalf to explain what happened to Arlin.

Thankfully, he does not hold us responsible but has doubled his efforts to find anything related to the dark magic we are dealing with."

Thank the Gods for that. I guess that is kind of good news. We were preparing ourselves for backlash while planning memorials on our end for everyone we lost. We waited days to find out if one of the other courts would attack us for what happened. They were supposed to be safe here. We've now doubled the guards, and they watch everyone like hawks. The only trusted people now are me, Rodan, and Warrick. We all have our suspicions, but there are so many people we hardly know where to begin. We can't even trust my parents' regular advisors now. Many of them are parents of the men here. Many advisors are also on the list since they reside in the castle.

So much for romance, I groan as I settle back in my seat.

"Warrick, what is the report on those not present at the ball at the time of the attack?" Dad folds his hands in front of him and looks at Warrick. Warrick moves away from the door and stands before Mom and Dad across the table.

"Sir, as you know, Owari and Yudoku were found out by the pond, bleeding out. It seems that the monster attacked them first. It emerged from the pond while they swam, but they managed to escape, thanks to Owari's piranhas buying them some time." Warrick clears his throat. "Sorrel says he was out in the garden with Calazar and Hyacinth. Seeing as Hyacinth didn't speak to anyone here before she left, and Calazar is missing, I can not confirm. As for Calazar, Sorrel says he walked off alone and didn't see where he went."

"And your guards?" Rodan asks, not looking up from the stack of documents before him, taking notes on everything.

"All were accounted for that night," Warrick states.

This is like a worst-case scenario: we have three fae dead and one missing. No one can account for him after he left the ballroom.

I don't know whether I should suspect him or worry that he got eaten.

Because of everything that has happened, Mom lifted the enchantment on Warrick so that he was as familiar with everyone as the rest of us. He was pretty pissed off when he found out Rodan and I knew the whole time, but he forgave me when I showed him what hot chocolate was, thanks to Jade's apt description. His sweet tooth is insatiable.

"None of this sits right with me," Dad grumbles. "You said Jade was making some headway with something?" He looks at me. I know he's humoring me, but like she totally was headed in a helpful direction. She is super savvy when it comes to research.

"Yeah, she was looking at records predating the war. She found a bunch of propaganda that the Sorcerers were telling people to get them on their side. She also found the documents listing all the people who were imprisoned and compared them to the birth records."

"What do birth records have to do with anything?" Rodan looks up at me.

"She said that there are children of the prisoners who are unaccounted for. They would have been in their teens and twenties back then."

"Why do we have Eneara's records?" Warrick asks.

Mom creases her brow in thought, all cute. "They were part of the accord. We share all records. Their books and ours are enchanted to have a twin in each other's libraries. That's why the records area is so vast. Ignorance may be bliss, but knowledge is power." Her eyes glow to make her point. Warrick's eyes grow big with understanding. Mom is so wise. "It's an interesting theory, Killian. She could be onto something if someone was overlooked. Please collect those books for me, as I'd like to see them for myself."

"No problem," I smile at her. I'm super proud of Jade for finding a lead.

Chapter 26
Jade

I hate running. I hate running with the fiery flames of hell. What in God's name had I been thinking? Every morning, Killian gets me up at fucking dawn to start my day with *a quick run around the castle to get the blood pumping*, he'd said. Then, off to the training field to lift weights, do core training, and balance work before offensive techniques. I am really beginning to regret asking him to train me.

Every muscle in my body hurts. I was shaking so badly I couldn't even lift a teapot yesterday. After a month of this, the running is getting easier, but my pace is slow. At least I don't feel like my lungs will explode today, maybe tomorrow. I follow the wall around the perimeter, chastising this fabulous idea as I approach the training area.

Cat is growling at Ryker as he flies around her. Undoubtedly, he got her up and dragged her out here before dawn as well. He shifts into his fae form and stalks up to her. "You can do this. Just focus," he growls at her as I run past to the weights, where Killian is leaning casually, waiting for me. Sweat glistens off his shirtless chest. Okay, that is a big perk to this. Those abs make me feel all kinds of ways.

"What did she turn into this time that's got them at it again? I thought she almost had it yesterday." I ask as I gulp down air and lie down on the mat. They can put my gravestone here because I'm never moving from this spot.

Killian snickers. "It was some sort of shark bird. Like an enormous bird, but it had shark teeth and a fin." He turns away, trying to hide his laugh as I grimace at the visual.

Poor Cat, every time she shifts, if she gets the littlest bit distracted, the animal gets messed up. She says she will focus on a cat, but at the last minute, a snake will pop into her head, then poof mutant creature.

I stand to move into the fighting stance he told me to begin in, muscles barking in protest. Killian pushes the stationary target forward. Today, I learn to throw punches at a target, or at least try to. This has been a very slow process since I was very out of shape when we started.

Killian stands beside me and guides my arm through the movement as he shows me how the rest of my body follows the motion. We work on the flow of it before he steps away and has me put some force behind it.

"Don't drop your elbow," he corrects. "Loosen up, or you'll hurt yourself." He comes behind me, pressing into my back and moving his body slowly, making mine mirror the movement. "Like this," he says low. "It's like a dance."

I have to fight the urge to lean into him. I want to collapse into his warmth. However, I asked for this, and he's taken time out of his morning every day to teach me. It's hard, but I feel stronger than I did before.

Things have been quiet since the ball, but Killian, Rodan, and Warrick have all been busy trying to find out who is responsible. I guess they all agreed that I'm not a threat. Killian told me the king is holding multiple councils every day. Each one has different groups, the idea being that the culprit is in one of the groups. Different information is passed to each group, with various vulnerabilities being presented as traps. So far, they've gotten nowhere, but it leaves almost all the guys pretty busy and all the ladies hanging out with each other instead. Later, I'll have lunch as usual with the girls.

"I'd like you to hit the target today." Killian cuts through my thoughts. "Just like we practiced, don't tuck your thumb in your hand." He smiles. "Step, step, jab. Go slow. Speed comes with practice."

Sure, no problem. I focus on each movement.

Step, step, jab. Stay balanced.

Step, step, jab. Don't drop your elbow. Okay, I'm ready. Next, hit the target.

Step, step, jab.

Concentrating on putting power into my punch, I throw my right fist hard at the target. It misses the mark that is still too far away. Fuck. I missed it by like five inches. It was right there. I groan.

"Did you just miss a stationary target?" Rodan's amused voice comes from behind me.

I drop my arms and turn, giving him an innocent look. "It moved." I shrug.

His eyebrow raises, and a smirk curves one side of his mouth. "It moved?" he grounds out. "Go back, reset. Do it again. I'll hold it still for you." He gives me a challenging look as he walks over and puts a hand on the shoulder of the dummy.

Damn it, why did he have to see that? I've barely seen him for the last month. I try to shake off the embarrassment as Killian gives me a warm smile. Running back through the motions, I get into position. I can do this.

Step, step, jab. I punch Rodan's hand and pull mine back, wincing in pain at the same time Rodan swears.

Oops.

Killian doubles over, laughing as Rodan shakes his hand, and I hold mine to my chest. Knuckles fucking hurt to punch.

"Missed again, Trouble." Rodan smirks.

"No, I hit my target," I say flippantly over my shoulder as I grab a glass of water, drinking it down greedily. I hear Rodan grumble something incoherent under Killian's laughter.

"I thought you were teaching her how to defend herself." Rodan turns to Killian.

"I am. The same way I was taught." Killian looks at him, confused.

"She's not gonna defend herself like that. Has she made any progress with magic?"

"No. No signs of it yet. So I was going through basic hand-to-hand and swords," Killian explains. So much for the theory that all fae have magic.

Rodan's face goes dark as he considers his words. "May I?"

Killian smiles. "Yeah, of course."

Rodan walks to the middle of the sparring mats and curls his finger for me to follow. I set down my water and move towards him. What fresh hell does he have planned? I ball my fists and try to stay calm.

"I think you need to learn how to get your opponent off of you and to the ground. So far, you've been learning offensive maneuvers. What you need is defensive," he says as he moves around me in a circle. He walks up behind me, wrapping an arm around my shoulders. "Get me off of you," he purrs in my ear. Sending heat through me. What if I don't want you off of me? Damn it, down girl. This is the biggest problem with training with these guys. Hormones come out to play more often than not.

I struggle in his grip and try to stomp on his feet, flailing my arms wildly, before I groan and slump. "You're too strong," I grumble.

"No, I'm not," he growls. "Grab my arm with your right hand." He guides my hand up and presses it into place. "Now quickly shift your weight, bending your left knee. While moving your hips to the right. Pull and use the momentum."

I do what he says, but stumble. He steps away and guides me through the movement. Stepping behind me, he presses into me and holds me again. "Get me off you," he purrs again.

Quickly, I run through the movements, grabbing his arm and throwing him with all my might onto the ground. I stare down at him in shock before I dance around, whooping in delight. I did it. I got him off me.

Rodan is suddenly on my back again, arm wrapped around my shoulders as he runs his other hand across my stomach in slow, tantalizing circles. His hand ever so slowly moving down. My breath hitches when he hits my bare stomach right above my pants.

A low growl rumbles through him. "Are you just gonna stand there, Trouble? Or are you going to stop me?"

Snapping out of my stupor, I kick into action and throw him down on the mat.

"Good girl. Again." He grins as he springs to his feet.

We do this another ten times before he sends me to the weights with Killian. I'm already shaking with exhaustion, and I still have strength training to do.

"When you're done, flip Killian a few times. I'll be back tomorrow to teach you more," Rodan says before striding away.

I grin at Killian as he moves the weight bar to the bench. "Thank you for making time for this. I know you've got a lot going on." I feel stronger already, thanks to him. Plus, I can finally swing a sword, albeit a small one, and make dents in the wooden targets. I'm not great at any of it, but I'm not entirely helpless anymore. Definitely no monster slaying in my future.

Lunch today is in the drawing room closest to the female wing of the palace. It's a beautiful room straight out of a Jane Austen novel. Everything is in pastel shades and light wood finishes.

Lyra smiles as Cat and I enter the room, our hair still wet from bathing. Lyra's spirits have been better for the last few days. Losing her best friend has taken a toll, though. She still has dark circles faintly dusting her under eyes, but the color has returned to her cheeks.

"Hello darlings, how was wrestlin' in the mud with the boys today?" She smiles as she pours a cup of tea from a tall metal kettle.

I sit in the chair across from her, draping my hair over the backrest, hoping the fireplace will help it dry. "I threw Rodan on his back, so it was pretty productive." I smirk as I reach for a teacup, cursing my wet hair as it slaps against my back again.

Cat picks up her teacup and takes a sip. "I tried to bite Ryker," she says, baring her teeth and snapping them. We all laugh at her antics. "But I'm still turning into mutants."

"You really should decide on an animal before you shift," I say.

"I know, but I can't commit. I always think of something better right before and become a weird abomination of both."

Lyra considers this. "Have you tried to mimic an animal that's in sight? Like Ryker when he's in falcon form? Or Killian when he's a wolf? Maybe if you oogle one of them, you won't lose focus."

"It's an idea. Although he may be the reason I keep losing focus," she sighs. She's still a little miffed with me about wanting to stay. She was given the option of going home, but didn't want to leave me here. I think the main reason she wanted to leave wasn't the attack. It was Ryker. He's gotten under her skin, and she's already broken all of her rules with him. The big one being: no more than three dates. She doesn't want to get attached. She wants to bail because she has feelings for him.

"Ya know that man ain't ever letting' ya slip his talons, sugar." Lyra gives her a soft smile. Cat groans and puts her face in her hands. Lyra shifts her attention over to me. "So, Rodan finally came out of hiding again? When are you gonna pull him and Killian into your hen pen?"

I almost spit out my tea. "What? I'm not. I am taking things slow with Killian. Rodan has made it very clear he's not interested." Even if his touch makes my body get all hot and flustered. His infuriating voice sends chills down my spine and makes me think about how it would feel to let him ravage me. Stop it. You can't daydream about Rodan when you are building something real with Killian.

Cat laughs. "Yep, that was so clear when he had his hand down your pants."

Lyra's eyes grow wide as she looks between us. "Hush your mouth. When did that happen?"

Cat snorts as she takes in the scathing look on my face. "At the beach, she got his electric treatment right before the dragon did."

"Who got an electric treatment?" Scarlette asks as she comes to sit next to Lyra. I feel all the blood rush to my face as Cat grins widely at me. "I feel like I'm missing something here."

Lyra turns to her, handing over a cup of tea. "Apparently, Jade had a romp with Rodan on the beach and didn't tell us." She lifts a brow towards me. "We're all adults here; no need to be so chaste about it."

"I didn't have a romp." I almost laugh at the term. "I lost my mind for a minute, and there was some heavy petting." Trying to make it sound less hot than it was. They all give me knowing smirks as I sink down into my chair.

"I thought you were dating Killian?" Corsac sits next to Scarlette, giving her a kiss on the forehead.

"I am. I think? I don't know. We are taking things slow. It's been over a month since he kissed me, so I have no idea what's happening," I say in exasperation. It was such a deliciously sweet kiss that left me wanting more.

"I think with Rodan, you have passion, hot, steamy passion. But Killian, you have something else, more sweet," Lyra considers, while I try to stay calm. I don't know why my love life is the topic of conversation. I don't know what to make of it myself. One wants to be with me but doesn't make a move, and the other avoids me like the plague, but it was like fireworks when he made a move.

"How are you two doing?" I look to Corsac and Scarlette, wanting a change of subject.

Scarlette smiles. "Well, Corsac's family has offered for me to move to Wilkno with them. I haven't exactly talked to my family yet. They were kind of expecting me to marry a prince." She blushes.

"I'll be your Prince Charming." Corsac nips at Scarlette's ear. They both giggle. "Any news on the curse?" She looks at me.

"Not since we talked to the Fates. No mentions of any special stones or anything else in any of the books I've looked at. I don't think they are any closer to finding a solution than they were before," I say, looking down at my tea.

"I still can't believe you went without me." Cat gives me a pointed stare.

"I know. I'm sorry. How many times can I say it?" I pout.

"Just a few more." Cat smirks, taking another sip of tea.

"Everything is all weird now. I was fixin' to make a decision on a man. Now they are too busy for lovin'," Lyra sighs, looking into the fire. "I feel as useless as moss on a boot without Arlin."

Cat and I crack a grin at each other. "Just ask one of them to have a late dinner with you. I'm sure they will say yes," I say.

"Bless your heart, darlin', I don't chase. A lady is meant to be wooed," she says, looking offended.

The doors to the parlor open, and trays of food on carts wheel in. The scent of chicken and rosemary fills the room. Scarlette looks over at it longingly before turning back to Lyra. "You do make a good point."

"Have the twins forgiven Edgar yet?" Cat asks no one in particular as she looks over at the food being placed on the table.

"For pissing himself and shoving them in front of him at the ball? No. Last I heard, they were making arrangements to go home."

Corsac pipes in with a smirk on her face. "I mean, I get not having a useful power in that situation and running, but to use the women you're dating as shields is just–yikes," she scrunches up her nose in distaste.

We all stand to make our way over to a table to eat. We spend the next hour eating and chatting. It's probably the most we've seen Lyra smile since Arlin died. I'm glad she's looking forward again. Maybe I'll tell Killian to pass a hint to Sorrel and Puck to ask her to dinner.

I walk towards the doors leading out to the pink garden. The beautiful day is the perfect setting to walk off some of the food I just ate. I'll go pick up some books from the library later.

The routine I've found myself in is strange. Working out in the mornings with Killian. Lunch with my friends in the afternoon and then researching with Cat. It's an odd sort of peace I've found here. I do wonder if, in time, they will send us back home or if we will find a place here among the fae. Lyra offered to let us stay in her kingdom if things don't work out here. So why go back? I'm sure I could arrange to see my family at some point. Or bug Warrick until he takes me.

I roam my way through the wooded path, enjoying the light that dances through the branches. The faint murmurs of voices as I approach the garden have me slowing my steps. I move to the side of the path and peek around a tree when I hear men talking. I spin around, pressing my back against the tree, heart hammering when I spot who's in the garden.

I've managed to avoid Bravos with the girls and Killian's help, making sure not to cross his path. But there he is with Hunter, Ellis, and Sorrel. I need to get away from here, perhaps go to the night garden.

"Isn't Killian after her?" Sorrel drawls.

"Jade is mine. I'll go to her soon, and no one will get in my way," Bravos boasts, stopping me in my tracks. What the hell is he talking about? Has he seriously not gotten the point? I've avoided him for weeks.

"Why do you even care about some half-breed?" Sorrel asks.

"She's exotic—that hair, that body. She's the best choice. And I deserve the best. Sure, she reads too much, but that will be the first thing to go. Like I said, that girl will be mine. I'll make her my wife," Bravos snaps. My heart is thundering in my chest. You have got to be kidding me. I swallow over the lump in my throat.

"Nothing good comes from that girl reading," Ellis grumbles. "I'd be glad to see someone put her on a leash. However, haven't you been fucking Beatrix?" he asks.

"Hasn't everyone?" Hunter pipes up.

"Exactly, my princess is untouched. She's been an intriguing hunt. I shall catch her, mount her, and mark her as mine." Bravos laughs. The world goes quiet around me, the roaring in my ears filtering everything out.

"She's too much of a prude if she hasn't spread her legs yet," Hunter quips, making my blood boil. What is wrong with these guys? My hands curl into fists as I heave air into my lungs.

"Oh, she will. She will be my little sex slave." My heart plummets as familiar words dance through my head. "She will be my wife. She will submit to me. She will cook and clean like a good little wife." No, no, not again. "She will have my babies and worship my cock every night like a good little slave, waiting on me hand and foot." I can barely hear him over my pulse pounding in my ears. "I'll own her." He laughs as I turn and stumble down the hill away from them, away from the castle.

The world closes in on me as I lose myself in the trees. Tears stream down my cheeks as his words fill my head. As memories flood my mind, I try to gulp down air, but it's no use as my throat closes. I run through the trees, my steps crunching through the brush. Blackness tunnels my blurry vision as I struggle to breathe.

You are my wife. I own you.

Not again.

Not again.

I stumble and collapse in a heap, curling my body over my knees and folding into a ball, hiccuping air, as the memory takes over.

The sun is setting, light shines through the window in the kitchen. I can smell the pot roast simmering in the crock-pot. Potatoes roll on boiling waves in the pot on the stove. Dinner is almost ready.

Doing one final wipe of the counters, the kitchen is clean; the sink is empty, and waiting for tonight's dishes. I'm so tired. I still need to shower and do laundry after dinner. My husband yells at the TV. He must be watching football. Ace is at least four shots into the bottle of vodka on the counter. I wish I could dump it down the drain.

As I finish mashing the potatoes, I take stock of the dishes I'll need to clean after we eat. Still, so much to do. Work was rough today; mandatory fourteen-hour shifts are going to kill me. Long days like this mean late dinners and even later bedtimes. I wish he'd help. But he says he works harder at work than I do, so it's only fair I do most of the housework. I used to fight him on it, but it's easier to give in. Fighting is worse.

He eats his dinner with a side of four more shots in front of the TV. I wish he didn't drink so much. "How was your day?"

"What, you actually care now?" he snaps.

"I always care." I blink at him in surprise.

"Well, it's not like you ever ask. I ask you every day. And every day it's bad. I try to help and fix the situation for you, and you still whine that it's stressful and bad." His idea of fixing things at work just makes things worse. I don't tell him anything anymore because last

time, he got me fired.

"Okay, well, I'm asking now."

"It wasn't great; there was a power outage, and the whole building was shut down for four hours. So I just had to sit there and do nothing; people would come in, and I'd have to turn them away. Does that sound fun to you? I was so bored, I just played games on my phone for half my shift."

"Sounds pretty bad. Sorry you had such a shit day." I pray for a power outage at work tomorrow. What a nice break that would be. One hour—that's all I ask.

Clearing the coffee table of our plates, I quickly run to the kitchen to rinse them and put them in the dishwasher. I get the laundry started a few minutes later, and now I can shower. Finally, five minutes of peace.

The water is scalding hot in the best way, as I relax under the spray. It's amazing how good a shower can make you feel. Just melt away the world and listen to the water.

The shower door flies open, and Ace jumps in. "Ah, why is it so hot!" he yells while he reaches for the knob, turning it down till it feels cool against my hot skin. Fuck my life. He runs his hand up my thigh while grabbing a handful of my breast. I sigh, but it doesn't come out as a contented sigh; no, it's exasperated. Shit, I'm too tired to even fake it.

"Seriously!" he shrieks at me. "All I did was touch you! I thought it would be romantic," he rants as he gets out of the shower. "You're never in the fucking mood anymore. You're always too tired or too stressed. What about what I need!"

Giving up on my shower, I turn off the water and grab a towel, wrapping it around myself. "I've been working twelve to fourteen hours a day for three weeks. Of course, I'm tired. I was just trying to take a shower," I try to defend myself.

"And I was just trying to make love to my wife." He storms into the bedroom, picks up his Bible from his nightstand, and flips pages.

Fuck me, I don't care what your book says, I'm positive you're probably interpreting it just to suit your needs. "Look," he stops on a page and jabs his finger at a line. I just stare at him. "It says right here the wife's body belongs to the husband." He slams the book shut and throws it on the floor. That's probably sacrilegious, but I'm not about to point it out. "You belong to me. Your body belongs to me. We had a verbal contract. You said we'd have sex every night." I said no such thing. "Every night!" He punches the wall to punctuate his statement. My heart is hammering out of my chest. I was trying to avoid a fight. Trying so hard. And now I can't think straight; he's talking so fast, and I've missed half of what he's said. "Because you always complain that you are sore the next day. Well, if we had sex more often, your body would mold to the shape of mine, and you wouldn't get sore."

"That's not how the female body works." What the actual fuck?

"I read about it; shit, I know more about your body than you do!" he screams.

"Then your book is wrong because vaginas do not just mold to fit over time. You have to be relaxed and use lube, and chances are it's still gonna be sore the next day!" Ok, I'm losing my shit because seriously? What planet does he live on?

"We had a verbal contract!" He punches the wall again.

"I swear if you put a hole in the wall..."

He cuts me off. "What? What's gonna happen if I punch a hole?" He punches the wall harder and harder. Then he turns and walks over to me. Getting right in my face, "Nothing," he growls as I lean back, trying to avoid his ire. "Because that's all you do—nothing. But you will submit to me and be the good little slave you promised me," he growls, and then he tears the towel away from my body. Grabs my hips and flips me over, my face in the bed. No, no, wait, no! But I can't fight. I'm frozen with fear. My body has stopped responding. He kicks my legs apart, and my mind fades to black. Nothing to see here.

They say everyone has a primal instinct of fight or flight. What *they always leave out is freeze.*

Crack.

"No, no, no," I wail, trying to distance myself from this reality. It's all happening again. I'm trapped. I can't get away. There will be no escape this time.

"Who hurt you?" A gentle but gruff voice comes from behind me. I jump at the sudden voice, but I'm frozen in fear. I'm alone in the woods. Oh god, what have I done? "You're shaking. Please tell me what happened." A gentle hand cups my shoulder and unfolds me from my knees.

"Please, no. Don't, please," I beg before a finger lifts my chin, forcing me to meet his eyes.

Rodan is kneeling before me, his face a mixture of anger and worry. "I won't hurt you," he whispers, face soft with concern.

I let out a sob and lunge my arms around his neck. He pauses briefly before sinking to the ground and pulling me into his lap. "Breathe." He pets small circles on my back. "Gods, you're shaking. Please breathe, Trouble."

I'm so deep in panic, my head is fuzzy. "I can't do this, not again...not again. Please help me," I sob out against his chest.

"Trouble, deep breath, look around, what do you see?" he coaxes.

"I can't see anything with my face buried in your chest," I mumble into him.

He lets out a huff of a laugh. "Please turn and look."

I slowly do as he says, laying my head on his chest. "I see trees." Tall, beautiful green trees surround us as we sit on golden pine needles in a small clearing beneath the branches.

"And what do you hear?"

Trying to filter through the pulse hammering in my ears, I listen. "I can hear your heartbeat; it's beating really fast." I breathe as he stiffens. I close my eyes and listen to the thump, thump, thump of his heart.

"And what do you feel?"

Your arms. Your warmth, every hard plane of your chest as you breathe, "Umm, you. Warm."

"What do you smell?"

You. I take a deep breath. "I smell pine and dirt and...you." I breathe in that ozone smell, the calm of the rain washing over me. How can someone smell like the air before rain?

"Can you breathe again?"

Yes, I'm no longer spiraling and hyperventilating. I slowly nod my head. Somehow, he's helped me come back to myself. I know the technique, but I find it difficult when I'm that far gone. "How did you learn to do that?"

He hesitates for a moment. "The woman who raised me a long time ago. I was afraid of a lot as a child," he mumbles. He was afraid? "Can you tell me what happened?" He tips my chin up to look into my eyes. "Please, let me help."

"I just had a panic attack." I sniffle. He doesn't need to be burdened with my problems.

"Do you get them a lot?" he asks, continuing to rub my back.

"Sometimes, I used to get them a lot before I came here. This is the first time my past has returned to haunt me so badly," I sigh, feeling the rise and fall of his chest.

"Who hurt you, Trouble?" he coaxes again.

"Someone said they owned me, and I'd be their sex slave. I...I thought...he'd given up. I thought things would be different." He gently wipes the tears from my cheeks that fall with the admission. When I look up at him, I'm surprised to see anger painted on his face.

"Who said it?" he growls low.

"Which time?" I drawl sarcastically, laying my head back on his chest, listening to the thump, thump of his heart. Honestly, I never thought I'd be cradled in this man's lap, let alone be content to do so.

"Tell me all of it, everyone who's said that to you," he growls.

"Why do you care?"

"Tell me," he pleads gently.

So I do. I tell him every sordid detail about what Bravos has done since I got here, leading up to my panic attack. My voice cracks, and I feel his stare on me the longer I talk. I don't know how well he knows Bravos, but the incident in the hallway makes him tense. My pulse quickens as I recall the terror that pulsed through my veins. Then I dive into the memories he triggered and the fight with my ex. I tell him everything. I sob as I relay the memory and all it entailed. Tears stream down my face as I let out my secret shame to the man who holds me.

He listens intently and wipes away my tears as they run down my cheeks. I don't know why I'm telling him this. Maybe I want him to understand why I reacted like I did. Maybe I needed someone to understand. Maybe it's simply that at this moment, I feel safer than I've felt in a long time. Maybe after all this time, I couldn't keep it bottled up anymore. Maybe I wanted someone to know. But now I feel vulnerable in a different way, and I'm wondering if I should have kept my mouth shut.

"Fucking Bravos, of course, that asshole would say something that depraved. I should kill him for putting a finger on you. I'm so sorry he brought up such terrible memories," he growls. "I don't know how you withstood being married to someone like that for so long. How could a man do that to his wife?" he pauses, taking a deep breath. "Please tell me that ex-husband is now six feet under."

"Unfortunately, no, but he also can't get me here. So, silver lining of being kidnapped by fae, I guess," I huff a laugh. He flexes his arms tighter around me and rests his head on mine. I snuggle into his warmth, breathing in his scent, letting the calm flow into me.

"If I ever get the chance, I'll make him suffer greatly before I kill him. Men like him don't deserve a quick end. He's why you didn't want to go back," he muses.

"That's why I didn't want to go back," I confirm, nodding.

"I know I asked, but why would you tell me all this? It's not like I've given you any reason to trust me," he murmurs.

"Because you already think I'm weak and pathetic, at this point, I don't care if you know just how right you are."

"That doesn't show me you're weak. It shows me you're a lot stronger than I realized. Showing vulnerability is a strength. You are not weak, Trouble. You get up every day and say fuck you to the world that's hurt you. You might break down occasionally, but you always pick yourself back up and try again." He pulls me in tighter.

"I'm broken," I choke out.

"Aren't we all?" he sighs.

The birds are chirping, and the forest feels alive around me. I'm not sure how long we've sat here like this in silence. How long have I sat here listening to his breathing and the forest? "Thank you," I murmur.

He sighs and shifts underneath me. "For what?"

"For coming and saving me from my panic attack. For listening." He grunts in response. "I know you're not fond of me, but I appreciate it all the same. I usually have to sleep it off, or I'll be a mess all day," I say softly, trying to hide my embarrassment at the admission.

"We should probably head back. I'm sure people are looking for us by now. I'll tell Killian to keep Bravos as far from you as possible," he says as he lifts his head from mine, giving me the signal I should get up.

"Okay." I guess we are back where we started. I probably gave him even more reason to want nothing to do with me. But I'm grateful he was here today, that I wasn't alone.

Chapter 27
Killian

Jade is curled up in a chair by the fire, looking cozy with a blanket and Pop on her lap. She lazily strokes his head as she reads the book she's propped on the armrest. I watch her over my book, content to be near her. She's so cute, and I love that Pop has taken a liking to her. He's such a good judge of character.

Rodan told me what Bravos said about her. He looked murderous as electricity crackled all over him. I don't know that I've ever seen him so angry. Jade must have been badly shaken. I knew Bravos was bad news when he gave her that necklace, but now I'm worried. Do I place a guard on her at all times? Should I sleep in her room? No, that would be inappropriate, and I don't know that I could keep my hands to myself. I'm at a loss for how to keep her safe. She's gotten under my skin, and I want to keep her there.

I peer over my book again as she tucks a strand of hair behind her ear, exposing the long column of her neck. I want to lick it. I want to lick every square inch of her body. I stifle a groan as I shake my head. I need to be a gentleman and take things slow. The fates told me to take things slow, and I will not go against their advice. I kissed her way too early, and now I need to wait an appropriate amount of time. I will build my friendship with her and wait for the sparks to fly. I grin behind my book as I think about my perfect plan. I get butterflies just thinking about it. The beast never rushed beauty, and I don't plan on it either.

Training her in the mornings has been torture. Sometimes when she's running, I want to chase her and ravage her right there on the path. The idea gets me so hard that I usually run ahead so she won't see. However, after the run, she's all sweaty, and I watch the drops run over her toned body. Every curve of hers is getting tighter with the exercise. My mind returns to thoughts of licking her all over again.

Damn it.

I look at the book in my hands, flipping through, trying to find any mention of the curse on Shadow. If we can figure out who cursed Shadow, we can get somewhere. Although my parents have been trying to find answers for decades, I'm not sure if there is anything new to discover. It's been weeks, and there haven't been any more attacks, and no new leads.

Ellis has been in his quarters more and more, buried in books. Sorrel has stated multiple times that the endeavor is pointless. Some of the men are getting frustrated and want to return to normal, tired of not having time to court the ladies. Oberon has been staying in Maysant's room, so I guess they figured out a workaround for the men being busy. Honestly, Mom has been giving out random tasks to all the councilors, lords, and dukes to see what they will do. I think she's running out of ideas, though. It has been a quiet month. Talks of resuming the courtship activities have begun.

I look up as I hear someone approaching. Rodan strolls into the room and stops as he looks at Jade and me. He tips his chin to me and walks over to Jade as I close my book.

He pulls a small velvet pouch from his pocket and tosses it onto Jade's lap. She looks down in confusion, mirroring my own.

"What's this?" She looks up at him. I lean forward, my interest piqued.

"It's to spice up your books." He smirks and winks at her before striding away through the stacks again.

Huh?

The look on her face says she's as confused as I am. She looks down at the pouch and picks it up. Her eyes grow wide, and then she laughs. It's a musical sound. She's laughing so hard she has tears glistening in her eyes.

"What? What is it?" I am so lost. I want to know what the joke is.

"That pain in the ass." She giggles. "He knew this wasn't what I meant." She looks down at the bag again as she tries to compose herself, but devolves into more giggles. "It's cinnamon," she takes a shaky breath. "I made a joke weeks ago about spicy books. He knew this wasn't what I meant." She puts the little bag down on the table and continues reading her book. Looking up occasionally and smiling at me.

About an hour ago, she put down the record book she was looking through and picked up one of Mom's mortal romance books. There's a whole section of them in the library. Warrick brings them back for her, along with newspapers from the mortal realm. I think the one Jade is reading is pretty heavy on the sex. Occasionally, her jaw drops, and she flushes as a small smile spreads across her face.

"It's nice to see you smile, Emerald. I miss that sometimes. You are captivating."

She flushes red as I watch her. I'm half tempted to throw all my gentlemanly rules out the window as she bites her lower lip. No, Killian. She had a bad day, and you don't get to throw away all you've been building to jump her in the library. Women like to be romanced. They don't want guys barking up their skirts. Keep it in your pants.

Pop jumps off her lap in a huff as she pushes the blanket off.

She slowly stands and walks over to me as I set my book on the small table beside me. I look up at her, unsure of what she's doing. She bends down, putting her hand on the backrest of my chair, making my breath catch as her sugary scent wafts over me. She picks up her skirt, moves onto my lap, and straddles me. My heart goes haywire as my dick comes to attention.

"I don't feel like reading anymore." She bites her lip as she settles into my lap. I grip the chair as I try to keep myself under control. "I've been waiting for you to kiss me again," she breathes. Am I dreaming? My breath becomes shallow as I try to keep control of myself.

"A gentleman doesn't rush things," I grumble.

"What if I don't want a gentleman?" She says in a low voice, a hair's breadth from my lips.

Fuck.

I run my hand down her side, digging my fingers into her hip as she grinds down on my dick. A growl escapes me as my other hand wraps around the back of her neck, keeping her from moving.

"You don't know what you ask, my lady," I growl.

She groans in response, and I lose control, pulling her into me as I kiss her. My wolf surfaces as the need to claim her overtakes me. I deepen the kiss, sliding my tongue through her lips and tasting her. She moans as my hand slides up her side, and I run my thumb over the thin material covering her breast. Her nipple peaks under the fabric as she rocks her hips, grinding down into me.

I pull her in tight as I shift her so I can reach her neck and slowly lick and kiss down to her collarbone. Her breath catches as I roll my hips beneath her. My need to claim her as mine drives me. Her hands run down my chest, eliciting another growl from deep within my chest, my desire to be inside of her growing. She shifts her weight, and her hand strokes over my length, desperate to be free of my pants. My body quakes under her touch.

"Should we go somewhere more private?" she whispers in my

ear before nipping it.

I stare at her, trying to comprehend her words as reality floods in. I am going to regret this, but I don't want to just be a distraction. "We should stop," I groan out through clenched teeth. "You've had a long day, and I don't want you to do something you might regret." I am an idiot. Prince Blue Balls at your service, my lady.

She stares at me and slumps over, resting her forehead on my shoulder. "Did I misread you?" she murmurs.

I huff a miserable laugh. "Not at all. Trust me, I want you. But I want it to be at the right time."

"You, good sir, are a tease," she mumbles against me.

"I don't want to rush things," I say, lifting her back up to look at me. "Plus, I don't think you are ready. When I have you, I'll want to claim you." I give her a serious look as she pouts. "When a wolf claims a mate, it can be intense. I need you to be sure about me."

She scrunches her brow in thought. "So...you can't have sex with me for fun? It's like an all-or-nothing situation?"

"Not with you." I look down, a little embarrassed. "I don't think I could control myself." I run my hand over her cheek and down her neck. "I've never felt the need to claim like this. It's why I've been taking things so slow. I don't trust myself, and you need to have the choice."

"If you claim me, is it like permanent?"

I gaze deep into her eyes. "Wolves mate for life. If I mark you as mine, there is no going back. Please give me a chance to prove to you that it will be worth it. Try not to think about it. Let's keep doing what we are doing and let me earn your heart."

She offers me a soft smile as she leans in and bestows a gentle kiss. "You are too sweet," she sighs as she turns and repositions herself in my lap, curling up against me as I hold her in my arms. "So no funny business because wolfy-boy can't control himself," she snickers.

I look down at her, smile, and shrug. I hope one day she will be my mate. I can feel myself falling for her a little every day. There is a tug in my chest that I can't ignore when I'm around her. I'm hoping someday she'll be open to it. It's gonna be a long night thinking about her, though. Because I wish I'd just buried myself balls deep in her and risked losing control.

Chapter 28
Jade

I wake to the bed shifting and crack my eyes open to see if it's Void. Although I usually don't feel him crawl into my bed, I only know he's been there if I wake up in the middle of the night. Otherwise, he steals in and out of my room like a ghost, leaving no trace. Void isn't beside me, though. The bed shifts again, and I feel weight near my ankles.

A figure leans over my legs at the foot of the bed, causing my heart to leap.

Killian?

"Decided you couldn't wait?" I say tentatively, still groggy from sleep.

"I'm tired of waiting, Princess." A low growl fills the darkness as the blanket recedes from my body. An icy chill takes my breath away.

Oh god.

Nonononono.

Bravos.

I dive out of the bed, sliding onto the floor, catching my fall with my hands, and kicking the blankets from around my ankles. Scrambling, I try to stand and stumble for the door. My shoulder hits the nightstand in the dark, and my water glass crashes to the floor.

"Enough of these games, Princess. I've waited long enough for you," he growls.

He's too fast and has me around the waist in seconds.

"You don't seem to understand, Princess. You are mine, and tonight, I finally get what I want," he growls, holding me tight against his chest. "I grow tired of the suspense."

Not again.

I feel my soul fracture as memories flood my mind.

"I'm tired of waiting. At this rate, you'll never be ready," Bradley sneers. I beg him to stop, but he pins me down. I thought we were in love. I thought he'd always take care of me. You were my first love.
Crack.

"Let go!" I scream as I pound against his chest. Memories of my past pour through me.

He grabs my sleeve and rips my nightgown. I hear it tear down my back as the cool air kisses my skin. I shriek in fear as I reach up and punch him as hard as I can in the jaw, sending a shockwave of pain through my hand. He goes rigid as he stares down at me.

Not again.

Ace slams me up against the car in the garage. I wasn't expecting it. "This is gonna be so hot," he whispers in my ear as he kicks my legs apart and pulls down my pants. No, please stop. Not again.
Crack.

Bravos drops the torn fabric as I push away, only getting a step back before his hand slaps across my face, and he pulls me in again. The sting of his palm radiates through my cheek. His arm is an iron bar across my back, caging me in. I scream in defiance as tears coat my face. I work tirelessly to get free of his hold, panic taking over.

Not again.

Theo said to come over, but he's not answering his door. We are gonna miss our dinner reservation. What if something happened to him? I creak open the door and see him passed out on the couch. I know we've only been out once before, but I doubt he fell asleep on purpose. I walk over and slowly nudge him. He reaches out and pulls me down onto the couch forcefully. He's on top of me before I can react. This is my fault. I should have left. I never should have entered his apartment.

Crack.

My cheek stings with pain as I struggle against him. He rips the top of my nightgown from my neck, exposing my breasts as I frantically try to push him away. The tatters of the gown fall around me as he gropes my chest. He leans in to try to kiss me, but I turn my head and scream again as I fight. He holds me tight as he reaches between us and undoes his belt and pants. Nononono.

"You cheated on me!" Ace roars. No, no, I didn't. I wouldn't. "You know what, it's fine. You did what you had to do, and I did what I had to." He pushes me down—an angry glint in his eye.

Crack.

Not again.
Not again.
There has to be a way out of this. I can't do this again.

I wake with my head pounding in a bedroom I don't recognize. Trying to remember what happened, I'm assaulted with flashes of being out drinking and getting really dizzy. Then, waking up to a strange guy on top of me with a poster on the ceiling of a half-naked girl. I look up to see that poster staring down at me. "Looks like the drug wore off, and here I was hoping for a round three," a gruff voice says behind me. A hand snakes around my waist from behind, pinning me to the bed.

Crack.

No. Not again!

Focusing on being small and feeling the telltale tingles as I shrink into my otter form, falling from his arms as he scrambles to catch me. He roars in frustration. I fall to the ground with a thud, knocking the air from my lungs as I hurry to right myself and run under the bed. My body aches from the fall. I limp as I move under the cover, trying to catch my breath.

"Change back!" he booms, lifting the mattress and throwing it onto the floor. "Change back, you bitch!"

I make a run for the door, hoping I can change back and open it before he catches me. A sharp, searing pain erupts from my leg, only a few feet from the bed. I collapse onto the floor and look at my bleeding leg in horror. A knife juts out of it as blood pools on the floor. My vision goes blurry as the room begins to spin.

In agony, I pull myself back into the corner, trying to keep my weight off my leg as I feel my body change back to normal. There's a knife sticking out of my thigh, and my nightgown is in shreds around me as I cower in the corner. I stare up in terror at Bravos. He threw a dagger at me. I can't run. There is so much blood. Hot tears run down my cheeks as hopelessness fills me.

"Now look at what you made me do," he sneers.

"Stay away from me," I croak out.

He paces back and forth, snarling, "You just had to make it difficult, Princess," he spits.

A loud bang sounds from across the room. I jump, my heart thundering as I try not to lose consciousness. The world is growing cold around me. I shiver, but I don't know if it's from fear or the cold air licking my skin.

A loud snarl pulls my attention as Void appears in front of me. He snarls again, and his hackles rise as he puts himself between Bravos and me. Shadows fill the air, circling around the giant cat, whipping around like tendrils of night.

Crouching before me, Void is enveloped in the shadows, and out of the darkness, Rodan walks out.

Chapter 29
Rodan

"What the fuck do you think you are doing?" I growl at Bravos, taking in the scene around me.

Trouble is on the floor, bleeding out, and half-naked. Blood pools around her leg, and I can see the streak of it across the floor. He must have hit something vital, for how much blood there is. The one night, I was late getting to her. I should have been with her hours ago.

Rage fills me.

The world is in shades of red.

"This isn't your fight, asshole. She's mine. I was just reminding her of that," he growls back at me, taking a step towards her.

I clench my fists as he steps forward, obviously oblivious of who I am. No matter, I'll remind him so that he knows who stands before him before he dies. I surge my power out at him, winding it around the walls of his mind and lifting the memory block. He screams and clutches his head as the wall falls. I could have been gentle, but this monster doesn't deserve nice.

He sneers at me as he straightens; recognition fills his gaze. "If it isn't the bastard son of the king himself." Of course, that is what he knows about me. No one knows the truth of who I really am except the king himself.

"Close enough." I sneer. "You will never lay another finger on her."

He takes another step forward. "This doesn't involve you," he growls.

"Oh, it most certainly does, seeing as how she's—*my mate*," I snarl as I launch my shadows towards him. He flies across the room with a look of shock on his face. Slamming into the wall before horror crosses his features. I guess he didn't notice the shadows in the dark. A grim satisfaction courses through me. I no longer have to hold back. The cat is out of the bag.

"Shadows," he whispers, "Impossible. The shadow wielders are dead." He stares in disbelief at the tendrils whipping around him as he stands.

"Not all of them." A dark grin spreads across my face. "But for what you've done, you soon will be." My shadows close in on him as he gives a roar of defiance. They encompass him, immobilizing his arms and pulling him to his knees. "I want you to look into the eyes of your mortality. Know who ended your sorry excuse for a life," I growl as I stalk closer. "I am Death, and I've come to reap your soul."

"No. Please. I'm sorry. I didn't know. I didn't know," he begs, panic falling over him as my shadows squeeze. I bet she begged. I bet she cried, and you showed her no mercy.

I look behind me at Trouble, who is crying silently on the verge of passing out. Frost is crawling up the walls and creeping out across the floor around her. The white glints in the pale moonlight, the air growing colder. I can see her slow breaths billow in the air. Not good. Not good at all.

A low growl radiates through my chest as I turn back to the scumbag in my shadows. His eyes are wide as he takes in the state of her. I'm done with this man in front of me. I'm done pretending that he's not a threat. He touched what belongs to me, and I will make sure he pays the price for it.

I slowly push my magic forward, reaching into his mind and snagging hold of the electricity flowing through his body. Every electrical impulse fights my control as I collect them. One by one, I start to pull. The electricity within the body is fascinating. All those impulses relayed through the brain and down through the spine to every part of a person's body.

I can control them all.

He screams in agony as I push through the shields of his mind, cutting off his ability to see. Next, his hearing—our conversation is done anyway. I tug the following line and feel when his body goes limp within my shadows' hold, unable to hold himself up anymore. This would be an excellent place to leave him. Paralyzed, blind, and deaf. It wouldn't be much of a life—a terrible fate, really. This is where I would leave him if he hadn't thrown a dagger at her.

The world is still red, my rage not sated.

It's not enough.

With a snarl, I stop every electrical impulse at once. I watch as my shadows recede and drop him in a heap on the floor. He's not just brain-dead. I stopped every function of his body. Not even the most skilled of healers could bring him back. No one ever thinks about what would happen if all the electricity were removed from a body at once. If I had wanted it to be quick, I could have done it. I didn't even need the shadows to hold him. I didn't want it to be quick, though. I wanted him to suffer. I would have stretched it out over hours if I had the time.

I quickly turn and go to Trouble. Half of the room is now covered in a thin layer of frost as the temperature drops.

Fuck.

I need to get her out of here. I need to heal her.

I just killed a lord's son in the castle.

Fuckfuckfuck.

I reach down to scoop her up, wincing at the cold. Her breath has gone shallow, and her eyes glassy. The steady stream of blood continues to pour from her leg.

"Hold on, Trouble," I murmur to her as my shadows surround us, glimmering with blue light, and I walk through with her in my arms.

The shadows recede as I walk out into the outpost of the Dracomore Mountains. I quickly take Trouble over to the cot in the corner and pull away the scraps of her nightdress around her leg. A dagger juts out of her leg, thankfully slowing the bleeding, but in deep. Thank the Gods she's passed out because this is going to hurt. I pull the knife out, swearing at the length of it. I'd kill Bravos all over again for this.

Pressing my hand to the wound, light fills the dark room. Magic weaves the muscles of her leg back together while the walls of her artery are rebuilt. I run a check over the bone and mend the gash I can feel there. Grateful for all the time I put into learning how to heal. It's not long before a light pink line is all that mars her flesh.

Frost seeps out from underneath her on the cot. She shivers as the frost continues to crawl up the walls around her. Her lips turn blue as she shivers on the small bed. Her breath still comes out ragged.

Damn it. Hold on, Trouble.

I turn to the fireplace and arrange wood in the small stone structure. Thankfully, I've kept this outpost stocked. A warm glow illuminates the space as the fire takes the logs. I walk over to the chest on the other side of the room and pull out a thick blanket. It's got a few holes from years of use and neglect, but it will have to do. I put the blanket over her and pull the cot towards the fire. I've got to get her to warm up.

As the frost creeps along the blanket, my heart drops. "Oh, Trouble, what a time to manifest your powers." I scrub my hand over my face, then lean over her, cupping her face in my palm. "Trouble, I need you to wake up."

She moans, and her eyelashes flutter. "Not again," she mumbles. "Please stop."

Fuck.

I groan as I look down at her. She's not waking up, and her mind is trapped somewhere bad. I can't let her power keep leaking out of her like this. We will both freeze to death if I don't do something. Killian's power would be helpful right now, but I can't go back for him and risk her.

Mind made up, I strip off my shirt and pants, leaving only my underwear on. I slowly lower myself onto the cot, pulling Trouble on top of me and the blanket over us. The shock of her cold skin is almost painful. This was a dumb idea. She's gonna freeze me to death. Fuck, it's like cuddling an ice block.

I methodically draw circles over her back, trying to get the tension to lessen. I'm sure I'm minutes away from frostbite or hypothermia, but I continue to hold her. Finally, the frost recedes from the cot as the heat of the fire warms the air. Her breathing has gone even as her skin warms to mine. I breathe out a sigh of relief as my own body begins to warm again. I hope she doesn't hate me when she wakes up half-naked on me.

As I lay there, the story the old crone told me floats through my mind. The memories are clear as day once again, as if a lock had been broken. Pieces fitting together from the things that Trouble had told me earlier. I think that was her life I saw. That feeling of hopelessness lodges in my chest as I look down at this magnificent creature. It's time to come clean. It's time to face my fate. She doesn't deserve another tragedy in her life.

Chapter 30
Jade

Things are going well. I've finally got everything in order. My routine with cleaning and cooking, my job, my marriage. I'm finally in a place where I've worked it all out. I haven't even been fighting with Ace as much. I've compromised on the sex. While it's not what he wants, it's often enough that he doesn't start fights over it anymore. And he's promised to stop counting how many times a year we have sex. Overall, I think everything is improving.

I smile as I plate up my dinner. Okay, this, I really don't want to eat. I'm so sick of steak and potatoes, I could cry. But I'm starving, and it's late. I sit down to eat dinner, but Ace is still in the bathroom. It's been almost an hour, and I don't want my dinner to get cold again. So I start eating. I'll eat, clean up, and then take a shower and let him have his quickie before bed. It's the only way.

He enters the room and begins eating. No words, I guess we'll just eat in silence. It's not the first time. Last year, we didn't speak for six months.

"Can we talk?"

"Of course." My heart rate is going up. I'm struggling to swallow, so I put down my fork and give him my full attention.

"Things have been going really well for the last few months, and I'm really happy about that." His eyes flick away from mine.

"Me too." I try to give a soft smile, but I know the ball's about to drop.

He looks really uncomfortable. I'm not sure what to think. He's fidgeting and shaking his knee up and down. What the hell is going on? Is he nervous? He takes a deep breath while I hold mine with a smile. "I love you, but I don't know if I'm in love with you."

My smile slowly falls away. What? What does that mean? I nod as I have no idea how to respond. He gets up and picks up his plate, looking at me mournfully. I don't understand. What does this mean? I sit there dumbfounded. "We can talk more tomorrow after you've had some time. Good night." And he's walking away.

I look at my half-finished dinner. I guess I should finish eating. Chew, focus. Why do I feel numb? I feel nothing. Text Cat—maybe she can help me understand. Did he just break up with me? Is this how a person ends a marriage?

Crack

A tear slips down my cheek as I come out of sleep. It feels like I've been hit with a freight train. Every lousy memory is so fresh in my mind, so close to the surface, that I feel exhausted. My body hurts, and my head is killing me. I try to shift my weight only to feel skin beneath me. My arms curled up along someone's chest.

Who?

What?

Bravos flashes through my mind, holding me, tearing my clothes off, throwing a knife into my leg. My heart starts hammering in my chest as I suck in a breath.

"Shhh, calm down, Trouble. You're okay." Rodan's calm voice washes over me as my heart stops. He has one arm draped over my back and brings the other to my face, brushing a lock of hair behind my ear. "You were gonna freeze us both to death if I didn't warm you up. I promise I didn't do anything to you."

"How would I have frozen us? You mean it was so cold that we needed body heat to stay warm?" My body tenses as I realize I'm practically naked under the blanket.

"Not exactly. Apparently, you wield frost, and it decided to leak out of you last night while you were passed out. I didn't know what to do or how to make it stop," his voice is uncertain, pained. "All I could think to do was warm you up and hope you didn't freeze me."

Oh, my god.

"Great, I'm a fucking cartoon princess. My mom always called me the ice queen, but that was because I didn't cry at all her sappy movies." I bury my face in his chest. He silently laughs, his chest bouncing under my nose. He's so warm, and I take in a lungful of his ozone scent.

"Wait—where are we?" I snap my head up, looking at the small, dusty room. "What happened? My leg—Void. What the hell happened last night?" I push up to look at Rodan, who still has his eyes closed.

He pulls me down against him and wraps his arms around me. "Your leg is fine. I healed it. You'd be in a world of pain if I hadn't," he sighs. "Bravos is dead. I shadow-walked us to the Dracomore Mountains. We are in an abandoned outpost on the border of Shadow and Amara."

My eyes grow wide as he talks, his tone lazy and matter-of-fact. I try to remember more of what happened, but everything goes hazy after—Void "You—turned, Void. Oh my god, you are Void." I try to push up off of him as realization hits me. "You've been sleeping in my bed this whole time?" I growl in outrage at him as he holds me firmly in place.

He cracks an eye open, looking down at me, with a slight tilt to his mouth. "Someone had to look after you, Trouble."

"But I–Oh god, I spilled my guts to that stupid cat," I groan and bury my face in his chest again, mortification flooding my veins.

"I know," he chuckles.

I elbow him in the side, cutting off his snickering.

"Careful, Trouble," he growls with an edge of amusement.

"Why?" I croak, unable to look at him.

"Why, what?"

"Why did you sleep in my room every night as a cat?" I ask.

He takes a deep breath. "Because on your first date with Bravos, he gave you a necklace. It was a collar meant to control and claim you. Killian had to melt it off of you." His body tenses. "I was afraid that he would try something while you were asleep, so I started sneaking into your room every night and leaving before you woke. As a panther, I figured you would be less freaked out." He runs his hand in slow circles on my back again.

I rest my head on his chest again, listening to his heartbeat. "Why?"

"Why did you wake up crying every night?" he growls.

"Don't change the subject, and you know why. Void. I told you all about my nightmares and fears and—how I was feeling about being here," I growl back. I try again to push up off of him, but he tightens his hold. It's a half-hearted attempt, and the warm touch of him stroking my back melts me. "Why?"

His body is tense beneath me before he sighs. He draws the blanket over my shoulders as he sits up, scooping me up and setting me next to him. He tugs the blanket more firmly around me, covering my exposed body. I miss his warmth immediately, but don't protest. I pushed him too far, and now I'll deal with it.

He stands. I didn't realize that he was almost naked, as I take in the sight of him in nothing but shorts. He moves in front of me before kneeling and placing his hands on my knees. "Because I don't hate you. I can't stay away from you. You infuriate me. At every turn, I find I can't ignore you. You research your way into understanding my world that I never thought you belonged in. Yet here you are, carving your way into it. Forging your path forward like you were always meant to be here. I fought the pull I felt for you, but you intoxicate my senses. I'm drawn to your orbit, and your fire just intensifies it. The more I fought you, the more you pushed back, the less control I felt. I see eternity in your eyes. I've waged a losing battle with fate from the moment I made eye contact with you. I knew who you were; I knew, and it scared me. Jade, I did it because you're my mate."

"What?" I breathe as I remember him saying the same thing to Bravos last night. He reaches out to cup my cheek. "But you wanted me to leave." I don't understand. I'm his mate? As in meant to be? His eyes look so sad as he looks at me like regret is destroying him. All this time, he was avoiding me because I'm supposed to be with him. What the hell kind of logic is that?

"That first time we met, I felt the pull of the bond when our eyes locked. So I ran because it scared me. I tried to push you away. Gods, I tried to push you away. I thought you would be safer in your world, better off. I didn't know how bad things were for you in your realm. The crone told me of your life, but did something to make me forget. The more I learned about your life before, the worse I felt about how I treated you. I should have put it all together sooner with your nightmares. I wanted you to be happy, even if it meant I wasn't. It doesn't matter; I'm an idiot, and I was scared of my fate. I've lost everything that would have mattered to me. I was furious with fate for stripping me of everything I should have had, so I fought against it this time, but I can't fight anymore. I'm in love with you, and the world can burn if it means I can keep you."

I have no words as I stare into his fathomless green eyes. All this time. I battered down my feelings for him, this draw I had to him, because I thought it was one-sided. He let me believe he didn't want me here and pushed aside his feelings because he didn't want me trapped in a world I didn't belong in. Only for him to tell me now that he loves me. I take a deep breath as I take all this in. My chest is tight around my lungs as I swallow down the lump in my throat. Anger wars with the sense of relief I feel. All this time, he burned hot and cold; he left me feeling worse for the draw I felt for him. A tear slides down my cheek as I stare at him in shock. I can't change the past, but I can finally face the feelings that I've bottled up.

"You've definitely fucked this whole thing up," I sigh.

I reach around his neck, lacing my fingers through his hair, and slowly pull his lips to mine. He kisses me softly as I sink into the feeling. Every touch tentative, not the hungry tension of the beach. Warmth spreads through me, along with a sense of calm. The tug on my heart floods with serenity. Like all the pieces are falling into place, the lost piece of the puzzle found.

He pulls back and leans his forehead against mine. "I'm sorry. It was selfish of me to distance myself from you. I am fated to be with you, yet forced you away at every opportunity."

"Not every opportunity." I smirk at him. My heart flutters in my chest.

His eyes darken as his mouth tilts into a whisper of a grin. "I'm an idiot."

"Yes, but I don't care," I say, pulling him toward me, kissing him hard, letting myself get lost in the feeling. He deepens the kiss as I pull him up and back onto the bed.

Chapter 31
Rodan

I laid my soul bare to her, and she didn't turn me away. After everything I've done to try to get her to go home, after every fight and cold shoulder, she didn't leave. I don't even know what to make of the soft smile she gives me. My heart thunders in my chest as I gaze upon her, uncertain of what she wants of me.

She pulls me on top of her on the small cot. I settle one arm above her head, trying not to crush her. She breaks the kiss, struggling out of the tangle of blanket holding her captive beneath me. I lean to the side to give her more room to unwrap herself.

"You don't have to. I know you went through a lot last night. You can cover yourself." I'm at a loss for what to do as she glares at me.

"I need this blanket off of me, this blood-stained nightgown gone, and to do things on my terms," she growls, throwing the blanket off her front.

A low growl escapes my chest as I take in the sight of her exposed upper body. The delicate lines of her collarbone lead to the beautiful curves of her breasts. She grabs my arm and pulls me back on top of her. I settle between her legs as I look at this being of beauty before me. Her breathing is uneven as she looks into my eyes.

"Kiss me," she whispers her demand, and I answer, crushing her lips beneath mine. She tastes like sin and dreams and everything beautiful in the world. Her skin is soft under mine, and it takes all of my self-control not to lose myself to her. I want to be in her orbit and simply exist here in her arms.

She runs her nails down my back, causing me to roll my hips into her and a groan to escape me. She moans as she feels me grow hard against her core. I move to kiss her neck as her spine curls into me; she grinds against me in the most delicious way.

"More," she whispers.

I grin as I lick a path up her neck, flicking my fingers to bring out the shadows. The tendrils wrap around her wrists and pull them above her head. Her eyes go wide as she sees what I'm doing. The intoxicating scent of her arousal grows more potent, but I'll release my shadows if she doesn't like it.

"Do you want me to stop?" I cock an eyebrow at her.

"No," she says on a breath. The pheromones she is releasing fill my lungs and need pulses through me.

"I want to taste every inch of you," I whisper in her ear, then lick a trail down her neck to her chest, stopping to suck on her nipple.

She lets out a short gasp, and I log that sound to memory. I want to memorize every little sound she makes. I continue kissing my way down her stomach, finding the remains of her nightdress still tangled around her waist. I grab it and slowly pull it down her legs. Once it's off her, I throw it into the fire and let it burn. I want to remove every trace of everyone who has ever hurt her. I watch her face as I run my hands up her legs. When I reach her knees, her face flushes red, and I take in the beautiful color of her flush. "May I touch you?"

"Yes," she breathes.

I grin as I move her knees apart again, slowly trailing kisses up her inner thigh. She makes little whimpering sounds as I climb higher. I find a perfect little smooth spot on the inside of her upper thigh. I take note of the area, drawing circles around it with my finger. "One day, if you accept me as your mate, I'll mark you. Right here," I purr.

Her breath hitches as I look at her. "Do it," she breathes, shivering under my touch.

"What?" I lift up to get a better look at her. She can't truly mean that. My heart pounds in my chest in anticipation of her answer. She couldn't know what this would mean. But maybe I'm wrong, and she feels the bond as strongly as I do. "It would declare you as mine."

"Mark me. I've been yours this whole time."

"But you need to know...what that means–"

"Every impulse in my body is telling me it's right, and I can't explain it. So shut up and do it before I realize how angry I should be with you."

A low growl from somewhere primal inside me erupts as I move on top of her once more to claim her mouth with mine. I roll my hips into her core as she kisses me back with ferocity. I need this woman like I need air. I break the kiss and move back down her body. I use my shadows to stroke the insides of her thighs and hold her legs open to me. Her scent is provocative as I lean into her perfect pussy. I slowly run my tongue from her opening to her clit as she lets out a moan. I can see exactly how wet she is for me, but I want to take my time and savor this.

She moans and bucks as I lick and nip at her clit, circling my tongue around the little nub. I hold her legs apart and suck, letting one of my shadows lick at her wet heat. She moans louder as I let it slide inside of her; the sensation sends feelings of her warm slickness to my dick. I've never used my shadows this way, and I moan as I revel in this feeling. My dick strains against my shorts as I lose myself in the taste and feel of her.

I curl the shadow to hit that sweet spot inside of her as I nip at her clit again. Her back arches as she cries out. I slow, not letting her peak just yet. I gather another smaller shadow and slowly push it to her back entrance. She takes a sharp breath and clenches down on both shadows, sending a shock of pleasure through me.

"Relax," I coax, licking up her center. "I won't hurt you." Some of the tension in her body relaxes into my hands again as the first shadow pumps in and out of her, growing inside to stretch her. Her body responds to the attention, back arching and a whimper leaving her mouth. The second shadow is small, but I increase its width every few strokes as she relaxes into it. She is panting hard as I work her, ready to tip over the edge. I lean down and suck on her little nub and send a small shock of electricity into the sensitive bud. Her whole body falls apart as she convulses, screaming my name.

I continue sending little shocks through her little nub, forcing her body to keep riding the ecstasy, replacing my tongue reluctantly with my thumb. I move to that little spot on her that I'd noted earlier. I send another shock through her core before she's fully come down from her orgasm, spiraling her into another. I lick the spot on her thigh before sinking my fangs into her flesh.

Every shudder of her climax rocks through me as the bond is formed. She moans loud and long as her body is caught in the throes of the bond snapping into place. My mark sealed on her flesh and branded in pleasure. Her moans are a symphony to my soul.

"I need to be inside you," I pant, looking up at her. I'm so hard it hurts. To finish the bond, I need to be inside her, the collision of our souls taking shape. She nods, and I slowly pull my shadow from her core, as I pull my shorts off and line myself up with her entrance.

"The other shadow is still there," she whimpers.

"Does it hurt?" I say, pushing a few strands of hair out of her face.

"No."

"Trust me," I purr as I struggle to hold myself back. I free her wrists, and she wraps her arms around my shoulders.

She looks down at my dick, primed to enter her, as I run it across her slickness. I look down into her eyes. "Um, go slow. You are really...big."

"I told you I'd ruin you. But I'll go slow."

Sliding inside of her is ecstasy. She is tight, but so wet that I know I got her ready for me. She lets out little gasps as I slowly seat myself in her. When I'm about halfway in, she moans and pulls me to the hilt. Her nails dig into my back as her body flexes around me. I groan, feeling like I'm gonna pass out from it. I reach down and kiss her with ferocity. She is fire and electricity. She is the air I breathe. She is everything—the spark that's ignited when fate comes to fruition. My heart pounds as I look into the deep ocean of her eyes.

"Oh god," she moans.

"Good girl," I growl as I thrust into her, slowly at first, but as her moans grow, I move faster, trying to keep rhythm with her pleasure. I send a shadow to play with her clit as I thrust into her wetness. She moans louder, saying she can't come again, but I disagree, as I have my shadow give her a little shock that sends her over the edge again. She clamps down so hard on my cock, I see fucking stars. The little shock radiates through her and through me as I come apart, roaring as the bond fully snaps in place, heightening the climax both of us shudder through.

I remove my shadows from her body before lying at her side, kissing her slowly. What did I do to deserve such a wonderful creature that would accept a bond with me?

Chapter 32
Jade

I lay in Rodan's arms as I try to piece together the events of the last twenty-four hours. I have so many questions, and I don't know where to start. He kisses my forehead as he moves to get up, picking up his shorts and stoking the fire. He dresses quickly, walking over to a trunk in the corner; he rifles through it and pulls out a shirt and pants, tossing them onto the bed for me. The pants are a bit big, but with the belt he slings towards me, I manage to keep them up.

I still feel like a limp noodle after what he just did to me. I never knew it could feel like that. Now I understand what the hype is about, and I feel a bit cheated by my exes. The pull towards Rodan is much more significant than it was before. Like if he were to go too far, it would be painful. I want to stay wrapped in his arms forever. However, a small part of me still feels guilt and a pull towards Killian. I made my decision, though, and I'll stand by it. Everything weighs heavily on me as I survey my surroundings.

"Okay, so where are we?" I ask as I tuck the shirt into my pants and look around the small space. The room has large windows that wrap around it, looking out onto the mountains and trees below. In one corner is a small cupboard that looks like it's seen better days, with the doors nearly rusted off the hinges. Rodan rifles around, pulling things out. Behind him is a large chest that he pulled the clothing from. I sit on the bed near the fire, and on the other side of me is a small desk overflowing with papers that look like they have been recently placed there on the dusty top.

"This is an old outpost that borders Amara and Shadow. Look out over there, and you can see where the fog covers the land of Shadow." He motions out the window.

I walk over and see the expanse of trees that abruptly stops where a thick fog begins. The mist reaches out as far as the eye can see, swirling and dense.

"I come here sometimes, keep the food stocked and extra clothes on hand. I've been going into Shadow when I can, looking through the documents left in the Shadow King's office," he says as he opens a can and motions to the desk.

My stomach sinks. "What about the death curse?"

"I shadow in and out quickly, grabbing what I can. I don't go often. The curse takes time to take hold. I could probably stay a week or more before it took me. I don't risk it, though. We don't know enough about it to risk more."

Shadow? Wait, what? My eyes grow wide as he pulls the chair from the desk over by the bed, motioning for me to sit. He hands me a bowl of fruit and a piece of bread as I sit on the bed and look at him.

"I have a lot to explain, I know," he looks down and sighs. "I was born in Shadow. My parents were the king and queen. When the curse hit, my father was able to hold the castle for a very long time, but with every death, the curse grew stronger, and his power began to fade. From what I was told, my mother died, and my father grew ill. My nursemaid brought me here, to the edge of the kingdom, in hopes of saving me." He rubs his brow, looking lost. "King Corbin came here to check on the border and found us. He said that she gave me to him, and he promised to raise me as his own so that one day, a true Shadow heir could reclaim the country if the curse was lifted."

"Why would he agree to that?"

"Because he was friends with my father. My father's ledgers say as much until the curse. As I grew up, King Corbin told me more and more about how they had been allies. He never understood why my father would accuse him of cursing Shadow. So, I grew up here in Amara alongside Killian. The people all believed I was the king's bastard son, which I guess helps keep me safe from whoever wanted Shadow wiped from the continent. It's why no one knows about my shadows or that I'm a shifter." He takes a bite of bread and waits for this information to sink in.

"So you are the Prince of Shadow?"

"Technically, I'm now the King of Shadow," he sighs. "But seeing as how it's still cursed, I'm just a bastard prince," he grumbles. "So I hide here in plain sight, trying to find a solution to both cursed kingdoms. I found all the plans my father made to get his revenge on Amara and how he did it. I know how to break the curse on Amara."

My hands stop and hover over the fruit bowl, and my eyes grow wide at this admission. "What? How? Why don't you tell anyone?"

He slumps down in the chair. "The king knows," he breathes, "to break the curse on Amara, the curse on Shadow has to be lifted. I found it in my father's last ledger, but seeing as how we can't find a way to lift the curse on Shadow, we are back at square one."

"Holy shit," I breathe, "but what about the prophecy that the fates gave us?"

He leans back and pulls a paper from the desk. "When the last shadow fades, the valley of the moon will fall," he reads off. "I believe this means that when I die, Moradi will fall."

My stomach drops. "What? How do you get that?"

"I am the last Shadow, the last heir. And Moradi means City of Radiant Moonlight. Since Moradi is the city that rules Amara, it stands to reason, I think, it's a warning. I believe the first half of the prophecy is what will happen if we don't break the curse. The second half is the how, but we haven't figured that out yet," he says with a grim look, tossing the paper back on the table.

I stand up and look out the window again towards Shadow.

"The blight has killed almost everything. My kingdom is a graveyard." He walks up behind me, wrapping his arms around my waist. "It took just over twenty years for the blight to kill everyone. I still don't understand how they got me out before it took me too."

"You were just a baby?" I lean my head back on his shoulder.

"Yeah, Queen Aleena and King Corbin raised me as their own. I grew up with stories of my parents. They told me that they were set up. They never figured out who would want to drive a wedge between the kingdoms. If we can break the curse, Killian and I plan to restore our kingdoms to their former glory. The two together were once a formidable force. I wish I'd known it that way."

"Do you think our recent problems are related? That the monsters could be tied to everything else?"

He takes a deep breath. "I don't know. It's a pretty long stretch to link something that's been going on for sixty years to random attacks only now just happening."

"But fae have long lifespans. What if the curse didn't go as planned, and they have just been waiting for the right time to strike?" I muse.

"It's possible, but it doesn't narrow down the field. Just adds to the questions. I wish I had the answers."

We are quiet for a long time as I consider all he's told me, staring out into the fog. "So, panthers?"

He chuckles and holds me tighter. "Why did you call me Void?"

"Because you disappeared into a void when you curled up with all that black fur," I giggle.

"I see," he grumbles. "I really meant no harm."

"You were guarding me, I get it. But you could have said something before I spilled all my secrets to you," I huff.

"And where would be the fun in that?" he purrs.

"Jerk."

He laughs and kisses the top of my head.

"Any other magic I should know about?"

He takes a deep breath and hesitates. I wait, wondering what bomb he's gonna drop on me next.

"So you know how Killian can make people spontaneously combust?" he asks as visions of those constructs exploding pop into my head, and I shudder as I nod. "That is the power of the royal lines. I can do something similar only with electricity. I can shut down or manipulate electrical impulses in the body. Royal lines with earth magic can manipulate the metals in the body. Water magic the blood. All of them are closely guarded secret weapons held only by royal lines."

"That is disturbing." The implications of that are horrifying. It would explain a lot about the things I've seen and felt him do, though. "Um, is that the zappy thing you do in bed?"

"Zappy thing?" He laughs. "If that's what you want to call it, yes. I direct your electrical impulses where I want them." He leans to my ear and whispers, "I could make you cum from across the room without touching you. Continuously." He nips my ear. "If I felt the inclination."

My breath hitches as butterflies dance their way south in my stomach. My god, he's a monster. What have I done? What if he does that while I'm talking to someone? He wouldn't. Would he? My heartbeat ramps up as a flush coats my cheeks.

"Don't worry, Trouble, I'm not as mean as you think I am. Plus, I won't share the little noises you make with anyone."

"What do we do when we go back? Are they going to arrest you for killing Bravos?" I turn in his grip to face him, sweeping his hair over his shoulder as I look up at him.

"No, Trouble. We will be fine. He didn't have your consent. Killian would have had his head as well." He leans his head down onto mine. "You accepting my bond is going to be an interesting conversation, though." He lets out a breath.

"I feel bad. I don't want to hurt him." Tears well in my eyes as I struggle to swallow.

He tips my chin up to look at me curiously, pain crossing his features. "You still feel a draw to him." It's not a question. "I never told him who you were to me. I knew that first time we met. I should have told him. I'm sorry. With the mate bond in place, I believe your feelings for him will fade in time. But I don't know. I've never heard of someone still retaining feelings for another after the bond is accepted. Fuck, I pretty much let my brother date my fated mate like it was no big deal. Now I have to tell him the truth."

"I don't know what to do. Why did you have to make everything so complicated?" I look up at him.

"I was scared that if I let myself fall for you, I'd lose you like everyone else." He leans down and kisses me gently. I wrap my arms around his neck, deepening the kiss. He bends me back against the window, his breath becoming heavy.

A rumble goes through the tower as the ground shakes, rattling the walls. Rodan breaks the kiss and looks out the window. His brow furrows as he lets go of me and walks the perimeter of the room, searching for answers through the glass. He stops at the far window, looking towards Amara, placing his hands on the frame as he stares at the billowing smoke that has begun to waft above the trees.

"What was that?" I ask as I rush over to look. In the distance, the trees shake, and the ground rolls toward us like a wave on the ocean. The whole tower sways as the ground rolls beneath us. I brace myself on the windowsill, trying not to fall as I look at Rodan in horror.

"I don't know, but it's not good," he growls.

"Does anyone know we are here?"

"No." He glances my way and then turns his attention to the

smoke that has begun shimmering purple.
My stomach drops as dread settles into my soul.
I have a bad feeling about this.

Chapter 33
Rodan

"Stay here," I growl, looking over at Trouble. She looks out the window in horror, the purple smoke growing denser in the distance.

"But—"

I cut her off. "Stay here. It's not safe. I need to get a closer look." I give her a look that brooks no argument. Her face is pale as I grab my sword and strap it to my hip. "I'll stay back far enough so as not to be seen. It will be fine." I take a deep breath and look back at her face as it falls. "Once I have an idea of what is going on, I'll return, and we will get reinforcements."

"Why don't we just go get them now?"

"I don't want to get them if it's nothing." I desperately hope this is the case.

"Does that look like nothing to you?" She puts her hand on her hip as she motions out the window. No, that definitely looks like trouble. I have a sinking feeling in my gut, but I need to see what is down there.

"Stay here. Everything will be fine," I grit out, hoping that she will listen. Maybe it's some pixies having a massive party. Sure, keep telling yourself that.

The tower rocks and shakes again as I move towards the door. I pull her into me and brush her hair aside as I lean into her neck. "I'll take care of it," I promise, nuzzling into her. She pulls back and looks into my eyes, concern pulling her eyebrows together. I reach up and run my thumb down her bottom lip before leaning in and kissing her softly. She is mine, and I'll protect her. Our bond tugs tight in my chest at the prospect of leaving her side.

She breaks the kiss with a gasp, clutching her chest with wide eyes.

I place my hand over hers and put my other on my heart. "We are bonded. Strong emotions can bleed through. I'll feel you no matter where you are in the world, and you'll feel me." Surprise and awe fill her face as she looks between our hands. I lean down and kiss her again, dreading walking out that door.

When I break the kiss, she looks up at me. "Come back to me," she whispers. I nod and turn to the door, walking out before I can think better of it.

Something is wrong, very wrong, and I need her as far from it as possible. Running down the steps that spiral the outside of the tower, I can't help but feel like I made the wrong choice.

As I reach the bottom, I turn towards the purple smoke that has begun to shimmer in the air.

My mind goes blank. Like I've forgotten what I was about to do. Odd. I'm panting like I ran down the steps, but can't remember doing it. I scratch the back of my head; why the hell was I at the tower?

A melody plays through my mind, a soft song carried on the wind and birds. My muscles relax as the song moves through me. Damn, I've never reacted like this to music. Where is it coming from? I close my eyes and take in the soothing sound. When I open them, I'm walking through the trees, the tower already yards behind me.

This must have been what I was doing. Looking for the source of this beautiful music.

Pain lances through my chest, and I clutch it. What the fuck. I feel a pull that is so powerful it nearly brings me to my knees. Determination keeps me on my feet, moving forward. A haze of purple takes over the forest, making the trees glow pink in the sunlight. It's mesmerizing. I never realized that this part of the forest was so magical. The music guides me on.

A sharp pang of agony pierces my head, causing me to spin and drop. I clutch my head as I lie on the ground, writhing in agony as my brain tries to escape my skull.

An ethereal face moves into my vision, singing that magical song. The glow of the sun makes her look like an angel of lavender and moonlight.

The world goes blurry.

Everything turns black.

Chapter 34
Jade

It's been hours. Where is he? I pace back and forth in the tower, looking out the windows, but there is no sign of him. The cloud of purple smoke stopped shortly after Rodan left, and I figured he'd be back soon. But that was this morning, and the sun is well past noon now. I have no idea what to do.

There are no portals. No horses. I don't have any useful magic; I can't even get it to work at will. I tried to use my power, trying to feel for anything different in my body. Held an empty can for ten minutes, attempting to picture it frozen. I even tried to hold my hand in front of me and shoot magic out. Nothing, the room didn't even get cold, not that I want to freeze to death up here. I like the cozy fire just fine.

I look back out the window in the direction that the purple smoke was in. I know that the city of Moradi is in that direction. How far is it on foot, though? And how dangerous would it be for someone who can't use magic? Nope, traversing mountains in a strange land by myself is going to be a no-go.

Shit.

Okay, this is the first time that I've genuinely missed a cell phone since I arrived. I have no way of contacting help.

I'm sure by now someone has seen the state of my room and

the body that Rodan left in his wake. Cat has got to be freaking out, and Rodan is the only one who knows where I am. In hindsight, I wonder why he brought me all the way out here instead of somewhere else in the castle. Did he need the dramatic backdrop to tell me the truth about himself? Fuck, now I'm questioning his motives? I need to calm the fuck down. He will come back.

Vertigo spins my head as searing pain rips through my chest. I collapse to the floor on my hands and knees, gulping in air. The pain pulses through me again, and I scream, falling to my side and clutching my chest. Blades drive into my heart as it beats furiously in my chest. I writhe on the floor as my voice goes hoarse. Spots cloud my vision, and blackness seeps in. I am going to die. I don't even know what is going on. Another pulse runs through my body, my chest on fire as agony steals my breath away.

"Interesting," a male voice reaches me through my screams. "Why didn't your song work on her?"

My head pounds, adding to the torment in my chest. "Strong mind," a female voice purrs. "But broken soul, my song slips through the cracks like water through a broken glass." Her voice is melodic and familiar.

Another burn of agony sweeps through me as I rasp a scream on the floor. The pain is so severe I can't move. It's blinding. I want to pull my heart out of my chest just to make it stop. I want to plead and beg them to help me, but I can't.

"Darling, what did you do to her?" the female purrs.

"Nothing yet. I wasn't expecting to find her in this state. I need to find the explanation before I dispose of her," he says.

And then there is nothing.

"Wake up, little mortal," a singsong voice cuts through the haze of my mind.

I pry my eyes open, a blurry image taking shape before me. Big, round eyes meet mine as Owari breaks into a smile. I'm sitting in a chair in a dark room, illuminated by torches. "What happened?" I croak out, my throat sore and raw. I go to lift my arm, finding I can't move, invisible hands holding me to the chair. My eyes grow wide with the realization.

"Hum." She taps her chin. "I'm not sure; you were screaming when we found you. My dear one is looking into it."

"Why can't I move?"

"For your safety, I'm afraid. You kept thrashing even after I put you to sleep," she says flippantly, walking over to a table on the side of the room. She picks up a vial and inspects it before setting it down.

"So let me go. I'm awake now."

She giggles, the sound like tinkling bells. "Oh, that would be a terrible idea indeed. He would be very cross with me and then wouldn't fulfill his end of our bargain."

"Bargain?" I need to keep her talking while I try to figure out a way out of this. The walls are made of stone, like the ones in the castle. I can only hope I'm close in my guess. Whatever is going on, it can't be good.

"Yes, I am to produce an heir. I need his seed to do that. However, I don't want the male to rule beside me, you see," she says as she flips through a book laid out on the table. "My court is matriarchal; thus, I don't need a husband. Just powerful seed." Her flippant tone makes me shudder.

"Who?"

"Ellis, of course, who else? You've seen us courting this whole time." She giggles.

"What does Ellis get out of this bargain?" I rasp out, barely able to make a sound.

"Something to do with the King of Light and the kingdoms of Shadow and Amara. Really, I wasn't listening. He has some grudge about his family in Eneara. Or some such drama. He gets my song and information. I get his seed. It's a simple trade." She smiles to herself, the damn cat with the canary.

Ellis? The King of Light? As in the Kingdom of Light? Shit. Is Ellis the sorcerer we've been looking for? I try to move my feet, looking for a weakness in my binds, but I can't. Every part of me is locked in place. The only things I can move are my neck and head. I can't even scream because my voice is so hoarse already. I need to get out of here and tell Killian. If the Kingdom of Light is in on this, they need to be warned. God, does that mean Scarlette and Beatrix could be in on it too? That's their kingdom. My head spins with the implications of everything Owari has told me.

Ellis walks in through an archway and looks at me. "Interesting," he says in a bored tone. "Owari, please stop touching things. You are disturbing my work." He places his hands on her shoulders and directs her to a chair in the corner. She turns and sits with a huff.

"When you are done with her, I'd like you to fuck me against that table, darling. I like it when you talk about work," she purrs as she slinks into the chair, practically drooling.

Ew.

Ellis drags a stool over to me and sits, looking pointedly at me. "These are not ropes. Stop trying to wiggle your way out. It's pointless." His frosty glare makes my heart speed up.

He pulls a vial from his pocket that glows yellow in the dim light. "You'll drink this, or I'll make it painful." I look at the vial in his hand and gulp. Terror seizing me, I glance over to Owari, who is inspecting her nails.

He pops the cork off the top and leans into me. "It won't kill you if that's what you're worried about." He rolls his eyes. "Now open," he demands as he brings the vial to my mouth. I close my eyes and open my mouth; the liquid slides down my throat as I swallow. Warmth radiates, spreading down my body in a wave. I hear his footsteps as I wait for something to happen. When I open my eyes, he's walking back with a clipboard and sits on the stool again.

He leans over, scrutinizing my face before writing something down. He places the clipboard on a tray to my left that I hadn't noticed. "Good, it's working," he mumbles as he moves his hands in small circles. "Now, let's see." Shimmering golden threads come out of my chest as the warmth in my body intensifies. He pulls them to himself and holds them in front of his face, inspecting them. "Interesting," he murmurs as he slides his fingers over the threads. Occasionally, he stops to write something down on his clipboard. I don't even know what to think of what I'm seeing.

He is cold and clinical. A mad scientist in his lab.

I'm broken out of my shock when he laughs. "Oh, this is rich," he says, dropping the threads. They curl back into me as if they were never there. "You bonded with him." He stands and walks over to his table, flipping through the open book's pages. "Quite recently, it seems. Who would have thought the half-fae was his mate?" he chuckles. My heart sinks. Why do I have such a bad feeling about this?

"It seems that fit of pain I walked in on was because of that bond." He straightens his glasses and then rubs his chin, reading intently from the book. "You will make a fun experiment."

"Where is Rodan?" I rasp out, fear filling my veins. I don't want to be an experiment.

"Gone," he grumbles.

"What did you do to him?" Tears run down my cheeks as I speak. He can't be gone. I beg anything that might answer, sending prayers to any deity of this world.

"He's not dead if that's what you are worried about. Plans have changed, and he is of more use to me alive right now," he sighs, not looking at me. "Although this bond of yours gives me an idea." He turns, holding me in his stare with a wicked grin. "Killing is a messy business. I prefer to do things with a higher purpose in mind." He looks over to the bookcase next to Owari, and a book slides out and flies across the room into his waiting hand. He places it on the table and flips through. "I want to know what happens when you separate a bonded mate. Indefinitely. It stands to reason that if you were nearly torn apart by removing him from this realm, a permanent separation would be worse than death." He turns back to me, his face serious. "You really were a nuisance. I'm glad the fates were less than helpful."

"Why not just kill us?"

"I don't like to get my hands dirty. It makes dark magic less manageable. Corrupts it. I'm not willing to risk that on a couple of bumps in the road." He sneers.

"So you send monsters to do your dirty work?"

"Enough. You've wasted enough of my time," he barks.

"Why are you doing this?" I whimper.

"Like I'd tell you."

My heart thunders as I sob. I don't want to be separated. I don't understand what has happened to Rodan. Killian will never know what happened to us. Terror has me frozen as I stare at him, unable to speak, unable to comprehend what is going on.

I'm going to lose Rodan. I sob at the thought. He will never know what happened to me. My heart breaks. I never even told him I loved him.

I thought we had time. Time to figure all this out. Time to be together, time to fix what we screwed up. I feel my soul crack and shatter within me. Somewhere deep, I feel the pull towards him, and I sob harder, tears soaking my shirt.

A fire blazes to life in a hearth across the room as cabinets I couldn't see in the gloom fly open. Small vials and other things spill into a big glass pot, one by one, moving of their own accord. Ellis stands at his desk, looking intently at a book, occasionally glancing up and looking at the pot. I feel the power before I see it. Ellis walks over and stands behind the pot, pouring power into the mixture that makes my hair stand on end.

Tremors rack my body as I watch in horror. Ellis is a sorcerer and a powerful one. So much for him having weak air power. This fucker is intense. Even I can feel the darkness within the power rolling across the room. It bleeds from his hands like black sludge, and sheer terror fills my chest.

I am going to die here, in this dungeon, and no one will ever find me. I'm racked with sobs again. I hope Cat finds happiness with Ryker.

Ellis stands at the pot as a vial fills itself and drifts into his hand, the menacing red glow illuminating his face. "Owari, come," he barks at her as he walks over to me.

"Rules are the same, Mortal. Open."

I purse my lips and look at him wide-eyed. Once was bad enough. Doing this twice seems like a bad gamble.

His brow furrows, and he reaches out a hand and twists the air.

Pain laces through my chest as I see the threads pulled taut and wrapped around his fist. He gives another yank that knocks the breath out of me. I gasp in agony, and he dumps the vial down my throat, holding my mouth shut with his hand. The bonds that hold me to the chair tighten, bruising my arms and legs and compressing my chest so I can't breathe. I try not to swallow, but he yanks the threads again, and I have no choice; involuntarily, it slides down my throat.

"Owari, block out all her memories since she left the mortal world," he directs her as he walks away.

"No," I rasp. I never got to tell him. Nonono, they can't do this. What will happen to Cat? I can't warn her. She'll be alone here. What will happen to me? My heart drops, and nausea rolls through me. Once again, I've made a dire mistake that has cost me everything. Only this time, I'm taking everyone I care about down with me. I choke on the sob lodged in my throat.

She steps forward, places a hand on my temple, and closes her eyes. Her face scrunches. "I don't know if it will hold. I can feel my power slipping through the cracks." The room spins as she speaks. It's like being drunk without the fun part.

"That's why I gave her the potion," he grumbles. "So long as I keep them apart, your song shouldn't slip through the cracks. Although I feel like I'm missing an opportunity to study the effects of trauma on siren song. No matter. Get it done."

Owari begins to sing, her melodic song filling the room, echoing back in the cavernous space. Her voice dances back in an eerie chorus to her melody, creating the illusion of multiple singers.

Searing pain shoots through my head as I scream. My vision goes foggy as memories start playing through my mind. The pieces are short and choppy as they fall into an abyss.

Rodan kneeling in front of me, telling me he was in love with me...

I love you.

A wall goes up, and the memory melts away.

"No!" I scream. Something I know was precious to me is now gone.

Killian teaching me how to fight, running me ragged every morning. Nuzzling my neck in the cool morning air as he showed me my next stance...

Slam. The wall blocks it off.

The ball, everyone running and screaming...

Slam.

"No! Please stop!" Pain lances through me, my back arching as I struggle in the restraints.

The Fates' warning: "For you will shatter before the curse is done. And what has shattered can never be undone."

Slam.

Rodan sitting next to me out in the garden while I cried myself to sleep...

Slam.

Killian telling me a story after the dragon attack...
Slam.

I scream and scream, but everything melts away into nothing. I sob uncontrollably for things I can't remember. My memories play in reverse, undoing everything I had grown to love.

Dancing with both of them, that feeling of contentment. The excitement of meeting these men who make my heart flutter. Wonder and fear of this new world I've found myself in...
Slam.

Meeting Warrick in the Bar...
Slam.

Chapter 35
Jade

Beep.

Beep.

Beep.

Groggily, I rouse from sleep to this incessant beeping. Groaning as I try to open my eyes. Everything hurts. As my eyes adjust to the light in the room, I focus on the heart rate monitor next to me. Pale beige walls greet me as I look around in confusion.

This is a hospital room. I lift my arm and see an IV strapped to it; the line leads up to a drip.

What the hell?

I attempt to sit up, but every muscle barks in protest. Bruises line my arms, dark and menacing.

Was I in a car accident? How the hell did I end up here?

"Oh, good, you're awake." A woman in scrubs walks in and checks the monitor by the bed. She moves over to the IV drip and adjusts something.

"How did I get here?"

"You were found on the beach, unconscious. Someone called it in, and you were brought here." She looks down at me, face going soft. "Do you remember how you got there?"

I try to think, but my mind comes up blank. The last thing I remember was driving to the courthouse to pick up my divorce decree. "No. I have no idea." I shake my head slowly, trying not to aggravate my splitting headache. "How long have I been here?"

"A couple of days, you were pretty beat up. You came to, just long enough to give us your name. Do you remember that?"

"No."

"Well, we called your emergency contact on file. They've been here day and night, worried about you. Now that you're awake, I can talk to the doctor and see about letting you go home. Looks like you had some bruising and a few cuts, but nothing life-threatening. He'll probably want to talk to you and run a few more tests, but you'll probably be let go by the end of the afternoon."

I make a noncommittal noise as I try to remember how I'd ended up on a beach, watching as she strolls out of the room, leaving me alone. I struggle but manage to sit up, ignoring the pain in my ribs and dizziness. I lean over, pulling the chart from the end of the bed. Hopefully, there will be something in it that might jog my memory.

I scan the documents for any familiar words. Bruises, lacerations, bruised ribs, and a possible concussion. Written in a small notes section at the bottom of one of the pages is:

Missing person. Police state missing for over two months. Have patient call to interview after discharge.

Two months? I've been missing for over two months? I read the date at the top of the document and gasp in horror.

How did I lose over two months of time?

What the hell happened?

"Glad to see you're finally awake."

I look up quickly at the familiar voice.

No.

Cold sweat chills my body. Ace leans against the doorway with a cup of coffee. My heart pounds violently as I look at him.

"Hello, Jade."

Books By J. Grenz

Labyrinth of Crimson

<u>Shattered Moon Duet</u>

Soul of Fractured Fate

Fate of the Broken

About the Author

J. Grenz is a self-published author living in the Pacific Northwest, where she hopes to one day fall into a fairy realm or bump into a vampire. Her love of romance, fantasy, and whimsical places lead to her debut book, Soul of Fractured Fate. Her husband and teenager help keep her grounded in reality, while her four cats and two dogs pretend they don't understand English.